Elliott Hall was born in 1978  lives in London.

Praise for Elliott Hall:

'To work, satire has to be subtle . . . Elliott Hall does this wonderfully' *The Times*

'Political satires set in chilling dystopian futures don't usually call for sequels . . . Hall's pizzazz ensures you want to know if Felix makes it' *Daily Telegraph*

'Redolent of *Watchmen* and *Blade Runner*, this futuristic thriller has its own mordant energy. A knockout debut' *Guardian*

'This debut crime novel is best read under a sweltering sun as its depiction of a dystopian near-future chills the blood . . . It is ingenious and witty' *Daily Telegraph*

'The first in a trilogy . . . Hall's novel combines pacy storytelling with a disturbing dystopian vision' *Mail on Sunday*

'An outstanding first novel by a new Canadian author we should hear more of' *Independent*

'It's a really good, traditional private eye story coupled with a subtle and believable picture of a fundamentalist state' *Morning Star*

THE
RAPTURE

Also by Elliott Hall

The First Stone

THE
RAPTURE

THE INNOCENT DISAPPEAR FIRST

ELLIOTT HALL

JOHN MURRAY

First published in Great Britain in 2010 by John Murray (Publishers)
An Hachette UK Company

First published in paperback in 2011

1

A CIP catalogue record for this title is available from the British Library

ISBN 978-1-84854-074-3

Typeset in Plantin by Servis Filmsetting Ltd, Stockport, Cheshire

Printed and bound by Clays Ltd, St Ives plc

John Murray policy is to use papers that are natural, renewable and recyclable products and made from wood grown in sustainable forests. The logging and manufacturing processes are expected to conform to the environmental regulations of the country of origin.

John Murray (Publishers)
338 Euston Road
London NW1 3BH

www.johnmurray.co.uk

For the Lord himself shall descend from heaven with a shout, with the voice of the archangel, and with the trump of God: and the dead in Christ shall rise first:

Then we which are alive and remain shall be caught up together with them in the clouds, to meet the Lord in the air: and so shall we ever be with the Lord.

– 1 Thessalonians iv, 16–17, King James Bible

Transcript from Felix Strange debriefing, day nine
Recorded at: ████████████████████████████,
Agent(s) Present: Gabriel Tan and Todd Baines

(Begin Transcript.)

STRANGE: We've been at this for two weeks. How many different ways do you want me to answer the same questions?

TAN: Let's start from the beginning: when did you first become aware of Brother Isaiah's death?

STRANGE: When that shitbag Ezekiel White had me dragged to the late minister's hotel room.

TAN: I've told you before the profanity is unnecessary, Felix.

STRANGE: I call him a shitbag only for the purposes of identification.

TAN: You had no prior relationship with Ezekiel White before that first meeting?

STRANGE: Never met the man. I've had a run in or two with his Daveys-

TAN: For the record, you are referring to officers of the Committee for Child Protection.

STRANGE: Yeah - Daveys. Kids fresh out of Christian college who've been kept in ignorance their whole lives. I've met costumed strippers who more closely resemble cops. I doubt they recommended me to White for the job.

TAN: You had no idea why White chose you to investigate Brother Isaiah's death?

STRANGE: I didn't know why either of us was there. White was the Elders' pit bull; he should have been yelling 'slut' at any woman showing knee, not doing a real job. It felt wrong from the beginning. Anyway, he gave me some spiel about his Daveys being watched. It was bullshit, of course.

TAN: Yet you accepted the case.

STRANGE: I didn't have much choice, did I? White had an almost unlimited scope for making my life hell.

TAN: Talk us through your initial investigation.

STRANGE: Again? White slipped me the crazy file, and the only name—

TAN: Back up, Felix. We need the whole story.

STRANGE: Have we talked about the Crusade of Love this time round? I'm getting confused.

TAN: We haven't.

STRANGE: You ever wonder why the Council of Elders persuaded Brother Isaiah to bring the Crusade back to the States? If you're looking to create a roving witch hunt, tapping an organization that did charitable work in Africa is a weird fucking choice.

TAN: We aren't here to discuss politics.

STRANGE: You say that every time, agent. I don't see how the topic can be avoided, since it's the reason Brother Isaiah is dead.

TAN: Continue.

STRANGE: The Crusade's policy of finding every piece of dirty laundry it could and nailing it to the mast made it a lot of enemies. I looked through the letters sent to the organization, and only one was a plausible assassin: a Holy Land vet called Jack Small. When I went to interview him, I walked straight into somebody else's war.

TAN: The police report of the incident finally arrived yesterday. Forensics identified three different calibres of shell casing at Jack Small's apartment.

STRANGE: That sounds about right.

TAN: So three men try to kill you, and you have no idea why?

STRANGE: As I said when I told ▓▓▓▓▓▓▓▓ I think they were after Jack Small, and I got caught in the middle. To be honest, it isn't the first time I've nearly been ventilated by complete strangers.

TAN: It's a good thing Jack Small had friends. Weren't you curious about the people who had saved both your lives?

STRANGE: Of course I was curious, and grateful, but I had enough on my plate at the time.

TAN: Did Small introduce you to any of his friends?

STRANGE: A man called Cal, who was tending bar at the time. That's it. It wasn't that kind of happy hour.

TAN: And that was the last time you saw or had contact with Jack Small, or any of the others?

STRANGE: Cross my heart and hope to die, agent. Why don't we move on to Marcus Thorpe? I'd like to get this over with before lunch.

TAN: We can start with how you got on to Marcus Thorpe in the first place.

STRANGE: I've told you and the record about the Corinthian four times already.

TAN: You described him as: 'an international criminal broker, a walking, talking crime against humanity'. The Bureau would know if someone like that existed.

STRANGE: The Bureau claimed the Mafia didn't exist. Try Interpol, if you're still on speaking terms.

TAN: You seem certain about this man.

STRANGE: Of course I'm fucking certain, I used to—

TAN: Used to what, Felix?

STRANGE: Nothing. It isn't the first time I've had dealings with the Corinthian, let's leave it at that.

TAN: Isn't it more likely that this Corinthian is a fabrication, and your source was the woman you were seen having dinner with at the Starlight Diner?

00011

STRANGE: Jesus Christ, agent, I've told you that woman was not involved, and I'll keep repeating myself until doomsday.

TAN: The diner is still an open crime scene, Felix. Between yourself, the two shooters and the bystanders who became involved, we have one gun unaccounted for. If that gun was in your mystery woman's hand, she is a suspect. It's in her best interest to come forward and clear her name.

Silence. Three seconds.

TAN: Look at things from the Bureau's perspective, Felix: half your story is told in ballistics reports. The Director

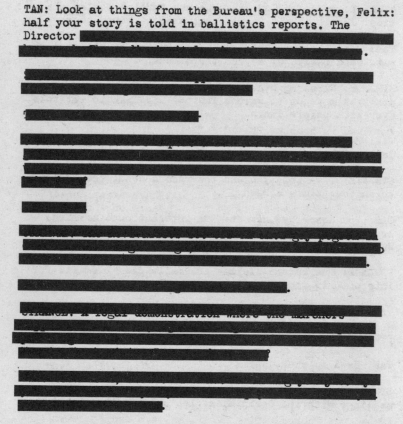

STRANGE: We both know that's bullshit, agent. This whole exercise is designed to figure out what I'm worth on the open market.

TAN: Don't be ridiculous, Felix.

STRANGE: Has the Director personally told you he won't sell me to the Elders?

TAN: I haven't received that assurance.

███

███████████████████████████████████

STRANGE: And that's why I'm protecting my sources.

TAN: It's in your best interest-

STRANGE: We're done.

Interview suspended.

TAN: Resuming debriefing interview with Felix Strange. Also present are Special Agents Tan and Baines. You were initially sceptical of the idea that Marcus Thorpe was involved in Brother Isaiah's death?

STRANGE: The guy's fabulous wealth depended on no-bid military contracts. I thought he had too much to lose, and rich men usually have easier ways of settling things. Thorpe's involvement didn't make sense until I learned that Brother Isaiah had evidence of Thorpe's son selling drugs. It wasn't the first time Thorpe Junior had been in trouble, but that's what money is for. The problem was, Brother Isaiah was one of the last men in the country who actually meant what he said. He wanted Junior to join his church. Thorpe refused, and he brought in some talent from Los Angeles to settle things the Chicago way.

TAN: These were the men who attacked you in the Star-light Diner.

STRANGE: Yes. Thorpe's right-hand man - I knew him only as Mr Lim - decided that they weren't up to the task of killing Brother Isaiah, and so he did it himself. He filled in the details about the feud between Isaiah and Thorpe. White had brokered a deal between Isaiah and Thorpe. Brother Isaiah would come to Thorpe's cabin upstate and speak to the son personally. When Brother Isaiah arrived, Lim was waiting.

TAN: Why did he confide in you?

STRANGE: He wanted to have a chat before he got round to murdering me.

TAN: Yet you killed him, despite being tied up at the time.

STRANGE: I got lucky.

TAN: You mean you got help from your mysterious source. Your friend left a lot of shell casings at the scene that couldn't have been fired by you. We'll leave that alone for the moment.

STRANGE: That would be smart.

TAN: Did White know Thorpe planned to murder Brother Isaiah?

STRANGE: He said he didn't, but I wouldn't have taken the man's word about tomorrow's weather.

TAN: It's convenient for you that he can't talk to anybody now.

STRANGE: You've got a fucking interesting definition of the word 'convenient'. White would have killed me as soon as I found some evidence of Thorpe's involvement. That's why he hired me. The minute I dug up the evidence he needed as insurance, I became a liability. Are you really going to hold it against me that I beat him to the punch?

TAN: Again, for the record, you killed both men.

STRANGE: Yes. In both cases it was about as justifiable as homicide can be.

TAN: Forensics is still going through the scene. We'll see about that.

STRANGE: I guess we will. Now, what's for lunch?

(End transcript.)

ONE

'I have a proposition for you,' the young lady sitting across my desk said, and crossed her legs.

She wore a light summer dress whose floral pattern didn't disguise the sheerness of the material. Her auburn hair was swept back to display skin just brown enough to suggest a hot climate or a sunbed. The eyes resisted inspection, pushing you towards a mouth that was wide, painted and knowing. There wasn't much subtlety in her figure, but I saw how it could make a man forget his obligations.

'What can I do for you, Miss . . .?'

'Call me Mary.' The smile she gave me was toothy and completely insincere.

'Mary Smith?' I enquired.

'If you like. Before we get down to business, I'd like to know what kind of work you do.'

Maybe she'd missed the sign on my front door. 'I'm a detective, Miss Smith. Female clients usually want me to clear up certain doubts about their husbands.'

'So you ruin marriages for a living?'

'I put marriages out of their misery.' I'd once broken up a wedding hours after the vows had been taken. The father of the bride had waited too long before deciding he wanted a little due diligence on his future son-in-law. He'd paid me to see what the groom had been up to in his old home of San Francisco, and the answer made him indictable in several jurisdictions. I flew back on her special day to ruin a reception that probably cost more than I made in a year. It was best for the bride in the long run, but I hated to see all that good food go to waste.

'It sounds like we're in the same racket,' she said.

Ever since I'd seen her leaning against the door jamb, I'd been trying to figure out what I didn't like about this woman. She was easy on the eyes, and projected an eagerness to please in all the right and wrong ways. She was the kind of dame a guy could fall for if he didn't pay attention. It would be as easy as going down an open manhole: one wrong step and you're in the dark.

'So what's your proposition?' I said.

'I know a certain hotel in the city where men tend to check in with friendly women. I need your help to stop these horrible crimes.'

'Take it to the police,' I said. 'The NYPD love pointless cases that make them look good with the new mayor.'

The guy we'd actually elected hadn't lasted long after the Battle of Christopher Park last year. If you'd been asleep for the last ten years it might have looked like democracy in action: the mayor taking responsibility for not stopping an urban war that had left dozens in body bags and a lot more injured. He had held back the police while militias attacked his own constituents for the crime of being gay.

The mayor had held the NYPD back on the orders of the Elders, the assholes who actually ran this excuse for a republic. We still had a Congress that anybody could run for, but every man there (and it was all men now) and even the President never would have gotten elected without their help. Some of the Elders had moved into government, but most stayed at their megachurches and foundations, content for their power to be an open secret. I sometimes wished that they'd just move into the West Wing and be done with it, but America thought too highly of itself to admit that it was a dictatorship.

It was surprising that the Elders had forced the mayor out, considering he'd done what they wanted. It was their foot soldiers, the Revivalists, who had strolled into Greenwich Village with automatic weapons, whether the Elders had ordered them to or not. Maybe they blamed the mayor for the residents fighting back and putting Revivalists in some of those body bags.

'I don't want to go to the police,' Mary said. 'I was raised to believe in the power of forgiveness.'

'Especially if that repentance comes in the form of small, unmarked bills.' Mary didn't bother trying to look shocked. 'You're taking quite a risk approaching me with this idea.'

'You come highly recommended,' she said.

'Who's been singing my praises?'

'Little Nicky.' Nicky Provenzano fancied himself a wise guy because his name ended in a vowel. I'd stopped some thugs from kicking his ass all the way down Fourteenth Street a while back, and he made good by putting my name in the girl's ear. If you wanted to spread some loose talk, all you had to do was mumble in his direction.

'So I thought we'd split things seventy–thirty,' Mary said.

'Is that so?'

'I'm going to be the one scaring up the business. All you have to do is take the pictures. This place is too classy to bug, but I've got an in across the street. It'll be a lot of money just to do this,' she said, and flexed her index finger.

'A judge won't see it that way,' I said. 'When it comes to the sentence on a blackmail rap, it'll be share and share alike.'

Mary chewed on that for a while. 'Sixty–forty.'

'I might bite if it was just photography,' I said, 'but I get the feeling you have more active work for me in mind.'

Mary shrugged. 'Some men don't want to reform. They might even react with hostility to my suggestion. If that happens, I'll need you to protect me.' She was still young enough to play the endangered little girl, but there wasn't enough innocence left in her eyes.

'If you want me to be the muscle as well, it's an even split or no dice.'

'Fine,' she said, with the petulance of a child forced into the tub.

I have this bad habit of feeling sorry for people. It usually comes in the afternoon, like an attack of indigestion. I wasn't surprised that Mary traded on her looks. If a dame had a lot of lights on upstairs, the country would do its best to turn them off. Law firms didn't have female partners any more, and businesses didn't want a vice-president without a Y chromosome. It was too much trouble whenever a Revivalist official walked into the room, fixed the female professional with a stare, and asked if she was married.

Given Mary's options, trading beauty for money wasn't a bad idea. Cash would appreciate over time, not fade into lines, wobbles and bitter longing for younger days. Mary could turn heads, but she wasn't beautiful enough to be exploited in the more respectable ways. I couldn't blame her for trying to play the hand that had been dealt her. The problem was that she was in the wrong game.

'There are easier ways to make a buck,' I said. 'The authorities come down especially hard on this kind of thing nowadays.'

Mary flashed a know-it-all smirk, and I figured out why this woman rubbed me up the wrong way. She'd ruled the town where she grew up with a manicured hand, the object of desire and envy for everyone inside the county line. Her reign of terror had given Mary an outsized opinion of her own beauty and intelligence. She thought she knew all the angles; it was written all over those high cheekbones and baby-blue eyes. The wisdom Mary affected to was going to come to her the hard way.

'That's sweet of you, but I'm a big girl.'

I couldn't argue. She was old enough to smoke, vote in our sham elections, and dig her own grave.

'I'll call you when I'm ready to go,' Mary said as she stood. 'I gotta bounce.' And bounce she did, down the stairs, out the door, and past the men on the street who pretended not to notice.

I had another hour before I was scheduled to meet my client. I looked at my inbox, and the email I'd been avoiding since this morning. It was the monthly update from the 82nd Veterans' Association, the official one that the government funded and kept an eye on. I guess no one had told them the army had taken a look at my medical expenses and thrown me out on my ass. The email usually went in the trash as soon as it showed up, but today I'd given it a reprieve for no reason I could name. Fresh out of distractions, I had no choice but to take a look.

The news about my fellow veterans was as predictable as it was depressing. I didn't recognize any of the names. These men were Holy Land veterans, not the ones who'd gone through Iran with me. The lucky ones had found work with Stillwater, manning checkpoints in the Holy Land or guarding bases. Some ended up with the second-tier security firms standing in front of train stations. A few got out of war fighting entirely, not too easy now that you had to serve ten years before the army would kick in for college. I think it was those few success stories that stopped me from blocking the emails completely.

I was about to delete the message and find another way to waste my time when the penultimate item caught my eye. Isaac Taylor had been reported missing by his fiancée Faye Grant.

Anyone who had seen Isaac recently was requested to contact the association. It was easy to walk off the grid if you were destitute or had post-traumatic stress disorder, but most of the men who went that way didn't have any family, or a fiancée. Neither outcome sounded like Isaac, but I hadn't seen him in ten years. Nobody had to tell me what a decade could do to a man.

I got the secure phone from the bottom drawer of my desk and called Benny at the FBI's New York office. Someone picked up, but all I heard was crackling on the other end of the line.

'Hello?' More static, and then I heard a big gulp that solved the mystery. 'Eat or talk, Benny. Pick one.'

'I don't see why I should, since you're the one spoiling my afternoon kugel break,' he said. 'Is this a social call, or are you in prison?'

'None of the above.'

'Since I've got you on the line, we should go through the checklist. You're overdue as usual.'

'Fine,' I said. 'Let's get it over with.'

'How's your health?'

'Is it your wife or the Bureau that's concerned?'

'Both,' Benny said. I doubted the reasons were the same, unless Miriam also viewed me as her property.

'Have you got all the medication you need? You know, the blue ones and the others, I think they're green, what are they called . . .'

'Benny, we do this twice a month. I would have thought you'd remember the names by now.'

'It ain't my responsibility to keep track of your personal rainbow of pharmacology,' Benny said. 'Just go through them so I can tick some fucking boxes.'

'The blue pills handle the nausea and the green are for muscle pain. The red pills stop me from going into a seizure-induced coma. Any of this ringing a bell?'

'Yeah, yeah, yeah. So you're okay?'

'I continue to bask in the Bureau's generosity.'

When the army cut me loose rather than pay to find out what had happened to me in Tehran, I didn't expect to live long. The Veterans Administration had found a cocktail of drugs that kept the symptoms in check, but they couldn't pay for it. After ten years of everyday scrambling to get the money for the medicines I needed, having the Bureau as my sugar daddy was a great relief, until my condition started to change.

'That's not what I asked,' Benny said. 'If you keep evading the question you're going to make me suspicious, and you know what that does to my digestion.'

'I've been having some side effects lately.' Last night I woke up on the bathroom floor with no memory of getting there or how long I'd kissed the tiles. The shower curtain was ripped, there was a hole in the wall and the razor and prescription bottles that lived on the sink had joined me on the floor. It had all the hallmarks of a seizure, but that didn't make any sense. I'd been taking the pills with my usual devotion. If it had been a seizure I wouldn't have woken up on my own. It wasn't like a bad hangover that went away after lunch.

'Side effects?' he said. 'What do you mean?'

'I'm not exactly using this stuff as prescribed, Benny,' I said. 'The VA didn't know what was wrong with us; they were making it up as they went along. Listen, it's no big deal. A little nausea is all. It's a listed side effect of my anti-nausea medication.'

'Unbelievable,' Benny said. 'It's the twenty-first century, what are you gonna do?'

'Move on.'

'Okay, okay,' Benny said. 'Now you know the second part: has any Revivalist threatened, harassed, offered to suck your dick, or contacted you in any other way?'

'As far as I know, they're holding up their end of the bargain.'

I suppose I had the Elders to thank for my current relationship with the FBI. If Ezekiel White, the head of the Elders' morality police, hadn't hired me as a ready patsy to investigate the murder of Brother Isaiah last year, I wouldn't be so valuable to the Bureau now. Millions had listened to Isaiah's religious broadcasts, and he was still fondly remembered as a man too good for this world. If word got out that White had been involved in the murder, the Elders would end up covered in something more noisome than glory.

I didn't know the specifics of the deal FBI Director Sands had made with the Elders. The negotiations had happened while I was sitting in a motel room in south Florida, surrounded by a dozen agents for my own protection. Every evening the agents would take me for a walk to the same roadside diner that had the same special every day. They couldn't make coffee worth a damn. I had plenty of time to pace the faded carpet, look at the swamp that lay beyond my window, and consider the relative value of my life. I was just a bargaining chip to Sands, another piece of currency no different from the coins that jangled in his pockets. In the end, he decided not to cash me in. My continued health was exchanged for keeping shtum about the location of a few significant corpses, and how they got that way.

'Nothing weird or out of the ordinary at all?'

Benny usually trusted my instincts enough not to make me repeat myself. 'Is something wrong?'

'No,' Benny said. 'I think there's been some rumbling in law enforcement lately. A lot of old-timers are retiring, one way or another.'

'The Revivalists are forcing them out?' I asked.

'Someone in the administration is. We don't know where the orders are coming from. The police commissioners of Chicago, Las Vegas, Salt Lake City and Sacramento have all been replaced in the last month. When you go down the ranks to deputies, chief of detectives and other brass the list just gets longer. As for the Department of Justice, forget about it. Half the attorneys general have been given the boot.'

'Well, they serve at the pleasure of the President,' I said, 'and he was elected at the pleasure of the Elders. What's the official story?'

'Six different flavours of bullshit. Anyone who's refused to go quietly has been charged with incompetence or burial in dirt.'

'Have they come after the Bureau?'

'They wouldn't dare, not after what happened last year.'

Benny didn't say anything for a while. The Brother Isaiah murder had been a big case for him, even if he couldn't brag about it. It had brought him to the attention of the director and fast-tracked his career. That didn't mean either of us looked back on it with fondness.

'Do you remember Isaac?' I said, jumping into the silence.

'You mean my cousin in Florida?'

'No, Isaac Taylor. He replaced Ortiz when we were holding down the Butcher School.' It was our nickname for the Medical Sciences Building of the former University of Tehran. It had been the home of our company for most of the war.

'Oh yeah, that skinny Garden State kid. I remember him. Nice enough, if memory serves. He followed you around like a lost puppy.'

'I don't remember that.'

'You wouldn't have noticed,' Benny said. 'You were too busy being an asshole.' Benny finished the last of his kugel, and belched to eulogize its passing. 'Kid had those big Bambi eyes. How snipers resisted them I'll never know.'

'You keep calling him kid,' I said. 'He was only two years younger than us.'

'Yeah, well, you grow up fast under automatic fire. Why are you calling me about this guy out of the blue? He's not dead is he?'

'His fiancée has reported him missing,' I said. 'It's probably nothing, but would you mind taking a look for me?'

'If I say no, are you going to let the matter drop?'

'You know me better than that.'

The sound of Benny's squeaking chair censored some of his obscenities. 'Okay, Taylor, Isaac, let's see what you've been up to.' There was some typing, a pause, and then some more. It was taking longer than it usually did to dig up someone.

'Is something wrong?'

'I don't know,' he said. 'Gimme a minute.'

I waited while he abused his keyboard.

'That was Taylor with a "y", right?'

'Yeah.'

'I can't find him.'

'You're saying the army has no record?'

'No one has a record,' Benny said. 'Army, IRS, banks, credit companies; it's natch across the board.' A person was in a database from the day they were born. If you learned how to drive, got a job, filed a tax return, got sick, took a mortgage, did pretty much anything besides relieve yourself, it was noted by someone, public or private. The distinction didn't matter much, since the former and the latter now shared everything anyway.

'We've seen this before, Benny.' About a year ago, when I was investigating the death of Brother Isaiah, Jack Small and I ran into some thugs who drew blanks in the usual databases. I'd never gotten around to figuring out why they were after Small and his friends. I'd had one or two other things on my mind at the time. 'It stinks.'

'Of course it stinks,' Benny said. 'It reeks in a way we both recognize, and that's why we're going to forget about it.' It was no simple matter to erase a man's life. A lot of arms would have to be twisted, and a few broken, to do a job this thorough. Only a Revivalist up in the thin air of power would have that kind of authority, maybe even one of the Elders themselves. 'Don't you remember what the director said when we pulled your nuts out of that fire up north?'

'I gave the Bureau the best scoop it's ever had, there was nothing charitable about it,' I said. 'Besides, I've been a good boy since then. I've stayed away from the administration and it's stayed away from me.'

'Well, that's what's got me worried,' Benny said. 'You've gone a whole year without doing anything stupid; I'm worried you're saving it all up to do something truly fucking idiotic. Do us all a favour and drop it, okay?'

'You know I can't do that.'

'So you served with the guy. Big deal, we served with a lot of people.'

'He saved my life, Benny.'

'So what? People save each other's lives all the time in a combat zone; it's fertile ground for that kind of activity. Why do you have to take it as some sort of obligation?'

'I don't know,' I said. That was the funny thing. I hadn't thought about Isaac for ten years, and now I felt I owed him something. 'That's just the way it is. I saved your life, and look at the shit you let me drag you through.'

'About that, I cannot disagree.'

'I'll go and talk to the fiancée,' I said. 'I'll probably find Isaac chained to the quarter slots in Vegas.'

'Will you at least promise me that you'll back off if it looks like the Elders are involved?'

'Of course I will.'

'Yeah, and I'm the fucking Pope,' Benny said, and hung up.

I took the subway to Rockefeller Center. I was early. The afternoon was bright and warm for the time of year, but there used to be more people in the plaza during a blizzard. There were still visitors from every corner of the world, snapping pictures and looking at the space where the tree stood every Christmas, but tourism had followed the rest of the economy down the toilet. The locals were doing what they usually did: everyone struggling to get past everyone else, their heads locked forward and their feet moving quick-time. People had changed in the last year. They made a more conscious effort to keep to themselves beyond the usual, cultivated big-city indifference.

I caught a glimpse of a woman threading her way through the tourists by the statue of Prometheus. Dark, wavy hair fell against a tan raincoat, her aerodynamic legs taking the woman away from the Center at speed. It wasn't her, of course. I'd only caught a glance of the woman's face in profile, her sunglasses keeping out the light and my gaze. It wasn't Iris, but I started following her anyway.

She walked east down Forty-ninth, maybe towards Saks. I weaved between the streams of foot traffic but never seemed to get any closer. She had Iris's talent of making crowds part for her. We got to Fifth Avenue and she had to wait at the corner. I caught up with her, trying not to run, afraid what I would summon if I said Iris's name out loud. When I got within a stride of the woman my arm reached out all on its own, and at that moment I caught her eye in the store window beside us.

We stared at our reflections. The woman turned, took off her sunglasses and confirmed that I was a fool. She was older, her face etched with fine, careworn lines you couldn't see from a distance. Her small blue eyes had a look of fear I never thought I'd see on a crowded New York street in the middle of the day. A look of fear directed at me.

'I'm sorry,' I said, and let my hand drop. 'I thought you were someone else.'

The woman kept staring, expecting me to do I don't know what. Finally she put her sunglasses back on and crossed Fifth

Avenue at double her previous pace, looking over her shoulder to make sure that I was receding into the horizon. I turned around and went back to Rockefeller Center, kicking myself all the way.

My client had arrived while I was busy chasing ghosts. Jose Arquez was the head of security for the Union Metropole, a hotel near the Gershwin Theater. He was a short man with a shaved bullet head and an expression of equal congeniality. Whenever I saw Jose I couldn't help but look around for the cannon they were planning to shoot him out of.

I approached while he was pretending to snap pictures of the plaza. I looked at a giant video screen and didn't make eye contact, as agreed. 'There are less cinematic ways of meeting,' I said.

In my peripheral vision I saw Arquez smile. 'Have you met the whore?' he asked.

'We are now acquainted. She told me her name was Mary.'

'Mary to you, Lucille to our doorman,' Jose said. 'She must have one of those name-of-the-day calendars. What was her proposition?'

'A standard-issue blackmail operation. I take pictures from across the street while she works her magic. The lady also expects me to play the heavy when she puts the squeeze on.'

'Broads like that never do have much imagination.'

'How do you want me proceed?'

'Let her call the tune,' he said. 'We need to catch her red-handed.'

'It's going to be messy once a John is involved,' I replied. 'It would be easier just to ban her. If Mary is arrested for solicitation on the premises, your hotel will be on a list of suspected houses of ill-repute till doomsday.'

'I'll make sure the police never get involved,' Jose said, 'and the Committee for Child Protection is no longer a problem.'

It was a neat trick the Elders had played when they made Ezekiel White's death public. Every organ of the media and state had lionized him for 'solving' Brother Isaiah's death and giving his life trying to apprehend the culprit. They'd repaid White's selfless courage by dissolving the committee – or Holy Rollers as everyone called them – firing most of his agents and rolling the rest into the Department of Homeland Security. It was a fate that the committee richly deserved.

'Are you sure she bought your story?' Jose said.

'She's on the hook; the only question is how long you want her to dangle.'

'The wrinkle in this situation is that she's corrupted one of my employees. That's why the hotel is willing to go to all this trouble. You string her along until Mary – or Lucille – fingers the Judas. After that we'll make sure the problem goes away. Whatever unlucky sap ends up being the John won't be in a position to complain. Has she given you a timeline?'

The screen I was watching switched to the news. Behind a podium emblazoned with the seal of the Department of Homeland Security was a man I hadn't seen in ten years, and had never wanted to see again. The Congressional Medal of Honor hung tight around his neck, falling right into the centre of the camera. His hair was whiter now but still cut to military length, exposing skin pockmarked by age and trauma. His eyes seemed crowded by his new face, compressed into something powerful and dark. The sound was off, but I could hear his voice in my head, the way he used to sound. It was impossible to forget that voice when he turned it on you. I'd heard he spoke differently now; a side effect of being shot in the head.

It had happened while he was serving in the Holy Land. The bullet had entered just below the right eye and left for other business out of the left side of his neck, taking his jaw along for the ride. He'd died on the operating table halfway through surgery,

and would have stayed that way if not for the miracle of defibril-
lation. After he'd stabilized, it had taken six separate procedures
to put his head back together. Most of his jaw was titanium and
the teeth ceramic, the same material they'd used to rebuild the
bones of his face.

The top left of the screen was owned by the ubiquitous
'Remember Houston!' logo. In the past year the Elders or their
media lackeys had decided that the words alone weren't enough,
and had added a small overhead picture of the devastation.
Fallout had ensured that everything was the same as it had been
ten years ago: the same buildings half destroyed, the same cars
thrown and overturned, the same craters where people had lived
and worked. Only the bodies had been removed. The area had
been designated a national monument, to preserve the day
Death had arrived in Houston with a nuclear device in his
luggage.

The picture was supposed to provoke righteous patriotic rage,
but next to that man all it did was remind me of another broken
city. The centre of Tehran hadn't disappeared like Houston; the
buildings we hadn't bombed still stood, the streets still recogniz-
able. It was the people who had disappeared, American and
Iranian alike eaten from the inside by radiation. A group of us
had survived, damaged but still alive, and the reason why was a
mystery no one wanted to solve.

When I didn't respond to Jose's question, he turned to see
what I was staring at, and then the look on my face. 'You know
him?'

The news byline read: 'General Simeon Glass, Director of the
Department of Homeland Security'. I couldn't say the name out
loud. 'He was my commanding officer in Tehran.'

I felt a tremor. It came up from the ground, through my shoes
and gave my bones a little shake. I was worried it was another
side effect until I saw the look on Jose's face. 'Did you feel that?'

'Yeah. Was it an earthquake?'

I shook my head. It was something worse. 'Get back to your hotel,' I said. 'They're going to need you.'

Jose yelled a question at my back, but I was already on the run.

Shock had started to give way to chaos on the streets. 'Do not be afraid,' the Public Address Safety System said. 'Stay in your homes, return to your places of work,' the dispassionate, vaguely female voice said from every television and speaker in the plaza. 'Do not panic. Stay indoors. You are not in danger. Do not panic. "Though I walk through the valley of the shadow of death, I shall fear no evil . . ."'

People weren't inclined to take her advice. Shoppers who had boarded planes and subways to haunt the stores and boutiques now protested at being herded into those same establishments by NYPD and National Guard units. The troops had their hands full with the crowds, but it wouldn't be long before one of them packed me in with the others. I could see black smoke rising in the south, but no more explosions. There was only the sound of sirens and people on the edge of panic.

I left Rockefeller Center going south and got to Forty-eighth Street. Everyone on Fifth Avenue was running the opposite way. There was an underground parking garage on my left, with another entrance on Forty-seventh. I ran through it, the attendants assuming I was another panic-stricken citizen worried about the health of his car.

Forty-seventh Street was empty. A few dozen people hid behind the windows of the jewellery stores. Hemmed in by luxury on velvet, they looked at me like I was on the moon. An officer on horseback rode by on the Avenue of the Americas, He paused and looked down Forty-seventh, the eyes beneath his riot helmet falling on me. I jack-rabbited into the new Lamont Hotel before he had the chance to grab me for my own good.

The lobby was pure chaos. Luggage had been piled in the front entrance like a barricade. Panicking tourists besieged the front desk, demanding in ten languages information, compensation and a way out of the city, right now. The three clerks had only their professional smiles as a defence. The head of security and two bellhops were trying to restore order but nobody was listening. Normally I would have slowed my pace to blend in, but even at a full run I was the most sane-looking person there.

The Lamont's service entrance opened on to Forty-sixth Street. On my right was an office tower. It had a little park in its grounds so employees could eat their lunch in natural light. I kept my pace, still unsure of what I was running towards. The cloud of smoke was growing.

There was a building site on Forty-fifth, sealed up but accessible once I applied my shoulder to plywood. Inside there was nobody to give me trouble, so I slowed down a little. The chorus of sirens was comforting, insofar as it drowned out the emergency PA's inspirational scripture. Helicopters were somewhere overhead, the sound of their blades joining with the charred smell in the air to bring up a lot of unwelcome memories.

I broke out on to Forty-fourth and stopped in the middle of the street. On any other day it would have been suicide. In front of me, so close I could feel the heat of its immolation, half a building had disappeared. It had been replaced by a burning absence doing its best to consume what was left. In better times brokers would have fought like animals over office space around here, but the recession had left a lot of prime Midtown real estate unoccupied. Rented or not, I couldn't imagine why anyone would want to wipe such an innocuous block of grey off the map.

I felt a hand on my arm. It belonged to a short cop in riot gear. 'What the hell are you doing, buddy?' he screamed at me through his plastic face shield. 'You got a death wish or something?'

A black rain fell on us, a toxic mix of incinerated wood, plaster and human flesh. I had seen the movie too many times: in Tehran and twice before in this city. I caught a glimpse of a burning shred of an Adamson memorial poster before it was consumed.

'Move it,' the cop said, pointing in the direction of Sixth Avenue. Tape was already stretched along the length of the street. Fire crews were putting on suits and air tanks, while SWAT teams stood by in case the building made a run for it. When I didn't budge, his nightstick found its way into his hand. 'Move, one way or the other.' The cop led my body towards the tape, but I kept my head where it was. The smoke had covered the sliver of sky visible between the two blocks, plunging the afternoon into an unaccustomed darkness.

I stared at the burning building, and felt something new and terrible on the move.

ISAAC

And he said, Take now thy son, thine only son Isaac, whom thou lovest, and get thee into the land of Moriah; and offer him there for a burnt offering upon one of the mountains which I will tell thee of.

- Genesis xxii, 2, King James Bible

TWO

Ten years ago

'Welcome to Tehran, gentlemen,' I said.

I stood in what remained of a lecture theatre in the Medical Sciences Building of the former University of Tehran. It was now part of Camp Able, the official name for the campus we and several other army and marine units occupied. Fresh meat from the States sat in any part of the room that wasn't completely fucked up.

I looked at the men and felt their faces already disappearing from my mind. I didn't know their names and something about them already bothered me. 'Before we begin, where the hell are your jump wings?'

I saw mostly blank faces, until a voice in the back said, 'We haven't gone through jump school yet, sir.'

Benny – now Sergeant Profane as of last month – rolled his eyes. These men were the new additions to the 82nd Airborne, and they couldn't even jump out of a plane.

Our last sergeant, Brown, had taken some shrapnel in the head during one of our many pointless search-and-destroy missions in the city. An Iranian had taken a few shots and led us into a booby-trapped alley. Most of the time we saw that trick coming, but you couldn't be right all the time. Brown was recuperating stateside. The doctors still weren't sure how bad the damage was.

I swallowed my disbelief and got on with it. 'If you have any questions about billeting or phoning home, ask someone else. This is an intelligence briefing,' I said, by which the army meant a two-page handout that I read aloud, accompanied by PowerPoint slides.

'Our area of operation is the western sector, which extends from the Mehrabad Airport to the old bazaar. Our mission is to secure the road from the airport to the university, to ensure men and supplies can enter the city without being ambushed or blown up.'

Our original mission had been to drop into Iran and secure the airport while the army advanced from Iraq. A logistical SNAFU had kept our planes on the ground for thirty-six hours. By the time we arrived the airport was already secure and Tehran was being bombed flat. We joined units fighting what we thought were holdout elements of the Revolutionary Guard.

I changed to the next slide, which showed the military's overall strategy. That was the name they gave to sixteen text bubbles and about thirty arrows that now crowded the screen. I'd given this lecture five times already, and I still had no idea what that flow chart was supposed to represent.

'As you can see from this diagram, what we do in the western sector is a vital part of the overall mission to' – I checked my notes. We'd been given three different versions of this story since we invaded, and I kept getting them mixed up – 'our overall mission of bringing the mullahs to justice for their crimes against humanity, and putting their nuclear weapons permanently beyond use.'

Everyone in the room knew what our real purpose was. We were here for payback, plain and simple. Houston would be glowing in the dark for a thousand years, and we were turning this country into a parking lot to say thank you. Both sides called themselves armies, but the psychology at work was all street gang.

The next slide showed several photographs of enemy combatants. Some were dead, and the others were about to join their friends in paradise. 'There are two groups that form the majority of enemy contacts. The first is the Basij, a kind of militia.' We called them 'Kids with Kalashnikovs'. 'Before the war, their job was beating up anyone in danger of having a good time. They're young or middle-aged, barely trained and equipped with little besides rifles and rocket-propelled grenades. They're dangerous only if you underestimate them. When someone points a gun at you, don't hesitate because they're young. We lost a man last week to a sniper who was twelve years old.'

That caused some murmuring until Benny shut them up.

'The real enemy is the Revolutionary Guard, the Pasdaran. They are practically their own state, with a separate navy and air force, and they answer only to the Supreme Leader. We've fucked up just about everything they had on four wheels, but they have access to all kinds of current-generation infantry weapons: machine guns, mortars, laser-guided missiles, and lots and lots of rockets.'

'How much action are we likely to see, sir?' said a young private with a Minnesota accent.

'He's not a sir, Private,' Benny said. I could hear the strain of control in his voice. 'Do you see any bars on that uniform?'

'As to action, that depends on your definition,' I said. 'If you're looking for a big stand-up fight, you'll be disappointed. Right now we're playing the biggest hide-and-seek game on earth, with guns. Next?'

'How does our sector compare to the others?'

'It could be worse. The eastern sector includes the Khomeini Mosque and the bazaar. We've shelled both since the start of the war, and the rubble is the perfect place to mount ambushes and mortar attacks. The north is even worse. It used to be the rich part of town, but now it's the end of the Haji Highway, a link between the Alborz Mountains and the city.' The consensus of the international papers was that arms sold to the Iranians were coming across the Caucasus or the Caspian Sea, and then through the mountains where the Pasdaran and what was left of the government were holed up like bank robbers on the lam.

'Were you at the siege of Khomeini Mosque?'

'Yes,' I said. Benny and I exchanged looks. I didn't trust myself to talk about that, nor did I want to. 'If you're looking for war porn, get it somewhere else. Any other questions?' The room was silent. 'We're done.'

The soldiers took the hint and shuffled out of the room. Benny gave me a slow handclap.

'Why do you keep showing up to these, Benny, other than to make my life miserable?'

'Every time you stumble through the script you get a little closer to telling the rookies what it's really like here, and I don't want to miss it when you fall off the cliff.'

'I suppose you could do better.'

'Here's all you have to say about the mission: we're here because some major-league assholes blew up Houston with a nuclear bomb. Those assholes got said bomb from the assholes that used to run things here.'

'So our mission is to kill the second set of assholes.'

'See?' Benny said. 'That wasn't so hard.'

'What about the other assholes?'

'Which ones?'

'The major-league kind.'

He shrugged. 'They're in an undisclosed location being ass-raped by dogs if there's any justice.'

'I'd leave that last part out,' I said. 'New regulations prevent me from saying ass.' The word rape, however, was a-okay.

Benny looked down the corridor where my class had gone, as if they'd left a trail of stupidity and inexperience only he could see.

'So they've sent men who can't jump to an Airborne unit.' Benny shook his head in disgust. 'I think I saw some tricycles out back; maybe we should start calling ourselves an armoured division.'

'Basic's been shortened twice already,' I said. 'They need warm bodies here as fast as they can, and nobody's jumping out of planes any time soon. I'd be happy if they could tie their shoes and recognize an officer at twenty feet.'

'Poor bastard probably just assumed you were one.' In the army's time-honoured tradition of shit rolling downhill, these orientation briefings had fallen from a Military Intelligence officer, to a sergeant, to me. I wasn't in intelligence, but I did have special training in human intelligence collection that qualified me to read from a script. I was supposed to be supporting Airborne units by speaking to the populace. I'd struggled through Arabic for a year, and the army rewarded me by invading a country that speaks Farsi.

'Everyone in intelligence is too busy chasing after the Golden Detainee,' I said. It was our name for the man everyone was looking for, the Pasdaran who could tell the brass where the mullahs and nukes were hiding and generally shit little nuggets of intel on demand. The worse things got, the stronger civilian and military leaders believed in this intelligence Santa Claus. To think otherwise would be too dangerous to their sleep and careers, so they sent kids like us out into the city, to hunt the great white whale of Tehran.

Benny's radio beeped. He mumbled a question into it, and then got up.

'Captain wants to see me,' he said.

I swore. The only time Captain Elks wanted to see Benny was when he wanted us to do something stupid.

'He said you can tag along.'

'Lucky me.'

Halfway down the hall, Benny put a hand on my chest. 'We've got something to discuss before we see the captain.'

'Really?' I said. I had a fair idea of what was coming, and made my face as innocent as possible.

Benny held out his hand. 'Give 'em.'

'Give what?'

'My fucking cigarettes. There were seventeen in my pack yesterday. Three have disappeared.'

'Who would steal only three cigarettes?'

Other soldiers in the hall overheard the conversation, and offered suggestions of their own.

'Maybe it was the rats, Profane.'

'Yeah, or the cockroaches.'

'It was vermin all right,' Benny yelled to the crowd. He knew the longer he dragged this out, the more fun everyone would have at his expense.

'You don't even smoke. Do you know what that makes you?' Benny said, jabbing his finger in front of my face.

'Healthy?'

'A fucking sadist, that's what.'

Benny marched off, and I followed.

We went down two flights to the company's command post. Outside the room were two soldiers from the Marines' First Recon, speaking to an Iranian translator wearing a balaclava. All translators wore them at all times. If the Pasdaran ever found out that they were working for us, they'd kill the man's wife and children in front of him. The marines gave us a brief eyefuck, and then pretended we didn't exist.

'Have you met our new neighbours?' Benny asked.

'I must have missed the housewarming.' The marines were from a group called Task Force Seventeen. They'd moved into the old Central Library in the centre of the university compound. They were an odd collection of units: marines, a company of rangers, and a shitload of Stillwater mercenaries and intelligence contractors. 'They're the new task force hunting for the weapons of mass destruction, aren't they?'

'That's what I hear. They're hinky fuckers,' Benny said, a bit too loud. They didn't react. 'They don't talk to anyone outside the task force, even guys from their own outfits. It's a standing order from Colonel Glass.'

I'd never met Glass, but it wasn't hard to get a picture of the man from the stories that were told. He'd done four tours in Iraq and two in Afghanistan, racked up so many medals he had to rent another guy's chest just to put them all on display. He'd never been before a congressional committee and had shown no interest in politics before Adamson slow-walked into the White House. Now he was a regular guest in the west wing. It was Glass's special relationship with the Commander-in-Chief that had clinched his command of the task force. We'd been in the country a year and a half and had yet to find any evidence of the weapons that had annihilated Houston.

'I wonder what a cache of WMDs looks like,' Benny said. 'Every time I try to visualize it, all I see are old James Bond movies.'

'Whatever it looks like, I hope they find it. We could use some good news.' That great emptiness at the centre of our enterprise was worse than just embarrassing: it was costing us the few allies we had left.

'It's not like you to be optimistic.'

'Yeah, well, scepticism is treason these days.'

The marines finished speaking to the translator and walked off. We went into Elks's office.

The captain was waiting for us in a large room that had once been administrative offices. Staff officers had set up laptops, LCD displays and satellite phones on any desk that still had four legs.

We stood to attention and saluted. Captain Elks gave us our ease. He was a rounded man deep into his thirties. The glasses he wore couldn't help but bring out the sharpness of his features. Word around the base was that he'd joined the reserves years ago, with the idea that it would help with some vague political ambitions. How he'd ended up in the Airborne was a story I'd never heard.

'How is Lieutenant O'Day?' Elks asked, which was about as close as he got to small talk. Our lieutenant had taken some shrapnel last month, and was still recovering in hospital. The army didn't expect him to be out of action long enough to warrant a replacement, so while O'Day was recovering there was no one to protect us from Elks's big ideas.

'He's fine, sir, getting stronger every day,' Benny said.

'Good, good,' Elks said, barely listening. 'I want you to have a look at something.' A large flat screen had been mounted behind him. Playing on a loop was what looked like footage from a Predator drone. We had fleets of the unmanned vehicles flying over the city, watching the world in black and white.

'It's not much to look at,' Elks said. He had a habit of moving his tongue around his mouth while he was thinking about something, as if he were literally chewing on what was being discussed. 'The building you're looking at is about seven hundred and fifty yards away from the university compound, on the far side of Felestin Avenue.' Enough of the sign was left to identify it as an electronics store. The second storey was gone, the remains of the upstairs now serving as a roof. One of the corners facing us sagged dangerously. A strong cough in the wrong direction could send the whole thing to the ground. There was a large pile of debris near the entrance, far more than could have come from the building itself.

'The National Security Agency has been running algorithms on the Predator footage, trying to see what's changed. The computer spat out this. That pile wasn't there a week ago. What do you think it is, Sergeant?'

'It looks like concrete dust,' Benny said. We'd ground up so many buildings and roads with high explosives that a fine layer of it was everywhere. It got in our guns, over our food, in our lungs and up our ass cracks. I'd promised myself then that I'd find a nice forest when the war was over, somewhere a hundred miles from a parking lot or an interstate. I'd meant to keep the promise, until I discovered what the takeout options were in the middle of nowhere.

'What do you make of it, Strange?' Elks said, turning to me. 'You're an intelligence specialist.'

'I can't say, sir,' I said. 'The dust could be from a tunnel under construction.' The Iranians had built a large underground network before the war. It was how they moved men and weapons between the city and the mountains, and popped up out of nowhere to try their luck in an ambush. Every once in a while we'd find a tunnel and dynamite it, but by then their army of young boys would have dug five more already. 'Or it could be the building getting ready to collapse in on itself. It might even be civilians scavenging.'

'There are no civilians in our sector, Corporal,' Elks said. Technically, that was true. President Adamson had given the people of Tehran a fortnight to leave before the invasion. At the time, no one had taken it as anything more than the usual effort to make headaches for the mullahs and minimize collateral damage. When the standoff in Tehran calcified into stone, Adamson declared that anyone still in the city would be treated as an enemy combatant. Tehran became a free-fire zone, and anyone who hadn't been able to load up the minivan and traipse off to a country home was caught in the middle.

'I can't order an airstrike on a pile of dust,' Elks said. 'That search-and-destroy last night used up most of our week's quota.' The heady days of unlimited munitions in the US Army were over. There were too many things that needed blowing up. It must have sounded like a wet dream to the air force, until they realized the money spigot wasn't going to turn another notch.

'Sergeant,' Elks said to Benny, 'reconnoitre the area. If you find a tunnel, call down an airstrike. If you find any high-ranking members of the Revolutionary Guard Corps, detain them.' Prisoners were the highest priority of all operations. Any captured Pasdaran officer was traded between the various military and civilian intelligence services the way prisoners barter in cigarettes. A Golden Detainee could make a man's career, and Elks was no stranger to that fact.

We saluted and let Elks get on with whatever he did. The rest of the unit was in the mess hall for dinner by now, and they had to be told the bad news.

We set out at nightfall. We didn't leave the university compound during the day if we could help it. The Iranians had bought some night-vision equipment off the Russians and Chinese, but what they had wasn't even close to our numbers or quality. Downtown Tehran was pitch black after dark, and being nocturnal animals we liked it that way. The US Army owned the night.

I was on point. Benny guarded the rear. Between us was Gradowski, Henderson, Mitchell – who was insane enough to go to war so he could become a lawyer – and a Tennesseean named Webb. Right behind me was Isaac Taylor, who we still called the new guy, even though he'd been with the unit for months.

It was only eight hundred yards to our target, if we were in the mood for suicide and walked straight there. Procedure was to take a leapfrogging tour of any rock still on top of another in the wasteland between the university and Felestin Avenue. A pile of rubble was a shelter, an intact corner of masonry a blessing. The terrain was so broken it was practically impassible to any vehicle except a tank, and they stood out like a brontosaurus on the White House lawn. This ground belonged to us tiny human mammals, scurrying from one bolthole to another.

Using night vision always felt like entering a parallel world, a green underwater nightmare never clear enough to make you feel at ease. The first thing I looked out for were mines. We were close enough to the university that anyone trying to set up trip-wires or other traps would get a bullet for his trouble. The Revolutionary Guard had mined the city as they withdrew, and they were still able to sneak nasty surprises under our noses using the sewers and the tunnels they connected to. Spotting a mine or a bomb was an inexact science. I was looking for something out of place, which was pretty much everything in this ocean of wreckage and debris.

Snipers were the bigger problem. A day patrol could expect at least one shoot and scoot – some jackass with a Kalashnikov taking a few shots and running for his life. There was less chance of an encounter at night, but anyone we ran into might be real soldiers, trained to hide in the shell of a skyscraper with night vision and a rifle. I didn't spend as much time looking for them, because they'd probably shoot me long before I had the chance.

It took an uneventful half-hour to get near the electronics store. Felestin Avenue was a wide boulevard that ran north–south for miles. Deprived of its trees, it was an open killing ground for anyone who watched it. We waited on one side like nervous foxes in front of a highway, silent except for Benny, who was whispering requests for updated intel. After a second he pointed me forward. I crossed the avenue at a low run, the squad's canary, or its lamb.

I was on the other side and still alive. I took a look around and signalled all clear. The rest of the squad came over. Benny signalled the others to fan out while he, Webb and I took up breach positions around the electronics store. We lay against the wall and listened. Silence. Benny went in first and I backed him up.

The interior was everything you'd expect a bombed-out building to be. Looters had taken whatever hadn't been destroyed. The only intact piece of furniture was a cashier's counter. It was too large to be shifted with ease, which was probably why it was still there. Benny shrugged and signalled to get out of dodge, but stopped when he saw I wasn't following.

Something was wrong with the floor. It was covered in chunks of masonry, cardboard and other bits of nothing, except for a square in front of the counter almost its size. I pointed at the clean space, and then the counter. Benny nodded, and we each took an end. It was lighter than I expected.

Beneath the counter was a hole just big enough for a man. A ladder knocked up from bits of wood beckoned me down. I signalled to Benny where I was going. He indicated no. I signalled again. Benny was now my superior, and could order me not to go down there. He had also felt the full brunt of my stubbornness, and would have to answer questions when we got back if someone didn't investigate. He finally shrugged, which was his form of permission.

I took my time descending. I wanted to be as quiet as possible, and didn't trust the ladder anyway. At the bottom was an unlit tunnel just big enough for a man. There wasn't enough ambient light for my night vision, and I wasn't about to say hello to everyone by using my torch. I put a hand on the wall and felt my way along.

After a while the wall disappeared. I covered my torch and risked a little light. The tunnel had opened into an antechamber. It was big enough to store a mortar tube and some rounds in a wooden box. On top of it were papers I had neither the time nor the light to read. I stuffed them in a pocket and was about to go back when I heard a scrape.

It came from further down the tunnel, close enough that I didn't like my chances if I bolted for the ladder. I flattened myself against the wall of the antechamber and waited. There was another scrape, and the crunching of trainers on new earth.

A man stepped into the antechamber. Cheap tobacco and old sweat had worked its way into his clothes. He was breathing hard, but not moving. Now was as good a time as any.

I shone the torch in his eyes, nearly blinding myself into the bargain. He had enough time to gasp before I pinned his nearest arm and butted him in the head. His head bounced off mine and into the wall, and he collapsed into my arms like a vaporous debutante. I held my unconscious prisoner under the armpits and walked him back towards the ladder.

Benny swore with surprise and levelled his gun when I reappeared with another man. 'What the hell are you doing?' he whispered.

'Getting the captain off our backs,' I said. 'Help me with this asshole.'

Benny lay on the floor and took the prisoner's arms, while I pushed from below. When Benny had him, he laid the man on the floor and tied his hands with zip cuffs. I threw the prisoner over my shoulder and we set off back towards the campus.

We covered the ground in our usual leapfrog way, Benny leading this time. I was in the middle with Isaac behind me, the rest covering our withdrawal. Benny was on the radio detailing the site and what I'd seen of the tunnel. No one had noticed us so far, but the night was young.

Isaac pushed me forward before he yelled, 'Incoming!' The three of us fell into a large shell crater. I felt an explosion nearby, but the two bodies on top of me made it impossible to see anything but dirt. I yelled Isaac's name. He signalled he was okay by getting off me. I gave myself a quick once-over and checked our prisoner.

It was the first time that I'd actually seen my trophy. He was in his thirties, a little emaciated but in much better condition than most of the people we ran into. He was breathing and had no visible signs of trauma, which was good enough under the circumstances. The night vision made it difficult to get a sense of his face; between the lack of depth perception and the way it made eyes phosphoresce, everyone looked like the unquiet dead. The insignia on his shoulder identified him as a major.

'Are you okay?' Benny was yelling over the channel.

I poked my head out of the crater and saw a burning car where I had planned to take cover. 'We're fine. What the hell was that?'

'RPG.'

We had been close enough to the campus for the strong points on the roofs to see the attack and unleash hell. Rifle, machine-gun and 20mm shell fire tore up the remains of any building near the point of attack. Isaac and I put a few shots of our own into the largest building nearby, but it was pissing in a rainstorm.

We began to take fire from another position to the right of the first building, and returned the favour. We rarely saw the men we were shooting at, just their muzzle flashes. I'd aim at those little points of burning powder, pull the trigger and hope a slug found its mark. I was too focused on doing my job to realize something was wrong right away.

'Do those sound like AKs?' I shouted to Benny. The university had shifted its fire to the new contacts.

'What?'

'Those aren't AKs,' I roared. 'Friendly fire.'

'Bravo One,' Benny said, 'does anyone know who's shooting at us?' He had a look of strained patience, like a man waiting for a train that was five minutes late. No one responded for a moment, and then a general ceasefire went out over the radio. We waited, in case more enemies had arrived or my ears were wrong.

I felt Isaac looking at me. He'd saved my life. He wasn't expecting praise, but I still felt like I should say something. 'How did you see that RPG coming?'

'I don't know,' Isaac said. 'I just knew. It was Providence.'

Benny signalled us forward.

'Do you know what destiny is, Corporal?'

I stood in front of Colonel Glass. He'd given me my ease, but I certainly didn't feel it. We were in his office in what had been Tehran University's Central Library.

He sat at a salvaged wooden desk and listened to the sound of his subordinates through the walls. Smoke from his cigar curled towards a shell-hole in the ceiling, the only source of light and ventilation in the room.

It had been a week since I'd pulled that man out of the tunnel on Felestin Avenue. We were on light duty after that; a pat on the head from the captain. I'd been taking it easy until a man from Task Force Seventeen had shown up with a summons I couldn't refuse.

'It's things that are meant to happen, sir,' I said. 'Things that we're meant to do.'

'Exactly, Corporal,' Glass said. 'People use terms like Providence and historical forces, but it's all the same. At one time it was the destiny of the British to command an empire. They ran the banks and kept the seas open for trade. The world depended on them, and accepted their leadership gladly. Now that task has fallen to us. The world wants us to walk the beat, Corporal, and if we have to get the nightstick out once in a while, it doesn't matter as long as we keep them safe.'

Glass's cigar sputtered and went out. While he rifled through his pockets looking for a match, I tried to figure out where this conversation was going.

Glass found his light and took a few puffs to resuscitate his cigar. 'Have you ever heard of the Leviathan?'

'Sir?'

The abrupt change of subject had caught me completely off guard. Over the next six months I'd grow used to Glass's style, which was more lecture than conversation. He made these leaps often, only connecting the two subjects later at his convenience. If that meant some people were confused, they were acceptable losses.

'The Leviathan. It's a mythical sea creature in the Bible, a real son of a bitch. "Behold, the hope of him is in vain: shall not one be cast down even at the sight of him?" Were you in college long enough to read Hobbes?'

'I studied history, and only for two years, sir.'

'Pity. Hobbes was an English philosopher, wrote a book called *Leviathan*. See, Hobbes really understood human nature, unlike most pinhead academics. He said a nation should be controlled by one absolute ruler, a Leviathan, whom no one dared to oppose. That was the only way to keep people in line. Do you follow?'

'I don't think I do, sir.'

Many versions of this meeting had gone through my mind when I was summoned into the colonel's presence. Most of the scenarios weren't good: I'd assumed my stunt in that tunnel had clashed against one of their operations, and I was on my way to catch hell. Of all the possibilities that had gone through my mind, discussing a long-dead English philosopher had not been one of them.

'I'm trying to explain why we're losing this war. Have you ever wondered why the Iranians keep on fighting?'

I hesitated.

'You can speak freely in front of me, son,' Glass said. 'Ranks don't mean anything here.'

I should have known then that he was a liar. Glass could pretend to be a man of the people because he knew respect for that eagle on his collar had been drilled deep into my unconscious. When an officer tried to get chummy, you knew he was either incompetent or dangerous.

'This is their home, sir. They have nowhere else to go.'

'That's only half the answer. You studied history; you know it's littered with conquered peoples. We've blown their cities to hell. They must be living like beasts up there in the mountains: no power, no running water, nothing. Still they fight.' There was admiration in his voice, whether Glass knew it was there or not.

'They know how our country does things: walk into a place, say some pretty things, destroy a building or two, and then it's on to the next stop. They know the American public is a big fat baby: selfish and easily distracted. All they have to do is wait around and the liberals will do us in with their whining about civilians, or the penny-pinchers will complain about the cost. Either way, we'll pack up inside the year. Then the mullahs will emerge from their caves and declare victory, no matter what the country looks like.

'We fought in Iraq with one hand tied behind our backs. Every time we tried to take the gloves off and do what needed to be done, some fag liberal slipped them back on. Our new leaders are just the same, except for the President. He knows what must be done, but he's surrounded by cowards. Do you know why they won't order a full-on attack on the Alborz Mountains?'

'The casualties, sir?'

'Sure, there'd be casualties. We'd be fighting a larger enemy on their terrain; I'm not saying we wouldn't get our hair mussed. But that isn't what really worries them.' Glass stared at the lit end of his cigar, pausing as if he were just making up this speech now.

'Our leaders are afraid. If we go into the mountains in force and come out with nothing, we'll look ridiculous. If we go in and get thrown back, we'll look ridiculous and weak. That's what they can't face. But what do they think we look like now, running around this shithole like headless chickens?'

Glass swore to himself and spat out an errant tobacco leaf. 'Do you know what we do here, Corporal?'

Another sharp turn, and I was equally unprepared.

'Task Force Seventeen's mission is to acquire high-value targets and search for weapons of mass destruction, sir,' I said.

'That's what our orders say, Corporal, but we have a more important job: I'm here to end this war. The mullahs think they can't be touched up there in the mountains. As long as the Cabinet has their panties in a knot, they're right. Maybe we'll get lucky and kill a few, but it won't do enough damage to make any real difference.' Glass leaned a little more over his desk, like he was telling me a secret. 'The weapons are what we really need.'

I decided to see how candid Glass had been when he told me to speak freely. 'I've never understood about the nuclear weapons, sir.' He motioned me to continue. I could see he was intrigued, and that kind of interest from a full colonel was more flattering than I'd like to admit. 'We know it was an Iranian weapon that destroyed Houston. So, beyond putting them out of use, what will finding the nuclear material do?'

'The fucking Russians and Chinese have never taken our word for what happened to Houston, or they believe us and don't care. We know the Chinese are selling them guns. The Pasdaran was hoarding oil for a rainy day like this, and the Chinese need it as badly as we do. The Russians just enjoy fucking with us. We bring those nukes to light, and the whole world turns against mullahs. Everyone will be too scared to sell them weapons or protest about humanitarian bullshit. With a smoking gun, we might even convince some Europeans to get off their asses and help us. Either way, we can say we got what we came for and go home.

'We simply can't afford to look weak this time,' Glass continued. 'The United States must become the Leviathan in this region: it's the only way to prevent another Houston. The only way to do that is to break this country in front of the world. That's the job the President has given me, and I don't intend to disappoint him. Your country needs your help, Corporal.'

'Sir?' I wasn't entirely sure I'd heard correctly.

'I read your file,' Glass said. 'You belong in intelligence, maybe even the Special Forces, and you'd be there if it wasn't for that assault conviction.

Before I joined the army, hospitals had been given unspoken permission to demand proof of the ability to pay before they loaded the uninsured into the ambulance. The flunky they'd sent along for the purpose had asked me for a credit card while my father died on the front lawn of our foreclosed house. My response was to break his jaw. If he could've talked, I'm sure the man would have said he was only doing his job, just like everybody else.

'The file doesn't say what happened, and I don't care. It's ridiculous to look for killers and then expect the men you find to be saints. We can make it go away; I've cleaned up a lot worse.'

'Sir,' I began, not wanting to look stupid but unable to avoid it since I didn't know where he was going, 'I'm not—'

'You're wasted here, Corporal,' Glass said. 'We both know chasing the Pasdaran isn't doing any good. It's emboldening our enemies and getting good men killed for nothing.'

I hadn't disagreed with anything he'd said so far, but that didn't explain his offer.

'I'm told you speak good Arabic, and your Farsi is almost passable,' he said. 'That makes you gold dust in this man's army to begin with. What you did on Felestin Avenue showed intelligence, perception and most of all initiative. That's Special Forces thinking, son, which means you might be able to keep up with my boys.'

Glass's voice was genuinely paternal. Seventeen was famous all over the army for the bond between the colonel and his men. They were a band of brothers or a cult of personality, depending on whom you asked.

'When you want someone hunted down like a dog, there are no finer men in the world,' Glass said. 'The problem is finding the target in the first place. When one of my teams goes after someone, I want you there to speak to the family and observe the area. You've got an investigative mind, Strange. That's what I need.'

'What about the men in my unit, sir? We're short-handed as it is.'

It was the first thing that came into my head. I said it as much out of concern for the others as a defence mechanism until I figured out what to think.

'I know you think you're abandoning them, but that isn't true. When that battalion from the 1st was transferred to Basra, nobody called them deserters. Besides, you'll do more good for your friends in a month working for me than if you stayed with them all year. The best way to keep them safe is to end this war, and I'm the only one who can do it.'

I made the mistake of giving him more silence to work with.

'You come work for me, your whole life will change. You'll be doing important work with the finest war fighters in the world. After all this is over, you could transfer to intelligence or go back to college. The only record you'll have is one of proud service to your country. Write your ticket however you want.'

Maybe it was the last part that got to me. I had seen my future, and it looked pretty bleak. Even if I got to college on the back of the GI Bill, my record would never leave me. I'd be ground down by dead-end jobs, dying a little faster than everyone else until my body acknowledged the obvious and gave out. Everyone dreams of stepping into a brand-new life, and that was what Glass offered me.

'What do you want me to do?'

Glass smiled. Someone had told me that he was only thirty-eight. I hadn't believed them at the time – it was a ridiculously young age to be a full-bird colonel – but standing in front of him I did now. His brown hair was frosting along the edges but still full. Weather not time had lined his face, leaving his recruitment-poster good looks intact. I barely noticed anything else; he had a way of drawing your eyes to his own, and keeping them there.

'Just what you've been trained to do, nothing more. Translate for my men, liaise with the local population, and keep your eyes open.' Glass stood up. He was almost exactly my height. 'America needs us to end this war, Felix,' he said.

A weird kind of energy went through me at the use of my given name.

'Will you help me?' Glass extended his hand.

My hand found his. A second was all it took.

I left his office in a dream. Everything looked blurred, but I felt exactly the opposite. My back was straighter, my breathing calm. In my heart stirred something that might have been called happiness.

'Felix?' Suddenly Benny was in front of me. I was halfway to our post at the Butcher School. 'What the hell happened to you?'

'I'm not sure.'

'Isaac told me a Seventeen shitbird showed up with a summons from the colonel. What happened?'

'He wants me to work for him, Benny.'

'Work for Seventeen?'

Benny was shocked, and then he laughed, and then he was amazed. 'Well, I guess you told him to go fuck himself in the most deferential way possible, right?'

Words wouldn't come. I stared at Benny like a dumb puppet, waiting for someone to pull my strings.

'Felix, what have you done?'

'He agrees with us, Benny. Everything we say about the war, he just said the same thing.'

'So what?'

'So, it's never going to end this way. When our enlistment is up they'll extend it. More of our friends die while we chase kids. We go on missions that make no sense because our officers need to look busy. None of it will ever change.'

I was losing Benny: the shock at what I'd said was giving way to something worse.

'Have you forgotten what his reputation is, Felix?' Benny said. 'Do you remember that guy Seventeen brought in last week?'

'He was an enemy.'

'His back had second-degree burns,' Benny said. 'They tied him to the hood of their Humvee like a fucking deer, and he cooked in the heat. Is that what you want to do?'

'I want the chance to do what I was trained for. If I stay in the unit, you and I both know that will never happen. The colonel sees the bigger picture. He's got the ear of the President. He might be the only one who can change things, and he wants my help.'

Before I opened my mouth, I thought I'd accepted Glass's offer for venal reasons. His offer to clear the assault conviction had been enough to override my spinning moral compass. Once I'd finished talking, I knew it was much worse. I actually believed in the colonel's mission.

Benny didn't say anything. I expected accusations, confusion and a lot of profanity. Instead he looked at the overcast sky. On his face was the saddest expression I'd ever seen.

'Benny . . .' My voice died.

Benny turned and walked away. He didn't look back.

THREE

Isaac Taylor's fiancée and I faced each other across her coffee table. A small tray with two cups and an aluminium coffee pot rested on its chipped beech surface. To my left was a patterned cotton sofa, occupied only by ghosts. We didn't say anything, so the borough of Queens spoke to us through the thin glass of the walk-up's windows.

It was not comfortable.

'Your front door sticks,' I said, which was not the first thing I'd planned on saying.

'I'm sorry?'

'The front door of your building. It's a little warped and the latch sticks. Someone should probably have a look at it.'

'Thank you,' she said.

I was supposed to be asking about her fiancé. 'When was the last time you saw Isaac?'

'A month ago,' Faye said. She poured a cup of coffee and handed it to me. I waved away milk and sugar. 'I see him less and less now because of his new job. He works all hours, and they don't give him much notice.'

Faye stirred milk into her coffee. For a moment the mixture was the same colour as her hair: a light chestnut that whitened past her shade as the milk spread from the centre. She was in her mid-twenties, with a slim figure and a professional's soft tapered hands. She wore little make-up and needed even less. Faye had what talent scouts called 'the wholesome look', a fresh face and trusting blue eyes. Besides a modest engagement ring she wore only a gold cross as simple as the one that adorned the wall.

Jose had called the day before to kill the operation against Mary. She hadn't been seen at the hotel since the bombing. After the attack every traveller, tourist and conventioneer had left the city as fast as JFK could put planes on the tarmac. It was a good bet that she'd followed her marks and skipped town, moving on to Chicago, LA or some other pasture greener than our own.

'Where did he work?'

'Titan Security. I have a card somewhere.' She rose and went into the bedroom.

My mind drifted back to this morning. Benny had shown up at my office at an ungodly hour bearing breakfast and bad news. He'd flopped into my visitor's chair and looked at the greasy bag in his hand for a long time before he spat out what was on his mind.

'You know that explosion in Midtown?' he said.

'I was there.'

'Kirov was inside.'

I blinked at him for a second. Benny took a bite out of his bagel while he waited for my brain to wake up.

'Jesus,' I said, once the dots connected. 'Piotr Kirov?'

Piotr 'Pete' Kirov had been the States' Attorney for the Southern District of New York, one of the most prestigious Department of Justice postings in the entire country. Anything in New York City that was deemed a federal case – terrorism, drugs, public corruption – was handled by him and his attorneys. They also handled civil rights complaints, but what that meant had changed in the last few years.

Benny and I had both become acquainted with Kirov last year. He was the fourth person in law enforcement to be informed of the murders of Thorpe and White. When Benny and his boss, Assistant Director in Charge Presmore, had arrived at Thorpe's cottage, the first thing they'd done was call the director of the FBI. Once the director had been briefed, he called Kirov. At the time I hadn't understood why, since the murders happened out of his jurisdiction. He might have argued that the conspiracy to assassinate Brother Isaiah started in New York, but it would have been a legal traffic jam if any of it ever saw the light of day. Even more confusing was why the director trusted the guy at all. I'd had no choice but to go along with it, as the Bureau was the only friend I had in the world.

'He had kids, didn't he?' I said. 'Two boys.'

We'd shown up at his house at four in the morning. I was struggling to remember what the man looked like, but I had a clear memory of his living room. It was ordinary suburban chic: bright throw pillows on the sofa, sturdy wooden department-store furniture, cream wall-to-wall carpeting. Utterly forgettable, but it stuck in my mind more than the man who owned it. I do remember him standing in the centre of the room while I laid out the whole fiasco. We whispered, because there were children upstairs, and in a few hours Benny and I might become wanted men.

I only got the full picture later, when I was sitting in that motel room in Florida. Kirov had become an unlikely liaison between the administration and the few sane men left in the country. He was the son of Russian refugees, fiercely Orthodox and ferociously anti-Communist. Those attributes, combined with his law and order record, gave him enough credibility to be listened to by some of the Elders. At the same time he was as professional as he was pious, and his position as a US attorney had given him more than one example of the problems of governing on faith alone. The director had known a deal would have to be struck, and Kirov would be the perfect go-between.

'What the hell was he doing there?' I asked.

'It was a raid,' Benny said. 'The building was vacant. Kirov's office got a tip that four men were squatting there, and had turned it into a bomb factory. He was part of a SWAT assault on the building when the place went up.'

'US attorneys don't go on raids,' I said.

'Kirov liked to lead from the front, that's where the TV cameras are.' A reputation for fighting terrorism could be traded in for a congressional seat or maybe even the Attorney General's office. All that grandstanding must have seemed like a great idea at the time.

'Do they know who did it?'

'They got nothing. That's why it's being kept off the news. Homeland Security is tiptoeing around whispering about "national security" and "need-to-know", but it's guarding an empty house. It's got a lot of chutzpah bringing up need-to-know, since the Bureau should have been in the loop in the first place.'

'It didn't tell the Bureau about a major terrorism case?'

'Not a word. The Bureau and Homeland Security have never exactly been kissin' cousins, but now we barely talk. It's gone from suspicion to hostility.' Benny shook his head. 'If I didn't know how incompetent the DHS is, I'd think it was up to something.'

'So who has the case?' I asked.

'Right now, it thinks it does. I don't know who it's planning to put on it; the Transport Security Agency is too busy frisking nuns, and the Coast Guard has other shit to do. I'm amazed an adult hasn't stepped in and spanked some asses, but so far nothing's moved. Our director's going to take a break from screaming bloody murder up in DC to come down and visit us.

He says he wants to see the site for himself, but it's probably some morale-building waste of time. Anyway, he may want to see you when he gets here.'

'Me?' I said. 'What have I got to do with this?'

'Everyone thinks Kirov caught a bad break,' Benny said. 'But there is a chance that more than just glory-hounding caught up with him. The director wants to have a talk with you, in case the deal with the Elders has been broken.'

'Fine,' I said. 'As long as he buys me lunch, I couldn't care less.'

Reminded by the reference to food, Benny held out the sodden paper bag like a junk-food Santa Claus.

'Whatever that is, I don't want it.'

'Suit yourself,' Benny said, pleased with my refusal. He stood and paused to light a cigarette. 'Keep an eye out. It ain't time to shit our pants just yet, but we don't know where this is going.'

I blinked, and saw a business card from Titan Security Services being held in front of my face. Faye smiled.

'I'm sorry,' I said.

'Wherever you were, I hope it was warm.'

'Not unless mundane has a temperature.'

Titan Security Services was Stillwater's mid-range subsidiary: a step above rent-a-cops, but definitely not the killer elite that wore the flagship name. The company guarded banks, some minor government offices, and bulked up a station's security presence during random checks. It was a company card of the kind given out at trade shows and the like, and someone had written the name Tony Scalia on the back. The name felt familiar, but I couldn't place it.

'May I keep this?' She nodded, and I slipped it in my breast pocket. 'Have you called this number?'

'It's disconnected. I called Titan's switchboard and they said it was company policy not to discuss any of their employees.'

'That's not unusual for their kind of work,' I said. 'I'll see if they're more cooperative with me. Have you spoken to Isaac since you saw him last?'

'He called me about two weeks ago.'

'What did you talk about?'

'Nothing important,' Faye said. 'What I was doing, how he was, how much money we had. We save the same amount every month, and it never amounts to much. It was just a good excuse to talk about when we're getting married.' Faye didn't cry. I didn't want her to see I was relieved.

The work of many elbows was visible on the sofa arms, and time had taken its share out of the countertops and cupboards in the little kitchenette that Faye tried to hide with a curtain. The apartment wasn't luxurious, but it was clean. The dusted corners and clear windows spoke of decent people living on the knife-edge of their means. Politicians and talking heads called people like Isaac and Faye 'the salt of the earth'. They patted them on the back and congratulated them for their dignity while they groped for the fleshiest part to stick the knife.

'He didn't mention anything new?' I asked. 'He didn't sound agitated or worried in any way?'

Faye shook her head. 'Isaac sounded the same.'

'What about his friends?'

'We don't have many friends. He mentioned one or two names from church . . .' Faye searched her mind. 'Bill something, that's all I remember.'

'Which church is that?'

'Glorious Redemption, near Rutherford. He's very close to the pastor there, Richard Aftergood.'

'No friends from work?'

She gave me an embarrassed smile that said that question was part of the larger mystery of his employment.

I made a note of the church while I worked myself up to the

next part of the standard questionnaire. I didn't know where this sudden reticence had come from, but it had already worn out its welcome. Last week I'd asked a woman if she could estimate how many prostitutes her husband visited per week, and done it without all this high school blushing.

'Did Isaac ever tell you we served together in Tehran?'

'Yes. He spoke about his tour there a few times,' she said.

We're told not to lie from an early age, but break the commandment for nothing more than basic courtesy or an eagerness to please. No wonder people found it so hard to tell the truth when it actually mattered.

'I haven't seen him since then,' I said. 'I'm not very good at keeping in touch.'

She smiled and waited for me to continue.

'The reason I mentioned it is I want you to know I have a personal stake in finding him. That's why I'm asking these questions, so I need you to answer me as honestly as you can.'

'I'm a big girl,' Faye said. It was an echo of Mary's words, and had the opposite effect of what she'd intended. 'Ask whatever you need to.'

'Was Isaac depressed or worried about something?'

'You mean, was he suicidal?' Faye asked. 'Why would he be? He's getting married.'

I moved on. 'Was he drinking more than usual, or taking drugs?'

'A beer now and then, nothing worse that I saw.'

'Do you think there's another woman in his life?'

'We spend so much time apart, I couldn't say for sure,' Faye said, 'But Isaac isn't really the type, is he?'

There weren't any men's coats on the rack by the door, nor shoes below them. The few books on the shelves were quasi-religious self-help texts, not the spy novels Isaac had devoured when I knew him. I couldn't be sure until I looked in the bedroom, but everything was too neat and tidy to suggest a man had lived here for any length of time.

Faye saw me giving the apartment another once-over with my eyes, and answered the question in my mind. 'He doesn't live here. He has a room in Flushing, in one of those boarding houses.' She wrote down an address and gave it to me.

Boarding houses had made a big comeback in the last decade. In earlier times, young single men unable to care for them-selves had found a furnished room and a surrogate mother. Cohabitation had changed all that, until the government started asking questions about unmarried people whose mail fell on the same doorstep. Room-mates of the same sex could lead to mis-understandings of a worse kind. So people rented small rooms of dubious comfort, a mailing address for everyone's peace of mind.

'Have you been to the boarding house?'

'I went there a few days ago when Isaac hadn't returned any of my calls.' She made a face. 'From what I saw of the outside, I don't know how he stood it.'

'You didn't go in?'

'I didn't have a key and the manager wouldn't let me in. He said he hadn't seen Isaac. He's a nasty character,' Faye said. 'He claimed Isaac owed him rent, and wanted all of it before he'd let me in. I wasn't going to give in to extortion.'

'On the subject of money—'

'I can pay you, don't worry about that,' Faye said. 'I have our savings, and what Isaac kept from his re-enlistment bonus.'

I usually didn't have a problem taking money from someone, especially when I was going to earn it with the sweat of my brow. In my business you couldn't afford to be coy about much, espe-cially not the size of your per diem. Most people who arrived at my door rode in on some kind of misfortune, and the extra expense just added to the injury. Being acquainted with the client and a general rustiness at missing persons accounted for some of my discomfort, but not all.

Much as I hated them, there were advantages to infidelity cases. By the time I showed up, hope was holding the door for me on its way out. The women (it was almost always women) were heartbroken or vengeful, depending on how the coin toss fell that morning. Sometimes they took their anger out on anyone carrying an unlicensed penis in the vicinity. Tears and spite rolled off me in pretty much the same way, familiarity breeding numbness instead of contempt.

Missing persons were another matter. Some potential clients were looking for their exes. It was usually for child support or alimony, but I always had to check that restraining orders weren't involved. Runaways were the worst. Their parents felt fear for the missing, anger at the abandonment, and shame for feeling what they did. Suppressed, it was a toxic cocktail, but it was easier to take than the hope that leaked out of their pores. On the whole, I preferred insurance fraud. I could almost convince myself it was a public service.

'Did you report him as a missing person?'

'Yes.'

'When was that?'

'I went to the police after that manager wouldn't let me into Isaac's apartment. They were absolutely no help. I told them all about Isaac, but they didn't believe me. They were too polite to say so, but they thought I was making it up.'

I wasn't surprised that the police hadn't launched a dragnet. Faye had walked into the station and asked them to find someone who according to their records didn't exist. As soon as the search came up blank, it was natural for the unlucky detective to start thinking Faye was crazy. They assumed that they'd be chasing nothing more than the wish-fulfilment fantasy of a disturbed young woman.

Thousands of missing persons were reported every year – most of them juveniles – and only a fraction of the cases ended, if not happily, at least without the suggestion of foul play. A lot of adults left because they simply didn't like their old lives. That was happening more often now that divorce required proof of infidelity, insanity or homosexuality. Watching the clock at a job you hated, so you could return to a family you despised, it was easy to think of getting in the car, giving the finger to your usual exit, and driving into a glowing sunset unclouded by work days or child support.

Of course it never ended that way. The Internet had made it the work of an average lunch-hour to find someone, if you had the access. Now that the fingerprints and DNA of every American were on file, most detectives could turn up someone on the way to finding their ass with both hands. If the police found them, they were over eighteen and didn't owe child support, the cops had to respect their privacy and leave them alone. That was where bottom-feeders like me usually came into the picture.

'You waited about a week and a half before you reported him missing?'

I didn't have to spell it out for her. 'I know it sounds strange that I'd wait so long. You have to understand, Isaac's job kept him away for weeks at a time. He usually told me before one of his assignments came up so I wouldn't worry. For the first week, I told myself he'd been stuck with something and didn't have time to warn me.'

She was pleading with me a little. When someone disappears, the people around them begin to look at the past forensically. The squabbles and petty disappointments of everyday life bloat and darken under the magnifying effect of the search for meaning. Did she run away because I forbade her to see that boy? Did he abandon me because I've gained ten pounds? Faye wanted to ask if it was her fault, wanted me to say no and absolve her, but pride kept the words chained to the tip of her tongue.

I was out of questions, and her small store of answers had been exhausted a long time ago. Faye's eyes drifted around the small circumference of her living room, waiting. The silence lengthened. The coffee cooled. It was hardly the time to start a chat about the weather. I stood up and put us out of our misery.

'Thank you for the coffee,' I said. 'I'll be in touch in a couple of days, sooner if anything interesting pops up.'

'Thank you,' she said, offering me my coat and hat. 'It sounds strange, but just meeting you has made me feel better. I couldn't face going out or seeing anyone. Rattling around here all day, I started to think the police were right, that I had dreamed him up. But you've met him, you know he's real.'

She saw me to the door.

'One more thing,' I said. 'Do you have a recent picture of Isaac?'

'Of course,' Faye replied. She went into the bedroom for a minute and came out with a single photo. Ten years later, and Isaac still looked young for his age. He'd kept his hair military length, and his skin was softer than anyone I'd ever met who'd spent so much time in the Big Sandbox. He stood in front of Titan headquarters, in their uniform. The smile on his face was the same wide, innocent one that I remembered, but it no longer reached the eyes.

'He must look very different than you remember.'

'Less than I expected,' I said, 'in a good way.'

We stood at the doorway for a moment, looking at Isaac together, before exchanging mumbled goodbyes.

It had begun to rain. My hat did the best it could, but was hard-pressed by cold, hard droplets that hit the brim like buckshot. Some people on the street had been blessed with the foresight to grab an umbrella on their way out the door. The rest of us had no alternative but to soldier on. I took a quick look at Faye's window, found it vacant, and went on the hunt for a cab. It was her hope, not the weather, that bent my head against the sky.

I started with Isaac's room in Flushing. Faye had been too charitable when she described the place to me: it was at the front of the pack in the dive Olympics. A neon sign had once announced the dirty grey building it sagged against as the 'Grand Royal Hotel', until half the vowels burned out and dirt transformed the rest into hieroglyphics. One glance at the lobby was all I needed to know that if they boarded anyone here, it was by the hour.

Decades of whores' high heels had ground the pattern out of the green wall-to-wall carpet. A few ladies of that occupation reclined on the two couches set against the wall, flouting city law by smoking indoors and life by looking so bored and broken. A quick once-over was all it took for them to realize I wasn't in the market for their wares, and after that I might as well have been invisible.

The front desk was a warren of cubby-holes and trash encased in wire mesh. The only trick the animal inside could do was play dead. The manager was a slight, middle-aged man with a little white hair, most of it on his eyebrows. The suit he wore had settled on grey after suffering everything except dry cleaning. The red marks on his neck weren't down to bad hygiene any more than the purple bruise on his face. Someone with large hands had been emphatic with the man, and not long ago. I let him sleep while I counted the stains on his tie.

The manager stirred, and when his eyes focused on me he nearly choked on his breath.

'He ain't come back, I swear,' he said, getting off his stool. His voice was thick with old tar and fear. 'I would have called you guys if he had.'

I don't know who he thought I was: pimps wore flashier suits, and the Mob's were better made. I decided to see where this case of mistaken identity would take me. 'I wanna see Taylor's room.'

'The other guys have been over it,' the manager said.

'I haven't.'

The manager heard the threat in my voice and got out from behind the desk as fast as he could. He led me up two flights of bare concrete to room 309. The manager opened the door with a large keyring on his belt and then stepped aside. He did not look me in the eye.

'I'll see you downstairs,' I said. I let him walk past me and into the stairwell before I went inside.

Room 309 was not a cosy place. The single bed against the far wall was an institutional box-spring number. A bare, discoloured mattress rested on top. A mini fridge was beside the head of the bed for easy access, and a closet with no door took up the wall to my right. Were you to stand in the middle of its warped wooden floor and swing a dead cat, the point of impact would have been the flat-pack dresser in the corner.

Standing in the centre wasn't possible at the moment, because someone had piled everything in the room that could be moved there. The dresser drawers had been pulled out and thrown over, two breaking apart under the strain. Under them I found a small pile of men's old clothes: T-shirts, a pair of faded jeans, briefs with tired elastic waists. The only contribution from the closet had been three wire hangers. There were a few plastic takeaway cartons and some empty beer bottles. There weren't any flyers, receipts or paper of any kind. A hotplate crowned the little mountain.

The police weren't this destructive, even when they were told to take a place apart. They might have pulled out the drawers, and ripped open the mattress, but they wouldn't have put everything together; that would wreck any evidence they were hoping to obtain. A man with a warrant had all the time in the world, but this looked rushed. It was a toss job, done by people who didn't care what the place looked like afterwards.

I went through the room looking for something to tell me who had done this, and what they were looking for. I came up empty on both counts. There wasn't a single thing in the room that could be called individual. I'd never been in a dirty place that was so clean. It didn't take long for me to feel closed in by the bare walls, a palette on which lime-green paint and years of smoke, grease and dirt had mixed together. The shade that came out was often found in the gutters outside a bar after closing.

Isaac may have lied to Faye about that security job. It wasn't the first time a man had spared his pride by hiding things from the people he loved. Even if he were unemployed, Isaac wouldn't have lived in this much filth. The man I had known had more dignity than that. If he had lived somewhere else during the long absences from Faye, Isaac hadn't left a clue to it here.

I stood by the door and looked the room over again. It reminded me of Jack Small's place, that hole where those thugs with no records had tried to give me a few extra breathing holes. Room 309 was the starter option of the brand called poverty, the fastest growing franchise in the continental United States.

I hadn't seen anything new but I did one last circle of the room anyway, more out of frustration than anything else. Something on the floor caught my eye. I squatted by the foot of the bed and looked at two cuts on the floorboard. The floor was covered with marks and scratches, but these were fresh and deliberate. Someone had been slipping a knife between the boards, and once in a while they'd missed.

I pulled the punch dagger from the sheath on my ankle and eased it between the boards. I probed a little, loath to damage the blade. The knife didn't hit anything. I pushed it a little to the right, and the left board came free. I pulled it off and found a small space between the floor and the concrete beneath it. Inside was a small black book wrapped in plastic.

I didn't even have to open it to know what it was. Isaac had carried that book with him the whole time he'd been in Tehran, sealed in a steel waterproof case. Like everyone else I'd assumed it was his pocket Bible, until I saw him writing in it a week into his deployment. He was the first person I'd ever met who kept a diary, or at least the first who would admit it.

I stuffed the book into my coat, stamped the floorboard back into place, and said goodbye to room 309.

The manager snapped to attention as soon as he saw me coming down the stairs. Now that I'd had a look at the room, I decided I could risk pushing him a little harder. 'Has anyone else been up there?'

'No,' he said. 'I didn't let anyone else near, just like your boss said.'

'What about the girl?' I said. I left it vague, in case someone besides Faye was in the picture.

'She bought my song and dance about rent. She ain't been back since.' He struggled to say more. I let him wrestle. 'You suppose I could rent the room out now? It ain't makin' money, being empty like that.'

If anything changed, whoever had tossed the place might find out I'd been there. I had to put that off as long as I could. 'What do you think?'

He nodded and stared at the carpet. I caught the faces of the lounging hookers as I turned towards the door. The old man's spook had got in them too, turning their early indifference inside out. Every single one of them looked at the ground, and made sure not to move.

Isaac had been here, more than once to go to the trouble of hiding the diary. Maybe that meant there was something in there worth concealing after all, a line on where he'd gone. I'd gotten what I wanted, but not in the way I expected. I didn't much like the tough guy act: I wasn't big enough to make it easy, and there were smarter ways to handle things. I'd come in expecting to spin a yarn or two and maybe dole out a little cash if there was information worth buying. Instead the old man took one look at me and assumed I was with whoever had worked him over, assumed it so bad he didn't want to ask me a single question. I wondered what he'd seen in my face, what other shadow lurked there, out of reach of the bathroom mirror.

FOUR

Some errands took me over to West Manhattan. The one pharmacist who the FBI trusted to fill my prescription was near St Vincent's on Fifty-first Street. It was part of a chain, no different from its siblings. I don't know why the Bureau favoured the place. The pharmacist refilled my prescription every time I showed up, no questions asked, so to me he was pretty damn special.

I'd been getting my prescription a little more frequently than I needed to. It wouldn't be enough to get back to the FBI, but I had managed to build up a small cache in case of emergencies. If something went wrong there was enough medication to keep me in shape for about three months. I hoarded out of more than just baseline paranoia: I'd lived a hand-to-mouth medicinal existence for so long I was determined that it would never happen again. I felt like a man who hid crusts of bread years after being released from the gulag, convinced he would starve no matter how many feasts were set in front of him.

Since the office was the first place someone would look for me, I didn't store anything I really needed there. I kept the stash in a tan leather suitcase and moved it around to lockers in different storage companies. A dozen had sprung up around Grand Central since they'd removed all the station's left luggage for security reasons. Along with the medicine, I kept some money and a panic kit the Bureau gave me for a rainy day. So far I hadn't needed to put it to use.

Though I'd told myself I was off the clock, my mind must have been on Isaac. I never would have passed the corner of Forty-eighth and Ninth without a serious distraction.

'Strange,' a familiar voice called out to me. I looked up from my study of the pavement to see Rose beckoning me from the Starlight's open door.

'Hi, Mrs Rose,' I said. I hadn't been back to the Starlight since Iris and I shot it up trying to stay alive. I couldn't face it.

'You haven't been by for a long time. I was getting worried.'

I made no move to come inside.

'Come on,' Rose said, still holding the door open. 'Nobody's gonna bite.'

Rose had one of those open faces you didn't see around much these days. It was too expensive and too dangerous for most people to be so honest. If Rose was aware of the risk, she wasn't the type to care. It was what made her such a class act, and impossible to refuse. I took off my hat, and let her tiny hand nudge me inside.

'Your usual booth is occupied,' she said with an apologetic smile. 'I try to keep it open . . .'

'I lost my squatter's rights a long time ago. I'll take a pin at the counter,' I said, sliding on to one of the stools fixed to the floor.

'So where you been?' Rose asked, coming over to the other side of the counter and pouring me a cup of coffee.

'You could say I've been on holiday.'

She gave me a sidelong glance as she replaced the coffee pot in a row of four stainless-steel machines behind the bar. 'Are you going to tell me her name?'

I laughed. It had been a while since that had happened. 'If only I could lead the fabulous life you dream for me, Mrs Rose,' I said.

'What can I get you?' Rose said, holding up her hand to keep me silent. 'The beef brisket on rye.'

'You should take that act on the road.'

She waved away my words with one hand while the other wrote down the order and passed it through the window to the kitchen. 'It's all you ever order.'

Rose drifted along the counter to serve some other customers. I used the mirrors on the walls to look the place over. Everything was the same: the slugs were gone from the walls, new panels covering any holes that remained. The windows were unbroken, the long counter under my hands restored to its previous glory. The plants were still plastic and every bit of aluminium shone. Billie Holiday was on the jukebox, covering the waterfront with her mournful voice. It was exactly like the old Starlight down to the last detail, except it was no longer my second home.

I didn't recognize any of the faces at the tables. Most of the workers had gone back to the office with the end of the lunch rush. There were a few tourists poring over maps and looking at their cameras. The rest were locals with time to kill, sipping bottomless coffee and talking among themselves.

A young couple occupied my old booth. I would have known they were foreign, even if their English voices hadn't carried in the gap between songs. They didn't have that awareness, an almost extrasensory perception of who was around and how much they could hear. I'd first seen the phenomenon in my kung fu teacher who'd fled the Cultural Revolution. There were people in this city on the lam from every petty tyrant and dictator on the planet. I used to see their fear of anyone with a badge as the symptom of a tropical disease, a sad thing that happened in other parts of the world. Now I saw that look every morning on the subway, and it wasn't because the immigrants had brought it in their luggage. This strain of the disease was home-grown.

A plate of shredded cow arrived in front of me, barely held in check by two large slices of rye bread. A pickle rode shotgun. I closed my eyes and breathed in the smell of the meat, though it reminded me of the full cost of my self-imposed exile.

'I never got the chance to thank you,' Rose said, watching me eat with obvious pleasure.

'Thank me for what?' I asked when the beef had cleared my windpipe.

'For what you did here last year,' Rose said. 'Your average Joe would have hit the floor and not looked up, me included,' she said. 'You fought back against those bastards.'

The bastards in question had only come to this particular diner, on that particular day, because they knew I'd be here watching the world go by. They'd been sent here to make sure I wasn't a nuisance to Mr Lim or his boss Thorpe, and they wouldn't have darkened the Starlight's doorway if I hadn't been a regular.

'I was just trying to defend myself,' I said, hiding my feelings in another mouthful of brisket.

'Don't be modest now,' Rose said. 'There are a lot of people who are walking around today because of you. They told us those two men were terrorists targeting Christians or some nonsense. I say they were just crazy. That's the only way I can think of it, coming into a place where people are trying to eat and turning it into the OK Corral. If you hadn't killed those lunatics, I believe in my heart they would have shot every man, woman and child in here.'

'I'm sorry it had to happen here,' I said.

Of course she didn't get my meaning, and shrugged. 'You know I was off visiting my sister in New Jersey that day? Poor thing had had cancer for a long time, and it was finally coming to the end. That was the first week I'd missed in ten years, since my Benjamin died. I don't believe in angels the way Christians do, so I guess I'll have to call it a funny kind of luck.'

'I couldn't think of a better way to put it.' I gave her the best smile I could, and silently thanked the man in shirtsleeves two stools down when he asked for a refill.

The TV behind the bar was turned to the news. Most establishments showed only sports updates. It wasn't safe to show foreign news in public, and American outlets were equal parts depressing and an insult to the intelligence. Having the lies in front of your face, especially where alcohol was served, might persuade someone to mouth off about the wrong people. At least the sound was turned down.

They were showing footage of the bombed building in Midtown, for ever burning inside the thirty-second loop of footage. They still weren't releasing Kirov's name, nor saying anything about the dead SWAT men. The administration's official stance was not to comment on an ongoing investigation. However, unnamed sources within the administration were hinting that a Palestinian terrorist group was responsible. No one in American journalism had a leash long enough to sniff out information on their own. The Elders were using their surrogates to prepare the ground for laying blame. I didn't know why they were taking so long to point the finger; it was their favourite pastime.

The anchor switched to the other top story of the day. Another round of Military Commission trials were under way at Guantánamo. The trials happened on a schedule that was impossible to understand. One month there would be a flurry of indictments that built into a media circus, culminating in confessions and convictions. Then the court would adjourn for months, with no explanation given.

The subtitles said that the man on trial this morning was part of a larger trial of Holy Land saboteurs. Years into our great adventure, the Temple was no closer to being rebuilt than in the time of the Crusades. Ground hadn't even been broken, which would require dynamiting the Dome of the Rock. Although the presence of a hundred thousand American troops and generous subsidies had greatly expanded the settlements, millions of Jews refused to come home. They stayed in the countries of their birth, spoke the languages they had been raised in, and paid as much attention to Israel as they wished to. This lack of gratitude caused great gnashing of teeth among the men whom the government had decided were theological scholars.

Faith hadn't yet had much effect on the practical problems that stood in the way. Even hardline Israelis couldn't have been thrilled with the idea of levelling the Dome. There hadn't been a general Middle East-wide uprising when we'd invaded Iran, but the implosion of Iraq and Lebanon plus a campaign of bomb-ings all over the world had definitely made it seem that way. No one knew how the region would take the destruction of one of Islam's holiest shrines. It was an abstract question to people over here, but Israel had to live in the neighbourhood. So did our troops, and I imagine that the Pentagon was exerting some pressure in the direction of reality.

That put the Elders in a difficult position: set the whole region on fire and destroy what was left of the economy, or admit they were wrong and call into question the divine blessing under which they ruled. They were fortunate to have a loophole that had been exploited for centuries, and he had horns. It was assumed that Satan and his agents would be working against the mission in the Holy Land. Lucifer knew better than anyone that it would inevit-ably lead to his final defeat, and Christ's glorious return. The minions of Satan must be found, and they must be punished.

The detainee was in his early twenties. When he'd arrived in the Holy Land, he would have looked like any other well-fed American boy. His dark hair would have been longer and the cheeks full instead of hollow. It was the eyes, pale green, that got to me. They were broken on the inside, and I knew how that was done. I couldn't stop myself from wondering why he'd been cast in this role, and how long they'd held him underwater until he agreed to play the part. It was a professional curiosity I could not suppress any more than I could cease breathing air.

Very little of the actual trial was ever shown. Excerpts, edited for content like the other dirty movies the Elders found objectionable, were released to news networks. No journalists were allowed to attend. Every detainee paraded before the cameras had confessed, to both secular and higher powers. If the amazing interrogation techniques the chaplains used at Guantánamo ever swam ashore, half the homicide detectives in the country would be out of a job.

'The mission given to me was sabotage,' the detainee was saying. For a moment I wondered what his voice sounded like, and thought of asking Rose to turn up the volume before I realized I didn't want to know. 'I adulterated concrete, sabotaged cameras and sensors, and took every opportunity to damage the heavy equipment used to build the settlement's security fence.'

'Who gave you this mission?' the prosecutor asked.

'The Children of God, an Islamofascist terror group. They were just the means; the person really directing me was Satan.' The detainee's pause for effect lengthened as he tried to remember his lines.

'Did he give you any other instructions?' the judge prompted.

'Last year, I was told to steal maintenance uniforms and IDs. The Children of God planned to sneak into the settlement and murder as many innocent people as possible, before they homicide-bombed themselves.' He stared out at the camera, his broken green eyes waiting for the next lie from the prosecutor. Below his face, where it always was, were the words: 'Remember Houston!'.

'Come on, Rose, aren't the Yankees or the Knicks playing?' I said, though I was interested in neither. 'I'd take a game of pinochle over this.'

Rose came over and switched to an all-sports channel showing golf.

I finished off the sandwich, took my anti-nausea meds and opened Isaac's diary. I felt a twinge of remorse for violating his privacy, but it was mostly for form's sake. Before the Elders, people had been competing to spill their guts to anyone who would listen, like an overexcited dog pissing on the floor to get attention. People weren't so eager now, when it was too late to take it all back. The only reliable way to keep something secret was to lock it inside your head, and even that wasn't a sure thing. If your poker face slipped for a moment, there was no telling what would come tumbling out.

I skipped to the end, less interested in high school crushes than in his current whereabouts. The last entry was dated after he'd come back from Tehran:

I re-enlisted today. Pastor Aftergood knew I was up, and asked me to come in for a talk. I thought he wanted to ~~talk to~~ counsel me about what I should do after the army, but he told me about the Holy Land project instead.

'It's a beautiful story,' he said. 'God's people returning to the land He gave to them in covenant. It is the duty of every Christian to help them.'

When the pastor convinced me to enlist the first time, he said I'd been called to fight a war for God. I thought that was Tehran, but the pastor said the war for ~~God~~ Jesus didn't end until He returned. Some are called to have Godly children, others to spread the Word, others to fight His enemies. The pastor reminded me that he had fought before he spread the Word, and maybe I would do the same. But he said right now the army is like my family, and I had to take care of them.

It doesn't feel like family. Most of my unit is out, transferred or dead. Sergeant Profane is going to join the Bureau.

Judge is out. I haven't seen Strange since he transferred. One day he was with us and the next, gone. I know he went to Task Force Seventeen, but I never found out why. I knew better than to ask Sergeant Profane about it. The way he acted, it was like Strange was dead, not just with another unit.

I heard later Strange was in Tehran on that day. He's alive, but they're holding all the survivors in some kind of secure hospital. He ~~prote~~ looked out for me when he didn't have to, and now the VA won't even let me say thank you.

Pastor Aftergood showed me a brochure from one of the new settlements they're building in Israel. He said it would be different from Tehran. Each settlement is like a fortress, and I'd be safe inside with all the comforts of home. The concrete walls, razor wire and guard towers reminded me more of a prison than a community. The pastor said five were under construction, but there was a plan for a network of secure settlements all over the Holy Land, as soon as more Jews returned.

I asked him if the Jews didn't want to return, and he smiled at me the way he did when I was a child. 'Jews are stubborn people, son,' he said, 'otherwise they would have already accepted our Saviour. American Jews are the worst: frightened, interfering, liberal. I tell you, if they weren't part of God's plan . . .' He laughed. I didn't know if he was making a joke. 'We'll make them remember their promise to God, you'll see.'

Pastor Aftergood had all my re-enlistment forms with him. The bonus was twice what I expected. I guess Tehran had made the army more desperate than I thought. He put the pen in my hand. I couldn't disappoint the pastor. He's done so much~~, but~~ for me.

I'm on my way to the Holy Land next month. What else could I do?

It wasn't the forwarding address I'd been hoping for. I turned the little book over in my hands, trying to divine some meaning in the cover's cracked black leather. I didn't know why Isaac had set up in that flea-bag, or why he'd taken the time to hide a diary that ended years ago. It made about as much sense as his sudden erasure.

Silence pulled my attention from the leather. The jukebox had gone quiet. No forks touched plates, no voices passed over table-tops. It was completely silent, except for the group behind me.

They wore starched forest-patterned camouflage, and their military boots shone with love and zeal. The oldest was nineteen, the other four hovering somewhere in their seventeenth year. They were the guardians of our moral purity, and most of them were too young to vote.

When Ezekiel White had formed his Committee for Child Protection, they'd infiltrated our lives with the claim that it was the only way to protect the children. After his fall from grace, the Elders had decided to cut out the middleman and let the children protect themselves. That duty fell to the kids who came out of the David Programme. It was the Christian schools' equivalent of the Reserve Officer Training Corps, meant to train the next generation of holy warriors.

The nation had high hopes for these kids; they were touted as the first unspoilt generation since breasts had appeared on television. Their parents had been raised at home or in Church schools, but sooner or later they'd had to confront the wicked modern world. Now that the Elders had stuffed that particular toothpaste back in its tube, it was assumed that there would be no conflicting thoughts or strange feelings to distract them from fulfilling God's plan.

'Five cheeseburgers,' the youngest one said, in a voice that was still a little high. He was a slight boy with close-cropped ash-blond hair and cruel hazel eyes. He had given the order with none of the old-fashioned courtesy the sacred schools so often bragged about. Instead, his voice had the hard edge of entitlement that only came from learning how to fashion money into a cudgel from an early age. By the way the other boys deferred to him, it was obvious he was leader.

The Sons of David whispered among themselves while they waited for their order. Each one carried a sub-machine gun, which they checked and fondled in a way we'd joke about once they were gone. They were gathered around the oldest, who was holding a Personal Digital Assistant. He was a husky young man who wore glasses and kept running his hands through what little the razor had left of his dark brown hair. The captain's bars on his lapel were supposed to signify that he was training for a command in the army without actually being in harm's way. That was the real purpose of the Sons of David: a way for connected Revivalists to support the Holy Land project without sending their own children to enforce it. He'd already abdicated his authority to the cocky blond, so for his future soldiers' sake I hoped he did stay home.

A low murmur returned to the diner. The jukebox stayed silent: the 'Star-Spangled Banner' wasn't on the playlist, and no one was willing to venture anything else. By an unspoken vote the patrons decided to eat and wait them out, like a bad storm.

I couldn't imagine that even the Elders had planned to enforce their morality with children, but White's death had left them scrambling for an alternative. Able-bodied men who were willing to fight were already in short supply, and needed in the Holy Land. The Elders hadn't risked a draft yet, but it was only a matter of time. They distrusted the police and FBI even more now, suspecting treason from every man with the wrong ecumenical credentials. The purge Benny was talking about was proof enough of that. The only option left was to send a boy to do a man's job.

The Sons of David were empowered to issue fines for blasphemy, disrespect to the nation and lewd behaviour, the latter meaning whatever their fertile adolescent imaginations could come up with. Whereas the Committee for Child Protection had been a mockery of a police force with the pretence of investigation, the Sons of David were just Boy Scouts with automatic weapons. The combination was frightening and ridiculous at the same time.

Whatever was on that PDA had their panties in a bunch. The captain and the blond boy were exchanging heated whispers while the whole group took turns to look at the couple in my old booth. They were joining in the general bemusement displayed by the other tourists. After a few days of historical sites, galleries and a Broadway show, half of them suspected the whole scene was being put on for their benefit. Here was an example of the new school of American repression, happening right before their eyes. I had the feeling those two Brits were about to find out just how genuine it was.

The blond-haired boy grabbed the PDA from his captain's hands and marched over to the booth.

'Come with us,' he said. 'There's a warrant for your arrest.' I didn't know the Sons of David had the power to serve warrants, but I wasn't surprised. The government had stopped making clear what their agents could and couldn't do a long time ago.

I caught a glimpse of the screen before he shoved it in the man's face. It was an e-fit, and a particularly bad one. The computer-generated mug could have been half the men in the diner. I wondered why he'd picked the British man. Maybe it was because his girlfriend was black, or because her shirt's V-neck was too deep, or maybe it was just the way the pair had looked at them when they first walked in. In the end it didn't matter. He could do it for any damn reason he liked.

'I'm sorry, I don't understand,' the British man said, pausing at the end of his sentence. He didn't quite know how to address the angry boy in front of him, whether he was an 'officer', 'inspector' or 'private'. It seemed silly to call someone ten years younger 'sir'.

The boy shoved the e-fit in the man's face again. 'This is a warrant. This is you. Come with us peacefully, or we will take you to the nearest precinct by force.'

It finally dawned on the man that the boy was serious. 'What am I being charged with?'

I hadn't seen anything about charges on the screen. From the look on the boy's face, it was obvious he didn't know either. Adolescent insecurities caught up with him: he became conscious of all those pairs of eyes on his body, laughter maybe hiding behind them. Crimson began to spread across the fair skin of his face. 'Come with me now.'

'Listen,' his girlfriend said, 'we flew in yesterday. How could he be the man you're looking for? You've made a mistake—'

Inside the near-silence of the diner, the sound was louder than a gunshot. The boy, in almost a spastic motion, hit the young black woman across the face with the back of his hand. Everyone, myself included, was stunned: Mrs Rose, the other diners, the couple, the Sons of David, even the blond boy was a little shocked at what his hand had done. He'd already felt humiliated, and to be shown up in public by a woman, who he'd been taught should be submissive to his will, was more than he knew how to take. The woman didn't cry, cover her face or scream. She just stared at the boy, open-mouthed, still caught in the grip of disbelief no matter what her cheek said. I felt Rose's eyes on my back. She wanted the big hero of the Starlight Massacre to book a return engagement. It didn't matter that the boy had an automatic weapon, and that wounded pride had already driven him so far around the bend that any further provocation might persuade him to use it. It didn't matter that he had four friends who would back him up because he was one of them, no matter what they thought of his actions. It didn't matter that attacking a Son of David would be treated as an act of terrorism, as was any assault on a representative of the state. I was so ashamed of what had happened last year, I started to consider doing the stupidest thing of my dumb and soon to be shortened life.

The captain touched the boy on the shoulder, but he shook him off.

'Come on,' the young captain said. 'We're not supposed to mess with tourists, remember?'

The boy broke his gaze from the booth to stare at his superior with hatred.

'Let's go.'

The boy turned back to the couple, and at first it looked like he wasn't going to move. 'You'd better learn how to keep your whore under control,' the boy said to the man. 'Her big mouth will get you in trouble.'

The boy stalked out of the diner, hitting the front door open with his palm. The other Sons of David followed.

There was a silence. Even the girl, who was now crying so hard the sobs sent spasms through her body, did it without a sound. Her boyfriend held her close, eyes numb with shock. I caught his eye, and we shared our powerlessness like broken bread. A customer, I'll never know which one, picked up his fork. Another followed suit, and before long there was the sound of eating and then drinking. The tourists were more shocked than the locals, but it wasn't because we were used to it. We knew something they didn't: things like that didn't happen in America, no matter what our lying eyes said.

Rose turned on the jukebox. 'Strange Fruit' began to play. Nobody said a word.

FIVE

I was awake. I was sitting in the chair behind my desk. My gun was in my hand, pointed at the door. It was the early morning.

I had no idea how I'd gotten there. I tried to remember but there was a hole in my head, a blank spot in my memory. I remembered eating lasagne at an Italian place a few blocks uptown. I remembered turning on the news, sitting down, and looking at the diary. I remembered pouring myself a drink. The rest was darkness.

Isaac's diary was on my desk, along with a shot of Scotch and the bottle that was its origin. I'd acquired the bottle earlier that night, and it was a finger lighter than expected. There was no second glass. Even if I'd worked my way through that whole bottle, I never would have left the diary in the open for anyone to see. I sniffed the glass. It smelled like whisky and nothing else.

One of the desk drawers was open. The junk I'd thrown in there over the years all looked accounted for: used batteries, some old receipts, paperclips, a few promotional pens, and an old magnifying glass I kept in a felt case. The latter had belonged to my grandfather, but there was nothing valuable about it. I couldn't remember the last time I'd opened that drawer, and there had never been anything in it worth stealing.

In preparation for the sting on Mary I'd installed a hidden camera in the office just above the front door. The footage came in handy for cases like Mary's, or when a client's cheque bounced. It sent the footage to my computer, which had enough space to record continuously for a year. If I was lucky it had captured my lost minutes.

I turned on my computer and looked at last night's footage. I scanned to the last thing I remembered, the beginning of the one o'clock news bulletin. I was sitting behind my desk reading the diary. There was no one else in the room. The angle was wrong to see what page the diary was open at. The FBI's drug plan had left me enough breathing space to buy a few toys, but a camera good enough to read Isaac's words on the page was still far out of my price range.

I saw myself look closer at a page of Isaac's diary. There was a quizzical expression on my face, a hunch forming there but not yet confirmed. I kept one hand on the page while the other rooted around in my desk. That must have been when the drawer was opened. Before I'd got very far, my body went slack. The searching hand fell to my side, the other kept on the book only by gravity. My eyes rolled back and took the whole head with them. I watched myself take a deep breath, and then begin to shake.

It was a seizure. At first it looked no different from the others; shaking so powerful it had taken three large orderlies to hold me down when I was in the VA hospital. I fast-forwarded and the shaking looked even worse. I'd pushed myself back from the desk but managed to stay in the chair. I fast-forwarded some more, waiting for whoever had saved me to come in. Instead, the seizure began to subside. I looked like a dying fish, each desperate flail for water weaker than the last. Instead of expiring, I fell asleep. A while later I woke up, eyes half mad and on the lookout for enemies that weren't there. I was as surprised as my video double, and began to hunt around the floor for my chin.

Coming out of a seizure on your own was impossible. That's what the doctors at the VA had told me, and my own experience had borne it out. Nothing but an intravenous dose of the anti-spastic drug in the red pills could bring someone around. That was why I'd assumed my nap on the tiles last week was a blackout or new side effect. I suppose I should have been happy about it, but I was too busy wondering why the drugs hadn't stopped the attack in the first place.

I rewound the tape back to the moment before and looked at my face. There was concentration there, but no premonition of what was coming. Seizures cause short-term memory loss during the episode, and sometimes a little before. That might explain what I saw on the tape but didn't remember.

I went into the bathroom, stripped and looked for wounds. I'd come out unscathed except for two buttons on a new shirt. It was dangerous to have an attack while alone and unrestrained. I'd met other patients who had fractured limbs and given themselves concussions in the midst of an attack. A prolonged seizure lasting several hours could even be fatal: the patient goes into cardiac arrest, their nervous system exhausted and shutting down.

When the self-examination was done, I picked up the phone. There was only one man who could explain what had just happened, and after four rings I was on his voicemail.

'You have reached the office of Dr Julius Brown. Our hours are . . .' I let the receptionist's recorded voice drone on. I hadn't expected them to be open shortly after dawn.

'Doc Brown, it's Felix Strange,' I said after the beep. 'I know it's been a while since we talked, but your favourite guinea pig has just done something unusual, and I know it will interest you. Give me a call and let me know if you'll be in New York.'

I hung up the phone and went through the desk drawer again. The only useful thing inside was the magnifying glass. When I wanted to look at something up close I used my camera. It had a powerful telephoto lens, the scourge of adulterers everywhere. Maybe the magnifying glass would have been good enough to discount the hunch that had been forming in my mind at the time. I looked through the diary cover to cover, not reading the words but examining the pages. There was nothing unusual or extraordinary. I couldn't see whatever had caught my eye the first time, or it wasn't there.

I leaned back in my chair and watched light throwing itself against the blinds. The old flip clock on my desk said it was seven. There was nothing more I could do with the diary right now; my eyes swam every time I looked at it. I'd have to hope that whatever I'd seen would attract my attention again. My worry over the unexplained seizure was almost overtaken by my anger. There had been a break in Isaac's disappearance, and I had no idea what it was.

I hid the diary and took a shower. I made some coffee, put on a fresh shirt and my best suit. It was time for church.

Isaac's house of worship was outside Rutherford, New Jersey, just off Route 3. A cab would have marked me as an odd duck to the other worshippers, so I rented a car for the day and drove over. One of the demands I had made on the Bureau was that they reinstate my driving licence. I'd made several specious arguments about the need to fit in and move fast if the administration came looking for me. They made a bigger stink about the licence than they did about the medicine, but they gave me both in the end.

From the road, the church looked like just another mall sucking on the teat of the highway system. It was two storeys of steel and glass, large signs for the businesses inside fixed to its side. What set it apart was a four-storey cross marooned in the concrete sea of its convenient parking. It was a busy morning, the lot almost full. I chased my tail for a while before I found a place to park.

Before I could get out of the car, my phone rang.

'Felix?' Faye said. 'I'm sorry to call you like this, but it's been a few days, and . . .' she trailed off.

'I should have called you earlier,' I said. 'I kept putting it off until I had something to tell you.'

'So no news then,' Faye said. She sounded more disappointed than sad. 'Did you go to his apartment?'

'I got the super to let me in,' I said. 'You were right, the place is a dump. Isaac definitely rented a room there, but I doubt he stayed in it very often.'

'How do you know he stayed there?'

'I found some personal effects—'

'"Personal effects?"' The phrase couldn't support the weight of Faye's hopes and fears.

'Just some old clothes and things,' I said. 'I found his wartime diary as well.'

'Do you think that will lead anywhere?'

'Everything in it is at least ten years old.' I wasn't going to tell her about my forgotten eureka moment until I knew what it was about. 'It's only been a few days,' I said, when she didn't fill the silence. 'I'm sure something will turn up.'

'You're right,' she said. 'I'm sorry, I shouldn't have called.'

'It's fine,' I said. 'I'm about to visit Isaac's pastor. I'll let you know if he says anything.'

'Of course,' Faye said. Her voice was about half the volume it had been at the start of the conversation. 'Thank you, Felix.'

'I'll talk to you soon,' I said, and hung up. I took a deep breath, and wished I were going anywhere besides a church.

Congregants were gathering for the ten o'clock service. The people who walked past me were nothing but solid citizens. There were a lot of young families in their Sunday best, a tradition that had come back into fashion. My suit held up well against the sports coats and chinos that a lot of other men mistook for formal wear.

Just inside the front doors was a small commercial row. There was a dry cleaner's, a drugstore, and a cheque-cashing place that also did pay-day loans and foreign exchange. A sign in each window announced that it was a 'Christian Business', though it didn't say what that meant. I wished I'd brought along a couple of shirts, just to see if garments dry-cleaned with the help of the Lord smelled any different from the regular kind.

Fresh-faced kids in the uniform of the Sons of David flanked every set of double doors that led to the main hall. After what had happened at the Starlight, I suppressed the urge to turn around. These Sons of David were doing nothing more than smiling at every person who came in, calling out to most with their first names. I joined a larger group and tried to look pious.

'Sir,' one of the Sons of David said, touching my shoulder and smiling.

'Yes?'

'You're new here, aren't you?' the young man said. I waited for him to ask for my papers, but instead he extended his hand. 'I'm Hank.'

'Fred,' I said and took his hand.

'Fred, would you mind going upstairs to the balcony?' Hank said. 'It's a little crowded on the ground floor.'

'No problem,' I said, and followed his pointing hand towards the staircase.

I guessed that there was room for around five thousand people in the hall. I looked over the edge of the balcony and saw that most of the ground floor was already full. We sat in box seats used in every movie theatre in the country. The hall had been designed to make a raised platform at one end the focal point. The eyes were drawn to the glass podium emblazoned with a gold cross, the seats for the choir just behind, and the two massive American flags looking down from either side. Right now the platform was empty except for the band, a quintet keeping the congregation entertained with hymns and a few popular pieces of classical music.

I was about to strike up a conversation with the patriarch of a large family next to me when the music doubled in volume. Everyone stood and I scrambled to follow. They sang 'The Lord is my Shepherd', most without hymn books. I mouthed along and tried not to look too out of place.

A procession came down the centre aisle. A boy holding a Bible aloft was followed by a double rank of people in white robes that must be the choir. Behind them came the Reverend Richard Aftergood and his two assistants. He was a short, powerfully built man who had just overshot fifty. Aftergood had some paunch but a lot less than you'd expect of a man his age. He wore a hand-made black suit, and something glittered from his wrist and the centre of his tie. From this distance he looked more like a corporate vice-president than a man of God.

Aftergood joined in the hymn as soon as he reached the podium. When it was over we sat down. He gave his flock a long look and smiled.

'My friends, welcome to another glorious Sunday in the service of the Lord,' he said.

I tuned out about then. I hadn't been to church since my father died. That had been a very different affair, Protestant and sombre, and not just because it was a funeral. Here there was a forty-person choir, live band, video and a lot of dancing and shouting for the Lord. Although I participated as little as possible, I could see the appeal. The traditional Churches just didn't provide enough entertainment.

As the last hymn died down, Aftergood began to arrange

some notes on the lectern. I perked up a little. The sermon would tell me what kind of man I was dealing with.

'They say there will be no Rapture,' Aftergood said, without warning. 'They *say* there will be no Rapture. They say you are sick, they say I am crazy. We are deluded, we are gullible. Mockery, persecution, contempt. It's the price we pay for our love of Jesus, and it's the best bargain on this earth.' Aftergood paused for applause, and wasn't disappointed. 'I know you ask yourself: why? Why do they say these things?

'Put yourself in the shoes of a denier. Just a moment now; more than that is dangerous. You live in a big city. You don't believe in God, or country, or marriage. Maybe you're a little . . . you know.

'So imagine one day you're running errands. They do that too. You're off,' he said, mincing around the stage to enthusiastic laughter, 'to get your granola, and some pornography, maybe stop off at your friend's house and "score" some drugs. But today isn't just any day.' The man next to me leaned in a little in anticipation. 'Today is the day of days, the glorious beginning. Suddenly, all the people you hate – the married couple who take their children to church, the girl who saves herself for marriage, the scolds, the "squares" – you see them all floating in the air. "Then we which are alive and remain shall be caught up together with them in the clouds, to meet the Lord in the air." First Thessalonians four, verse seventeen. And it's happening everywhere, my friends. Everywhere. Highways are blocked by empty cars, pilotless planes fall out of the sky. Millions of people gone in the blink of an eye, up to meet their maker. This elevator only goes one way, and it's up, up, up!'

Aftergood mopped his brow, but that was just an excuse to let the crowd die down a little. 'We are gone, and who is left? Pagans, homosexuals, Muslims and the stubborn deniers of Christ.'

I wasn't sure if he meant Jews or the very sceptical. Thomas had doubted Christ, and Peter had denied him three times. Things had worked out okay for them.

'And for just a moment' – Aftergood squeezed a small space between his fingers – 'that liberal is in paradise. There's no one to tell him to pray, to think of someone besides himself. No one to say he can't get high, marry a horse, or sleep with his sister. If it feels good do it, right? And there's no one left to say no. Without us, America is a shadow, and Godless Europe, the new Roman Empire, reigns in the name of the Antichrist. It's everything a liberal has ever wanted, and they rejoice, because they don't know what's coming.'

Aftergood's hapless stereotype may not have known what lurked around the corner, but the congregation did. There was an expectant silence in the great hall, everyone waiting for the punch line of a joke they already knew and loved more with each retelling.

'Fire, flood, blood. Say it with me: fire, flood, blood!' The room echoed with the chant. 'What will our atheist say when the earth shakes and the rivers boil? It's freak weather, mass hallucination, global warming.' Aftergood laughed. 'Anything but an Act of God. As the trumpets sound and seals are broken, as a third of men upon the earth perish, and famine, disease and death come calling, what will they do?' He was obviously enjoying himself, and so was the congregation. They hung on every apocalyptic word. 'Brothers and sisters, I don't know. I will not be there on that day, nor will you. Where will we be?'

'With the Lord,' came the ecstatic cry.

'Where?'

'With the Lord,' they said again as one.

'Thessalonians again: "and so shall we ever be with the Lord." We will mourn those left, as we must mourn all sinners, but we will not join them. These plagues, these wars that will wash the earth with blood up to a horse's bridle, must be borne by those who have turned against God.

'And when horror piles upon horror, when the divine purpose of this misery cannot be denied, who will the unbeliever run to? Lawyers? "Send a cease-and-desist letter to God. Put a restraining order on Jesus,"' Aftergood said in the most prissy voice he could manage. 'Well, I've got news for them: there is only one law, and it is the law of Jesus Christ the Lamb of God, and He is judge, jury and executioner. Matthew twenty-four: "they shall see the Son of man coming in the clouds of heaven with power and great glory." He is coming, and you'd better get out of his way.' The organ played a few notes to let Aftergood catch his breath. The man on my left was grinning from ear to ear. I didn't find much to smile about in the end of the world, but in this place I was a minority of one.

'He is coming to judge,' Aftergood continued. 'He is coming to cast down the sinners and the blasphemers, the fornicators and the adulterers. John the Revelator says that Jesus will rule with a rod of iron, and you'd better believe there will be no right of appeal. There will be no Supreme Court to tell us when we can't praise Him, no one to take down our commandments from the courthouse and the school. It will be Jesus's law in the morning, afternoon and evening. It will be His rules, north, south, east and west, and anyone who stands against Him will join Satan and his host in oblivion.

'And when He comes, who will be by His side?' Aftergood asked. 'Will it be you?' He pointed to a member of the audience. 'Or you? You too?' He pointed all over the congregation. 'Who will wear the white raiment? Who will be a guest at the wedding when we give ourselves to the risen God? It's time for you to decide: are you with Jesus or against Him? Answer that question, brothers and sisters. I know some here haven't. I know you're hedging your bets, saying, "tomorrow, tomorrow." Well, I say to you: do not delay. Do not waver. Do not falter. Because there is one thing I know, deep in my heart and soul, deeper than my own name. It's a secret.'

Aftergood leaned and looked around furtively. I could see faces in his congregation wanting to shout out the words before he did, like over-eager children.

'Messiah is coming,' Aftergood said, and the room instantly sent the words back to him. 'Messiah is coming,' he said again, and it became a chant. 'Messiah is coming.' Over and over we chanted those words. I kept my scepticism locked inside while my body did what was necessary to fit in. Having a second face was a regular feature of my work and I had a natural talent for it, but as the chant went on I found it harder to resist. There was joy all around me. My voice joined the others from the balcony as they met those from the ground floor. For a moment I felt a lightness in my body. The voices tugged at my sleeve, trying to carry me aloft with the others.

The chant died away. Wardens moved down the aisles with plates of gold, while Reverend Aftergood asked for a donation.

After the service, the crowd filled a meeting hall that was part of the complex. I wore down the linoleum going from average Joe to typical Jane, chatting about the weather and throwing Isaac's name around. No one bit. It was part of my job to be in places I wasn't welcome asking questions no one wanted to answer. Here I met nothing but civility. Everyone I asked ate their complimentary doughnut and replied politely in the negative. I had no reason to think they were lying to me. Isaac must have known someone here, but it was a cast of thousands. Sooner or later I'd have to go to the church administration.

The Sons of David who'd directed me upstairs appeared to solve the dilemma.

'Excuse me,' Hank said. 'Fred?'

'Yes?' I said, trying not to react when he touched me on the arm.

'Reverend Aftergood would like to have a word with you.'

Neither Hank nor his companion gave off even a hint of malice. I didn't think they were the kind to rough me up, especially in a church, but after what I'd seen at the Starlight anything was possible. Hank pointed towards a set of double doors. I followed.

They took me deep into the administrative side of the building. We went up a few flights of stairs, past a receptionist and then an old woman they called Marge. She indicated that the reverend was in his office. Hank frisked me before we went inside. My gun was down with the others in the church locker, but he took my wallet. I was kind of hoping that Captain America would try to pocket it, or at least take a look inside. Instead he opened the office door.

Richard Aftergood stared at me from the moment we entered the room. It wasn't the usual curiosity about someone new. He was trying to take me apart with his eyes, figure out which springs fed what gears. I didn't like it, especially since it was the way I usually looked at other people.

'Have a seat,' Aftergood said. He reached out to accept the offering of my wallet, large biceps sprouting from a powder-blue golf shirt. The biography on the church's website had gone into great detail about Aftergood's Special Forces background, and the medals he'd earned in the first Gulf War.

I took a seat in one of the steel-frame chairs facing his desk and looked around. The years I'd spent in other people's offices had made me something of a connoisseur. The carpet was off-white and covered the entire floor. Wall lamps hidden behind frosted glass provided illumination. Tall arched windows let in the sun on my left, but the only part of God's creation they displayed was the parking lot.

The concrete walls were painted to match the carpet, and covered in gilt-framed photographs. Aftergood was the centre of every single one. In family pictures his wife and kids were arrayed around him like the branches from a tree. The rest were group shots with members of the congregation, none of which featured Isaac. On the wall behind Aftergood's head were larger photographs of him posing with Revivalist luminaries. The only one I recognized on sight was F. Lincoln Howe, the Secretary of State.

'Something wrong?' Aftergood asked, looking up from my ID.

'I thought your office would be more impressive, considering the size of the building,' I said.

'I have a different office for receiving guests,' Aftergood replied, which gave me an indication of how this interview was going to go. 'Why are you here? Did the regional office send you? Was it the Inspectorate?'

I hadn't heard either of the terms before. Whatever they were, Aftergood was afraid of them, judging by the way his body tensed as the words left his mouth. I thought I knew every Revivalist organization there was, but new ones sprang up so fast from the bureaucratic chaos in Washington it was difficult to keep up. 'I have no idea what you're talking about.'

Aftergood leaned back in his chair and stared at me. 'I don't believe you.'

'I'm looking for a friend of mine. I was told that he's a regular here.'

'This isn't a bar, Mr Strange.'

'Ask your congregation what I talked to them about, see what they say.'

'I won't harass them any more than you already have.'

'The Inspectorate wouldn't send a private investigator,' I said, groping in the dark. The argument made a tiny hole in Aftergood's wall of suspicion. 'Especially someone like me.'

He knew what I meant. I was often mistaken for being Jewish: my mother's ancestry made me a Jew on a technicality. I didn't see anything in my features to suggest it, but the misidentification happened often enough that there must have been something. For once it looked like the misimpression might work in my favour.

'Who are you looking for?' Aftergood said.

'Isaac Taylor.'

I wasn't expecting a river of tears or a guilty confession, but the absence of reaction surprised me. Aftergood kept looking at me, the news barely rating a blink. From what I'd seen in Isaac's diary he worshipped this guy, and Aftergood was having trouble mustering any kind of reaction at all.

'How do I know you're a friend of Isaac Taylor's?' Aftergood looked at my ID for a moment, his mood not improving, before he handed it back. 'You could be some bottom-feeder just chasing reward money.'

'There's no reward,' I said. 'I'm looking for Isaac because I served with him in Tehran.'

'You're a veteran?'

'Eighty-second Airborne,' I said. 'You don't believe me, ask your secretary to look it up.'

He didn't pick up the phone, to check my story or have me thrown out. 'I like to think the best of people, Mr Strange,' he said, 'so I'll assume you're telling the truth.' Aftergood looked past me out the window, going through the files in his head. 'I haven't seen Isaac in church for six weeks.'

'You have a big church,' I said. 'Is there a chance you missed his attendance?'

'It is a big church,' Aftergood said, 'but I know the name of every person who passes my threshold. I like to circulate among my congregation after every service, talk to people, see what they need. I look forward to it. I'd be down there right now if you weren't here. Besides, if I hadn't seen him, one of the wardens would have, and there're cameras all over the church.' He glanced at the computer on the desk to his right. 'There's been no sign of him.'

'Isaac's a devout man,' I said. 'Didn't you think that was odd?'

'Sure it was odd. I noticed it myself, that's why I'm so familiar with the particulars. We do our level best to make sure the people who come here stay on the right path, and that includes coming to church. According to our records, the office called him a few times after he missed two Sundays in a row. They left messages but he never called back. After that we usually send out a delegation to their home, in case the person is having a crisis of faith.'

'Did someone go to Isaac's house?' I imagined a coterie of wives hitting that hotel lobby and had to suppress a laugh.

'No. We had the wrong address, and with his parents gone there was no other way to get in touch with him. There had been a mistake somewhere. We called Titan Security Services, which according to our records was where Isaac worked, and they'd never heard of him.'

'Who did you speak to there?' I asked.

'A Mr Scalia,' Aftergood said, looking at the monitor.

I hadn't recognized the name when I saw it on the back of the Titan card Faye gave me. The second time I heard it, an old memory fell into place. He would be my next stop.

'You were a Sergeant for Christ?' I said, pointing to a set of pictures on the wall. Aftergood was in the centre of them all, just like the others, but this time he was surrounded only by young men in uniform. Most hadn't yet seen their twentieth birthday. They smiled at the camera with choirboy eagerness, still ignorant of what wearing the uniform would entail.

'Was, still am and still proud. Why?'

The Sergeants for Christ was a national programme run out

of the White House's Office of Faith. It was designed to coordinate the Pentagon's recruiting efforts with patriotic holy men all over the country. Pentagon PR men helped pastors shape their sermons into ads for the military. The army got the warm bodies it needed, and any holy man from Palookaville, USA, could rise to national prominence if he introduced enough fodder to the cannon.

'Isaac told me you had something to do with his decision to enlist.'

'The military gave me direction, and I thought it could do the same for him. I felt it was every American's duty to make the mullahs pay for Houston. Isn't that why you enlisted?'

'I joined before the attack.'

'When the Holy Land mission began, Isaac understood it was his duty to help.' That wasn't the version that had been in Isaac's diary, but I could understand why Aftergood remembered it differently.

'His duty as an American or a Christian?'

The odd look Aftergood gave me said he didn't see any difference between the two.

'Why are you asking me these questions, Mr Strange?'

'Isaac valued your advice,' I said. 'I thought he might come to you before he made a big decision.'

'I don't reveal what my flock says to me in confidence. I can tell you there was nothing unusual or alarming in what he said.'

'No indications he might leave the Church?'

'As I said, nothing unusual or alarming.' Aftergood put his hands together on the table. 'Isaac is a valued member of this Church. We do our best here to care for our people and make sure they don't fall through the cracks, but we can't be everywhere. I wish I could help you, Mr Strange, but that's all I know.'

Aftergood stopped speaking and stayed that way. He was

either as ignorant as he said or determined to lie in that direction. I had no leverage to see whether he was telling the truth, but I did have one more question. I'd saved it until last, since it would probably get me thrown out of the office.

'Are you still in touch with any of the men in those photos?' I said, pointing again at the Sergeants for Christ publicity shots.

'Some,' Aftergood said. 'Isaac is before their time. Why are you interested in them?'

'Just curiosity,' I said. 'I was wondering how many of them are still alive.'

Aftergood's silence spoke for him.

'I won't take up any more of your time,' I said, rising. I often left my card behind when I questioned people. They usually ended up in the trash or between cushions, but once in a blue moon someone picked up the phone. That was more than enough to justify the cost. I didn't bother in this case: Aftergood knew exactly who I was, and if he knew something there was no way he'd call me.

'Will you tell Isaac to call me when you find him?' Aftergood said. 'We're all very worried about him.'

I nodded and started for the door. Aftergood didn't let me get very far.

'When will you be emigrating to Israel?' His tone suggested a friendly chat about an upcoming vacation, but the question was as innocent as the KGB enquiring about your health.

'Soon,' I said. It was an automatic response. A year ago I would have told him to check the weather forecast in hell first, but I wasn't so free with my opinion now. My name was on enough lists already. 'I have some things to finish here first, and finding Isaac is the most important.' Moving to the Holy Land was still supposed to be voluntary. I'd heard stories about audits, credit checks, even calls from the FBI to Jews who were a bit too vocal about their decision to stay. The stick was emerging from the shadow of the carrot. One call from a man like Aftergood might tie all those bureaucratic strings into a noose around my neck. 'If I went to Israel now, it would feel like I was leaving a brother soldier behind.'

Aftergood nodded, but my military appeal didn't dispel the look in his eye. 'I've been to Israel many times. It's a lovely country, so full of promise. I lead tours there every year for the congregation. Maybe I'll see you there next time, Felix.'

'Maybe you will.'

I opened the door, and found the two Sons of David standing outside. They smiled. I smiled back.

SIX

When I had met the man born as Tony Scalia, everyone called him 'Judge'. We'd served together in Tehran for months, but I only learned his real name when they gave me his post by mistake. If he was still working for Titan he'd be spending time at their New York headquarters on Centre Street. It would be best for both of us if I didn't approach him directly. I'd had a few run-ins with Titan in the course of sticking my nose into other people's business, and they hadn't appreciated it. One of their corporate vice-presidents had personally threatened me with bodily harm if he ever found me on a site they protected. As tempting as it was to stroll into their HQ and throw his name around, I had another plan.

The most popular spot for Titan employees to blow off steam was Petros's Sportsman's Emporium on Franklin Place. In the front was a thousand square feet of equipment for the modern hunter. A shooting range took up the back. I arrived around one, thinking I'd get in a little target practice while I waited to see if Scalia would show. Instead I found him standing in booth three, pointing a .380 automatic at his paper demons.

I waited for Scalia to finish his clip. He put ten rounds into the centre mass of his target, two into the head. He put down his weapon and leaned on the counter, head down. Scalia stayed that way for a while. I was about to say something when he took out his earplugs and turned around.

'Strange,' he said.

'Hello, Judge.'

'Nobody's called me that in ten years.' Tony didn't seem surprised or pleased to see me. He leaned against the counter and said nothing.

'I think you know why I'm here,' I said, competing with the guns going off near us. He shouldn't have been expecting me to fall out of the sky after ten years.

Instead of replying, Tony shifted his eyes to the left. The other five booths were full. Men in Titan uniforms fired identical service weapons at identical targets. 'Will you buy an old army buddy lunch?'

Tony led me to a sports bar around the corner on Leonard Street. The wall space that didn't have big screens showing highlights was shared by sports pennants and black and white portraits. It wasn't the sort of establishment whose door I'd normally darken, even if I didn't dislike organized athletics in any form. The only things it had going for it were deep booths and loud music.

On the way inside I ran into someone else coming out the door. He was a few years older than me and further down on his luck. He wore a tan sports coat frayed at the cuffs and elbows. Two drops of barbecue sauce were on the right side of his tie. He was shorter than me and had his head down when we collided, so he had to look up to see my face.

'Hey, buddy—' he started, but the attitude disappeared as soon as it had arrived. His stubbled, indistinct face filled with the fear reserved for hunted animals. The man stammered something I didn't catch and went off down the street fast.

'A friend of yours?' Scalia asked.

I shrugged and held the door open.

We slid into the back booth and Tony nodded at the waitress, a forty-year-old woman with the body of an OAP. She sauntered over and then shifted her weight from one foot to the next in front of us.

'I'll have my usual,' Tony said. 'You want anything?'

'You do hamburgers?'

The waitress grimaced in a way I interpreted as a yes.

'I'll have one of those.'

Tony and I studied each other while the waitress scribbled on her pad and then wandered off. The last ten years had not been kind to him, and Tomy hadn't looked that great to begin with. His black hair had begun to thin in Tehran, but now it was in full retreat. His skin was sallow and he seemed to pinch his eyes with the lids. He had a long, sober face that couldn't commit to a smile even when it wanted to. That mug had earned him the nickname Judge, as in sober and humourless as. He didn't exactly like it, but with a face like that a nickname was inevitable. At the time, Benny had tried to console him by pointing out that he was lucky not to be stuck with Droopy Dog, or Sadsack Motherfucker.

'You look like hell, Judge.'

Tony laughed, but it sounded more like a bark. 'Same old Strange. You were a prick then and you're a prick now. I guess they haven't found a cure for it.' By the time the last word left his mouth, Tony figured out what he was saying. His eyes widened a little and he cleared his throat. There was another silence, though the scream of the music made it impossible to hear. Tony didn't try to apologize, and I didn't want him to.

I decided to get to the point before the small talk got someone's nose broken. 'I'm looking for Isaac.'

Tony leaned back against the booth. 'I always expected someone to come. I gotta admit I didn't think it would be you.'

'Who were you expecting?'

'The cops, the feds, maybe even the army,' Tony said. 'Someone with a little standing.'

'No one else has asked about him?'

Tony shook his head. 'No one cares. He's out of the army, and Titan's got ten thousand résumés to choose from.'

'Did you get Isaac the job at Titan?'

'Yeah, I vouched for him. I brought Isaac in because he's a decent guy. You know how rare that is?'

'I have an idea.'

'You would not believe some of the sons of bitches I work with. Titan doubled in size last year, and I don't think anyone is checking up on these guys. I wanted a partner I could trust to watch my back. My boss had other ideas.'

'What detail did they stick him on?'

'Babysitting some fed's wife.' Tony could see I was confused, and enjoyed it for a while before he explained. 'Last year, Congress passed a law that said every federal official above a certain level had to have armed protection.'

I'd stopped paying attention to Congress around the time the Elders gave them rubber stamps. 'Did Congress say why?'

'They played the usual tune,' Tony said. 'Grave terrorist threat, clash of civilizations, et cetera,' Tony jerked off the air. 'It keeps the taxpayers on edge, makes them look powerful, and we cash in.'

'Who was Isaac assigned to?'

'A Homeland Security muckety-muck named Campbell. Isaac said he was a Special Investigative Aide to the director of DHS.'

General Glass was the director of DHS. I'd never heard of the position before, but any aide to my old CO would have a lot of dirt on his hands.

'What's a "Special Investigative Aide"?'

Tony shrugged. 'You ask me, they pick these names out of a hat. Whatever he does, Campbell has major suction. I was waiting to meet with our Vice-President of Operations when Campbell came down to sort out the assignment. He wanted to inspect personally the guy who would be spending so much time with his wife. When he showed up, the VP was bowing and scraping so much you'd have thought he was greeting the King of frickin' England. I caught a look at the VP's face before he closed the door, and he was scared.'

'DHS is a big contract. He was probably worried about screwing it up.'

Tony shook his head. 'It was a different kind of fear. He had that look in his eyes, a man about to walk into gunfire, you know what I mean?'

I nodded.

'It was fear for himself, his life. I never thought I'd see it on someone so connected.'

'Did Isaac tell you what it was like working for this bogeyman?'

'A little,' Tony said. 'He said Campbell was never there. The guy's wife was a real homebody, afraid of her own shadow. Isaac said he mostly patrolled the house and kept the lady company.' He saw the question coming. 'Some of Campbell's entourage were always around, and Isaac wouldn't get up to that kind of funny business.'

'I don't suppose he told you where Campbell lived?'

'Naw, he took that need-to-know stuff seriously.'

It didn't make sense. Titan sent Isaac on a milk run and he never came back. 'How did you find out Isaac was missing?'

'The VP called me into his office about two weeks ago. To be honest, I thought I was about to get canned.' Tony grimaced at the memory. 'Instead, he goes through this song and dance about operational security. The long and short of it was don't talk about Isaac and deny he ever worked at Titan. He never told me why.'

'You didn't ask?'

'The first rule of that place is you don't ask questions. If I'd pushed, he would have fired me on the spot. Are you gonna hire me?'

'I'm not trying to bust your balls,' I said. 'Could Isaac have been reassigned to something else?'

'I doubt it. Management's got a chip on its shoulder. The guys are second string and they know it. Whenever a job that requires a security clearance comes up they make a big fuss, give us the "loose-lips" talk and suggest the assigned guy's life is at risk. Most of the time, the guy comes back a week later and regales us with stories about standing in front of a different pile of bricks. This security classification bullshit is usually just one group of suits jerking off another. Isaac didn't have the clearance for a classified assignment, and I would have heard if he'd been moved to something else.'

I was too busy chasing an idea round my head to follow up. Tony let me stare at the table for a while.

'It looks like you got a theory,' Tony said. 'I think I deserve to hear it.'

An idea had begun to form in my mind. It had the advantages of being both simple and plausible. 'I've never met this Campbell; he sounds like a bad egg,' I said. 'Anyone who works for Glass has to have something wrong upstairs.'

'Yeah, you're an expert on that subject.'

I ignored him. 'Maybe Isaac saw something he shouldn't have.'

'You're saying . . .'

'Maybe. It's just a theory.'

Tony whistled through his teeth. 'I thought the worst thing that could happen was that I'd lose my job. I don't know what I was thinking talking to you.'

He started to rise but I grabbed his arm. I felt twenty pairs of eyes on us, and another ten pretending not to watch. 'He's one of us.'

'You've got a lot of fucking nerve coming out with that.' Tony shook off my arm. 'Where were you when I took that sniper round, or when Tennessee lost his legs?'

'I was transferred.'

'You were recruited,' Tony said. 'You went to work for Glass on your own; nobody put a gun to your head.' The way Tony looked at me, I could tell he'd thought about correcting that mistake. 'So what was wrong with you?'

'I was angry.'

'That's not an excuse.'

'I wasn't offering one,' I said. 'If you want to hate me, knock yourself out. That doesn't change the fact that I want to find Isaac, and you want him found.'

Tony calmed down a little. The anger was still in his hands, clenching them up, but at least he was breathing. 'Why are you doing this, Strange?'

'I owe him,' I said.

Tony let himself fall back into the booth. 'I brought him into the company,' he said. 'If something happened to him because of Titan . . .' Tony didn't have the heart to finish. 'You find out what they did to him, and the rest goes under the bridge.'

I put a few bills on the table. 'Thanks for lunch, Judge. It was something.'

Tony wanted to smile, and his face almost obliged him. 'Yeah, it was something. You don't want your burger?' he asked as I got up.

'Feed it to the poor,' I said and walked out, still followed by the eyes.

I headed for the subway while I turned my new theory over. It went like this: Isaac is hired through Titan to keep some DHS bigwig's wife out of the way. Somewhere in the line of duty, he sees something he shouldn't. If Benny was right about a newly aggressive Department of Homeland Security, then the shady high jinks could be official. On the other hand, the dirty laundry could just as easily be domestic. So many things had been criminalized or stigmatized in the last ten years, there were now more secrets in this town than cockroaches.

The theory explained most of what I'd found so far. Full-time bodyguard was a live-in occupation. That would account for the state of the flophouse: he kept it for appearances and emergencies, while actually living under Campbell's roof. If Campbell did kill Isaac, Titan would have a large financial interest in helping him cover it up. DHS threw a lot of money its way, and it would have one of the department's top men on the hook.

It was a great theory, except for all the holes. I didn't know what Isaac might have seen, where he saw it or whether he saw anything at all. I had only Scalia's word that Isaac had worked for this Campbell, and Titan wasn't about to supply corroboration. It looked like Campbell would have to be next on the list. I had nothing to bargain with; I'd have to see how far I could get on charm and good looks.

I guess it was about then that someone broke a two-by-four on my head.

I woke up not much later. I was in the same alley with some new friends, one of whom was holding me upright. In the crowd was the man I'd run into in front of the bar. I almost didn't recognize him; he looked much braver, now that he was backed up by seven men.

'You don't know who we are, do you?' he said.

'I'm sorry,' I said, 'should I have curtsied?'

The man hit me across the face. 'Look at us.'

There wasn't much to see. The men ranged in age from early

twenties to late forties. They were all white and all angry. Some were in the shabby business casual of my interrogator. One wore a dirty T-shirt, the rest uniforms from an auto shop, clothing store and fast food chain. It looked like one of those 'America United' posters the Revivalists put up had jumped off the wall and attacked me.

'What happened to them?' I said, pointing to the two on the ground. One was out cold with a nasty bruise on his face. The other held his leg and moaned occasionally.

'You don't remember?'

Bits and pieces started to come back. I remembered a collage of fists coming at me, most wildly thrown now that I had the time to think about it. That must be why I'd stayed up long enough to knock that guy out. I also recalled the feeling of my heel against the other's knee, the joint giving way and a scream. Whoever had hit me with that two-by-four hadn't done his job.

Adrenaline tends to mess with memory, even without a bump on the head. The body took control in a fight, muscle memory lashing out without waiting for orders from upstairs. Not being consulted, the brain tended to forget things had happened. Whether it did that to spare me trauma or make things easier in an interrogation room, only a neuroscientist could say.

'Both of them?' I said, just to be sure.

My interrogator nodded.

'I guess every cloud does have a silver lining.' I was hit by someone new.

'We're what's left of the Committee for Child Protection,' the man said. 'In New York anyway.'

'You killed Ezekiel White,' said a young man with severe acne scars. 'You dissolved the committee and ruined our lives.'

'First of all, he had it coming.' No one else knew that Iris had dropped White, and I was determined to keep it that way.

'Second, the Elders dissolved the Holy Rollers, not me. And third, if leaving the Rollers ruins your life—'

The acne-scarred youth stopped my lecture with a boot to the solar plexus. I wheezed and sputtered but the man behind me held me up.

'Why don't we just kill him?' the youth asked.

'Not yet,' the other man said. He looked at me for a while, searching for something. 'Why are they hunting us?'

I would have been less surprised if he'd told me I was the Emperor of China. 'What are you talking about?'

'We're disappearing,' he said. 'All the former Rollers, one by one. Friends of mine have gone to work, gone home, and never arrived at either. They're just gone.'

'The police take down our statements and then use them for toilet paper,' the youth said. 'They don't give a fuck.'

'Any one of us could be next,' the man said. 'One of us will be.'

'I don't believe in holding grudges,' I said. 'You have to believe me when I say that I've never heard any of this before. I know you're out of the loop now, but I'm not exactly the Elders' best friend.'

'You're going to tell us who's doing this, and you're going to do it right now.'

I caught a smell in the air: hot tar. A road crew must be working nearby. I considered calling for help, until I saw a man enter the alley with a steaming bucket and a pillowcase. The man – who was short, dissipated and dressed like a homeless regional manager – put down his bucket of tar and opened the pillowcase. It was full of feathers.

'You have got to be joking,' I said.

My interrogator watched me watch him stirring the tar with a stick. 'You may not hold a grudge, Strange, but we do. Killing White queered our meal ticket. Some of us even liked the guy.

Either way, you owe us. There are two ways we can collect.' He held the stick close, the heat of the tar cooking my face. Another few inches and it would take it right off. 'You tell us something worthwhile, you escape with a beating. You don't cooperate, and we got a lot of feathers.' He waved the stick in front of my face. The others laughed.

'I don't know what century you think you're living in,' I said, 'but you're not going to tar and feather me in the middle of the street.'

'Do you see anyone trying to stop me?'

The report from the shotgun startled my captor so much he nearly let me fall into the tar. Standing at the mouth of the alley was Jack Small. He held a shotgun on the ringleader, but in this kind of confined space he would sweep up nearly everyone.

I hadn't seen Jack since those mystery men had tried to kill us last year. It was a friendship that had lasted just as long as we were under fire. I hadn't wanted to know about or get mixed up in whatever Jack was doing, and he made clear that the feeling was mutual. I could explain his sudden appearance about as well as the men threatening to dispense feathered justice.

Standing next to Jack was a man I'd seen before. He was black and in his late forties. His moustache, thick and grey like steel wool, jogged my memory. He had been tending bar at that veteran dive where I'd had a drink with Jack. Everyone had called him Cal.

'Okay, shitbirds, listen up,' Cal said. 'You can walk out of the alley single file, or you can stay with your friends and wait for the sirens. Either way, nobody lays another hand on Strange.'

It was hardly a contest of wills. They were forming a line almost as soon as Cal finished talking. My captor let me go so quickly I nearly fell over again. This pack of dogs knew when it was against a wolf.

'I owe you one,' I said, when the uninjured ex-Rollers had left.

The other two were still on the ground; none of their friends had thought to pick them up during their single-file retreat. I tried to stand and almost succeeded. Jack and Cal steadied me.

'Take it easy,' Jack said. 'They fucked you up good.' They laid me back down on the ground. 'Sorry we can't make you more comfortable, but we were never here.'

'Where?' I said. My head was spinning.

Half the sky disappeared as the bald planet of Cal's head rose in the corner of my eye. 'Meet us at Grand Central, in front of track sixteen, noon in three days,' he whispered in my ear. 'We'll tell you what you need to know.'

The sky was full again, and I heard sirens in the distance. Jack and Cal were gone.

SEVEN

The hospital room I woke up in was better than an uninsured schmuck like me could afford. It was private for starters, with enough room for my bed and a visitor's chair. The walls and floor were blinding white. Both smelled of disinfectant. The window was open, but from my bed I could see only the tops of trees.

I'd spent the end of the war being shuttled around military hospitals in Kuwait, Germany, Korea and the US. I saw the world, but it always looked like this room. There were about fifty of us showing symptoms at the time. They kept us in isolation so I never saw the others. We were a fun diversion for army doctors; a curiosity to be studied like a mummy stolen by Victorian archaeologists. When the novelty wore off we'd be transferred to another hospital so we could be someone else's problem. Eventually I got dumped on the Veterans Administration, where someone made the mistake of giving a damn.

My convalescence grand tour had done more than make me an involuntary expert on hospital food. The first thing I did when I woke up was check the machines around me. An IV drip of anything but morphine was the medical version of interior decorating, and could be ignored. A heart-rate monitor was cause for concern, a ventilator a worry. A defibrillator left within easy reach was a far worse omen for your chances of survival than some hobo telling you to beware the Ides of March.

My personal nemesis was the EEG machine. It was always there, no matter which hospital I was stuck in that week. The electrodes made my scalp itch, even when they implanted them directly on my brain. The only thing my many doctors had ever agreed on was that the condition was neurological. They kept me tied to the EEG, hoping to crack the signals of my brain like they were encrypted messages. Even when it was turned off, I felt like the machine was waiting, hoping I'd have a seizure. Then it could have its day in the sun, charting with precise lines the Armageddon kicking off inside my skull.

The only machine in this room was a television, which re-assured me more than any doctor's bedside manner. I sat up and had to stifle a scream. My chest ached, and breathing made it worse.

On the bedside table was my phone, with a message waiting. It was from Faye, keeping in touch in case I'd found anything new. She tried to keep the tone light, but I heard the plea loud and clear. I'd planned on calling her anyway; Faye needed to know I'd be on forced rest for a few days.

She picked up on the first ring. 'Felix?'

'Hi.' I coughed, and had to swallow the pain.

'Felix, are you okay?'

'Not really. I'm in the hospital.'

'My God, what happened?'

'I was in the wrong place at the wrong time,' I said. 'It's nothing to do with Isaac, just some bad luck.'

'Are you going to be okay?' Faye asked. She seemed genuinely concerned about me, and not just the delay. It threw me off balance, but only for a moment.

Benny opened the door and stepped inside. I caught a glimpse of the hospital corridor and an NYPD uniform sitting in a chair opposite my room.

'Listen, I have to go. I have to take a few days off to heal,' I said. 'I won't bill you.' Before she could respond, I mumbled a goodbye and hung up.

'How do you feel?' Benny asked.

'I've been better,' I said. 'What's with the cop outside?'

'A little precaution insisted upon by the assistant director. Besides, knowing your opinion of hospitals, I expected you to make a break for it as soon as you could put one foot in front of the other.'

Benny pulled the room's other piece of furniture, a worn blue plastic chair, up to my bed. 'So what happened?' he said. 'Gimme the short version; I'm not interested in how long you begged for your life.'

'I ran into some old friends,' I said. 'They claimed to be ex-Rollers.'

'Claimed?'

'I don't know why anyone would want that honour, so I took their word for it.'

'What did they want?'

'Revenge,' I said, 'and some information. They wanted to know who was making their fellow alumni disappear.' Benny sat up straight, which he only did on special occasions. 'Did the Bureau get wind of this?'

Benny shook his head. 'Not that I know of. Did they say how many?'

'They weren't in the mood to give details.'

'Why did they come to you?'

'They assumed I was involved. Someone's got an inflated idea of my importance.'

Benny rapped his hands against the plastic chair. 'Did they mention the Elders?'

I started to shake my head, but pain shot up through my neck into my brain. 'It wasn't their style. If the Elders had wanted me out of the way, they wouldn't have sent clowns in cheap suits to lynch me.'

Benny nodded. He knew it would have been a bag over the head and a free trip to a foreign country. He rose and began to pace. 'When the director gets here, he'll sort it out. He might even know something about these disappearing Rollers.'

'I wouldn't hold my breath on that,' I said. 'Those disappearances could easily be a coincidence. An ex-Roller must have a lot of enemies.' The Rollers had been little more than a confederation of bullies under head tormentor Ezekiel White. The honest ones destroyed careers, ruined marriages, and proclaimed parents unfit to see their own children. The corrupt ones took money and other favours to do it to someone else.

'I see what you mean,' Benny said. 'If I were looking for their enemies, I'd start with the phone book.'

'Since the director is still coming, I assume Homeland Security hasn't seen the light about the Kirov case?'

'It's told us the casualties at least,' Benny said, as he picked at a crack in the floor with his foot. 'Kirov and twelve SWAT members. Two more are in intensive care and could go either way.'

'Fuck,' I said, because there were no other words. 'New York hasn't lost that many officers in one day since—'

'I know,' Benny said. 'Someone in DC better get their hand out of their ass soon. I wouldn't trust DHS to find my fucking dog, let alone solve something like this.'

Our conversation was interrupted by the entry of an attractive Puerto Rican nurse. She was in her mid-thirties and had beautiful dark eyes, made even darker by the circles under them.

'You're awake,' she said. The nurse took my chart from the

end of the bed and looked it over. 'Are you experiencing any dizziness or discomfort?'

'I'm not dizzy,' I said, 'and I was comfortable until this jackass showed up.'

Benny showed the nurse his ID. 'This man is a suspect in the unnatural violation of several city buses,' he said. 'Don't worry; he isn't dangerous unless you run on hydrogen.'

The nurse looked back and forth a few times and made the unvoiced decision to ignore us. 'You've sustained a mild traumatic brain injury.'

'What's mild about a traumatic brain injury?'

'The common word is concussion,' she said. 'You may experience dizziness, nausea and confusion for a little while, but there's no permanent damage.'

'There's not much in there to break,' Benny said, while he continued his assault on the crack in the floor.

'Stop that,' the nurse said to Benny. To my amazement, he did. 'I need to look at your stitches.' She undid the top buttons of my hospital gown so I could pull it down to my waist. The nurse inspected my torso and sucked hard on her teeth. 'What do you do for a living, play in traffic?'

The old wounds the nurse was admiring were the rewards of a decade of making a living the hard way. She touched a long white scar at the base of my neck, just above the collarbone.

'That was a cheating husband who didn't appreciate my photography skills,' I said. 'He jumped me with a hunting knife after I testified at his divorce.'

'Did he shoot you in the stomach as well?' the nurse asked. There was a small circular scar to the right of my belly button.

'No, that was a woman. She hired me to find evidence of her husband's infidelity, and when I did my job she blamed me for the break-up of her marriage. Lucky for me, the gun she used was small enough to fit in her purse.'

'That scar on your left side also looks like a gunshot wound.'

'A gift from a sniper in Tehran.'

'Where did you get hit during the siege?' Benny asked.

'You mean while I was saving your life? The ass.'

'Maybe you should check there,' Benny said.

She ignored him and felt around my ribcage with her fingers. I tried not to wince. 'You cracked two ribs, but they're still in position. You're doing pretty well, considering. I'd recommend you go home and rest for at least the next two weeks. You can check yourself out at the front desk when you're ready.'

I thanked her but she didn't seem to notice.

On her way out, the nurse paused to stare Benny down. 'As for you,' she said, 'call your mother.'

I tried not to laugh, because it hurt like hell.

'Are you going to take her advice and rest?' Benny said.

'Isaac is still missing.'

'I figured you'd say that. Have you gotten anywhere?'

'I've gotten somewhere,' I said, 'but nothing worth writing home about.'

'Have the Elders or their Revivalist henchmen come up?'

'Nothing yet.' I didn't have any proof of Campbell's involvement, so it was only mostly a lie. I didn't want to give Benny an ulcer until I had something concrete.

'Fair warning,' Benny said, 'you may not have much longer to wrap this up. The mood the director's in right now, when he hears about this he may put you back in protective custody.'

'I'm not going back to that motel.'

'It would be something more permanent this time.'

'I don't care. The Bureau will put me in a suburb in Arizona and leave me there to rot. What am I gonna do, Benny, play shuffleboard for the rest of my life?'

'At least you'll still be alive.' Benny picked up his hat and made for the door. 'Your clothes are in the closet, and your gun is down at the front desk. The Bureau has you registered as a Mr Charles Fox, so don't forget that when you sign yourself out.'

'I ran into Tony Scalia just before the Rollers showed up,' I said.

'Who?'

'Judge.'

'That's Judge's real name?' Benny whistled. 'How is he?'

'Scared.'

'Yeah, well, he can join the club.'

Benny left me to get dressed. My ribs complained every time I moved, and it was an ordeal just to get both legs into my trousers. In the corridor, I heard my protection snoring.

Back at the office, I followed the nurse's orders and stayed put. It was difficult to move, but I had all the time I wanted to think. It didn't do me much good. I wouldn't be able to follow up on what Judge had told me for a few days: my ribs made even a flight of stairs an ordeal.

There was a knock on the office door. My gun was on the desk, never far from my hand nowadays. The outside camera showed Faye standing in front of my door, holding a dish wrapped in foil. She was alone.

I wished I'd installed an automatic door lock when I bought those cameras. It took me longer than the average septuagenarian to get out of my chair and to the door.

Faye was waiting on the other side. She smiled and held up the dish.

'For your recovery,' she said. 'It's a casserole.'

'Thanks.'

'May I come in?'

I stood aside.

Faye looked around for a home for the casserole and didn't see any likely prospects. Every square inch of my desk was covered with papers, coffee cups and a gun-cleaning kit I'd already used six times to try to break the monotony.

'I'll take that,' I said, and went into the kitchenette. I shoved some dirty dishes into the sink so they could be with their friends, and left the casserole in their place.

When I came into the main room, Faye was taking her time looking the place over. I suddenly became conscious of the unswept corners and the overflowing bin next to my desk. I don't know why it bothered me; Faye hadn't hired me for my sense of hygiene.

'So this is where you live,' Faye said. 'It's nice.'

'It's affordable,' I said. 'Like I said on the phone, I need to rest for a few days. Sorry about the delay. Is there something I can do for you?'

'Oh nothing, I just wanted to see if you were okay.'

I waited.

'You said something about a diary when you called?'

'He kept it during the war.' Isaac wasn't alone in the desire to document the great adventure, but he was the only one to use such an old medium. There were almost as many video cameras as there were rifles in our company. My fellow soldiers nursed dreams of fame, fortune and capturing their badass exploits for posterity. Once it became apparent we were in a different war from the one that had been advertised, the cameras disappeared. No one wanted to remember, let alone have it on film.

'May I have it?' Faye asked. 'It's just that I have so few things of his,' she continued, when she saw my hesitation. 'He kept nothing at my place. I even hid my pictures of him, in case someone saw. I was so stupid. I have friends who keep pictures of their boyfriends around, even live together, and nothing happens to them.'

'That's courage,' I said. 'It's not the same as intelligence.'

'Either way, I want to make up for it,' Faye said. 'May I have the diary?'

'I need to hold on to it for a little while,' I said.

'Why? I thought you said it wasn't important.'

'To be honest, I'm not sure whether it is or not.'

'Felix, if you're keeping something from me because you think it will hurt me, or—'

'I'm not keeping anything from you,' I said, which was of course a lie. She could see I was being evasive about something. I had to throw her a bone. 'I found the diary beneath the floorboards of that flophouse room. I've gone through it and everything in there is from his time in the Big Sandbox. I don't know why Isaac hid the diary; maybe he was just trying to guard his privacy. I need it until I can rule it out.'

I could tell Faye wasn't happy about it: her arms were crossed and she had a look on her face more appropriate to a child denied ice cream. 'May I see it at least?'

She was pushing a little too hard, and I couldn't help but wonder what the angle was. I knew most Titan employees had a life insurance policy bought through the company. Faye would need proof of his death to collect on it. She'd also need some proof he'd been alive in the first place.

'Sure.'

I took the diary from its improvised hiding place. Faye flipped through a few pages, barely reading Isaac's neat hand.

'He never told me he'd kept a diary,' she said.

Faye skimmed a few more pages and then gave it back to me with obvious reluctance.

'If that diary means something, you'll tell me, right?' she said. 'No matter what.'

'You have my word,' I said. 'You have to trust me, Faye.'

'You don't trust me,' she said. It was surprising how loud she made my front door slam with such delicate arms.

117

EIGHT

Cal and Jack were waiting by track sixteen, right where they said they'd be. Cal was reading the *Times* while Jack kept *Soldier of Fortune* in front of his face.

My phone was as useful a prop as it was a communications tool. It gave me a reason to linger anywhere and be inconspicuous – just another hump checking his messages – and I could play with it a lot longer than my shoelaces. I stopped near them and pretended to press a few buttons.

A few sidelong glances gave me my first good look at the pair without the interference of head trauma. Cal was the same as I remembered. He topped six feet, with a shaved head and a thick moustache the colour of bone. From the lines on his face I guessed fifty was pushing, but he'd pushed back: he still had the broad-shouldered physique you developed while the army told you to hurry up and wait.

Jack Small had gained some weight he'd sorely needed. His hair was short and neat, and the new jeans and ski jacket let him fit in with the crowds around us. If he'd shown up at Grand Central looking the way I'd first seen him last year, people would be giving him change.

'You look a lot better than the first time I saw you, Jack,' I said, my face still directed at the crowd.

He surprised me with a smile. 'My cover isn't so disreputable this time.'

'Thank you for coming,' Cal said.

'It was the least I could do, considering.' I could feel the flock of closed-circuit cameras nesting above us. They covered every entrance and exit, every platform and waiting area, and had probably been secreted somewhere in the john. 'Grand Central isn't my first choice for a meeting. This station has more cameras than CNN.'

'They were installed on a no-bid contract,' Cal said. 'The resolution is so bad your own mother couldn't identify you. We're here because there's something you need to see.' Cal walked away from the platform, and Jack and I followed.

'How long have you been following me?'

'We weren't following you,' Cal said.

'Judge? Why are you interested in him?'

'Probably for the same reason you are.'

That stopped me.

'The idea is to be inconspicuous,' Jack said.

'We are. I'm going to tie my shoelace, and one of you is going to explain.'

'We're looking for Isaac,' Cal said. 'Since you aren't in the habit of looking up old army pals, I guess you are too.'

'Who told you Judge and I served together?'

'Isaac, who else?' Jack said. 'He told us all about his time in Ghost Town. The first time he mentioned you, I didn't make the connection; the way he described you, it sounded like a different person.'

'Is that good enough?' Cal said.

'For now,' I said, laces tied.

Cal led us into the main concourse, full of people as it always was. We stopped between tracks twenty-six and twenty-seven. The white wall had been covered in photographs, most of them adult and male. There were photos with the family, candid shots and a few official-looking photographs. Putting things up here was illegal, but neither the police nor the cleaning crews had disturbed the shrine.

There was a Houston memorial further down the concourse, as there was in every major station and airport in the country. It was a miniature replica of the old Houston downtown, made out of scrap metal by a famous artist whose name I couldn't recall. I did remember that he'd wanted to use the girders of Houston buildings, but that was impossible: they were still radioactive, and would be for a long time.

The shrine in front of us was improvised, and didn't declare what tragedy it represented. 'What am I looking at?' I said.

'The missing,' Cal said. 'Everyone on this wall has disappeared. They left no note, no body and no explanation.' Below each photograph was a name, contact details, and the date they were last seen. Candles shared space on the floor with poems and a few teddy bears. 'One day they found the edge of the world and just stepped off.'

'Or they were pushed,' Jack said.

I didn't know why they were showing me this, and I knew I wouldn't like the answer. 'I already have a case,' I said.

Cal handed me a portable video player. I saw a six-inch view of a desert that could be anywhere. Ten blindfolded Arab men knelt in front of a shallow ditch, hands taped behind their backs. Some were silent; the rest were crying, praying or trying to do both at the same time. Behind them were ten men in camouflage gear wearing balaclavas in the desert sun. Each one had a pistol in his hand, body tense with expectation. One man stood off to the side. He was dressed like the other men, but he wore a military cap and a handkerchief over his face.

The posture of the others made it obvious that he was in charge.

The leader was speaking, but the sound quality was too poor to make out the words. More of the men called out. The leader raised his hand. He let it fall. Before it reached his side, ten men were dead. The men in balaclavas holstered their weapons and rolled the bodies that hadn't already fallen in into the trench. The camera performed a shaky zoom in on the leader, just as he took off his handkerchief to mop his brow.

'What does this have to do with Isaac?' I said.

'Do you recognize the leader?' Jack said.

Foreign sun had cooked his skin to a deep brown, and adolescence had left a line of acne scars on each cheek. I'd had the opportunity to study his eyes while trying to stare them down. They were a blue so pale they were almost grey, and they crowded his nose in the centre. I couldn't see all that from the grainy footage I was looking at; the broad outlines of his face had been enough to call up a picture in my mind that I wished wasn't so complete.

'His name is Peter Stonebridge,' I said. 'He was attached to Task Force Seventeen when I met him in Tehran. Stonebridge was technically an employee of Janus Intelligence Services, but he really worked for Glass.' We all did. 'Stonebridge executed those men on Glass's orders?'

'I know you've heard the rumours,' Cal said. 'General Glass ran secret death squads when he was commanding the expeditionary forces in the Holy Land. They were called Citizens' Self-Defence Forces and a lot of other names, but not many were actually settlers. The officers were mostly Task Force Seventeen men Glass brought with him. For the foot soldiers, he put in a call to the scum of humanity, and they came running.'

'The army wouldn't have allowed it.'

'It didn't know. The Citizens' Self-Defence Forces was a

legitimate programme before Glass got his hands on it. He flew his thugs into American military bases disguised as labourers. Neither the American brass nor the Israeli Defence Forces even knew they were in the country.'

'I bet the Israelis were thrilled when they found out.'

'The IDF lost its mind. It was bad enough that there was an armed militia running around its country, but Palestinian resprisals for Glass's work killed Israeli soldiers and civilians. That's why he retired so quickly and went to work at Homeland Security.'

'How many did he kill?'

'I don't know,' Cal said. 'I doubt even Glass does. There was a formula, a sort of multiplication table. A single settler was worth so many Palestinians, an IDF soldier a few more. I've been told it was a long list, and at the top were American soldiers, worth ten Palestinian lives, twenty if the man was an officer.'

'Were they even guilty of anything?'

'These men?' Cal said. 'I don't know, and it doesn't matter. The executions were a message.'

Glass ran death squads without authorization, and now he runs one of the largest departments of the United States government. That wasn't a slap on the wrist; it was a massage. No one would have believed he had acted on his own. The Elders probably told Glass he could write his own ticket, as long as he left quietly.

'You still haven't told me what any of this has to do with Isaac.'

'Stonebridge is back in the country with a new name, courtesy of General Glass,' Jack said. 'Campbell.'

'This is your case, Strange,' Cal said, looking at the shrine again. 'Every single face. You're looking for Isaac, and he was looking for them.'

If Campbell really was Stonebridge, then I was sure he was

involved in Isaac's disappearance. Scalia's opinion of the man was too kind by several hundred miles. I could see now where Jack and Cal were going, and I liked it even less than I thought they would.

'Glass isn't running a death squad inside the United States,' I said. 'He isn't making people disappear for the Elders. They get up to enough mischief without us inventing conspiracy theories for them to dance around in.'

Cal and Jack showed me faces free of doubt.

'Where did you get this crazy idea?' I said, handing the video player back to Cal. I had no desire to see it again.

'The same man who gave us that video, who wanted Isaac to get close to Stonebridge and made sure he got the job,' Cal said. 'We know him as Jefferson.'

'As in founding father, author of the Declaration of Independence, Monticello Jefferson?' I said. 'He sounds like a modest guy.'

'I've never met him in person, but he's never lied to me, and he's never steered us wrong.'

'You know what Glass is capable of, so why won't you believe what we're telling you?' Jack said. Cal shot him a look and Jack lowered his voice. 'You know they've made people disappear before.'

'That was a handful of people, mostly foreign-born. I'm not saying it was right, but now you're talking about hundreds of people,' I said. 'Americans.'

'Did that matter at Christopher Park?' Jack said.

That I couldn't deny. Revivalist groups had used machine guns and RPGs on American citizens in Greenwich Village. I'd seen it with my own eyes.

'You and I know it's just one more step from there to here,' Jack said, dipping his head towards the memorial.

One more step, right off the edge of a cliff. 'Do you see any protests going on out there? Where are the speeches in the Senate, the civil disobedience, the revolutionary banners streaming down Broadway? People have decided to pretend that the Revivalists don't exist, to get along as best they can while they wait for the other guy to stand up. I'm not saying they aren't capable of it, but why would the Elders bother?'

'After people fought back in Christopher Park, the Elders got scared,' Cal said. 'They assumed that the fight was part of a vast conspiracy to end their rule, instead of ordinary people defending themselves. No matter what they're told, the Elders refuse to believe there aren't rebels moving against them. The fact that they haven't found evidence of the plot just means that it's been hidden well. They're afraid, just like we are.' All around us, at every station and on every street, were signs, flyers and banners, telling us to watch our friends, suspect our neighbours, and never, ever, close our eyes.

'Besides, even paranoids have enemies,' he continued. 'The way Jefferson tells it, he isn't the only founding father to reappear when his country is in need.'

So this Jefferson ran Cal, Jack, Isaac and who knows how many others. If he was telling the truth, there was an Adams, a Madison, definitely a Washington, all running cells of their own. I was happy to hear that there was someone out there disturbing the Elders' sleep, but only idiots assumed that the enemy of my enemy was automatically my friend.

'Now that Isaac has disappeared, what is your mysterious benefactor going to do about it?'

'Isaac knew what he was getting into,' Jack said. 'He thought it was worth the risk to expose what the Elders and Glass are doing. If I'd disappeared instead of Isaac, I'd want the operation to continue. I know he felt the same way.'

'Do you have anything solid to connect that video to this wall?' I said.

'That was Isaac's job.'

'We'd like you to pick up where he left off,' Cal said. 'Jack and I are too well known to the authorities.'

'In case you've forgotten, I'm not exactly a fucking stranger to them either.' I was reminded by my chest of the consequences of raising my voice with two cracked ribs.

I looked up at Grand Central's ceiling, though I'd seen it a hundred times before. The constellations had been painted above, the only way for a station that never sleeps to see the night sky. Gods and demons of antiquity looked down on us, their bodies nothing more than connected points of light. The stars had been painted backwards, and none of the explanations I'd heard had ever satisfied me. I was hoping one of that menagerie of deities would deign to throw me a clue, but they were as aloof and self-obsessed as they had been before the birth of Christ.

I tried to imagine what Cal and Jack were saying – the number of people who would have to be involved, to shrug off the kidnapping, torture and probably death of hundreds of their own people – but even my deep well of cynicism wasn't up to it. 'If you want to run around risking your life for a man you've never met in pursuit of this crazy idea, do it without me. I'll let you know the minute I have anything solid about Isaac. I owe you that much.'

Cal nodded. He didn't seem surprised by my answer. 'I know you understand what I'm saying, but you don't want to see it. That's fine. Jack and I didn't want to believe it either. All three of us have been kicked around some by the hallelujah chorus, but that's life. We thought there were still a few ground rules, that at the end of the day they'd remember we're all Americans. Everyone gets to shout a lot, and everyone gets to go home. Those days are over.'

'You really believe the Elders are taking Americans?' I said.

'We know,' Jack said. 'You follow Isaac's trail long enough, you'll know it too.'

Cal whispered some numbers in my ear, made me repeat them. 'Ask for Franklin,' he said.

I let them leave first. Commuters rushed past on all sides, paying as little attention to me as they would any other statue. I felt alone with those photographs. I couldn't look at them. An automated voice came on the PA, telling me to watch for anything suspicious.

I took the Forty-second Street exit and tried to walk no faster than the average organization man I resembled. The afternoon sunlight had brought me back to reality, and I started the long process of convincing myself that Jack and Cal were wrong.

I headed south on Lexington, going nowhere in particular. I liked to walk when I was working on a tough problem. The loco-motion primed the pump in my brain and kept me focused. To unravel what had just been dropped in my lap, I was going to need to walk half the island.

What Cal had said wasn't possible outside bad movies and dime novels. To make hundreds of people disappear required thousands of accomplices. Someone had to kidnap them in the first place, transport them to where they'd be held, and guard them once they were there. A bureaucracy would have to be created, and they would leave a paper trail of purchases, salaries and expenses. The people involved would have to never brag to their girlfriends, lose a battle with their conscience, or try to sell the story. The domestic press might be too afraid to say anything, but a foreign outlet would sell their mother for a story that explosive.

Even if the impossible happened and everyone did their job, perfect secrecy would undercut the whole idea. When govern-ments had done this before, people knew who sent their brother to Siberia, threw their father out of a helicopter over the ocean, or took them to a building from which no one ever returned. There was no point in terrorizing people if you didn't tell them who to be afraid of.

By the time I crossed Fortieth, I knew I was being followed. It's a difficult feeling to explain, more of an aggregate of instincts than a single thought. Most people who lived in this country were lucky enough to see dangerous animals – of the two- or four-legged kind – only on the evening news. They didn't need those older, darker instincts buried deep in the evolutionary chain. For those of us whose lives were threatened on a regular basis, they were indispensable.

Lexington's pavements were full. It would have been simple to use a knot of pedestrians to lose whoever was following me. That would be the safest choice, but it would also leave a lot of questions unanswered. If I'd picked up this shadow before I reached Grand Central, then Cal and Jack might have been fingered too. I also needed to know who was happy to waste their time following me. It was part of an ongoing effort to keep track of all the people who wished me harm.

I kept going south, waiting for my pursuer to make a mistake. I passed the Soldiers', Sailors', Marines' and Airmen's Club. It was a military hotel. I'd never stayed there, being a local, and now I never would. Their doors were closed to the dishonourably discharged, the bureaucratic term for the way the military had screwed me. Tag the walking wounded from Tehran with a 'personality disorder', and all those doctor's bills go away. A light burned on the second storey of the building's façade, in honour of those who had given their lives for their country. If I'd died that day in Tehran, I would have taken my place among the other fallen heroes, to be lionized on monuments and cried over when a politician needed a photo-op. Instead, I'd had the indecency to survive with wounds they couldn't understand, and for that sin I was cast out.

A few blocks down my progress was impeded by a gaggle of twelve-year-old girls spilling out from Yeshiva University. American yeshivas had done pretty well in the early years, sharing in the general largesse directed at all things Jewish and religious. In the last few years the Revivalists had started to pressure the schools in the backhanded way that characterized all their dealings with Jews. They said the proper place for a yeshiva was the Holy Land. After all, what better place would there be to learn the word of God? The Revivalists even offered to pay for American students to follow the school abroad. They found little enthusiasm among American parents for the idea of sending their children to study the Torah in a war zone.

My shadow still hadn't shown himself. He was good; almost good enough to get one over on me. The stroll hadn't revealed any accomplices, so my pursuer was probably alone. It was time to find a quiet place and introduce myself. I'd need that privacy to discover why I'd grown a tail, hopefully with a minimum of gunfire.

I turned on to East Thirty-third. The orange stone behemoth of Mormon Thomas High School was on my right. Set back from the street was the entrance to a loading dock. I paused at its mouth, pretending to take a call. In the distance, the Empire State Building watched over us all, the cross on its summit burning with neon light. Pretending to get away from the noise of the street, I walked into the alley, drew my gun and waited.

The footsteps that followed me had the high, staccato sound of heels. I'd never been pursued by a woman before, but that did nothing to reassure me. A pair of three-inch pumps had no effect on the action of a trigger finger.

The woman turned the corner. When she saw the gun she stopped, but didn't scream.

'Fancy meeting you here,' Iris said.

THE MISSING

Behold, I will send for many fishers, saith the LORD, and they
shall fish them; and after will I send for many hunters, and
they shall hunt them from every mountain, and from every
hill, and out of the holes of the rocks.

– Jeremiah xvi, 16, King James Bible

NINE

Nine years ago

'Mrs Rasjani, where is your husband?' I said in Farsi.

The woman stared at the floor instead of answering me. Her two children – a girl of about four and a twelve-year-old boy – held on to the folds of her chador. At that age I was mortified by physical contact with my parents, any sign of affection that might betray the fact that I was still a child. The boy was malnourished and already bore the scars of war. He didn't have the luxury of rebellion I had once enjoyed.

'Mrs Rasjani, where is your husband?'

We were in the northern suburbs of Tehran, what had once been the upscale part of town. I remembered seeing pictures of villas with manicured gardens hidden behind iron fencing. Or maybe I was thinking of villas in Spain. I'd never been here when Tehran was still a city, and there wasn't much left to go by.

The building we were in had been apartments, probably expensive ones judging by the footage. The top half of the building was gone, and what was left had been deformed by ordnance and stray bullets. The main living area that we were standing in was the only usable room left. The bedroom ceiling was full of holes, and the bathroom was a useless relic. There hadn't been running water or indoor plumbing in this city for a long time.

The apartment wasn't Mrs Rasjani's. Civilians learned to stay on the move, or they died. You could wake up one morning and find a Pasdaran rocket team setting up on the roof, or American soldiers clearing your building to use as a forward observation post. The bits of furniture in the room wouldn't be hers either, or the pictures of the ayatollah on the wall.

'Mrs Rasjani, where is your husband?'

She kept up her staring contest with the dirty floor. People here were less talkative than witnesses to a ghetto shooting back home. I couldn't blame them. The Pasdaran made it a general principle to kill anyone they saw as collaborators. Just being talked at by Americans could be proof enough to get her and her family killed.

I didn't have much to offer her to make it worth the risk. This wasn't Iraq; we weren't here to crusade for hearts and minds. We were here to break them, to somehow salve the wound of Houston by grinding the country into dust. Any concern for civilians somehow became a dishonour to those who had lost their lives in that attack, and most units had almost no contact with them anyway. Seventeen spent more time with Iranians, but the only form our community outreach took was a fist.

A lot of ink had been wasted before the war musing over how much ordinary Iranians hated the clerical regime. This fact wasn't seen as an opportunity to outmanoeuvre the mullahs, just another argument that the war would be a cakewalk. Iranians would be demoralized and unlikely to fight for a regime they despised. The great and the good of our country seemed genuinely shocked when we ran into old-fashioned patriotism, as if they'd never heard of the phenomenon before.

'Mrs Rasjani, where is your husband?'

'He is dead.'

It might be true, but the claim was almost impossible to verify. Rasjani might have been shot in the street, blown to pieces or trapped in a collapsing building. If he was dead, odds are she hadn't been able to give him a decent funeral. Either way, there was no government to issue a death certificate, and nothing short of a corpse would have been accepted by my superiors anyway.

'She says he's dead,' I said to Lieutenant Blake. He was an army ranger in his late twenties, the commander of the hunter-killer team I'd been attached to today. The shortage of Farsi speakers meant I worked with a lot of different units; Glass moved me to wherever he decided I would be most useful that day. This led to a lot of jokes in the task force about my promiscuity, but I preferred the teasing to being called the 'Haji Whisperer'. Knowing a little of the native tongue made me suspect in some soldiers' eyes. I was fortunate Blake wasn't one of them.

'She can say he's a fucking astronaut,' Blake said. 'You know what our orders are.'

There were three other rangers with us in the apartment. They were supposed to be looking for evidence of Rasjani's whereabouts, but were instead destroying what was left of the room in distracted spasms of violence.

'Miller, Sykes, Haig,' Blake yelled at the three, 'are you done?'

'Nothing here, sir,' Sykes said. He was the youngest in the unit, barely nineteen. He was a ranger, but he'd come to Seventeen direct from his training at Fort Benning and, like the saying went, there was no substitute for experience.

'Strange, do you think she'll talk?' Blake said to me.

I shook my head. I'd always known that if I ever got a chance to do intelligence work, circumstances would tie a hand behind my back. When it came to my stint at Seventeen, I felt like I'd been hog-tied, blindfolded and then thrown down a well. I didn't know who this Rasjani was or why Seventeen was interested in him. I knew nothing about his life, his views or his associates. It was Colonel Glass's standing policy to keep field men separate from the intelligence for reasons of security. All I had, all we were ever given, was a name, a face and a possible location. Labradors knew more about the sticks they were sent to fetch.

Without knowing something about why Rasjani was on our list, it was difficult to work the missus and impossible to turn her. I couldn't catch her in a lie or lead her towards something we wanted to know. That left the usual gun in the face, and they didn't need me for that. I spent most of my time just translating the CO's threats.

'Okay,' Blake said. 'We have to go to plan B then. Sykes.'

Sykes grabbed the boy. He tried to hold on to his mother's chador, and she to him. She was talking now, pleading that her son wasn't part of the resistance, that he'd done nothing wrong. Another ranger, I think it was Miller, stepped in and pulled Mrs Rasjani away from her child. The girl began to cry. Sykes struggled to get the boy's hands behind his back.

'Jesus Christ, Sykes, get on with it,' Blake said.

I tried to explain to Mrs Rasjani that this was standard procedure. Standing orders were that if a target refused to give himself up, we were to take the nearest male relative as collateral. That was the official term. I tried to tell her that we would hold her son until her husband gave himself up. The boy wouldn't be harmed, which was true unless you counted imprisonment and several days of interrogation.

She didn't hear a word. She was too busy hurling abuse or calling out to her son. The son was trying to calm his mother while Sykes bound his hands behind his back with zip cuffs. I was the only one who understood what they were saying, but it needed little translation. He told her not to worry. He was the man of the house now, and he would take care of her and his sister. He said the Americans couldn't hurt him, and he'd make his father proud. Those were the last words the boy got out before Sykes pulled a hood over his head.

Lieutenant Blake spoke into his radio to the rest of the unit outside. They were guarding the vehicles and looking for any interest in our presence. We were deep in the wilds, as Seventeen always was. The Pasdaran knew our insignia and made things as personal as we did. Every minute we were stationary was a risk.

'It's clear,' Blake said, 'let's go.'

Haig went out first. Miller let go of the mother to help Sykes with the boy. I was still throwing words at her, trying to explain where she could collect her son once we had her husband or his corpse in our possession. She ignored me and looked at her son, crossing the borrowed threshold, maybe never to be seen again.

The pistol came out of nowhere. A chador could easily conceal a weapon, a fact the person who had frisked her was supposed to know. She tried to get a bead on Sykes. I didn't have time to yell a warning or tell her to stop. I didn't think to try. I saw the gun, drew my own, and fired.

She didn't fall so much as meet the floor halfway. It was silent, and almost gentle. Mrs Rasjani lay on her back, eyes open and alive. The heavy fabric of the chador soaked in her blood, the same way its black colour drank the light that touched it.

Sykes craned his head to get a look at her. 'Should we get a medic?' he said when he realized she was still breathing.

The bullet had nicked an artery in her neck. Even if we could stop the bleeding, shock or blood loss would do the rest before we could casevac her anywhere. Blake looked at me. I knew what I had to do.

The second shot went into her skull and stayed there. Her son was crying. The tears mixed with the fear-sweat that had been soaked into the hood by a dozen other men. He sobbed, in silence but with such force that the inhalations drew the hood taut against his face, so I could see every line of his grief through the fabric. The little girl threw herself on her mother's corpse. We pretended not to notice.

'Who searched the woman?' Blake said.

Haig owned up from the hall.

'I'll kill you later. Good reaction, Strange,' Blake said. 'Aim a little straighter next time.'

Sykes looked at me. I could tell he wanted to ask about the girl. Another week with Seventeen and he'd know that we don't do charity work and we don't pick up strays, even when we kill their mothers. We filed out and left her there.

'What did she say to you?' Sykes said. 'Just before you shot her.'

'Those weren't words, Private.'

We got in our Stryker armoured vehicles and headed back to the university. Lieutenant Blake rode shotgun, while Sykes and I shared the back with the human collateral. We drove fast with our lights off, the driver steering with night vision. These Strykers were the new models, up-armoured with a reinforced top turret. Back in the 82nd, we were making do with whatever could be scrounged. Having the President of the United States as our patron had its advantages.

I'd been part of Seventeen for a year and twelve days. I knew the exact date because I couldn't believe it had been so little time. We had been close in the 82nd; it was unavoidable when you fought, ate and slept side by side. The same was true for the task force, but to an even higher degree. We didn't mix with the other units. That was Glass's standing order, but he needn't have bothered. Other soldiers kept their distance whenever we operated in the same area. I'd like to chalk the looks they gave us up to envy, because unlike my colleagues I didn't enjoy it when fellow soldiers were afraid of me.

The streets were quiet, as they always were. Tens of thousands of people still lived in the city, even if the government didn't acknowledge it. If I thought about it, and I tried not to, I wondered how any of them were still alive. This city was a good home only for rats and the uneasy dead. How did they get clean drinking water, food, heat when winter came? There was a black market in the city, but no visible way to earn currency to buy from it. Somehow, people survived. They always did.

It was three months into my new assignment that I'd started to notice the stars. It seemed like a silly discovery; they hadn't moved or jumped to get my attention. What had changed were my eyes. On the rare occasions that we left the Butcher School, we'd always travelled in the green underworld of night vision. Now I was out all the time and able to enjoy the night sky, disturbed only by the occasional light pollution from high explosives.

'Sergeant.'

It took me a moment to realize that Sykes was talking to me. I'd been promoted as soon as I joined the task force. Glass had pressed the stripes into my hand just before he sent me on my first snatch-and-grab, but after a year they still sat uneasily on my shoulder. Every time I heard my new rank, I expected to turn around and see Benny, smoking a cigarette and getting ready to curse.

'Sergeant,' Sykes said again. 'Are you okay?'

'I'm fine,' I said.

'If it's about that woman, you know you had no choice, right?'

'He said he's fine, Private,' Blake said from the front. He turned to face me, though he kept speaking to Sykes. 'It isn't the woman he's thinking about.'

Blake had taken part in Operation Golden Calf, the siege of Khomeini Mosque. He hadn't exactly told me, but I'd figured it out when we were shooting the shit a while ago. We'd shot a lot of women in that operation. They were armed, same as the men. It shouldn't have made a difference, but it did.

No one tried to ambush us on the way back. I was surprised, considering how long we'd been at that house and the noise we made in the silent city. I guess even the Revolutionary Guard took a night off once in a while. We dismounted on the south side of the library. About a dozen other members of the task force had just returned from missions or were getting on with something or other on what had once been a lawn around the university's library. Sykes got the boy out of the vehicle and led him in the direction of detention. Blake was reporting our arrival.

I felt the impact of the first mortar round in my teeth: a numbness and an invisible hand on my chest, both gifts from the explosion. I was under the Stryker before I gave myself the luxury of thought. It must have fallen only a few hundred metres away, maybe on the other side of the library.

Two more rounds fell. I couldn't see the explosions, just the running feet of my comrades taking cover. I saw the legs of the boy we brought in struggling with Sykes. Whether the boy thought this was his chance to escape, or the explosions had simply panicked him, he wasn't making Sykes's job of dragging him to cover easy.

A round hit right in front of me. I saw the flash and hid my face from the metal and dirt that played a tune on the Stryker's hull. I stayed down and waited. The rounds trailed off, and then stopped.

The all-clear sounded. I came out of my hiding place. Two of the support staff had found similar homes. Some soldiers came out of the library and the outbuildings, most getting on with whatever they were doing before metal started falling from the sky. I thought there hadn't been any casualties until I saw Lieutenant Blake staring at the ground.

There was a crater less than a hundred metres from where I'd been standing. If I'd stayed there, they'd be shipping me home with a few extra pounds of shrapnel in my gut. Around the crater were bits of flesh and a few fragments of desert camouflage and white cloth. That was all that was left of Sykes and our young detainee.

'Colonel wants to see you,' Blake said, without looking at me. 'Don't keep him waiting, Sergeant.'

You could see a thousand people die and feel nothing, but it was the one after that stuck in your heart and remained. Blake stayed where he was, staring at what could have been Sykes or the boy, only God and maybe DNA able to sort one from the other.

Glass was waiting for me in his office. The hole in the roof still hadn't been fixed.

'At ease, Sergeant,' he said.

I did the best I could. Blake hadn't told me why I'd been summoncd, but I had an idea. If I was right, this meeting would be uncomfortable.

'I just heard about Sykes,' Glass said. 'Do you know he was offered a scholarship to play ball for Texas A&M? He decided to serve his country first, and barely had the chance. What a fucking waste.'

It was surprising that Glass even knew grunts' last names, considering Task Force Seventeen was a chimera of different units and services. Sykes's scholarship was news to me, and I'd worked with him. I'd never met a commander who took such a personal interest in every one of his men.

'Do you know why you're here, Sergeant?'

'Does it concern the Egyptian, sir?'

The Egyptian was the nickname we'd given to prisoner 6319. Task force elements had snatched him while he tried to cross the border into Iraq. The dossier said they thought he was a bagman for communications between the Iranians and their Shi'ite brethren fucking things up in Iraq. In the hands of interrogators he became something much more.

'What the hell did you think you were doing?' Glass said, as he handed me a transcript.

```
CONTROL: You have told us you received money
   from Russian agents.
6319: Yes. A submarine landed them on the
   coast. I met . . .
Inaudible, one second.
CONTROL: Where did you meet them?
6319: I don't remember. I told the other man.
   Ask him. I told him about the Russians and
   the other.
CONTROL: The other? Who else was there?
Inaudible, three seconds.
6319: Satan.
CONTROL: Satan?
6319: Yes. I remember now. He met me at a
   crossroads.
CONTROL: Where?
6319: North of Karbala.
CONTROL: What did he look like?
6319: A great big man. Head shaved and crazy,
   burning eyes. No horns.
Inaudible.
6319: He gave me guns. He told me it was his
   will to fight the Americans. But first I had
   to swear loyalty.
CONTROL: Swear how?
6319: Oaths. Secret oaths.
CONTROL: Are you sure it was Satan?
6319: I think . . .
Inaudible speech, two seconds.
6319: What do you want me to say?
```

'Will I be court-martialled, sir?'

'Don't be a drama queen, Sergeant. The task force is a family; we solve our own problems.'

Glass took the transcript from my hands.

'You had no authority to conduct your own interview, Sergeant. Your role on the team was translation only.'

Each detainee was assigned to a 'Tiger Team' – an analyst, interrogator and interpreter. The Janus interrogator who had been assigned to 6319 was a man called Stonebridge.

'It was in my capacity as interpreter that questions arose about the interrogator's methodology, sir.'

The methodology in question was a mixture of action movies and pop psychology that did neither any credit. Before the interrogation of a regular detainee, Janus operatives would leave them shackled in a painful position for hours, just to make clear who was boss. After that came threats against the family, sexual humiliation, and guard dogs if the detainee got uppity; all before basic facts about the detainee had been established.

'We aren't in court, Strange. Speak plainly for God's sake.'

'The Egyptian was broken, sir, on the inside. It was obvious as soon as you looked at him. I had zero confidence in the efficacy of anything he said. I believed that if we pursued any of his so-called intelligence, we would waste time and endanger members of the task force. I raised the matter with Interrogator Stonebridge several times, and he refused to consider it.'

The Egyptian had been evasive and uncooperative, as you'd expect of a man who left his home to fight people he'd never met on behalf of a sect and people he didn't entirely trust. The Egyptian's tenuous relationship to the Iranians could have been worked at, eroded. He could have been reminded of his home, his family, that this wasn't his fight. Convince a man to turn of his own free will, and we would have had reliable intelligence about how Iranian forces were communicating with the Shia insurgents hammering our supply lines all over southern Iraq.

Stonebridge had entertained different ideas. The problem with information gained that way wasn't its content, but the fact that it had been traded, earned or given, not taken. Here the veracity of information was measured by how long its bloodied source begged for his life.

The Egyptian had said the meeting at the crossroads had come up during a previous interrogation. I should have been present at all of them, and I couldn't find a record of it. All interaction with detainees was supposed to be recorded, but the Central Library was a large and crumbling building. There were plenty of collapsed rooms and staircases to nowhere, ideal places to have a quiet word with detainees away from the prying eyes of international law.

Stonebridge wouldn't have done anything so gauche as tell the Egyptian what to say: he would have just kept the prisoner shackled naked in a stress position until he made up a story that fitted Stonebridge's leading questions. Fear of a repeat engagement would have kept the Egyptian on message, if Stonebridge hadn't damaged him so badly he couldn't keep the lies straight.

'Well, Stonebridge has had some complaints about your methodology.'

Glass picked up a sheet of paper on his desk.

'In a report to his superiors at Janus, Stonebridge stated: "Sergeant Strange has on a number of occasions expressed an unnecessary concern for the health of detainees, and has objected to lines of questioning he feels are too aggressive. Strange's inappropriate interest in the physical well-being of detainees has impeded the efficient working of the Tiger Team, and undermined my authority with detainees."'

Stonebridge was a contractor for Janus Intelligence Services, the firm that did most of the task force's interrogations. Some were former CIA and Defense Intelligence Agency men. The rest had found their security clearance at the bottom of a cereal box. Those men shouldn't have been in charge of a drive-through, let alone detainees in a war zone.

'Stonebridge isn't the only man to raise concerns about your humanitarianism, Sergeant. The other Janus interrogators share his view that you're a soft touch. The funny thing is, most of the 'gators still want to work with you. It seems that, like me, they are willing to tolerate some suspect empathy in exchange for your other gifts.

'I'm not questioning your courage; you'd proved yourself in the field long before I found you. It's the fact that they're unarmed and handcuffed that gets to you, isn't it?'

He held up his hand before I could speak to indicate the question was rhetorical.

'You see a lot of pain in those interrogation rooms, a lot of suffering and begging. You wouldn't be human if it didn't get to you. What you don't see are the men they've killed, our brother soldiers shot and torn apart. You look at the Egyptian and see the broken man in front of you, not the crimes on his soul.

'I think disagreements like this make the task force strong, Sergeant, but I can't let them go on for ever. Janus has recommended sending the Egyptian's intelligence upstairs. I need something more than empathy to persuade me otherwise.'

If they sent the intelligence up the chain of command, then sooner or later the man would follow. He'd be passed around every agency with an interest in intelligence, most of which had contracts with Janus as well. Maybe the Egyptian's intelligence would be believed, maybe it wouldn't. Either way, the result would be a lot of billable hours for the company.

'Nothing in the Egyptian's dossier suggests he would have access to the kind of information Stonebridge claims he knows.'

'You mean the nuclear technology?' Glass said. 'Finding the weapons of mass destruction is our job, Sergeant. I've seen you aim a knife at the dark on more than one occasion. Sometimes you even hit something.'

'Sir, I also accept when I cut only air. From the transcript, it is clear that anyone acting in good faith wouldn't have mistaken the Egyptian's ignorance for resistance.'

The 'good faith' part got Glass's eyebrows up. He knew what the formulation implied. 'What exactly are you accusing Janus of, Sergeant?'

'Sir, it's an open secret that large bonuses are written into Janus's contract, especially where nuclear intelligence is concerned. If this Stonebridge can convince the higher-ups that the Egyptian has that intelligence, Janus stands to make millions of dollars, some of which will go to him.'

'What's your point, Felix?'

'Once the Egyptian enters the system, half the intelligence community is going to take a crack at him. Sooner or later, someone will see him for what he is. When that happens, it won't be Janus with egg on its face, but us.

'I don't care what they did to him, sir. Odds are he's helped kill Americans. I just don't want what happened to 4th ID to happen to us.'

They'd picked up an Iraqi insurgent in southern Basra and touted him as a key member of the resistance. He was transferred to the 735th Military Intelligence's Interrogation Control Element, who realized in short order that the man was a brain-damaged fantasist with a mental age of twelve.

Glass leaned back in his chair and looked through the hole in the ceiling. I'd worked with the colonel long enough to read his face. The incident hadn't done much for the 4th ID's reputation, but they were in the war-fighting business, not intelligence. The consequences would be worse for us.

'Elite units don't make these kinds of mistakes. I was just trying to protect the task force's reputation.'

'I know, Sergeant. That's why your ass isn't in a sling. I wish you had come to me first before you pulled a stunt like this, but I suppose that isn't your style.'

Concerns wouldn't have been enough. Too many self-interested parties had decided that the Egyptian was valuable, and once that had happened the idea took on a momentum of its own. I knew if I let the Egyptian speak long enough he'd discredit himself. Afterwards I'd panicked a little at what I'd done, afraid his outrageous delusions would actually be believed.

'Did you get anything of value out of the prisoner?'

'From my time with him, I can tell you that the prisoner is paranoid, half lucid and full of delusions of grandeur we probably gave him. Janus has turned the Egyptian into a talking parrot. I'm sure he had some useful intelligence, but without more information I can't separate it from his torture-induced fantasies.'

'Careful, Sergeant,' Glass said. 'I'm not saying I disagree; the task force probably dodged a bullet thanks to you. But Janus has a lot of powerful friends, and if you keep using the T-word they'll hear about it. Take the edge off your assessment in the official report, and we'll wash our hands of the whole thing.'

'Yes, sir.' It was the best I could have hoped for.

Glass lit a cigar and said nothing. I could feel him studying me, but I didn't know for what purpose.

'I made a promise that you would have a chance to do what you were trained for. Circumstances have prevented me from making good. I've kept you on the hop this year, moving you between the field and interrogation. You've risen to the challenge, and that should count for something.'

Glass pushed a folder towards me. It was the case file for a prisoner number 6524.

'You've heard this before, Sergeant, but I want you to believe it because it comes from me. Prisoner 6524 is the most valuable detainee currently in American hands. I believe he has intelligence that will change the course of this war. Janus has been interrogating him for two weeks and they've gotten nowhere. I'm turning him over to you. It isn't exactly what you were trained for, but your practical experience is worth a lot more than a two-week interrogation course at Fort Huachuca.'

'You want me to be the interrogator?'

'Don't make me doubt your intelligence now, Sergeant. Pick an analyst you think you can work with. You'll have to do your own interpretation,' Glass said with a wry smile.

'Thank you, sir.'

'Don't thank me yet. You'll be behind the eight-ball. Everyone at Janus will be waiting for you to fail.'

I took the folder in my hands. I tried to calculate how long Janus had interrogated him, how many times he'd been beaten, how long he'd been isolated just by the weight of the paper, the number of reports. The Golden Detainee, that most elusive of all creatures, had just been dropped in my lap.

Task Force Seventeen had transformed the University of Tehran's Central Library stacks into holding cells. It was an ideal space: windowless and segmented. All we had to do was add partitions, beds and bolts to chain the detainees to.

The university cells were split up into several Interrogation Control Elements, each with its own team of interrogators. Glass kept the ICEs separate, officially for security but also to measure their performance. I had no idea how many prisoners the task force held in total. I wonder if even Glass knew.

Field men like myself didn't usually visit the cells. We were never told where our prisoners went after they were delivered to the captain in charge of detention. The only reason I had done interrogations at all was because translators were in such short supply. I had hoped that seeing both ends of the process would give me a better appreciation of the task force's work. It had given me something.

I changed to a civilian shirt before I entered the cells. It was standard procedure for all interrogators and translators to look like civilians, not to put our prisoners at ease, but as a further extension of the absolute control we exercised. A rank might give our detainees something to use, and names made pleas for mercy more effective. We pretend to know everything about our detainees, but to them we were gods who remained anonymous.

The MP guarding this unit of prisoners unlocked the gate and let me inside. He was nineteen, fresh from the States but at least he knew his job. We had too many prisoners, and not enough people trained to guard them. Add in twelve-hour shifts and sporadic attacks, and it wasn't surprising that the treatment of prisoners strayed outside the rulebook.

'Hello again, Sergeant.'

'I'm here to see prisoner 6524.'

There were eighteen cells in this ICE, each one full of men. A few cells were dark, but most baked under fluorescent lights. The detainees in these cells wouldn't get more than four hours of sleep a day. Most were lying on the bare floor, but a few of the healthier ones were sitting and staring at the wall. There was a constant hum in the room, a bit of white noise for our guests' entertainment.

The pattern of cuts and bruises would have been seen by the Red Cross as a map of abuse. I just saw it as paperwork. The use of every 'enhanced' method had to be approved through channels. The commander of the ICE could personally authorize hard slaps to the abdomen, shaking and various kinds of sexual humiliation. If you wanted to stage a mock execution or leave them naked in a freezing cell for twelve hours, the request went higher. Combinations also had to be authorized. How about stress positions and sleep deprivation? Or electric shocks and isolation? Mother, how many times may I waterboard the detainee?

All those requests crossed Glass's desk sooner or later. He had seen and approved almost every act of torture in this place. He took responsibility for his men and what they did. I'd heard that at the beginning he'd had to send some of the requests all the way up to Washington. That had stopped after the siege of Tehran was officially over. The President trusted his discretion, and his zeal.

The swelling on the faces of a few detainees was too clumsy even for a junior interrogator. When I was attached to the 82nd, it was an open secret that some soldiers went down to the holding cells to blow off steam. It was the same here, though it was hard to imagine anyone in Seventeen had steam they needed to release. They led lives of uninterrupted aggression, hunting amid the ruins for whatever scent Glass had put them on that day. I figured it was support staff: IT guys and private administrators. There was an eager glint in their eyes whenever we brought someone in, dead or alive. They came up here to show how tough they were, prove they were a loyal adjunct to the warrior elite.

I stopped in front of an emaciated man in his early thirties, though he looked at least a decade older. I'd dragged him out of a collapsed building in front of what was left of his family. It could have been near the old French embassy, but I wasn't sure. I definitely didn't remember the reason, because we wouldn't have been told. It was always who, where and how; never, ever why.

He had been silent until the zip cuffs went on. A detainee had about three seconds between restraint and a bag going over his head, depending on how many others were being taken at the same time. It was a bad moment to begin protesting your innocence. All he'd managed to say was that he was a cab driver. We said he was a terrorist. It could have been both or neither, and it didn't matter. Anyone could be anything here. If you didn't like who you were, there were the ruins of a million other lives on the ground just waiting to be picked up.

'Sergeant,' the MP said, noticing I had stopped at the cab driver's cell.

'Private, you were holding a prisoner 6319 here, weren't you?' That was the Egyptian, our last contestant for the role of Golden Detainee.

'Yes, Sergeant.'

'I don't see him here. Where has he gone?'

'They don't tell me where they go, Sergeant. One shift he was here and by the next he was gone.'

For a second, I allowed myself to think about my life before the army. The suburban street, my parents married to the end, getting drunk and trying to read Gibbon hung over. I tried to draw a line from there to this place, which I wouldn't have believed existed if I hadn't been standing in it. That normality to the smell of these walls, supersaturated with despair. It was a story with scenes I didn't understand, even though I had lived through them all.

'Lead on, Private.'

Prisoner 6524 was in an isolation cell behind another locked gate. He couldn't see me, and it wasn't just because of the one-way mirror between us. He was a man in his forties, bald and unshaven, a once portly figure now mostly folds of skin. I couldn't see any cuts, burn marks or other signs of damage on his body.

'Private, when was the last time the prisoner slept?'

'Approximately fifty hours ago, Sergeant,' the MP said.

The treatment of 6524 had been smarter, if not kinder. According to the file, he'd been kept awake by bright, disorienting lights and a medley of eighties stadium rock. He was interrogated for eight hours at a time, but the file hadn't included any transcripts. It was odd, especially since Stonebridge had been the control on this detainee before me. He didn't exactly have a light touch, but in this case he'd been careful not to leave any marks. Something else was going on.

Simple sleep deprivation might have led a layman to think Janus was going easy on the prisoner. Everyone had pulled all-nighters before, and it didn't seem like that bad an ordeal. Given the chance, the average Joe would probably say he preferred it to electric shocks, beatings or the other forms of physical abuse most people thought of as torture.

Back in university, I'd read about a torture used by the OGPU, Stalin's thugs. They'd put a prisoner against the wall and make him stand on tiptoes. At first blush it had sounded pretty tame for such brutal men, almost a fraternity prank, until I read about the results. Blood pooled in the joints, causing swelling and agonizing pain, permanent damage if they were left that way. After a few days the procedure could break almost anyone.

Imagine my surprise when I found out Seventeen used a variation they'd picked up from the defunct CIA. Detainees were shackled by their wrists to the ceiling with short chains. They had to stand or take their weight on their arms. The CIA had a category for the procedure: 'self-inflicted pain'. After the agency was disbanded, its people must have had a bright future in advertising.

'If you don't mind my asking, Sergeant,' the MP said, 'when was the last time you slept?'

'That's classified, Private.'

Sleep deprivation took a little longer, but gave the same result:

a person willing to say or do anything to make it stop. That was what the OGPU had wanted: confessions, not information.

'Has a doctor seen the prisoner?'

I had given instructions that prisoner 6524 receive food, rest and medical care. It was pointless getting angry with the MP. Someone higher up had overruled me.

'He came by six hours ago.'

'Did he do anything besides certify that the prisoner was still breathing?'

'I don't know,' the MP said.

'Who gave the order to keep him awake?'

Stonebridge came in, wearing khaki trousers, a white shirt and bulletproof vest. It was the unofficial uniform of the corporate douchebag in country, and Stonebridge wore it with pride. He barely noticed me, and made a beeline for my prisoner.

'No visitors,' the MP said, 'by order of the colonel himself.'

Stonebridge wasn't surprised. He was here to wait.

'Is this your doing?' I said to him.

'The corporation's, not mine,' Stonebridge said. 'Janus has concerns about intellectual property relating to this prisoner.'

For a moment, I was lost. Stonebridge enjoyed it.

'If 6524 happens to let slip something useful while you're holding his hand or whatever it is you do, we want to make sure our interests are respected as a stakeholder.'

'A stakeholder?'

'Janus has spent a lot of time and resources interrogating this man. We don't want you taking all the credit after we loosened him up first.'

'He's a man, Stonebridge, not a jar of mayonnaise. If that's an official Janus term, your company needs to come up with a better euphemism for torture.'

'Spare me the international chorus of human rights fags,' Stonebridge said. 'This guy was trying to kill your buddies.'

'You've never seen combat, have you, Stonebridge?'

'I served in Military Intelligence,' he said. 'Are you trying to call me a coward, Strange?'

'No, I'm calling you a moron.'

I got in Stonebridge's face. He wasn't used to it, and I enjoyed that. 'You're right; friends of mine are dying. They're getting killed by snipers and IEDs. This asshole might have been able to tell me about that, but right now he's so fucked up he'd probably finger Mickey Mouse. Colonel Glass brought me in because of your incompetence. He doesn't want another embarrassment like the Egyptian.'

Stonebridge's face darkened. It was long past the time when the MP should have intervened. If he'd been more experienced he would have felt an energy in the air, a tingle that preceded a prison yard fight. 'So you're the one who changed Glass's mind.'

I saw the swing coming. I had time to laugh, but I decided to punch Stonebridge in the face instead. He stumbled and fell backwards. He looked up at me, seeing red through a bloody nose. Stonebridge drew his sidearm. If he was expecting me to run or apologize, he was disappointed.

The MP grabbed him from behind.

'What are you doing?' Stonebridge said. 'This man assaulted me.'

I helped the MP get Stonebridge up, relieving him of his weapon in the process.

'What's going on here?' Colonel Glass said.

I wondered how long he'd stood by the security gate watching us. 'A disagreement over intellectual property,' I said.

Glass laughed. Stonebridge's face, already covered in his own blood, couldn't get any redder.

'Sir, I—'

'Save it, I don't care,' Glass said. 'I came here to tell Strange, but you might as well hear it too. I've listened to your corporation's concerns, and I think they're without merit. Janus can complain to its friends in Washington, but it'll find the answer is the same there. Strange is now prisoner 6524's handler. Results matter. You should know that better than anyone.'

Stonebridge mumbled an apology to Glass and made to leave.

'You're forgetting something,' I said. I popped the clip on Stonebridge's sidearm, ejected the round in the chamber, and handed it back to him. 'If you ever pull a gun on me again, I'll kill you,' I said, loud enough for just him to hear.

Stonebridge didn't reply. He left the cells nursing his nose and a grudge.

Colonel Glass watched me watch Stonebridge. 'I know what you're thinking, Sergeant,' Glass said. 'I let you both run wild for the same reason.' He looked at the detainee for a while, searching for something I couldn't see. 'What are you going to do with your new prisoner?'

As it happened, prisoner 6524 chose that time to look up. He stared at the one-way mirror, at his own beleaguered face, but his eyes went through the glass and through me. If I had met this man outside, I would have shot him without a second thought. I would have perforated the brain of any man on this floor, blown off their limbs, shredded their insides with shrapnel, and if I'd been lucky enough to get downtime I would have sunk into a deep and untroubled sleep. The next day it would have been a struggle even to remember their faces.

Today I wasn't on a battlefield, and had the freedom to see exactly what we'd done to a man who no longer posed a threat. Whether I had been the one or another member of the task force didn't matter. I went out into the city and found men, put a bag over their heads and told them where they were going in their own tongue.

I'd come to the task force because I had special knowledge. Most of the Farsi I knew had come from a book. The last six months had increased my vocabulary only where threats and orders were concerned. I could tell you some other facts I'd read or seen in presentations: the extent of the old Persian Empire before Christ, the approximate population of Tehran before we bombed it, some scraps of Shi'ite history.

When it came to the people, ordinary Iranians, I drew a blank. This man and the others in the cells outside were a mystery to me. I was the specialist only because I'd bothered to make the effort. We weren't trying to liberate this country, as we'd sort of tried to do with Iraq. We were here for revenge, and nothing else. That mission made everyone an enemy, and the United States didn't talk to its enemies.

'Sergeant?' Glass prompted.

I couldn't show what I was feeling in front of the colonel. He would see my hesitation as weakness, and my doubt as something worse: the beginning of disloyalty. Both were unforgivable. I found a hole in my heart and stuffed those feelings inside. I was a professional. Torture was ineffective and distorted whatever information the prisoner actually had. That was all I would allow myself to think about the matter.

'Let him rest,' I said. 'Then we'll see what he has to say for himself.'

TEN

I stared at Iris, still not entirely sure she was real. She wore the same tan raincoat I'd first seen her in; I could draw it from memory. Dark stockings ended in glossy black heels. An average woman would have saved them for special occasions of the kind that required no more than ten steps at a time, but Iris's poise made them look as comfortable as bathroom slippers. Her hair was red now – a dye job of such quality I could be persuaded it was real – and cut to frame her neck like the curtains on a music-hall stage. Her face hadn't changed a bit, and for that I was thankful.

'What happened to your hair?'

Iris laughed. I wanted to get it on tape and throw out my music collection. 'That's the first thing every woman wants to hear.' She was about to say something more, but by then she was in my arms.

'You shouldn't be here,' I said into the nape of her neck.

'I know,' she whispered back. We stayed that way for a while, both afraid to let the other go. 'Are you going to put your gun away? It's digging into my back.'

'Sorry,' I said. I let her go and holstered my weapon.

'Do you suppose we could go somewhere more comfortable?' Iris said, looking around.

'I know a place,' I said.

The owner had something of a love affair with oak panelling: it covered the walls and the partitions between tables. The floor was hardwood with a heavy coat of varnish. A diner and a log cabin had had a love child, and it was hiding out in Manhattan.

Business was good, but not many were staying to eat. It was no problem to get a booth in the back corner, away from the front windows and the door. The waitress hovered.

'Do you want anything to eat?' Iris asked. 'I'd like to order pie, but I don't want to tempt fate.'

I smiled, even though the memory was not a happy one. 'Just coffee for me,' I said.

'Me too.'

The waitress looked at us and decided we were both a little screwy. This decision didn't change her expression much; working in a place that was still open in the darkest parts of the night, she'd seen a lot worse.

'Aren't you hungry?' Iris said, when the waitress had gone.

'I ate a little while ago.'

Iris pursed her lips, a sign she didn't believe me.

'The FBI is my sugar daddy now. I've got all the medicine I need.'

'Okay,' Iris said, and for once she took me at my word.

Our coffee arrived, and we looked at each other for a while. Iris smiled. I asked her why.

'When I was in Africa, this is how I remembered you,' she said. 'Sitting in a booth with a cup of coffee in your hand.'

'Is that where you went?' I said. I hadn't known where she was after that night she shot Ezekiel White. It was safer that way for both of us. I'd told myself I had to give up hope of ever seeing her again. I accomplished it through the clever reverse-psychology of thinking of her every hour I was awake.

'The Lord called me to continue Brother Isaiah's work there,' she said. 'A village in Guyana also happened to be the perfect place to hide out.'

'Has the whole Crusade moved back to Africa?'

I'd read the news reports when the Crusade announced its intention to wind down its American operation in the wake of Brother Isaiah's death. It was the organization's second departure; Brother Isaiah had led the first exodus from this profane land. His death had made the end of its domestic operation inevitable. Without his holy stature it couldn't pull in as many recruits, and without his star quality it couldn't get the press it needed to expose people's lives.

'Most of us have.'

'If Brother Isaiah had stayed in Africa, he might still be alive,' I said.

'If Brother Isaiah had stayed in Africa, I would have died in the gutter.'

It took one look at her averted eyes to realize I was being cruel. My manners had gone downhill in the last year, and they hadn't been that good to begin with. I rarely spent time with people I liked; even Benny could be touch and go as far as that category was concerned. I couldn't bring myself to speak well of the old man, even for her sake. To eulogize Brother Isaiah now would be spitting in the faces of all the people whose lives he'd destroyed.

'I think you're selling yourself short,' I said. 'If you had the strength to get clean with him, you had the strength to do it by yourself.'

'You don't understand,' Iris said, as if she were talking to a child. 'Some things you can't face without the help of a higher power. Admitting you're just a human being isn't a sign of weakness.'

This train of conversation wasn't doing either of us any good, so I decided to get off before we found a cliff. 'You said most had left. What happened to the rest?'

'They had lives here,' Iris said. 'Some were pastors who couldn't abandon their flocks. Others had work to do.'

'Work?'

'Fundraising,' Iris said. 'We depend on the contributions of American Christians to fund our work in Africa.'

'Is that all?'

Iris avoided my eyes.

I should have known. Too many people in the Crusade had become too adept at spying on others to give it up entirely. 'So you kept some people in place for a rainy day.'

'The way the weather's been lately, wouldn't you?'

I gave her that. 'That doesn't explain what you're doing here. You're too pretty to be a bagman.'

'Some of our people have gone missing.'

The weird ideas Cal and Jack had put in my head began to bubble up. The problem with a conspiracy theory was that you could shoehorn just about anything into it. If I had bought what they were saying, I would be thinking how Iris's missing persons jived with my own. The potential to see everything as one big apocalyptic plot was one of the reasons I'd left their theory on the floor of Grand Central.

'Have you heard something?' Iris asked. From the look in her eyes, she had seen something behind my own.

'No,' I said. 'It's just an odd coincidence: I'm working on a missing person's case myself. Who are you looking for?'

'I have six names, but there's one man in particular I need to find. His name is Patrick Salda. He's very important to the organization.'

'They shouldn't have sent you.'

'They know I have experience,' Iris said.

'Experienced or not, not everyone in your organization has your history. They must have realized how dangerous it would be.'

'They don't know about that,' Iris said. 'Why I would tell them?' She was right, and smart. The fewer people who knew she'd ventilated a leading figure of American law enforcement the better.

'Besides,' Iris said, 'Patrick is a friend of mine.'

Iris used the present tense when she spoke about Salda, just like Faye when she'd talked about Isaac. I wanted both their hopes to be vindicated, but the world was rarely that kind.

'So what do you need from me?' I said. 'That is why you're here.'

'Play nice for once, Felix,' Iris said. 'I'm here because I wanted to see you.'

'You saw me all right,' I said, 'but you didn't speak to me. Much as I like the idea of being pursued by a beautiful woman, I can't figure out why you didn't just say hello.'

'I told myself I needed to know who was watching you, in case I put you in danger. The truth is, I knew when I met you I'd have no idea what to say.'

I took her hand across the booth, tried with a smile to be kind in a way I could never seem to manage when I opened my mouth. We stayed that way for a while, until the check arrived to break the spell.

'Do you have a picture of this guy?'

Iris nodded.

'Okay,' I said, and got up. 'I'll find a payphone and make some calls.'

'Why don't you just use your cell phone?' Iris said.

'Don't go naive on me now, sweetheart,' I said. 'It's about time you remembered which country you've come home to.'

An hour and a dozen calls later, and we were standing in the morgue. What had once been Patrick Salda lay on a bed of stainless steel. Asthmatic air conditioners thrummed behind us, keeping away the inevitable. Iris looked at him but didn't say a word. I kept busy handling my contact.

Steven Richard was a slight man in his early forties with a powerful squint and the complexion of an alcoholic. I don't think Richard was a drinker – he drove too hard a bargain – but he had the same red face, and his full shock of ginger hair didn't help. Whenever I met Richard I wondered if his ruddy cheeks were a biological reaction to the pale and lifeless flesh around him. I don't know how he ended up being a morgue attendant, but I assumed it had something to do with the misfortune of being born with two first names.

'The bodies are four-deep in the hallway,' I said, in what passed for small talk between us. 'Did somebody start another war without telling me?'

Richard shrugged. 'I just tag 'em and file 'em.'

'Has the Medical Examiner had a look at him?'

'She did the autopsy this morning,' Richard said. He handed over a folder.

'Police?'

'They haven't been by, and the techs didn't say much.'

I took out my wallet. 'And the other guy I asked you about?' I said, calibrating my generosity.

'I put the word out to the other orderlies and funeral attendants; if he shows up on a slab in the five boroughs, you'll know.'

There was still no trace of Isaac. At least he hadn't shown up on a gurney. I didn't have to crush Faye's small hope that he was alive just yet.

Richard maintained a dignified silence as I slipped a few bills into his lab coat's breast pocket.

'Give us a minute, would you?'

'No problem,' he said. 'The coroner's out to lunch. Don't worry about that,' he said, pointing to the camera in the corner of the ceiling. 'I took care of it. They've been on the fritz all week anyway.'

Richard left us alone with Salda and twenty other corpses on ice. I flipped through the report.

'Cause of death was two small-calibre bullet wounds to the head,' I said, paraphrasing what was on the page. 'The first shot was a contact wound to the back of the head.' That meant that the gun had been pressed against Salda's head. 'The second hole is on the side. No powder was found around that wound. They must have shot him once, and then made sure of it when he was on the ground.'

'Where was he found?' Iris asked.

'Underneath the Queensboro Bridge. He was dumped in his own car.' I turned the page. 'There are abrasions on his hands, from some kind of coarse rope. There are some wood splinters in the upper arms as well.'

The corpse had serious bruising all over the torso from knuckles made of flesh and brass, the worst around the kidney area. Three of the four fingers on his left hand were broken. He was missing four teeth and had a double shiner. His right ankle rested at a funny angle on the table. I didn't need to read the report to know it was broken.

'They tied him to a wooden chair and beat the living shit out of him,' I said. 'I guess someone still appreciates the classics.'

I'd let my mouth run on one sentence too long, but Iris didn't rebuke me. She was intent on the body, naked and alone on the slab. They hadn't been lovers; I knew that by her dry eyes. Instead she had a sad but resigned look I recognized. We'd worn the same face for our friends too many times in Tehran. You expected death to stop by, but that didn't make the visit any easier to take.

'Did he have a family?' I said.

'A wife and three daughters,' Iris said. 'The last time they saw him was six months ago. He couldn't tell them what he did. Now they'll never understand his sacrifice.'

'The Crusade won't level with them, even now?'

'I don't know,' Iris said. 'It isn't my decision.'

A gurney pushed open the double doors behind us. Richard was driving, and he stopped it next to me. 'I can only give you another five minutes. The coroner will be back soon.'

I barely heard a word he said. On the gurney Richard was pushing was a woman I recognized. It was Mary.

Richard noticed my interest. 'She was pretty hot, wasn't she?'

'What can you tell me about her?'

'Not much. They brought her in a few hours ago,' he said. 'According to the sheet she was pulled out of the Hudson. She's still a Jane Doe.'

There was a dark purple ring of bruised flesh around what had formerly been Mary's perfect neck. 'Strangulation?'

'Do I look like the ME?' Richard said, wheeling her into a spot in the corner. He pointed at his watch and then left the room.

Iris stopped taking pictures of Salda and watched me look at Mary's corpse. 'Did you know her?' she asked.

'Yeah,' I said. 'I was trying to get her arrested.'

Except for the bruises, Mary looked the same on the outside as when I last saw her. I wondered where all that self-assurance, sly intelligence and sex appeal had gone. There wasn't much of it here. Maybe, if you were there when her heart stopped, you could see a shadow of what she'd been melt into the air. More likely it had just disappeared for ever.

'Do you want to tell me about it?' Iris asked.

'It was just another job,' I said. 'Are we done here?'

'Sure,' Iris said.

'Then let's go. We don't have much time.'

'What about your friend?' Iris asked.

I assumed she meant Richard. 'He's not my friend. The only thing we have in common is a deep affection for the contents of my wallet.'

We took the elevator from the morgue and went back on to the street. I wasn't sure where Iris was going next. I wasn't sure if I wanted to tag along.

'You got any suspects?'

'Too many,' Iris said. 'I've got some other leads to follow. If I can find out what Patrick was doing in his last few hours, maybe I can narrow down the list.'

'You want me to come along?'

Iris shook her head. 'It will be easier if I do this alone. Thanks for your help.'

'Don't mention it. How can I get in touch with you?'

'I'm staying at the Memorial Baptist Church in Brooklyn.' Iris wrote an address and phone number on my hand. 'Tell them you're my cousin from New Canaan.'

We began to walk north towards the trains. Mary wasn't my problem, but I couldn't help thinking about her. The marks on her neck could have been from a trick gone wrong, but my gut nixed the idea. The bruises were too even to be a crime of passion. Someone had murdered her with malice aforethought. I wasn't surprised. Mary had been in the blackmail business, after all.

I stopped dead. Iris took a few steps before she noticed and turned back.

'What's wrong?' she asked.

Mary had just given me an idea. 'I'm going to ask you a question,' I said. 'I need you to be completely honest.'

'Okay,' Iris said.

'Was Salda running a blackmail operation?'

'What?'

'The Crusade needs money, and it has a lot of other people's secrets. The maths does itself.'

Iris rolled her eyes. 'How many times do I have to tell you we aren't the mafia?'

'Well, someone tortured your friend for information.'

'Information about the Crusade,' Iris said. 'You know we have many enemies.' She turned on her heel.

I'd done it again. 'Just keep it in mind,' I said to her back.

'I don't hate people as much as you do, Felix,' Iris said, 'but I'll do my best.'

Iris walked away from me, just like she always did.

ELEVEN

It was me versus the diary, round three. I sat in my office and stared at the ceiling.

There had to be something in there. It was all I had. Faye had left me alone the last few days. I hoped it was out of respect for my injuries. The last meeting I'd had with my client hadn't gone too well, but I didn't think I was fired. She hadn't asked for her money back.

If Faye did call I wasn't sure what I would tell her. All my leads so far had hit dead-ends. I certainly wasn't going to tell her about Cal, his crazy ideas, and Isaac's possible involvement with both. Whether it was true or not, she could get herself in a lot of trouble if she talked about it with the wrong people.

The diary didn't improve with a third reading. I'd often wondered how things might have been if I hadn't put myself in the wrong place at the wrong time in Tehran, if I hadn't come home with a condition no one wanted to talk about. I imagined a life without the constant fear of running out of medicine, a job I could be proud of, maybe a little house I shared with a dame who happened to look a lot like Iris. The grass on the other side of the fence had to be greener than the toxic brown of my own.

Isaac's time after Tehran had put a few cracks in those rose-coloured glasses. He was struggling for money, unable to find a decent job, drifting back into the army. He wasn't scrounging for a prescription, but other than that things hadn't been that different for us.

I flipped back to the end of the diary and looked at the last entry. I don't know why he didn't continue writing it during his tour in the Holy Land. There were blank pages at the end, and I doubt he'd seen worse than what we lived through in Iran. Maybe it had all been the same as our tour, and not worth putting down.

Outside, the world was settling into dusk. I turned on my desk lamp and it caught the diary at a weird angle. The full stop at the end of 'I'm on my way to the Holy Land next month' had an odd shine to it. I rubbed it with my thumb, but it felt no different from the rest of the page.

I looked at the page through my camera, zooming in on the full stop as far as I could. White lines were visible inside the dark circle, too regular to be anything but writing.

It was a microdot, a spy technique almost as old as photography. You took an image or some text and then shrank it to a tiny size using camera tricks. That made it easy to hide in a letter, or in this case a book. Isaac must have read about it in one of those spy novels he was always reading when we were in Tehran. It was a primitive technique in the era of digital encryption, and that was its attraction. Whoever had tossed Isaac's flophouse room would have been looking for hidden files on a computer, a thumb drive or an optical disk. Nobody paid attention to books any more.

I went through every other page looking for more microdots. It was laborious, boring work but it paid off. I found six more, for a total of seven.

One of the great things about living in Manhattan was you

could get just about anything on short notice. There was a scientific supply store uptown near Columbia. In two hours I was back at the office with a microscope powerful enough to read the microdots, and a little adapter for my camera so I could photograph them.

My God, what have I done? Adultery is a sin. 'Thou shalt not covet another man's wife,' it says so right in the Ten Commandments. I pray and I pray, but still I covet. When it first started, I thought it was just lust. I understand lust. God has given me the strength to manage it.

It's much worse. I think I'm in love. Whenever I'm near her, I have this strange feeling. I'm happy. Maybe it's just because she's the only person I know who doesn't look right through me. I guess it doesn't matter. I love her, she loves me, and that imperils both our souls.

It was Isaac's handwriting, the same as the diary. No wonder I hadn't been able to make out the words. Handwriting on a microdot was a weird thing to do, and smacked of improvisation. The text also didn't make a lot of sense. Was he talking about Faye? Had she been married before they met?

Yesterday he had some kind of seizure. I saw him through an open doorway. He was on the ground flailing and shaking.

I filled his prescriptions last week. I'm a gopher too. There were three different bottles. I didn't recognize any of the names, but I don't think they get you high. He never looks that way.

She was there. She just watched him. No call for help or anything. There was this look on her face, a mixture of hatred and sadness. I can't understand why she married him, and I don't think I ever will. Eventually his men came

in and injected him with something. He went limp after that.
I'll tell the others. They might be able to use it against him.

She's crying again. I wonder what that bastard has done to
her this time. She never tells me when I ask. Sometimes I
think about killing him, but nothing I could do seems bad
enough. I spent the whole day with her; he told me to keep
her out of the way. I wanted to comfort her, but there
were too many people around. So I watched her cry. It was
torture.

She's a saint, and not just because she stays with him.
She's kind, giving and peaceful. A good Christian woman,
married to the devil.

Ref. 14498

*Rabbi Michael Tenenbaum	413
Martin Spanoli	189
*Father Charles Fiore	199
*Eric Blair	199
Martin Drysdale	208
*David Emerson	825
Sarah Johnson	208
*John Darby	666

00026

Mr Stonebridge has gone to Washington. I know what that means now; she finally told me. He goes to DC on Homeland Security business. While he's there, he picks up a whore. He likes them to be Persian-looking. She said his men do the finding, and complain about it. There aren't many Persian-looking women in DC, and he never sees the same woman twice.

He beats them. That's all Mrs Stonebridge said, but he probably does worse. He never has sex with them. That way he can pass a polygraph if he's asked about his marriage. Adultery would damage his career.

I'll hit his office tonight. I know the safe code. The demon unlocks it with his door open. I'll find what they need, and she and I can run.

Not much time. They said they'd get us out. I've got to convince her, but first I have to get the list. They said the letter isn't enough. I don't know what to do. I can't sleep, can't eat. I don't want to go back there. It was dangerous enough the first time. I don't have a choice. I have to get us both out soon.

My right hand searched for the Scotch until the left stopped it. Cal was right. Or I was crazy. Or we were all crazy, which would have been best for everyone. As soon as I saw Glass's imperious scrawl at the bottom of that letter, I knew Cal was on to something. Glass's letter didn't say what would happen to the names on that list, but orders like that were never spelled out. The government lived by euphemism. When children died in an airstrike, the military called it 'collateral damage'. When the government locked up a troublemaker, it called it 'preventive detention'. Maybe I had believed him from the start, and hadn't wanted to admit it.

MEMORANDUM FOR: SIA Peter Stonebridge

Attached is an addendum to your task order. Most of
these were last-minute approvals. The asterisked
names are now your alpha priority; they supersede
everything from the original order, except for
CASSANDRA. Approval for the asterisked names was
difficult to obtain, so we must act before it is
withdrawn. Once clients are in the system, all
doubts become irrelevant.

Emerson is a special case. You'll need to delay
dealing with him, but be prepared to move immediately when the signal is given.

I have seen your request for more men. It is
denied. Accounting has already brought your cost
overruns to my attention. I appreciate that the
high cost of living in New York is a factor.
However, even taking that into account you have one
of the worst cost-per-client ratios in the country.
I have given you almost a company of men. It should
be more than enough to do your job.

Far too many pieces of paper with your name on it
have been cluttering up my desk lately. I have
given you an important mission in LEVIATHAN. Do not
make my trust in you one of the few regrets of my
life. Send any reports relating to Emerson or
CASSANDRA only to me. And remember what I said
about cost. We are serving our country and our God,
but this is still a business.

General Simeon Glass, US Army (ret.)

The mystery woman had to be Mrs Stonebridge. It was the only way the first microdot and this one made sense. Isaac was having an affair with the woman he was protecting. As motives for murder went, it was an absolute classic. Add the theft of documents from Stonebridge's safe and abused prostitutes and things only got worse. Whatever the final reason was, I didn't doubt that Stonebridge had murdered Isaac.

The seizure that Isaac described sounded like one of mine. I'd known Stonebridge in Tehran, but we'd lost touch after I threatened to kill him. I had no idea where Stonebridge was when the city was destroyed; he could have been inside the fallout zone. No one knew how many of us there were: several hundred at least, definitely fewer than a thousand. I was kept in isolation for most of my time at the VA, and I assumed the others had been as well. The cycle of seizure/restraint/sedation that had been my typical day hadn't left a lot of time to mingle. By the time the cocktail was developed, they were already cutting us loose. If he had my disease, that wouldn't change my opinion of him one bit. He was sick long before that day.

I left the office and used the subway system as one big Internet café. Stations were one of the few places where the only ID you needed to use the Internet or make a call was legal tender. Tourists didn't have social security numbers or driver's licences. A rumour had gone around a few months ago that the regime had considered mandatory passport checks for every Wi-Fi account or calling card. The mayor had found his spine and pointed out that tourists were already fingerprinted at the border and forced by law to produce their passport on demand. Any more regulation would have driven tourism even further into the basement it currently occupied. Reality still won out over paranoia once in a while, but only when a lot of money was involved.

I stuck around Midtown, walking between stations rather than riding the trains. It was safer that way: there were fewer cameras topside, and thicker crowds to get lost in. I blended right in with the tourists, remembering to stop and gawk at something as if I'd never seen it before. I didn't mind that part much; you can't look at the Chrysler Building too many times.

I checked one name from the list per station, and was never online more than five minutes. The NSA had supercomputers combing through all telecommunications traffic. My search for these names might raise a red flag somewhere, or it might pass by unremarked in that great tide of noise.

It was impossible to know how cautious I had to be. Better to err on the side of paranoia than take unnecessary risks. It was that hesitancy, that fear of looking at the wrong thing just in case someone might be watching, that was the real aim of the policy anyway.

Glass had shown a special interest in David Emerson, so I began with him. The first hit was a Department of Justice page. He worked for the Civil Rights division of the Southern District, right here in New York. That meant Kirov had been his boss.

The next hit told me David Emerson was twenty-nine years old. He had started at the DOJ right out of law school, married his college sweetheart Greta, and now lived in Park Slope, Brooklyn. All this came from an unimpeachable source: his father.

Under normal circumstances, a young lawyer on the federal payroll wouldn't have been able to afford a house in that part of town. It so happened that David was the son of Ignatius Emerson, pastor of the twenty thousand-seat New Life church outside Boca Raton, Florida. It so happened that Ignatius Emerson was a strong believer in the idea that those who tithed to his church would be repaired by the Lord tenfold. It so happened that the Emerson family was filthy rich.

Emerson's job, family and connections were all good reasons

for Glass to leave him alone, not single the man out for special persecution. I would have to figure out just what being a special case meant.

After Emerson I went back to Rabbi Michael Tenenbaum of the top of the list. The first hit I got was a notice for his funeral. He had been the rabbi at the Temple Israel Synagogue on the Upper East Side. It was a reform synagogue, the branch of Judaism the regime always looked on with suspicion.

His obituary noted that he'd been the director of the United Reform Council four years ago. I remembered something about the council attacking the government's incentives for Jews to emigrate. It had stuck in my brain, because by then so few people were still willing to criticize the Elders' policies in public. I didn't remember when the statement was released, so I couldn't be sure if Tenenbaum had been running the United Reform Council at the time.

The obituary didn't mention any controversy. It talked about his contributions to Jewish education and his tireless advocacy on behalf of the poor of all faiths. It mentioned his wife and two daughters. It mourned the loss for the world when a great man was taken at a young age, and so suddenly. Few men in excellent health die of a heart attack aged forty-eight.

Martin Spanoli, Eric Blair, John Darby and Martin Drysdale all came up blank. That didn't mean they'd disappeared like Isaac, just that they weren't that popular on the Internet. I'd have to use a government database to find out more. Benny was the only way in I had right now, and I didn't want to get him involved.

I found Sarah Johnson's name in a single place. It was a lawsuit filed in Manhattan against the government. The court had started charging to view even abstracts of cases a few years ago, a canny way to bury the legal process under another layer of privilege and track who was interested. I wasn't about to use a credit card to find out what the suit was about, but Johnson's title in the documents was a red flag. She was listed as a staff attorney for the American Civil Liberties Union, on whose behalf she was arguing.

I ended up at Columbus Circle when I got to the last name. Father Charles Fiore was the head priest at Our Lady of Grace Church in Park Slope. The church ran a girls' school that was highly sought after by young and upwardly mobile families. There was a number for the rectory on the website, so I gave it a call.

'Hello?' said a prim-sounding woman.

'May I speak to Father Fiore please?'

'I'm sorry, Father Fiore isn't available right now. He's. . . he's on a retreat.' Either this woman wasn't accustomed to lying, or they'd been writing the script on the back of an envelope when I called.

'When will he be back?'

There was a silence, ended by a long intake of breath. 'He will be gone for quite some time.'

'I see,' I said. I didn't know what to say. 'I'll pray for him.'

'Please do,' she said, and hung up before the tears could start.

I had one more call to make. I decided to walk up Broadway to Lincoln Center, hoping the walk would get the sound of that woman's fear out of my head. By the time I reached the center that catch in her voice was still there, hovering in the background.

I dialled the number Cal had given me. Someone picked up. There was no hello.

'I'm looking for Mr Franklin.'

There was a long pause. 'There is a smoke shop near West 125th and Lenox,' a female voice said. 'He'll see you there tomorrow at four.' She hung up.

Coates's smoke shop was a basement storefront on 125th Street. Green venetian blinds hid the interior from the street. When I opened the door, the afternoon light that followed me doubled the illumination inside.

Most of the place was floor-to-ceiling glass cases arranged in rows. Inside were specimens of tobacco leaf from all over the world, and in as many forms as human ingenuity could provide: cigars from Cuba, cartons of unfiltered Turkish cigarettes, loose Virginia leaf for pipes, and thick, wet chewing tobacco in stainless-steel drums. It was like a museum devoted to a cancerous habit the nation was trying to turn its back on.

The owner stood behind a polished wooden counter, attended by two friends. All three were black men pushing middle age. I could see the owner knew who I was, but he still waited for me to make the first move.

'I'm here to see Franklin,' I said. 'I have an appointment.'

The owner inclined his head towards the back door. I accepted the invitation.

Cal and Jack were waiting. The back room was bare concrete and crates stacked high. Both men sat on crates in front of a folding card table.

'What changed your mind?' Cal said.

Right to the point. That was fine with me. 'I found these hidden in Isaac's wartime diary.' I put the microdot enlargements on the table.

I pulled up a crate and watched them read. The entries made Jack angry and Cal sad, but neither was surprised. I filled them in on what I'd found out about the names in the letter.

'Why didn't you pull Isaac out?' I said to Cal. 'Stonebridge was on to him.'

'We didn't know that for sure,' Cal said. 'He was the only asset we had in place. I had my orders.'

'Don't throw orders at me,' I said. 'You know what they were worth in Iran.'

'We need that list. If we don't get it, more people will die, more will disappear. We're at war with the Elders, whether you want to see it that way or not. Isaac was a soldier. He knew the risks. We all do.'

I'd heard the 'we are expendable' speech too many times before. It got my blood up regardless of who said it, but slugging Cal and walking out wouldn't help anyone. That wasn't where my anger should live anyway.

'What's the next move against Stonebridge?'

'Hold on a second,' Jack said. 'We've levelled with you; it's time you did the same. Who's your client?'

Jack was doing his best to damage the good opinion I had of him. I'd formed it while being shot at by strangers, and tended to look favourably on anyone not following their lead.

'Don't go stupid on us now,' I said. 'I don't want my client's name on your lips if you're snatched off the street tomorrow.'

Jack stood up. 'Are you calling me a snitch?'

'Calm down, son,' Cal said. 'He's right. He doesn't know anyone from our end, and we don't know anyone from his. It's safer for everyone that way.'

Jack eyed us both and sat down again. 'We know where Stonebridge is going to be; why don't we be the grabber instead of the grabbee for once?'

'A little bird told us he'll be attending Kirov's funeral tomorrow,' Cal said.

'Kidnapping him won't do us any good.'

'Why not?' Jack said. 'He knows where the list is. I'm sure we can make him talk. Don't we owe that bastard for what he did to Isaac?'

'We owe him for a lot more than that,' I said. 'Suppose we do what you say. Maybe we get the list. It won't matter, because we'll be drowning in a flood of federal badges.'

'So he's a fed,' Jack said. 'That doesn't make him untouchable.'

'You think they actually care about a mid-level gopher like him? He's the help. We take Stonebridge out of play and there are a hundred other assholes waiting to take his place. We get next to nothing, and they get an excuse to tighten the screws even more.

'If you're going to kill Stonebridge, you need to have the will and the means to kill almost every Revivalist in government. I'm talking about the President, Vice-President, the whole Cabinet, every Elder, the heads of all the agencies, new and old. Everyone.'

Jack swore under his breath. 'You agree with him?' he said to Cal.

'Strange is right,' Cal said. 'We assassinate Stonebridge, we're just giving them the war they want to fight.'

Jack's face burned. He refused to meet either of our eyes.

'Don't take it personally, Jack,' I said. 'We both want a crack at Stonebridge as bad as you do, and ten years ago I might have tried my luck. I know how things work now. The sheriff can't just ride in and clean up.'

'Are you planning on being that sheriff?' Cal said.

'I thought of myself more as a deputy,' I said. 'I'm with you as far as Stonebridge; he's the only way I can find out what they did to Isaac. After that, we'll see.'

'Okay,' Cal said. He knew that was the maximum commitment he'd get from me. 'What do you suggest?'

I picked up Glass's memo. 'General Glass holds Stonebridge's leash. We're talking about the dog when we should be worrying about the man. Glass calls Emerson a "special case" and I'd like to know why. I think I've got enough to chase him down. This Cassandra is Glass's top priority. Does the name mean anything to you?'

Cal shook his head. 'I've never heard it before.'

'It might not even be a person,' Jack said. 'It might be an organization, or an operation. Leviathan sounds like one.'

'I've heard that word before, but I can't remember where,' I said. 'Does it ring any bells?'

It went right over their heads as well.

'I'll run the names past some friends and see if anything turns up,' Cal said.

'Okay.' I stood and grabbed my hat. 'Is that number you gave me still good?'

'Yeah,' Cal said. 'If we need you to get in touch, the woman you spoke to will call you about a box of cigars. You can pick them up here.'

'Okay,' I said. 'Anything else?'

'She'll say something else if we've disappeared: Your cigars have been lost in transit.'

'If you hear that,' Jack said, 'say thank you, put down the phone, and run.'

'You're going to Kirov's funeral, aren't you?' Cal said. He must have read my expression when he mentioned that Stonebridge would be there. The old man had better eyes than I gave him credit for.

'I won't do anything stupid,' I said. 'I need to see Stonebridge, make sure he's the man I knew in Tehran. I can't explain it. You've just started hating these men. I've been practising for ten years.'

Cal nodded. Maybe he understood. 'Be careful. I hear you do stupid things, whether you plan to or not.'

'It's a funeral,' I said. 'I'll be on my best behaviour.'

I went out through the front. The owner and his friends were in the exact place I'd left them. They looked straight through me. I banged the front door like an angry ghost.

TWELVE

Kirov's final resting place was Mount Hope Cemetery in Westchester. I rented a car (on my tab, not Faye's) and drove about an hour north of the city. Traffic was surprisingly heavy for a Sunday morning, all the way to the cemetery gates. A lot of people were coming north to pay their respects. Kirov was a public servant, but there was no way he knew this many people. Considering the twenty-four-hour coverage given to his case, I got the feeling television news had struck again.

State troopers manned a checkpoint at the front gates. They had sniffer dogs, metal detectors and a bank of X-ray machines for larger bags. A large sign told attendees that the machines were provided courtesy of 'Gauntlet Security Devices Inc. – as seen in the Holy Land'.

I joined the queue. Most of the people in line reminded me of Aftergood's parishioners. They wore suits and dresses in sombre colours that befitted a funeral, hats on both men and women. A few people went the other way and decided that a Giants jersey was the best way to mourn someone they'd probably never met.

A row of coaches was parked near the gate. Mourners had been bussed in like a junket to Atlantic City. Someone wanted to make sure that the numbers were large today. Rumours swirled through the line that the great and the good might make an appearance, but officials cited security in their denials. I didn't care who else was here, as long as Stonebridge showed his face.

I got to the front, showed my ID card and put my thumb on the fingerprint scanner. They patted me down but let me keep my gun. They were looking for bombs, not Caucasians with a sidearm.

I'd considered trying a false identity, but it wasn't worth the risk. You could get away with a forged ID at a traffic stop or an Internet café, but only expensive, quality work would get past this level of security. There was no reason to hide my identity anyway. The Elders already knew about my history with Kirov. That had been the whole point: Kirov was the honest broker between the Bureau and the Elders while they negotiated the price of keeping Brother Isaiah's death and White's complicity under wraps. I had more reason to show up at his funeral than most of the people here.

The crowds led me up a hill. The other side fell into a flat, manicured plain of gravestones. At the other end was what I assumed to be Kirov's gravesite. It was impossible to see through the security cordon around it. At least forty Stillwater men stood in honour guard in front of the grave. Every single one was cowboyed up: black fatigues to match the assault rifles cradled in their arms, dark wraparound sunglasses to hide their eyes. They wore that kit in the Holy Land to let the locals know who ran the show.

Behind the phalanx was a bandstand covered in red, white and blue bunting. It was a little festive for the occasion. The chairs on the bandstand and the lectern at its front were all empty. Above the bandstand was a massive video screen. On either side were speaker towers that wouldn't have been out of place at a rock concert.

After half an hour a motorcade approached the bandstand:

two Humvees front and back, four black SUVs in between. More Stillwater men exited first, and they screened the bigwigs in the SUVs from view. I focused my binoculars on the group, and got nothing but the occasional glimpse of an arm in an expensive suit for my efforts.

The bigwigs and their minders marched to the bandstand. Only when they mounted the stairs did they become visible, their guards swelling the ranks of the Stillwater men in front. The mayor and governor of New York sat on the left with the state's junior senator. The deputy Attorney General and two congressmen followed after.

Stonebridge was next. I focused in with the binoculars. He looked almost the same as the video Cal had shown me. In person, the circles under his eyes were darker, the lines in his face deeper. He wore a grey raincoat over a hand-made suit that was the colour of night. His head was bare before the eye of God.

Stonebridge was officially just a Homeland Security bureaucrat, outclassed by everyone else on the bandstand. The reason for his presence became clear a minute later: he was just the warm-up act. General Simeon Glass ascended to the bandstand, his left hand on a black polished cane he was too strong to need for anything but show. His suit was the same colour as Stonebridge's except for the wall of medals and decorations shining on his chest. I could see only his profile. It was the good, unscarred side, but the face still radiated power and hatred in equal measure.

I was so focused on Glass I nearly missed the guest of honour. The Reverend F. Lincoln Howe, PhD, Secretary of State, ascended to the bandstand and parked himself in front of the lectern. It looked like he would be the one to deliver the eulogy, not Kirov's priest.

For most of his career, Howe's church had been a rental unit in a strip mall in Santa Barbara and a post office box. He communicated with his flock via books, videos and anything else that could be ordered through the mail. He had little formal education – the doctorate was an honorary one from Dallas Theological Seminary, awarded last year – but that hadn't stopped thousands of people from asking him to run their lives. He was on record calling for biblical penalties for homosexuality and idolatry, but I'd never heard him endorse the same for adultery and coveting in the first degree.

The music died away, leaving a respectful silence. Above the left speaker tower, a large screen blinked into life. Howe, squinting through his glasses, looked out at the crowd from behind a face that was nearly a storey tall.

'Piotr Kirov was born in Brighton Beach. His parents were devout Christians fleeing Godless Soviet Communism. Young Piotr had a tough childhood. His family started with nothing. His mother waited tables and his father drove a cab. They didn't whine or demand a handout. They worked and pulled themselves up with God's help.

'Young Kirov worked just as hard. He went to Columbia on a scholarship, and then Yale Law School. Many other young men would see those blessings as a ticket to material wealth. He could have gone to work for a big firm, worn expensive suits, and forgotten his upbringing.

'Instead, Piotr became a prosecutor for the New York District Attorney's office, and then US Attorney for the Southern District of New York. My friends, Piotr Kirov was a success story that could only happen in America.'

Many members of the audience, upon hearing the name of their country, broke into applause. It was a reflex reaction, a fear that the next man over would clap when you didn't, and people would begin to wonder why.

'When I say Piotr gave his life to public service, it is a tragedy that that statement is literally true. Piotr was taken from us by the armies of Satan, men who work against God's plan in the Holy Land and on our own soil. These men, if that is what they can be called, have been corrupted by Islam, atheism and the sensual world. They are without mercy or conscience, and must be fought wherever they are found.

'Piotr never shrank from that responsibility, but that isn't the lesson God wants us to learn today. My friends, I know some of you are asking: Why did God let evil men take Piotr from us? Why does God allow terrorism at all? Brothers and sisters, let me read from the story of Abraham and Isaac: "And Abraham stretched forth his hand, and took the knife to slay his son. And the angel of the LORD called unto him out of heaven, and said, Abraham, Abraham: and he said, Here am I. And he said, Lay not thine hand upon the lad, neither do thou any thing unto him: for now I know that thou fearest God, seeing thou hast not withheld thy son, thine only son from me."'

Howe paused to take a drink of water and catch his breath. I looked around to see if anyone knew where he was going with this. The crowd seemed happy to follow along with the scripture and hold their questions until the end.

'Genesis continues: "By myself have I sworn, saith the LORD, for because thou hast done this thing, and hast not withheld thy son, thine only son: that in blessing I will bless thee, and in multiplying I will multiply thy seed as the stars of the heaven, and as the sand which is upon the sea shore; and thy seed shall possess the gate of his enemies; and in thy seed shall all the nations of the earth be blessed; because thou hast obeyed my voice." Because thou hast obeyed my voice,' Howe said again. He let the words travel around the crowd.

'My friends, Piotr Kirov feared God.'

He offered no proof for this assertion. I'd met Kirov only once, but I suspected that was one more time than Howe.

'He feared God's majesty and His power, as every good Christian should. That fear led to obedience, and that obedience allowed Piotr to be shaped by God's eternal plan. He had the means to drown himself in material things and the corrupt morality of our big cities. Instead, he chose the righteous path and was blessed with a career, a lovely wife and two wonderful daughters.' It was the first time Howe had gotten around to mentioning Kirov's family. I focused my binoculars on the wife. Her tear-stained eyes stared straight ahead, a deer caught in a thousand headlights. The sons cried in the folds of her mourning dress.

'Piotr Kirov heard God's call to punish the wicked and he answered it. He did not bargain. He did not question. He obeyed. For that reason, though we mourn his loss, our grief is tempered by the sure knowledge that this great man is looking down on us from heaven. He has gone to the final and greatest reward, to sit on the side of the angels when Judgement Day comes.

'We are not so lucky. Just as Piotr battled terrorists, we must battle Satan for our souls. Every day, this great country is assailed by the IED of greed, the insurgent called doubt and the suicide bomb of sexual immorality. Terrorism is another test inflicted on us by Satan, and God allows it. Why? Because fear makes us humble. Fear reminds us that we are nothing without God. Fear turns us to His worship and His ways. Just as a parent teaches his child to fear fire, so our Father teaches us to fear the breaking of His laws. And that is why we will prevail over the Godless men who took Piotr Kirov from us. Because here, right here' – the giant face of Howe filled with blood as he pounded his own chest – 'is the fear of a loving God, whose Son will lead us to eternal glory!' Howe raised his arms. Overhead, three jet fighters cut white lines in the sky.

The reason for those buses outside was now clear. The crowd

was mostly normal people, who out of respect and basic decency would never think of cheering during a funeral. The zealots they'd bussed in prompted other people to cheer, whether they wanted to or not.

While the crowd went semi-wild, Howe signalled the priest. He helped Kirov's wife up and steered her towards the coffin. The poor woman was still in a trance: the priest had to walk her forward like a puppet. It was Stillwater men, not marines, who folded the flag on the coffin and presented it to Kirov's wife. She clutched it to her breast with both hands, until the priest offered her a spadeful of earth. He guided her hand towards the last home of her late husband, and turned her wrist to dip its contents over the lid. The crowd applauded the entire time.

The worthies on the bandstand began to disperse almost as soon as the dirt hit the coffin. The faithful in the crowd took the hint, and the cheering began to die down. They let Kirov's wife and family exit first. I put the binoculars on Glass and Stonebridge. Stonebridge was whispering something in Glass's ear, and he didn't like what he was hearing. Glass said something short to Stonebridge, and then joined the procession of great men marching towards their motorcade. Stonebridge stayed behind, with the advance guard of Stillwater men and an entourage of his own.

The thinning crowd made it easy for me to get closer. I'd seen everything I needed to through the binoculars, but it didn't seem like enough. The mercenaries maintained the perimeter even though all the VIPs had left. They saw me coming, mistook me for a deranged fan, and got ready to crack my skull.

'Strange.' Stonebridge appeared from behind the wall of hired muscle. Up close, I realized I'd been wrong; he did look different. The desert tan was gone, leaving a sallow complexion and lines on his face I hadn't seen before. A few were scars, but the rest had been carved by worry.

'Come inside,' he said.

Some people still lingered outside the perimeter. Families took their time packing up children, gawkers waited for a glimpse of VIPs who had already left, and the itinerant lingered with no clear intent. Inside the perimeter were armed men and vehicles with darkened windows. That old story about the spider and the fly popped into my head.

'Why don't you come out.'

The ranks parted enough for Stonebridge and five men to exit. His entourage wore US marshal badges around their necks, but they were the most unlikely lawmen I'd ever seen. The new uniform seemed to be a neglected black suit. Two showed tattoos on the backs of their hands when they clenched their fists for my entertainment. I looked into ten eyes empty of conscience or restraint. They looked back.

'You deputize these men yourself?' I asked.

'They're loyal men,' Stonebridge said, 'and that makes them good men.'

That was the sound of his master's voice.

'Do you remember what loyalty is, Strange?'

'If you're talking about the army, I was thrown in the trash, not the other way around.'

He wasn't talking about the army, and we both knew it. 'The general says hello,' Stonebridge said. 'He's sorry he couldn't meet you in person.'

'I understand,' I said. 'He's an important man now.'

Stonebridge smiled. 'He's been an important man for a very long time. You may want to forget, but I'm proud of my service.'

'I don't look back with fondness on actions that in another war would have led to a trial.'

'Strange the bleeding heart,' Stonebridge said. 'I'll never understand why the general has a soft spot for you.'

'He said I was the only one who wasn't afraid to tell him the truth.'

Stonebridge scoffed with the back of his throat. He paced a little: three short steps and a full turn back to me. His men watched the crowd and the horizon. They didn't look smart, but their instincts had been honed in prison exercise yards, and that had to be respected.

'You ever wonder why you're where you are and I'm where I am? Two men: similar backgrounds, similar conditions.'

I wondered if he was referring to my, maybe our, illness. The fascination of meeting another sufferer almost overwhelmed my good sense, but I kept quiet. He'd insist on knowing where my information came from, and I didn't want to tip my hand.

'Both enter the private sector. One flourishes, the other fails. You don't see the work of a higher power in that?'

'The market for thugs has exploded lately,' I said. 'The only higher power I see is the invisible hand of greed.'

'I've prospered because I followed God's laws.'

'You've prospered because you've done anything Glass tells you.'

'Isn't that the same thing? To paraphrase the Good Book: "He is our God: we walk before him, and we are blameless."' Stonebridge smiled again. 'I'm an American success story, just like the secretary said. You could have had the same.'

'I didn't want it,' I said. 'I wasn't given the choice anyway.'

'That's not the way the general remembers it.'

'The general remembers things the way he wants to.'

'What did he say to you,' Stonebridge asked, 'that day when he visited you in the hospital?'

'That was a private matter,' I said. 'If he hasn't told you, he doesn't want you to know.'

'He didn't offer you help?' Stonebridge said. 'That's what he offered me. He knew it wouldn't be long before the military cut us loose.'

Us. I didn't like the way he used that word. 'You weren't part of the unit that day.'

Stonebridge tried for an angry smile, but what came out was a sneer. 'No, you saw to that. Janus ordered a group of us to follow, no matter what Glass said. We were halfway out when it happened.'

I'd met a few people who'd been near but not too close to Houston when it was destroyed. They couldn't shut up about it; where they were, what it felt and smelled like, since everyone had seen and heard it on recordings a hundred times. Every year dozens appeared on television to share their escape, to remind us of the others whose luck had gone the wrong way.

They didn't commemorate Tehran in the same way, at least in this country. There was footage of that day, but it wasn't shown on domestic television. Those of us who had been there, even those who'd gotten away clean, had trouble talking about it. Stonebridge had none of my misgivings, and even he couldn't come out and say it. With enough persuasion or alcohol, we might talk about before or after, but never that moment when the wounded city became just a collection of bricks. Both cities had been destroyed, but only one had been erased.

'I guess they wanted their employees to be in on the big score, no matter what,' he continued. 'The shockwave blinded our driver, and we went into a wall at high speed. I lay in that Humvee for six hours, waiting to die. Casevac found me instead. I was the only one who survived. When I found out about the syndrome, I wasn't surprised. I deserved it.'

'I thought you'd had your conscience surgically removed.'

'This isn't about right and wrong, Strange; it's about loyalty. Janus was my employer, but Glass was my leader. I betrayed him, and I paid the price.'

I should have known it wasn't the men he'd brutalized that haunted Stonebridge.

'The general came to see me after I was diagnosed. Janus had already stabbed me in the back: it paid a gang of fuckface lawyers to say the company's insurance wouldn't cover my medical bills for a condition that didn't exist. I had no one until he came. He forgave me, said I was just following orders. When everyone else had cast me aside, he offered me his hand.'

'What a touching story,' I said. 'He took you in, and offered you honest work torturing and killing in the Holy Land.' I wasn't giving anything away by talking about what he'd been up to over there: Stonebridge and I both knew they were the only two things he was good at.

'He did more than that. Did you know that the Pentagon kept studying the syndrome in secret? They were worried we'd been hit with some kind of biological weapon.'

Not worried enough to help us. 'How do you know that?'

'The general got me into the programme. He would have done the same for you, if you hadn't turned your back on him.'

'I guess the eggheads didn't trip over a cure.'

'No, but I was spared the Veterans Administration trials. The Pentagon study came up with a similar cocktail before the VA did. I was out of the hospital and working for Glass months before they let you out of that hospital in Kuwait.'

'If it had been a choice between the two, I still would have taken the latter,' I said. 'Did the Pentagon find out anything at all?'

'Scientists don't share their findings with lab animals.'

The crowds were thinning, and Stonebridge wasn't becoming any friendlier. I started to get antsy. 'Thanks for the history lesson, but—'

'You have something that belongs to me,' Stonebridge said, before I could move.

I looked around, and began to appreciate the full extent of my stupidity. All these squarejohns I'd relied on for witnesses would be nothing of the kind once push led to shove. If five marshals seized a (by then screaming) member of the public, what would they do, ask to see a warrant? They had careers, families and unbroken bones to think about. When the fireworks started, they'd paint all of us out of the scene with silence and denial.

'You must be mistaken,' I said.

'A pigeon told me you recently had a drink with an old army buddy.'

It would be a pigeon that would drop a dime on me: they were rats with wings.

'That's illegal now?'

'You don't have drinks with old army buddies. You know Scalia and a former employee of mine.'

Isaac knew me and we both knew Scalia. For someone with a brain it was a starting point, but for people like Stonebridge it was all the proof they needed. Since we knew Isaac, we must have been in on whatever he was up to. The same method could implicate my dry cleaner, or Faye.

Of course if you send enough rounds into the dark, sooner or later you hit something. Stonebridge would have been dead wrong before I started looking into Isaac's disappearance, and now he was still mostly incorrect. I remained unsure of what I'd gotten myself mixed up in, which should make it easier for me to lie to Stonebridge.

'Who's our mutual friend, and why would he be stupid enough to work for you?'

'Keep acting dumb, Strange, and I'll cure you the hard way. Isaac Taylor took something that belongs to me.'

'I haven't seen him in a long time, but that doesn't sound like the Isaac I remember. In fact, he was the opposite: if he saw something wrong, he wouldn't hesitate to report it.'

Stonebridge didn't take the bait. I guess he had learned something in the last ten years.

'You showing up here can't be a coincidence. Are you crazy enough to think you can sell it back to me?'

'I came to bury an acquaintance,' I said. 'This shindig was supposed to be a funeral.'

'If you don't tell me where it is, there might be a second funeral today. The general wouldn't like to see you harmed, and one of us still respects his orders. Tell me where it is, and you walk away.'

'I still don't know what you're talking about,' I said. 'If you've lost something, check under the sofa.'

'I'm glad I could show you to my men,' Stonebridge said. 'You're an interesting case. Glass once said the only God you worshipped was your own stubbornness. I could arrest you.'

'On what charge?'

He ignored me. 'You'd tell me what I wanted to know eventually; everyone breaks in the end. I'd do it just for old times' sake, but you aren't worth the effort. You'd dissemble and twist every question I asked until I couldn't tell your confession from the lies. When we come up against a hard nut like this one, we look for softer targets,' he said to the marshals, like I was the skeleton in an anatomy lecture. 'Children are the most useful; other family after that. The problem is, our Felix has none of the above. His parents are dead, he has no siblings, and certainly no wife and children of his own.

'The last option is friends. Even this born loser has managed to trick a few people into caring about him over the years. There's a war buddy in the FBI. He has a family.'

Stonebridge was fishing. I could feel the hook inside my mouth, tugging at my anger. I kept my eyes on him and flexed my face into a mask. I didn't know how much Isaac had told him. He might know about Cal and Jack. He might know everything, and just be toying with me.

'I read the reports from last year. You were seen in the company of a woman before you shot up that diner.'

At some silent command, his minions fanned out, encircling me with deliberate steps. I didn't give Stonebridge the satisfaction of reacting; it was long past the time to run.

'Would that woman go to the police if you went missing? I wonder,' Stonebridge said, 'if we arrested you today, would anyone come for you at all?'

I gave him a slow-motion ovation. It wasn't the smartest thing to do in the circumstances, but it was the best way to distract him, and he had it coming. 'Back in Tehran you thought a pair of pliers and a car battery would make people take you seriously. Now it's five guys and an ass-licking federal gig. You can put as many words in front of your name as you like, Stonebridge, but they won't change the fact that you're just a coward with a gun.'

Stonebridge's men looked at him, waiting for the word, but he stayed mum. If he was going to make me disappear, now would be the time. Stonebridge's hand crept towards his pistol.

'Do you remember what I said I'd do if you ever pulled a gun on me again?'

I was armed. I knew what was waiting for me if I came quietly, and would rather be a known corpse than a living ghost. We hadn't tangled in a long time, but the smart odds said I was still faster than him, and had no qualms about shooting first. Stonebridge should know all that, but he'd never been that bright.

His hand stopped just short of its goal. He nodded to the two goons behind me, and they stood aside. I turned my back.

'The Elders haven't forgotten what you did, Strange,' Stonebridge said as I walked away. 'I'm your only way out.'

I didn't respond. I had about as much regard for his words as the departed under our feet.

THIRTEEN

Iris called and asked me to meet her at a street corner in Brighton Beach. We didn't discuss details over the phone, but I assumed it was about Salda, the Crusade official in the morgue. I wanted my missing people and hers to be separate problems, but things were never that simple. If the Elders were taking care of the opposition, the Crusade wouldn't be far down the list.

I should have been on the trail of that man in Glass's letter, Emerson, not pushing down the pavement in Queens. As far as Faye was concerned, I was still on sick leave. She knew I was keeping something from her, and Faye wasn't the kind of delicate flower who would accept I was doing it for her protection. I'd have to come up with some kind of explanation soon, one that didn't make me sound crazy or put her in danger.

Iris hadn't arrived, and I had no idea why anyone would want to linger here. The street was a nondescript collection of storefronts that could be found anywhere in the country: a Laundromat, bodegas facing each other on the corner, an accountant's office, a failed print shop and a funeral home called Andronescu Brothers Bereavement Services. The name rang a bell. Before I could dig around in my brain for the source of the familiarity, a finger attached to an arm I recognized emerged from the window of a battered station wagon. The finger curled in invitation, and then it disappeared.

I got in the passenger side. 'Nice car.'

'A friend lent it to me,' Iris said. 'I never turn up my nose at the Lord's gifts.'

I did. A strange smell had soaked into the upholstery, and it was no more pleasant for being anonymous. I was about to ask her what we were doing here when I remembered where I'd heard the name Andronescu before. 'Please tell me you're not staking out that funeral home.'

Mike Andronescu was a pimp, thug and trafficker in all types of distressed humanity. He brought people in and out, and used coffins from his network of funeral homes both ways. Mexicans came north and Asians west, though the country had become a less appealing prospect of late. Moving people out was almost as lucrative a business as moving people in. Abortion was still legal in Mexico, and a woman of means wasn't going to bleed to death in some back alley like a regular girl. The 'brothers' part of the business was just marketing, and for that the world was grateful.

'I still have friends in low places,' Iris said. 'I asked around about Salda; I figured only lowlifes would torture a man like that.'

'Well, you came to the right man for that. You do know who he's connected to?'

Iris gave me a blank and pleasant stare. She was trying to provoke me, and it was working.

'He's an associate of the Corinthian. Don't you ever do your homework?'

Andronescu wasn't part of anything so formal and self-regarding as a mafia. He was just another point in the Corinthian's web of exchange, the strands mutual interest rather than blood oaths taken in back rooms. Little was expected in the way of friendship, and even less when it came to loyalty.

I'd been lucky enough not to see the Corinthian since I ran into him investigating the death of Brother Isaiah last year. The Bureau's patronage meant I didn't have to spend as much time in the gutter, but I heard things all the same. The Corinthian was in the city, buying and selling anything with a favourable margin. Anyone with more than a passing affection for their own lives never mentioned him directly, but you could see his hand in the ebb and flow of illicit goods and desires, the same way an atom could be observed by its effect on its surroundings. I'd done my best to stay out of his way, and now Iris had brought me within two degrees.

'I don't think the Corinthian has anything to do with it. No one has mentioned his name.'

'No one ever mentions the Corinthian's name, that's how they keep breathing.'

'Don't be so melodramatic, Felix. He puts his trousers on the same way everybody else does.'

'When you met him last year, he threatened to have us killed and condemned one of his employees to an even worse fate in the space of five minutes. Spend an hour in the man's company and you'll see things that will drive you to the nearest convent.'

Iris gave me a half-smile. 'I wonder if you want me in a convent so I'd be safe, or you like the idea of me in a wimple.'

'If the Corinthian isn't involved, then why are we sitting on a two-bit smuggler?'

'A friend's cousin overheard one of Andronescu's men at a bar who'd had way too much to drink. He said something about a "task order"and his friends practically gagged him with a cocktail napkin.'

'Task order?' I said. Glass had used that term in his memo. It sounded like one of the phrases business consultants occasion-ally vomited upon the world. I hoped the term was generic. The possibility of Glass and the Corinthian working together was too terrifying to contemplate just yet. 'Could that be another way of saying a contract?'

'Maybe,' Iris said, 'but people talk about contracts all the time. A body gets fished out of the river, and you're tripping over rumours and speculation. This is different. Some of the guys I talked to had done time in Russian prisons, which make ours look like wellness retreats. They were scared, and relieved they didn't know more.'

There weren't that many people capable of putting the fear of God into hard cases like that. General Glass could, if he was now free to do in America what he did in the Holy Land. The Corinthian was equal to the task as well.

Iris began to fiddle with what looked like a small radio.

'What's that for?' I said.

'I planted a bug or two in there a little while ago,' Iris said.

'You did what?'

'I posed as a customer,' she said with a shrug. 'A recently bereaved wife whose husband died fighting for his country and his God in the Holy Land.' It explained her sombre attire. She wore a long black dress with no jewellery. A pillbox hat of the same colour, now resting on the back seat, completed the outfit. I hoped she'd kept the attached veil on as much as possible. 'When I started to tell the funeral director about my heroic late husband, I realized I was describing you.'

'Thanks,' I said. 'I guess the sob story worked.'

'Every man loves a vulnerable young widow; he was drooling so badly they should have followed him around with a mop.'

'Have you heard anything?'

'I know more about the different linings available for caskets than I ever wanted to,' she said. 'They speak Romanian most of the time. At least, I think that's what it is.'

'So we're sitting in a car that smells like' – I struggled with the identification – 'wet basset hound, based on a single drunken outburst?'

'Just imagine we're on a date. We've got dinner,' she said. Arrayed on the dashboard were bags of potato chips and two sandwiches wrapped in butcher paper. Sodas clinked against her heels on the floor. 'And a movie.'

'If this is a movie,' I said, looking at the street, 'then it's one of those European art films that never goes anywhere.'

We settled in and waited. We ate the sandwiches. After a while, I thought up some light conversation to pass the time.

'I think you should leave the country.'

'You'd be surprised how often I hear that on dates.'

Iris had spent a lot of time in front of the mirror that morning, but make-up couldn't hide the shadows under her eyes. At first I thought she was scared, but it wasn't her style. Iris hadn't been frightened even when she should have been. She looked tired, and sad.

'You found out more than you're telling me, Iris.'

'If I tell you, you'll think I'm crazy.'

'Let me guess: you checked up on Salda's operatives. They've disappeared.' I said.

She turned to me in disbelief.

'Someone I know disappeared a few weeks ago. I've been trying to find him, but he's fallen off the face of the earth, and taken all his records with him: social security number, birth certificate, everything. It's happening all over the country.'

'How do you know?'

'I found something. A document. If it's genuine, and I think it is, Homeland Security is involved. It wouldn't do an operation like this without the Elders' approval.'

'Why are they doing this?' Iris asked. 'Why now?'

'I don't know. If Homeland Security has rolled up Salda's

network, then it probably has someone on the inside. That means they might know about you.'

'I can't leave yet.'

'Damn it, Iris, if they know about you, they'll come for you. It's just a matter of time.'

'It's not just the agents who disappeared,' Iris said. 'Wives, husbands, whole families are gone too. Some of our people left their children in Africa, just in case. What am I supposed to tell them, Felix? What am I supposed to say when they ask me where their parents are?'

I didn't have an answer, for her or when Faye would ask me the same question.

'Please, Felix,' she said, squeezing my hand. 'No more talking. Just keep me company for a little while.'

I said yes by shutting up. We waited. We watched the funeral home. Iris didn't say anything, and neither did I. Being beside her was enough.

An hour later, an expensive black sedan with tinted windows pulled up in front of the funeral home. Two gorillas stepped out. They wore wraparound sunglasses, earpieces and dark Italian suits cut to leave room for the body armour underneath. It was secret service chic, and it would be funny if they weren't so heavily armed. One scanned the street while the other opened the back door for his principal.

The Corinthian emerged from the car, dwarfed by his bodyguards. From a distance, the conservative dark suit and armed protection might have led an observer to mistake him for a high-ranking government official. On closer inspection, you'd notice that his attire was beyond the price range of any civil servant, and no public official could have pulled off the look of detached mastery permanently fixed to the Corinthian's ageless, unplaceable face.

'Nothing to do with the Corinthian, huh?'

Iris shrugged. 'You never told me what the history was between you and him,' she said.

'Like I said before; I used to find people for him.'

'There has to be more than that.'

'Let's just say that as far as I know, I'm the only man to lay a hand on him and live.'

The Corinthian headed inside. Iris flipped the transmitter between the bugs she'd planted, and got a mixture of static and muffled voices before she found one nearby.

'You didn't tell me you were coming.'

I didn't recognize the voice, but it had to be Andronescu's. I no longer minded the smell in the car so much. From the quaver in Andronescu's voice, I'd guess the crime boss had just shat himself.

'If I had told you, that would imply I wanted to come,' the Corinthian said. His voice still had that menacing serenity. 'Was something about Task Order 2389 unclear?'

'No, sir,' Andronescu said. 'We did like you told us to—'

'I told you to tenderize the meat a little before delivery to see what came out. It might have led to other sources of revenue. I was very clear about the need for restraint. Instead you destroyed it. That meat was to be delivered fresh; the task order was adamant in that respect.'

'There was an accident—'

'I don't care,' the Corinthian said. 'I am being asked to explain why not only were we unable to deliver what we'd promised, but that the carcass was found, and in an obviously damaged condition. I do not enjoy explaining myself.'

The silence inside that room was pregnant with fear. 'What can I do to make this right, sir?' Andronescu said.

'Tell me how you have contained the situation.'

'The men, by which I mean employees, have all been . . . let go,' Andronescu said. He was obviously struggling with the new business vernacular the Corinthian demanded of him. 'Any investigation will stop there.'

'Associates of mine will verify your due diligence,' the Corinthian said. 'Update me on the rest.'

'We've got five, and are waiting for delivery instructions. Three aren't in the city. Two are visiting relatives in Minnesota and Oklahoma, and another is on business in Chicago. Should we go after them?'

'No. Forward the details to me in the usual way, and I'll have local people take care of it. That leaves how many outstanding?'

'Six. We're working our way down the list, just like you told us.'

Another pause. I could almost hear Andronescu sweat.

'Are there any other accidents or surprises I should be aware of?' the Corinthian said.

'No, sir. It's all going to, uh, procedure.'

'Good. Then for your sake, I hope I never visit here again.'

One of the Corinthian's men came outside and scanned the street a second time.

'They're getting ready to leave,' I said. 'Have you ever followed someone in a car?'

'Don't worry,' Iris said. 'I had an unorthodox childhood, remember?'

'You have a question,' the Corinthian said, still inside.

Andronescu took his time. 'Did they tell you why we're doing this?'

'No.'

The Corinthian exited the funeral parlour, followed by his other bodyguard. Andronescu didn't come out to wave goodbye.

Iris gave them a block head start before she turned on the ignition and began to follow. It was a leisurely tail at slow speeds.

The Corinthian stuck to side streets and headed deeper into Queens, not towards his lair in Brooklyn.

Iris stared straight ahead and didn't say a word during the whole pursuit. It wasn't because of concentration. The discussion of Task Order 2389 had sounded too much like what had happened to Salda to be a coincidence.

After about fifteen minutes, the Corinthian's car stopped. Our luck held, and there was a parking spot nearby. We pulled in and waited. Our quarry idled for almost ten minutes. It made me uneasy, and I didn't know why.

The back passenger door opened, and shortly after my head began to spin fast enough to power the state.

'I recognize her,' Iris said, talking about the woman who was half out of the car.

'So do I,' I said. It was Faye. We could see the Corinthian's arm holding one of hers. They were having a spirited discussion, half in the car and half on the street.

'I think I saw her at the Waterfront a few times,' Iris said. The Waterfront was the Corinthian's Brooklyn club and office. It wasn't the sort of place frequented by nice girls from Queens. 'Is that where you saw her?'

'No. I don't have time to explain, but I need to follow her.'

'You take her, and I'll stay on him,' Iris said.

I nodded.

'If you find anything out, look me up at the Excelsior Hotel on Spring Street. I was endangering too many people staying at the church.'

'Think about what I said.'

'If I told you to stop looking for your friend and leave the country, would you?'

'Your friend is dead.' If I had found Isaac's body instead of Salda's, I'd have to know who killed him and why. Iris was no different.

I opened my door and crouched behind the line of parked cars. 'Take care of yourself.'

Iris winked, and I closed the door.

Faye had broken free of the Corinthian and started walking. His car pulled away and Iris followed. I wasted time watching her recede into the distance, following one of the most dangerous men I'd ever met.

I stayed with Faye. I couldn't afford a close tail. If she saw me I'd never be able to explain it, and I'd lose my only chance to figure out her connection to the Corinthian. We weren't far from her place. I gave Faye a two-block lead and hoped I was right about where she was going.

We reached her apartment and Faye went in. I wanted to confront her immediately, but my gut told me to wait and watch her next move. Faye stayed in her apartment for a quarter of an hour, and left with a large canvas bag. She walked two blocks and went into a Laundromat. Faye loaded up two washers and sat down to wait. She opened a dog-eared novel, and settled in to watch the clothes go round.

I retraced my steps. The lock on the front door was an electronic card reader of a type most buildings had installed ten years ago. There were ways to confuse them, but none of the methods I knew could be done safely in broad daylight. Luckily for me, I'd seen that the door itself was old and a little warped the first time I came here. The latch had a tendency to stick instead of fully entering the frame. I walked up to the front door and opened it with a strong yank.

Faye's door was more of a challenge, but at least I had some privacy. It was an old-fashioned key lock. I'd had a fair amount of experience with credit cards – as aids to unlawful entry rather than financial instruments. A few minutes probing the latch and I was able to slip the credit card in between the latch and the frame.

The apartment was exactly the same as last time: same fake leather chairs and patterned sofa, same chipped coffee table. I split the apartment into a grid and began to search.

When I was in Task Force Seventeen, I seemed to be the only one who could properly search a room. Some of the Special Forces guys knew what they were doing, but most hadn't been trained for the job. They acted like any normal person who was looking for something, and didn't care what state the room ended up in. They slashed mattresses, emptied drawers, and punched holes in walls looking for secret rooms. All that destruction was a part of the design. A visit from Seventeen was as much intimidation as investigation.

Here I had to be the opposite of my old comrades. If Faye ever figured out that I was searching her apartment, she'd never forgive me. I also wasn't eager to tip my hand in dealing with her. Now that I had seen her with the Corinthian, all bets were off.

The main room yielded no surprises. The furniture was clean, as least as far as I could tell without cutting it open. I spent more time than usual on Faye's meagre library. Nothing was hidden between the pages. I flipped through each volume, looking for the telltale shiny punctuation of Isaac's microdots. I found none.

The kitchenette was more interesting. I stood on a thin rectangle of linoleum that gave only enough space to turn. On one side a few fitted cupboards surrounded a counter and a sink. The other side had a refrigerator and a stove. I checked the fridge and freezer, and found only condiments, a little fresh fruit and the remains of last night's Chinese. The cupboards were almost bare as well: just some dried pasta and cereal.

On the counter was an old coffee can. Inside was a .25 calibre pistol. I lifted it up with a pen and looked it over. The gun was in good condition and fully loaded judging by the weight. I sniffed the barrel and smelled only oil. It was encouraging that Faye hadn't shot anything recently, but it hardly quieted my doubts.

I put the gun back where I found it and moved on to the bedroom. A double bed took up most of the space. Built-in closets claimed two walls; framed pictures of nature scenes decorated the rest. Beside the bed was a black plastic nightstand with an alarm clock. I opened its single drawer and found odds and ends. The faded receipts were footprints from day-to-day living, nothing more. I didn't find any contraception, but that wasn't a surprise. As a smart single girl, Faye would have known it was in her best interests to hide it.

There were a lot of empty hangers in the closet, the result of Faye's laundry trip. Pushed to the back were a number of outfits that didn't belong in the room they hung in. They were a mixture of dresses and evening gowns, all by foreign designers, all very expensive. Add in the shoes below and it was a few years worth of rent on the apartment. It certainly didn't fit the image of genteel poverty Faye was trying to project.

I found a shoebox hidden under some old clothes in the very back of the closet. I shouldn't have been so surprised at what I found inside. There were about a dozen pictures of Isaac and Faye. A few were taken in the apartment, the rest around town. Isaac and Faye were eating dinner in an Italian restaurant. Isaac and Faye were throwing rings and hitting the bumper cars at Coney Island. Isaac and Faye were in the park, holding hands. Isaac and Faye were building a life together.

I put the pictures back in the shoebox and buried it in the closet. I'd seen everything I needed to.

I walked around for an hour or two. I didn't know where I was going, and I don't remember where I went. I had two different images of Faye, and I couldn't reconcile one with the other. There was Faye and the Corinthian, the latter's hand on her arm. Then there was the Faye I'd seen smiling from all those photographs. I tried to imagine a single woman who could fit both those images, but I failed. I turned my footsteps back towards her apartment. I'd have to confront Faye with what I knew, and pay for it later.

'Hello, Felix,' she said, opening the door and letting me inside. I didn't take off my coat, and she noticed. 'Have you found Isaac?'

'Who are you?'

Her confusion was an almost perfect copy of the real thing.

'Felix, what are you—'

I grabbed her arm. 'I saw you with the Corinthian today. Let's skip the theatre of denial; we aren't getting any younger.'

Faye looked at my arm and played it cool. 'Are you going to hit me until I tell you what you want to hear?'

I let her go.

'Why don't we sit down?'

We sat in the same places as our first interview, looking at each other over the no-man's-land of the worn coffee table. The menu didn't include hot drinks this time.

'Start talking.'

'When I was younger, my father got sick.'

I saw a sob story on the horizon. For her sake I hoped it was a good one.

'It was cancer. He'd beaten it before, but our insurance didn't cover it. He ran a small market, and that was already mortgaged. I was desperate.'

'So you approached the Corinthian.'

'Not at first. My father had grown up with people who knew people. I went to visit a loanshark, but he said he couldn't help me, on the Corinthian's orders. I'd never heard the name before and still have no idea how he knew about me.

'I went to see him at his club. He said rather than lend me the money, he'd give me employment on "very favourable terms". Those were his words. He said I had the kind of fresh, innocent face he'd been looking for. I was afraid he'd ask me to prostitute myself, and even more afraid I'd say yes. He wanted me to do something different.'

'Something worse?'

'I didn't think so, at least in the beginning. The Corinthian has respectable friends – businessmen, state senators, police officers – and sometimes he likes to send them gifts. They were too valuable to go through the mail, and he couldn't send one of his own people.'

The Corinthian differed as much in manner and dress from his employees as a feudal lord from his shit-smeared peasants. He didn't have so many people capable of counting to ten that he could waste them on bagman duty. His organization was built on an army of the desperate and not-too-bright willing to do anything for pocket change. If one of them had walked into a state senator's office with that fresh from the gutter smell, the result would have been high comedy and jail time.

'What were you delivering?'

'I don't know. I was told to meet someone at a prearranged location. They would give me a purse. The Corinthian implied it would be better for me not to look inside and I didn't need to be told twice.'

'What was your cover?'

'Sometimes I was a family member, others the wife or daughter of a supporter. The man who brought the purse always gave me a few names and things to memorize. I'd go to the person's house or their office, make small talk with my memorized facts if anyone else was around, and always forget to take my purse with me.'

'Well, it could have been a lot worse.'

'It got there,' Faye said. 'One day I delivered Representative Reynolds. Have you heard of him?'

'He's a senator now.' Reynolds was a Revivalist golden boy.

He'd ridden into office on President Adamson's coat-tails just after Houston. Since then he had been a reliable embarrassment to our state, singing whatever tune the Elders gave him. I had no trouble imagining such a naked opportunist taking money from the Corinthian, but I didn't know what he would get back. 'What was the problem?'

'He decided I was part of the gift. I excused myself to the bathroom and called the Corinthian. I told him it wasn't part of our deal. Do you know what he said to me? "My friends stay happy, your father stays alive." I did as I was told. It became a regular thing after that.'

'Was Reynolds the only one?'

Faye shook her head. I didn't ask her to spell out the rest.

'I did it for a year and a half,' Faye said, 'until my father died. Then the Corinthian released me from our compact. He said I didn't look fresh-faced and innocent any more. Imagine that.'

That level of degradation sounded closer to the Corinthian's natural habitat, but it left something bigger unexplained. He didn't offer his employees a pension plan, because he didn't allow them to retire. You were useful to him, and after that you were dead.

'Why did the Corinthian let you live?' I said. 'You know a lot of inconvenient things.'

'And I did a lot of incriminating things,' Faye said. 'I guess he thinks I might be useful if one of his friends becomes difficult.'

I should have thought of that. The Corinthian's largesse always came with hidden chains. 'If you stopped working for the Corinthian, why go to him now?'

'Why do you think? I want to find Isaac. The Corinthian knows a lot of people. I thought he might be able to find some trace of him. I couldn't just wait around and hope you'd discover something more than how to get your ass kicked.'

I'd never seen her angry before, and Faye didn't like showing it. She buried her face in her hands for a moment, and was calm again when she emerged. 'I'm sorry.'

'It's a fair crack. What did the Corinthian say?'

'He hadn't heard anything but he promised to ask around, as a favour to an old friend.' She tried to laugh. It didn't come out so well.

I realized then that I'd made a rookie mistake: forgetting who my client was. I was so focused on finding Isaac that I didn't think about Faye. I'd stayed silent to protect her, and also to make sure she kept out of the way. She deserved an explanation, and it would have to come now.

I believed that two things were involved in Isaac's disappearance: the affair with Stonebridge's wife and his work for Cal. If I told her about the latter, it might get her killed. If I pinned the whole thing on the affair it would break her heart.

There was another way. There was still a chance that Isaac had been killed over something he'd seen; Stonebridge might have only discovered that the documents were missing later, and made a lucky guess that Isaac was responsible. I could use Stonebridge's extracurricular activities to tell a story that ended up blaming the right man. It might even be true.

'I didn't want to tell you until I was sure,' I said. 'What I'm about to say could put you in danger.'

Faye perked up a little. She seemed more eager than afraid. 'I don't care. Whatever happened to him, I need to know.'

'I told you earlier that Isaac was working for a man called Stonebridge, who now calls himself Campbell.'

She nodded.

'It turns out this man has some repellent hobbies. He picks up prostitutes and, well, abuses them.'

'That's horrible.'

'I think Isaac saw something he shouldn't have. Stonebridge is a rising star at Homeland Security, and if what Isaac knew came out, it would destroy him.'

'You think this man Stonebridge kidnapped Isaac?'

'Kidnapped or worse.'

'We have to go to the police.'

'We don't have any proof,' I said. 'Once we have that, we can use it against Stonebridge. This man is capable of anything. If he found out about you—'.

'He might already know,' Faye said. 'There was another reason I went to the Corinthian. I think I'm being followed. Maybe it was just you.'

'When did this feeling start?'

'A few days ago,' Faye said. 'It's nothing definite, just things I see out of the corner of my eye. Shadows.' She fell silent. 'I thought the Corinthian could protect me.'

The hen had asked the wolf to work the door of her coop. 'Listen to me,' I said. 'It's very important that you never go near the Corinthian again. I think he was involved in Isaac's disappearance.'

A shiver passed through Faye. 'How?' she said, forcing the words out.

I couldn't tell her the whole truth. 'He works with Stonebridge. The Corinthian cleans up his messes.'

Faye lurched forward. I went around the table and caught her in my arms.

'I was in his car,' she said. 'He held my arm. He told me to keep quiet about him.'

She sobbed but didn't cry. If the Corinthian had been given a task order for Faye then she wouldn't be here. Either Stonebridge didn't consider her enough trouble to be worth the effort, or the Corinthian was protecting her. The latter wasn't such a crazy idea when you knew that she was a living leash on a US senator. No woman, no scandal.

'Is there somewhere you can go?'

'No,' she said. The sobs died down. 'This is all I have. I'm not leaving.'

'Do you have a gun?' I asked, knowing the answer.

'Yes. Isaac showed me how to use it.'

'Okay,' I said. 'You stay close to home, and keep that gun handy. I don't care if you're just going around the corner to buy milk, bring it. I'll call in a few hours and check up on you.'

'Wait,' Faye said. 'I haven't slept much in the past few days. The slightest sound wakes me up. Would you stay here for an hour? I think I could sleep if I knew someone else was here.'

'Sure,' I said, and took off my coat.

'Thank you. Wake me in an hour, and make yourself at home.'

Faye went into the bedroom. I took off my shoes and sat down on the couch. I looked at the pictures on the wall, the few books on the shelves, all the little objects I had scrutinized so intensely an hour before. I knew every spot of water damage on the walls, and every scratch mark on the floor. Faye's apartment was starting to feel like home, and that worried me.

FOURTEEN

I let Faye sleep for two hours before I said goodbye. I had a lot to think about on the subway ride home. I kicked myself again for keeping things from her. I'd told a white lie or two to my clients, but it was a rare occurrence. People came to me when they wanted the ugly truth, about their employees or their marriage, and I was usually inclined to give it to them. If they were happy to live in blissful ignorance they wouldn't have picked up the phone. I couldn't protect Faye from what was coming any more than I could make the Hudson flow backwards, but I was still unable to tell her the truth.

I arrived home to find my door ajar. I drew my gun and pushed the door open.

My office was trashed. I checked the other two rooms. Whatever tornado had hit my place of business was long gone. If Stonebridge was here looking for his memo, then he left a disappointed man. I kept the diary and the microdot blow-ups hidden on my person.

The building superintendent, Tony Kankaredes, stuck his head in the door. He spent a moment appreciating the scene before he opened his mouth.

'You redecorating?'

'Something like that.'

Tony didn't like that answer, but he would have glowered as much at any other. The gregarious nature God had taken away from Tony had been repaid tenfold with body hair, his head left bare to remind him what his skin looked like.

'It's a . . . juxtaposition from your last set-up. I got a package for you,' he said, and handed me a box about the size of his head.

'When did this arrive?' I asked, trying to think how much plastic explosive could fit in it without showing the calculation on my face.

'Yesterday.'

'Yesterday? When were you going to tell me?'

'When I got around to it,' Tony said. 'Reason I got around to it today . . .' Tony took his time. 'Is we got some complaints from downstairs.'

Tony and I had what could be described as a strained relationship. He didn't appreciate the odd birds that knocked on my door at all hours, but I called them clients. There had been a few complaints about noise over the years, usually caused by someone trying to break my bones. As much as he disliked me, Tony had never tried to have me thrown out. Eviction could be a tedious business in New York, and I'd restored his faith in miracles by paying a whole year's rent in advance, courtesy of the FBI.

'I wasn't even here this afternoon—'

'Well, tell whoever's doin' your remodelling to keep it down a little. Mrs Kreznick from downstairs told me it sounded like they were tearing the place apart.'

Mrs Kreznick wasn't far wrong. The drawers in my desk had been upended, the closets cleaned, and everything thrown in a pile in the centre of the room. My chair was the victim of a vicious stabbing, stuffing leaking from six slash wounds. The television, computer and all my new toys were gone. A wild animal would have been less subtle.

'Listen,' Tony said. 'You're a professional, right? So am I. My profession is to keep the building clean, the trash out, and the tenants from each other's throats. Now, juxtapose that with your profession . . . matter of fact, I still don't understand what you do.'

'I'm a private—'

Tony waved away my words. 'That ain't important right now. What I'm gettin' at, is that you're makin' it hard for me to do my frickin' profession, okay?'

'Warning received,' I said.

In all the years I'd lived here, I'd never heard Tony use a word with a price tag higher than four dollars. I was curious about this outbreak of syllables. 'Did somebody give you one of those "word of the day" calendars, Tony?'

'Toilet paper, as a matter of fact. Why?'

'Your speech today is a juxtaposition from your earlier vocabulary.'

Tony eyed my compliment with the face of a man told to pet a reptile he's been assured is docile. 'Thanks. That's, uh, very magnanimous of you.'

Tony left me with the choice of opening the package or sorting through six months' worth of paperwork strewn all over the floor. I chose a third option: the blinking message light on my office phone. It had better be good news.

'This is a message for Felix Strange from Dr Brown's office. The doctor apologizes for taking so long to get back to you. He will be in New York attending a symposium at Javits Convention Centre. He can be reached at this number.' Brown's receptionist rattled off ten digits.

It wasn't exactly good news, but it was as close as I was going to get. I'd forgotten about the message I left for Brown. He had no reason to see me: he wouldn't profit from my visit, more likely the reverse, but he took his Hippocratic oath seriously. I'd show Brown that video of my seizure and see what he made of it. I was lucky I'd backed up everything yesterday, or the video would be out the door with my computer.

I returned to the package. It had no return address, and weighed about a pound. A pound of C4 would be more than enough to leave me in bite-sized pieces, and recent events hadn't left me in a trusting disposition. I put the package to my ear, but no cartoon ticking was audible. If I wanted a definitive answer I'd have to give it to Benny so he could run it by the FBI bomb squad. That would endanger a lot of people and cost me a lot of time. More than one person wanted to kill me, but none of them would do it in this way. It was too gauche for the Corinthian, and Stonebridge needed me alive until that memo was back in his hands. I didn't have a whole lot to live for anyway.

I opened the lid, and my organs stayed where they were. Inside the box was a satellite phone and a document, fronted by a letter:

```
Dear Felix,
Please give me a call. The number is on speed
dial. I have enclosed a gesture of goodwill.

Sincerely,
Cassandra

PS The phone is not a bomb.
```

It was kind of Cassandra to set my mind at ease, whoever he/she was. The only thing I knew about Cassandra was that Glass named it as his top priority. Considering the context, I assumed that meant capturing or killing whoever went by that name. Glass's enmity was a good reason to be interested in Cassandra, but not to trust the person behind the name.

The page below looked like a surveillance transcript.

Conversation 221

Recorded at Fisher Partners Board Retreat
The Eden Hotel and Casino, Las Vegas, ███████████

Present: General Simeon Glass, Secretary of DHS,
Mr Simon Tolliver (CEO, Fisher Partners), Mr David
Boycott (CFO), ██████████████████, Secretary Lincoln
F. Howe, Admiral David Trombley (ret.), Wing Com-
mander Hugo Davis (ret.), Revd Paul Franks, ████
██████████████████████████, Revd Percy Clayton

TOLLIVER: We've been posting steady, quarter-on-
quarter growth for the last five years. This year
the government is entering a new phase in the War
on Terror, and Fisher Partners has the primary
contract.

BOYCOTT: If you've seen our last quarterly report,
you know how well things are going. Billable
man-hours to the government are scheduled to rise
tenfold in this year. It's difficult to give you
an idea of just how meteoric our sales projections
are.

TOLLIVER: Have you seen the space shuttle take off?

Laughter/Crosstalk

BOYCOTT: That's about right. If you look at the
sheer increase in our clients from previous years-

GLASS: No need to bore them with details, David.
Stick to the money.

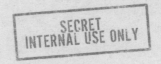

BOYCOTT: Yes, sir. As I was saying, we are on track for a fourfold increase in revenue, especially if ███████████████████████.

FRANKS: That won't lead to an identical increase in profit, will it?

BOYCOTT: It will be close.

FRANKS: I've heard some concerns about cost overruns at the new state and regional offices. ████ ████████ raised it with ███████████.

TOLLIVER: True, we have had larger than expected infrastructure costs, and I spoke to the board at our last meeting about chronic manpower problems. You have to remember that the only reason we even have these issues is because we've become victims of our own success. We now have offices in every state, and have opened in eighty per cent of our regional and urban centres. We are still experiencing a recruiting shortfall, but that is due to our own quality control. Fisher Partners has a reputation for reliability and discretion that I wouldn't want to see threatened.

FRANKS: That's not what I'm suggesting, Simon. I'm just worried about our position as

There was no second page. I wasn't sure what Cassandra expected me to get out of the document. I'd never heard of Fisher Partners before. Besides Glass, I recognized a few of the other people. Secretary Howe had recently ruined Kirov's funeral. Trombley and Davis had been chiefs of the navy and air force respectively, before retiring a few years ago. They were just career military as far as I knew. Franks ran a 35,000-member megachurch near Omaha. I'd heard his name mentioned as a possible member of the Council of Elders, but not from anyone I trusted.

It looked like the usual suspects who traded on their government contacts once they joined the private sector. It had been going on for decades, and seemed almost quaint considering what went on nowadays. The only way I was going to get any answers was to call Cassandra. It was time to see what he/she had to say for him/herself.

Someone picked up on the second ring. For a while there was silence.

'You're late.' The voice was altered, stripped of any kind of humanity. An elevator announced the floors with more warmth.

'Maybe if you'd contacted me in a less unusual way, the response would have been more prompt.'

'The reports said you had a sense of humour. I'm glad they weren't wrong. Did you read the document I sent you?'

'Yes.'

'Do you know what it means?'

'I know what you want it to mean,' I said. 'You've redacted some parts, and I can't prove the whole thing wasn't made by a twelve-year-old.'

'I removed some elements to protect my sources,' Cassandra said. 'I think you know enough by now to realize it isn't a forgery. You've seen the sharp end of the business whose growth they're celebrating.'

'I've never heard of Fisher Partners.'

'But you've seen what they leave behind. Those mysterious gaps in the public record are their work. They're like black holes: impossible to see until you're past the event horizon. One of your friends fell in, didn't he?'

I kept silent.

'Suppose the Elders became afraid after the Battle of Christopher Park. They thought there was a national movement to oust them, or worse.'

'But there isn't a national resistance movement,' I said. 'Is there?' Cal and Jack's organization was hardly an army in the shadows from what I could tell.

'The Elders believe there is, so anyone who tries to prove otherwise is either too incompetent to find evidence, or objectively disloyal. The only man they trust is General Glass; to them he's still the hero of Tehran. I'm sure he understands the true situation.'

'It's difficult to prove a negative.'

'Or investigate an absence, as I'm sure you're now aware. Since the rebel army doesn't exist, it must be created. Old political enemies are made the ringleaders, and there's more than enough room for supporting roles. Of course someone has to deal with these traitors. Men must be followed. They must be interrogated. They must be kidnapped, and they must be killed. The army won't do the job. CIA no longer exists. The police aren't up to it, and the FBI can't be trusted to do as it's told. The only option left is outsourcing. That's where Fisher Partners comes in.'

'Contractors deliver supplies and make food, they don't—'

'Interrogate prisoners? They did in Iraq and Iran. You worked with mercenaries snatching Iranians, why do you think it would be any different at home?'

Cassandra had me there. If the government was kidnapping

and torturing people, someone, somewhere, would argue that the private sector could do it for less. 'That transcript mentions offices in every state. How many people are we talking about?'

'I don't know. I can only see the outlines of what they're doing. The reason Glass doesn't want to talk about numbers is that the rest of the board doesn't want to know.'

'What do you mean they don't want to know? Aren't these assholes the ones who give the order?'

'Not directly. They're on the board to bring in new business and give the organization gravitas. Do you think they want gory details? They know it's happening, but they can't see it happening, so they can pretend it isn't happening. If they saw anything other than dollar signs, it might disturb their sleep.'

'So you're saying the Elders have created a movement in their heads, populated it with their enemies, and then demanded Glass destroy it in a way they don't want to know about.' The inside of my head was starting to look as crazy as the room. 'That's insane.'

'It's a case of moral cataracts,' Cassandra said. 'It's a common illness among men of a certain age and position.'

'Well, it's an entertaining story. I'm not sure I believe any of it.'

'You will,' Cassandra said.

'In the meantime, you said my friend fell into one of these black holes. Does that mean you know where he is?'

'Once an individual is eaten by the system, they don't come out the other side. You know that. You've seen how it works.'

So it was the same system as the one we'd used in Tehran, the same black sites and the same people. I don't know why I hadn't thought of it before, and I wasn't too happy about connecting those particular dots.

'If you aren't going to help find Isaac, I'm going to put an end to this small talk,' I said.

'No, you won't.' The mechanical voice made the statement even more matter-of-fact. 'The only chance you have of finding Isaac is to help me.'

'I've heard that before. I don't even know if you're a man or a woman on account of that gizmo you're using. I don't want to call you "it".'

'You'd only need to know if I'm a he or a she to talk about me to someone else. That would be unwise. If you want a character reference, remember how eager General Glass is to have me dealt with.'

Glass had named Cassandra as his top priority. It was impossible not to be curious why. 'If you want my help, tell me why Glass has such a hard-on for you.'

'A lovely choice of words, Mr Strange. My grudge with Glass is ancient history; everyone involved is either dead or should be. You have enough on your plate right now.'

I had the feeling Cassandra included him/herself in that list, but with the voice distortion it was impossible to be sure.

'You'll have to indulge me.'

'Look up the Rudashevsky Group. It's safe; the Elders are proud of it, God help them. You have a right to know about it anyway.'

'What do you mean?'

'Do you still have nightmares about what you did with Task Force Seventeen?'

'Fuck you.'

'I'll take that as a yes. Start with the Rudashevsky Group. Once you've done your homework, I'll fill in some details. But first, we must return to the present.'

'Fine,' I said. 'What do you want from me?'

'The list of all the clients in New York.'

'Clients?' I said. 'Is that what they call them?'

Cassandra didn't answer.

'What are you going to do with this list?'

'Expose them. That objective is where we part company with your military friends.'

'If you've really done your homework, you should know the army is no friend of mine.'

'Dancing isn't much fun when you do it over the phone, Strange. We're talking about your friends in the unofficial army: the young ne'er do well and his moustachioed father figure.'

Cassandra could only be talking about Jack and Cal. 'What do you mean, "unofficial army"?'

'It's called the Founder Initiative. The Defense Intelligence Agency is running networks of active-duty soldiers in the Holy Land and veterans at home. Jefferson, their handler, is DIA, slippery and not half as smart as he thinks he is. The mission is to look out for number one.'

'Those army friends saved my life,' I said. 'Last time I checked, the only thing you've done is send me junk mail. Assuming I do get this list, what makes you think I'll give it to you?'

'Because, Felix, sooner or later you'll need me.'

The line went dead. I put the phone on the desk, poured a drink and sat in my bleeding chair. My home was still in disarray. I didn't have the heart to clean it up.

FIFTEEN

The years had been kind to Doc Brown. The hair was gone, but a shaved head suited him, as it did many black men. He still had the physique of an infantryman though he'd stopped being a battlefield medic before I'd enlisted. The gold-rimmed spectacles were the same, and new lines couldn't obscure the essential decency of his face. We stood outside Javits Convention Centre, trying to match each other's current face with the one we remembered.

'Hello, Felix.'

'Doc.'

It was harder seeing Doc than I expected. I hadn't forgotten what he'd done for me, for everyone like me, and I was grateful. The problem was, every time I looked at him I remembered some of the worst days of my life.

'Thanks for seeing me,' I said.

'Forget about it. You're a welcome diversion. If this conference goes on much longer, I'm going to eat my gun.'

'What's the conference about?'

'Neuroscience and its possibly lucrative frontiers,' Doc Brown said. 'I'm working for a small biotech company looking for investors. I should be wearing a mini skirt and cheap lipstick.'

'Don't sell yourself short, Doc,' I said. 'I'm sure you're classier than that.'

Brown laughed. 'You look okay, Felix,' he said, 'better than I expected, to be honest.'

Doc's trepidation at our meeting must have been double that of my own. After all, he was the respectable doctor and I was the former patient thrown to the wolves. I could have been calling him for a prescription or a handout, and he met me anyway.

'There's something I need to show you,' I said. 'Is there a private room with a TV in there?'

'I know somewhere,' Brown said. 'If you're going to show me a stag film from your private library, I'd like to invite some investors. I might actually get somewhere with them.'

'Sorry, Doc, I doubt they'll want to see this.'

Brown led me into the convention centre. From the outside, Javits looked like the discarded crystalline shell of a giant insect. Inside, it was just a mall without the stores. Brown's convention was up on the top floor, in the Galleria and River Pavilion.

Doctors in plainclothes mingled with booth girls and sharp-suited company reps. I didn't understand a word of their pitches, but the hustle's shine was familiar from any billboard. Conventions were as fertile ground for the breaking of vows as a hotel full of ex-girlfriends. My professional eye couldn't help keeping a lookout for self-appointed Casanovas.

I saw more than one. They had a look of determined hedonism in their eyes, like students on holiday. They hid it better than the kids, but not from me, and certainly not from the women who would be haunting the bars of their hotels later. Mary would have been one of those girls. She'd have seen this place exactly like me: dollar signs in chinos killing time. When Brown walked into a booth walled off by curtains, I was almost reluctant to follow him. I felt like I was leaving good money all over the convention floor.

The booth was a showcase for the accoutrements of the bone-saw's profession. A cart laden with sharp implements of stainless steel sat next to a table of the same material.

'Did it have to be in here, Doc?'

'You wanted a TV,' Brown said, pointing to the large video monitor on an upright stand behind the table. 'This is the examination room of the future.'

'Well, it looks a lot like the one from the past.'

There were two or three contraptions on wheels near the table. I recognized one of them as an anaesthesia machine. My eyes had always seemed to rest on its face of blinking lights while I waited for the drugs to take effect. It was usually the last thing I remembered before they went digging for treasure in my skull.

'Forget the furniture and show me what you've got,' Brown said.

I hooked a video player up to the room's monitor and played the footage of my seizure. When it was over he asked to see it again. I gave him the player so he could watch it as often as he liked. I'd seen it too many times already.

'Tell me about your pharmaceutical regimen,' Brown asked, midway through his third viewing.

'I take the cocktail every day, just like you prescribed.'

'No changes in dosage?'

'None.'

'Even after these two . . .' Scientific caution, not delicacy, made Brown trail off. 'These two events?'

'No. You told me what might happen if I did.' When the doc had first explained the cocktail, he'd made clear that it hadn't been tested to his satisfaction. Changing the interrelationship between the drugs could cause serious side effects, maybe even death.

'How about the quality of the drugs?'

'They're all from legal prescriptions filled at a legit pharmacy.'

Brown took his eyes away from the monitor. He wanted to know how I could afford them, but was decent enough to take the time to form a more diplomatic question.

'I married an heiress. Let's leave it at that.'

'Maybe this rich heiress could also get you some real medical care.'

'Anyone they send me to will say it's all in my head. That's the American Medical Association line, isn't it?'

'I meant in Europe. They don't acknowledge your condition officially, but they won't say you're crazy.'

There was no way the Bureau would let me out of the country, especially not now. I'd have to be terminal before they'd even consider it. 'She's sweet on me, Doc, but not in love.'

I looked at the video. Brown had it paused right around the time my eyes began to roll back in my head. 'Have you seen this before?' I said.

Brown nodded, but he was still wandering around in his own thoughts. 'A few patients responded that way during our first trial of the drug cocktail. You remember that.'

'Oh yeah. Fun was had by all. Did you figure out what was causing it?'

'We didn't have time. We'd barely started looking at the results when the army shut us down. It could have been an abnormal reaction to the drugs, perhaps because of the patients' previous toxicology.'

'You don't sound convinced.'

'There was no single drug or earlier illness that linked all the patients. The only common factor we noted was age.'

'Age?'

'They were all over thirty, most near forty. None was older than that. At the time we thought it was just background noise in our sample. An older body can't withstand damage as well as a younger one, and we were losing a lot of people to good old-fashioned radiation poisoning. It may have been just that.'

'But you're not sure?'

Brown killed the video. 'Of course I'm not sure. Listen, doctors aren't fucking magicians. The only reason we understand diseases like tuberculosis, Parkinson's or cancer is because we do our homework. We experiment, conduct simulations and then clinical trials. It's a massive effort.

'We were at the early stages when the Pentagon decided to classify your disease as a mental disorder. We were just starting to get the shape of the thing, to tune out all the other variables. You know how many other things were floating around out there: depleted uranium from the invasion, asbestos and heavy metals from the destroyed buildings, and a host of environmental irritants from the burning oil wells. That's not to mention the fistful of drugs they fed everyone out there. Half the soldiers were using stimulants well outside guidelines to do long patrols. We still feared chemical or biological attacks, so everyone got anti-virals, vaccines and antidotes for various nerve agents. And then we come to the radiation of the actual explosion.'

He meant the explosion that turned Tehran into Ghost Town. It was the last thing I wanted to think about, but it reminded me of Stonebridge, and what he'd said.

'Doc, did you ever treat a guy named Stonebridge?'

'No. Even if I had, would you want me telling others about you?'

'Point taken. I heard he was in a Pentagon study of us around the same time, didn't know if there was any truth to it.'

'That's another dead-end, Felix. That study was shut down before we were.'

'Do you know what they found out?'

Brown sighed. He leaned against the table and took his time to

226

speak. 'I know they developed a drug regimen that could control the condition's symptoms before we did, but not what it was or how people become affected.'

'Why didn't they tell you and the VA, if they'd discovered a treatment?'

'It was a by-product of their research, not the goal, and they killed nine men doing it. Look,' he said, when he saw the swarm of questions gathering on my tongue, 'I haven't seen the files myself; what I'm telling you is all second or third hand. The point of the Pentagon study was to determine if you were the victim of a new biological weapon.'

That was the most popular conspiracy theory around the wards when I'd been in hospital. Alien experimentation had come in a close second.

'Were they trying to develop a defence, or weaponize what had happened to us?'

'From a research perspective, there isn't much difference. It was chaos after Ghost Town; no one knew who'd destroyed the city, we were drowning in casualties, and then we discovered you. Everyone was ready to expect the worst.

'It took a lot of fatalities, I don't know how many, to persuade them the syndrome wasn't caused by an agent. I've been told the Pentagon let the VA continue its work just in case we stumbled on something useful. Once their study determined that it wasn't a weapon that caused the condition, the Pentagon shut us down. If it was a weapon, your condition would be a national security issue.'

'And because it wasn't, we became nothing more than a human resources problem.'

Brown nodded.

'Is there anyone else I can talk to?'

'You want a second opinion?' It was a sad smile Doc Brown gave me, the smile of a man contemplating a lost cause. 'I wish I could recommend someone in this country, Felix, I really do.'

'There's no one.'

'No one who will speak to you. God knows, I shouldn't be.'

There was a tone in Brown's voice that I'd come across more than once in my professional life. 'Has someone threatened you, Doc?'

'The army doesn't threaten people, Felix. A few of us from the original study kept in touch. We were an informal working group trying to keep an eye on syndrome cases when they popped up. We weren't publishing papers or petitioning the government; it was practically a social club. The Pentagon started visiting us last year. They made it clear there would be professional consequences for our support of "junk science".'

'I don't understand,' I said. 'Why are they going after you now?'

Brown took off his glasses, so I knew to expect bad news. 'In the last two years, we'd noticed an increase in fatalities among patients from the study. We knew their names from our original notes.'

'I'm surprised the army let you keep them.'

'They didn't. I smuggled a copy out in my drawers.'

The army must have noticed the pattern too. I guess it was afraid someone would talk to us, see the pattern, and start to believe there was something there.

'Imagine,' Brown said, shaking his head as much in disgust as disbelief, 'they can level buildings from space, and they're worried about a few eggheads.'

'Were these fatalities because of the syndrome?'

'We don't know. No doctor is going to look for it as a cause. The cases I saw were heart attacks, strokes and a lot of cancer.'

'That sounds pretty normal. Aren't those the things that kill most people?'

'Cars kill most people,' Brown said. 'The stroke victim was thirty-three.'

'What are you trying to tell me, Doc?'

'I don't know,' Brown said. 'We don't have the files or the resources to figure out if this pattern is anything more than a coincidence. I shouldn't have mentioned it. May I have a copy of that video?'

'Sure,' I said. 'It's not doing me any good.'

Brown copied the file to a hand-held computer. I took a quick look through the curtains separating us from the convention floor. 'Is the Pentagon at this convention, or maybe the cops?'

'There were police outside,' Brown said. 'It's just security guards on the convention floor.'

'What company?'

'Titan, I think,' Brown said.

I'd have to be on my best behaviour then.

'Are you in trouble, Strange?'

'Probably. I don't know how bad yet. I'll leave first, just to be safe.' I watched the crowds and didn't see any uniforms. 'I've lived with this thing for ten years. These last few months were the first time I thought I had it under control.'

'I'm glad you're getting the care you need,' Brown said. 'I know I didn't bring you good news. I'm sorry.'

'You're the only reason I'm standing here, Doc,' I said. 'If you hadn't discovered the cocktail, they would have locked me in a mental asylum. I never forget that.'

'I wasn't the only one who came up with it.'

'Yeah, but the rest won't take my calls, so you get all the credit.'

We shook hands, and I went on to the convention floor. The snake-oil men and their pretty assistants still manned booths separated into neat rows. They passed out glossy brochures and branded pens, promising with each firm handshake a pocketful of miracles, none of which could help me.

*

On my way back to the office, I couldn't help thinking about what Cassandra had said. Delivering that satellite phone was theatrical enough to be the work of a paranoid or a fantasist, but I don't see why a lone wacko would pick on me. I wasn't famous, and I certainly wasn't important. What made it worse was the certainty I'd heard the name Rudashevsky before. This case was turning into one extended bout of déjà vu.

I stopped at Penn Station and looked up this Rudashevsky Group. Cassandra had said it wouldn't trip any NSA alarms, but I didn't find that mechanical voice reassuring. If it was nothing more than a crazy theory, I might at least get a few laughs I could use.

The first result was an old news story. A reporter – fresh from the immaculate conception of the make-up chair – gave the world a blank smile in front of the Capitol steps.

'The Senate Committee for the Investigation of Terrorist Attacks met for its tenth hearing today. CIA Director Foyle gave testimony that congressional sources are already calling "a smoking gun".'

The feed cut to inside the chamber. The network had decided to give only the highlights. Director Foyle, the starved-looking, bespectacled head of the CIA, was already in mid-testimony.

'Enriched uranium was stolen from several old Soviet warheads in Belarus and sold to Anatoly Rudashevsky through an intermediary. The Belorussian government had given us a sample from the uranium it still had to assist in its recovery.'

Clancy Dyer, an incredibly fat senator from Oklahoma, had the microphone. He was the ranking member of the Senate Intelligence Committee, seniority being the blowhard's only qualification to investigate the Houston attack.

'A cutout working for the Iranian Revolutionary Guard Corps met with Rudashevsky in a hotel in Bangkok,' continued Foyle.

'Nuclear material changed hands at this meeting?'

'Yes, sir. Due to increased tensions between Sunni and Shia countries, especially Iran and Saudi Arabia, Iran had become interested in acquiring a nuclear deterrent.'

'Why didn't Iran enrich the uranium itself?'

'It was afraid that the centrifuge construction would be discovered before it enriched enough uranium for a viable deterrent. The Iranian leadership also believed that the United States was about to supply Saudi Arabia with a deterrent of its own.'

'Is there any truth to that, Director?'

'Absolutely not, Senator.'

'Once they had the uranium, why didn't they just keep it as a deterrent, if that was their original plan?'

'The collapse of oil prices in June put a severe strain on the Iranian treasury. Dissatisfaction with the regime was at an all-time high. Certain radical members of the IRGC believed that domestic nuclear attack would cause so much economic and political chaos, the United States would be forced to withdraw from the region for a generation.'

'Didn't they realize an attack would simply bring out the best in the American people?'

'Senator, the IRGC, like all Islamist groups, sees America as weakened by sin and fat from corruption. It believed that a single, shocking attack would destroy our morale. The Japanese had similar ideas when they attacked Pearl Harbor.'

The tape jumped forward. The faces were the same, but the expressions on them had changed to a mixture of alarm and indignation. Dyer was keeping a lot of anger hidden under the façade of a professional statesman. Something very unsettling had taken place in those missing seconds, and the network wasn't going to tell its viewers what it was.

'Director,' Dyer said, 'for the record, could you be absolutely clear: have you established that the traces of uranium found at Houston are the same as the uranium sold by Anatoly Rudashevsky to representatives of the IRGC?'

'Yes, Senator. There isn't a shred of doubt in my mind.'

The testimony was perfect: no stumbling over words, cross-talk or irrelevant questions. A Senate committee from that time was usually just a chance for the senators to play to the cameras and the people giving testimony to advance an agenda. Any facts that managed to leak out were the result of one of the few good eggs briefly getting control of a microphone, happy accidents that President Adamson corrected after he founded the Council of Elders. Dyer and Foyle had led each other hand-in-hand through all the facts they wanted in the public record. As soon as I had noted the contrast in their body shapes, I should have expected a double act.

The camera switched back to the crowd outside, and it was ugly. People were screaming, chanting, praying and holding up a lot of signs: 'Nuke Iran now', 'God damns the mullahs', 'Bomb Mecca'. Some of the signs had been mass-produced by the same groups that had bussed people in, but for once there was a lot of real, spontaneous emotion in that crowd. Too bad almost all of it was fear, with rage coming a close second.

'While the committee won't officially deliver its report for another two weeks,' the correspondent continued in voiceover, 'highly placed sources in intelligence and the military implicated Iran before the committee had its first meeting.'

That had been Adamson's doing. He was only President-Elect then, but that didn't matter. Nobody listens to a lame-duck President, especially when he isn't saying what people want to hear. Adamson had an agenda and the networks were desperate for access. Everybody got what they wanted, at least the people who mattered did.

I hadn't been paying enough attention to know any of this at the time. My unit had deployed to Campbell Barracks in

Heidelberg, in preparation for a NATO joint exercise. Before the Houston attack, I'd spent most of my time trying to learn the German for 'I am lost,' 'A beer please,' and 'You have beautiful eyes.'

When the city was destroyed we moved to DefCon holy fuck and were confined to barracks. We'd huddled around televisions watching news broadcasts like this one, as much in the dark as the countrymen we had sworn to defend. Like them, we had too much anger and not enough places to put it. Most people refused to leave their homes; the rest took to their streets to demand safety and revenge. It was three hundred million people panicking at once, and it was terrifying even on television.

Unlike civilians, we were parts of a machine that should have been designed for situations like this. We knew we were supposed to be killing someone, but the brass was waiting for the suits in DC to say who. At least we had the discipline and routine of military life. It was boring in good times, but a wonderful refuge when the world suddenly became twice as confusing and scary as it had been the day before. We drilled, waited and tried not to kill each other in the meantime.

The file ended. There had been no mention of Cassandra, and I got the feeling that report hadn't contained whatever I was supposed to see. I took a stroll through some proxy servers, and then went digging in foreign press outlets. The BBC had taped the entire set of hearings. I found a report titled: 'Houston Commission has Contentious Tenth Hearing'. The hearing had only looked contentious at the end, and only if you looked for it. Maybe the BBC was going to fill me in on what had happened during those missing seconds, like a real news organization.

They shot the crowd from a different angle, but it was the same angry, terrified mob-in-waiting. The tape included more of Chairman Dyer's questions to Director Foyle. It was twice as boring but no more informative than the short version.

Dyer yielded the floor before he asked the last question I'd seen on the earlier report. It was the turn of Senator Russell Lee, a lame-duck senator from Minnesota who hadn't appeared at all in the earlier report, to speak. I had vague memories of him being one of those congressmen who had become institutions, and must have thought they had jobs for life until the Adamson deluge drowned them all.

'Thank you for appearing today before the committee, Director. I wonder, could you tell me how we found this uranium had gone missing?'

'We were informed by the Belorussian government.'

'And it also provided the sample?'

'Yes.'

'Did agents or other US personnel inspect the site of the theft?'

'The Belorussian government informed us of the theft as a courtesy, Senator. It was obviously very embarrassing for that nation, and we are not on such good terms with that government that it was willing to disclose the time of the theft or its location.'

'Do we know how the bomb entered the United States?'

'We believe it arrived in a container delivered to the port of Houston. The blast atomized most of the physical evidence, Senator. A full reconstruction of this atrocity will take some time, as I'm sure you know.'

'You testified that Rudashevsky met with a representative of the Revolutionary Guard while he was in Bangkok. My office has been told that intercepts recorded meetings between Rudashevsky and several other parties in Bangkok, but transcripts of these meetings haven't been made available to the committee.'

Foyle lost his composure for a second. It was nothing more than a few rapid blinks and a longer pause, but his voice made it clear that he was no longer reading from a script.

'Those meetings weren't relevant to the committee's work.'

'Could you tell us how many other people Rudashevsky met with during his stay in Thailand?'

Director Foyle went from hiding his surprise to concealing his anger. 'Senator, I'd like to remind you at this time that we are in an open session. If you continue this line of questioning, I will be unable to answer on grounds of national security.'

'I'm not asking for their names, Director.'

Dyer finally managed to struggle to his feet. His face was red – not the pink hue of a three-martini lunch, but the darker colour of a man who has just stumbled on his daughter's first foray into non-virginity.

'Russ, I wasn't aware you were going to ask these questions.'

'I have just been made aware of some of these facts, Clancy.'

'Then we should discuss them before putting more questions to the director,' Dyer said. The other committee members were watching the exchange with a mixture of horror and disbelief. It was clear by now to anyone with eyes that everyone else in the room wanted Lee to stop talking.

'Today is the director's last scheduled testimony, and I don't believe the facts of the CIA's case have been fully established.'

'That is for the entire committee to decide, Russ.'

Senator Lee started to respond, but found his microphone dead. Dyer took advantage of the fault to ask his final question.

'Director,' Dyer said, 'for the record, could you be absolutely clear: have you established that the traces of uranium found at Houston are the same as the uranium sold by Anatoly Rudashevsky to representatives of the IRGC?'

'Yes, Senator. There isn't a shred of doubt in my mind.'

The report ended with the BBC correspondent helpfully saying that he had no idea what Senator Lee had been talking about. None of their sources would talk, even off the record.

So all Senator Lee's questions had been deemed unfit for the

American audience. Again there was no mention of Cassandra, but I had the feeling that Lee's testimony was what I was supposed to see. I would have struggled to recognize any of the people in the videos without the news captions. They came from a time before the Elders, and their arguments seemed as alien and remote as the disputations of the Roman senate.

It took only a little more digging to find out that all three were dead. Dyer had suffered a widely anticipated third coronary five years ago. Foyle had died of a brain aneurism last year. Lee hadn't lived out the year that testimony was given. It was almost a mercy that he never saw what the republic would become.

Someone had fed Lee intelligence that the CIA hadn't given to the committee. A politician, like a lawyer, rarely asks a question he doesn't know the answer to. Foyle's testimony was the accepted history of the Houston attack, the one I'd heard at the time and for ever after. There had always been enough loose ends to give conspiracy nuts the horn, but no concrete evidence challenging the narrative. Lee's questions hadn't contradicted Foyle's version, but they would have created a lot of doubt if they had been broadcast and then left unanswered.

Cassandra seemed too sophisticated an operator to be a conspiracy freak, but I still knew next to nothing about the person at the other end of the phone. All I'd gained from this goose chase was more questions about something that had happened ten years in the past, not answers about the present.

It was time to stop fooling around with mysterious voices and get back to my real job, whatever that had become.

SIXTEEN

I sat on Emerson for three days. He worked at the new Department of Justice offices on Centre Street, an unremarkable grey building in Manhattan. A contact at a credit agency had given me a recent photograph, employment history, home address and marital status; almost everything I needed, except why Glass was so interested in him.

The first day, Emerson went into the Centre Street building in the morning and didn't come out until after three. I'd rented a car, but I had nowhere to put it. There was a small parking lot behind the building, but I didn't have a permit, and the area was lousy with cops. I stowed it a block away. The maze of one-way streets and police checkpoints would give me enough time to reach it before Emerson got away.

There was a small park between the lot and Emerson's office, so I grabbed a bench and waited. I'd haunted this block quite a few times. On the south side of the square was the New York family court building. Most of my divorce cases were settled between lawyers; the new laws required only 'strong evidence' of adultery, which a judge could sign off on in private. It was a nice loophole for the respectable citizens who wished to avoid the embarrassment the Elders said we all deserved. Sometimes the couple were so angry and self-destructive that they needed a court to tell them how to say goodbye. That's when I ended up here, cooling my heels outside a courtroom.

Around three o'clock, Emerson left his office and headed for the parking lot. I sprinted to my vehicle and was back before he'd left his space. Instead of driving south towards the Brooklyn Bridge and home, he went east, to my stomping grounds in the Lower East Side. He parked in the lot behind a tattoo parlour and waited.

I waited with him. Emerson idled in the parking lot for about ten minutes, and then another car, a federal-issue brown sedan, pulled in. The second car stopped next to Emerson's so that the drivers' sides were adjacent. I saw Emerson press a brown envelope into a babyish, ring-covered hand that emerged from the other window. The two cars drove off separately after that, with no time wasted on small talk.

I got the other car's licence plate, but decided to stay on Emerson. He drove back to his office and didn't move again until six, when he joined the army of commuters marching on Brooklyn.

Emerson lived in a townhouse that said money and not much else. My luck with parking spaces held, and I stopped not far down the street. In one way his homecoming was like any other settled family man's: his toddler daughter – a little angel with a curly mess of a golden halo – met him at the door. Unlike most other dads, a large man exited the townhouse as soon as Emerson stepped inside. The man was in his late forties, with a greying brush-cut and a blue bomber jacket that kept his body armour warm. Emerson, like Stonebridge, was a mid-level federal employee, and was thus provided with mid-level protection for him and his family. I didn't need my binoculars to know that the logo on the jacket would be Titan Security Services.

I ducked down, afraid the bodyguard was going to sweep the

street. Instead he took two steps from the front door and pulled a pack of cigarettes from his breast pocket. He seemed intent only on his addiction but I kept low on the off-chance he accidentally did his job.

The bodyguard discarded his cigarette in a bucket and stayed outside on the stoop. I shifted my focus to the happy family scene already in progress. The Emersons had placed their dining-room table against a large bay window on the first floor. They kept the chenille curtains open at all hours: a family with nothing to hide, or at least fear. Right now the little angel was doing some colouring. Dad was pitching in. Occasionally he would glance lovingly at his wife, who was splitting her time between making dinner and supervising the art, judging by the apron. She was a leggy blonde wearing a simple blue dress, an abundance of pearls and a happy smile.

From a distance, Emerson's wife looked like the kind of spouse Revivalists ordered in bulk from the Stepford catalogue. Their idea of womanhood was something pretty and un-demanding, like a seascape by a minor artist; a painting that could become wallpaper if you weren't in the mood to appreciate it. I doubted that was the reality, for Mrs Emerson or most other Revivalist wives. I'd seen more than one good woman cease sub-mitting to her husband's authority once she saw another do the same on tape. When she realized that all those years of swallow-ing her pride and strangling her dreams had bought her nothing with the man she'd married in the eyes of God, the lid came off pretty quick. I should know: I was usually there.

The family enjoyed each other's company for a little while after dinner. The floor above the dining room was the child's. I could see Emerson's silhouette reading a story to his daughter. She was enthralled, as all children are with their parents. I couldn't fault Emerson for his home life, at least not yet. I might have to give his marriage a little shake and see what fell out.

After the story, the house prepared for bed. The Titan man was brought inside like the family dog, and the lights of the townhouse went out one by one. I shifted in the car seat for the millionth time, trying to find a comfortable area the size of my behind. The night had grown cold, but I couldn't risk the heater. The Emerson family were snug in their beds, maybe embracing each other in their dreams. I doubted the man of the house was going anywhere tonight, but I had to be sure. I popped an Evalacet, watched the empty street, and waited.

The next day was the same routine. He was at Centre Street ten minutes before nine, and stayed there until six. There were no suspicious meetings in parking lots this afternoon.

Stuck in traffic six cars behind Emerson, I began to wonder if I was treating this guy all wrong. Glass could have it in for Emerson because he was doing something right, like leaking the DOJ's part in what the Fishermen were doing. Glass's response to betrayal was never slow, but maybe Emerson's position and his family were forcing him to tread carefully. That could be why the memo had called him a 'special case'.

Considering his father, I would have expected a home-schooled education, Christian university and a comfortable position in the Revivalist Empire. He was home-schooled, but after that it was Columbia, then Yale Law, and then the Department of Justice of all places. Emerson wouldn't have been the first son of a Godly man to switch his allegiance to Mammon (especially when his family's relationship with both was tangled), but he hadn't pursued private practice and its earthly rewards. I had a hunch that if I could figure out the missing piece in Emerson's life, I'd know why Glass was so interested in him.

The scene at the townhouse was a rerun of last night. Emerson went in, the Titan man went out, and everybody gathered around the dining-room table for family hour. The only thing that had changed was the wife's outfit. She wore capri trousers the colour of sunflowers. A white blouse was mostly hidden by the apron and pearls that must have been her uniform.

She'd made pot roast tonight. The curly-haired angel moved her colouring books from the table, and the Emerson family broke bread. I used street light to eat my second dashboard dinner in as many days, starting with a Delectil appetizer to make sure the food stayed down. A surveillance team of one was an exhausting and impossible job. I'd used some of my rainy day money to buy an automated pal: a GPS transmitter about the size of my thumbnail. As soon as the house went to bed I was going to plant it on Emerson's car.

I'd brought Cassandra's phone with me. That Rudashevsky video she'd sent me after had stuck in my head. Cassandra had said it had something to do with me, but I couldn't see how. I wasn't worried that Cassandra was an Elder plant: she (or he) was just too weird. More likely Cassandra was a nut who'd decided to cast me in whatever paranoid fantasy preoccupied her/it. The biggest danger to me was a waste of time.

Lucky for Cassandra that I had time to waste at the moment, and was too curious for my own good. Someone picked up on the third ring.

'Thanks for the history lesson,' I said.

'A man should know his past.' It was the same distorted voice, maybe the same person.

'I don't see what Rudashevsky has to do with me. I was cooling my heels in Germany.'

'Not Rudashevsky, the Rudashevsky Group. They were a committee set up to investigate Rudashevsky's connection with Iran. Everyone in the intelligence community was on it, in case there was blame to be shared.'

'Does everyone include you?'

'They debased some of my work for their own purposes, but other than that I was kept away. My scepticism wasn't welcome.'

'So you fed your doubts to Senator Lee. I'm surprised he made such a meal of it.'

'So was I. Politicians, like broken clocks, have the privilege of being right at least once. I don't know why his conscience chose that time to collect, but it was very good for me.'

'You're assuming he didn't ask those questions out of bitterness. The Revivalists had just made him a lame duck.'

'It doesn't really matter now. Lee and his suicidal courage are both just artefacts of history.'

Cassandra's choice of words interested me. 'Did the Elders have anything to do with his heart attack?'

'As far as I know, fried food and domestic beer were his only assailants.'

'I still don't understand what any of this has to do with me.'

'The Rudashevsky Group is where Task Force Seventeen begins. If they hadn't said there were nuclear weapons, you wouldn't have been sent to find them.'

'The WMD still would have been there, whether this Rudashevsky Group said so or not.'

Cassandra was silent.

'Are you saying they lied?'

'Nothing in life is so simple, Felix. It's a little difficult to explain over the phone.'

'You're doing pretty good so far.'

'Another time. I'm more interested in your progress.'

'Things are coming along. I'm a hard worker. You know that; I'm sure it's in my file somewhere,' I said. 'Suppose I get you this list. What are you going to do with it?'

'This country is an addict no longer able to control its disease. We still have friends in the world. If they know what's going on, what's planned, they might organize an intervention.'

'Or leave us to our fate. Even if you have the list, you won't be able to stop the Fishermen?'

'No one can stop them.'

'Not even the Founder Initiative?' I said. 'You told me the Defense Intelligence Agency had its own programme. If there's anyone who can bring the Elders to heel, it's the Pentagon.'

'Intelligence agencies hoard secrets, Felix. They don't expose them.'

The line went dead. Cassandra had said just enough to keep me interested. Not many amateurs can manage information that well. I was dealing with someone who had worked in intelligence, now or in the past. The talk about foreign friends might have been a hint. I could be dealing with British intelligence. Not many other countries still liked the US enough to make the effort.

The Emerson family darkened its windows at the same time as yesterday. When I was sure no one was moving, I started the car, drove a few streets over and walked back to the end of their block. It was a safe bet that surveillance cameras covered Emerson's car, especially since it was parked on the street. I took a deep breath, made sure my hat was on firmly, and began to do my best impression of a drunk.

I wandered down the block, swaying and muttering to myself. I hoped that by the time I got to Emerson's car I'd be convincing. I kept my head tilted away from his side of the street, and happened to stumble into the car. I grabbed on to the back wiper to steady myself, and planted the bug on its underside. I shuffled off towards my car, singing a happy tune in case someone was listening in.

On the third day, I took it easy. The GPS transmitter meant I didn't have to keep an eyeball on Emerson all the time. I followed his drive to work on a little screen, and then sat outside his office all afternoon. Emerson didn't leave, to meet his mystery friend or anyone else. The licence plate on the car that had met him came back to a retiree upstate, and the only description I had were plump fingers and a manicure.

My phone rang about three.

'Mr Strange?'

It was the woman who spoke for Cal. 'Speaking.'

'Your cigars have arrived, Mr Strange. Would you like to pick them up?'

'I could swing by after work,' I said. 'Are you still open at seven?'

'Yes. See you then.'

When Emerson left work I let him go. I was sick of staring at his happy home, and for once the private life of my target might not be relevant. I switched to the subway and headed uptown.

When I got to the smoke shop in Harlem, the same scene was waiting for me. The same men gathered around the proprietor in the same places and poses. The only difference this time was a shortening of the dance with the owner. As soon as he saw me he looked at the back door, and then went back to pretending I didn't exist.

Cal and Jack were waiting.

'What happened at the funeral?' Cal said, before I had a chance to sit down.

'F. Lincoln Howe was there. He gave the eulogy, if you could call it that. The Elders aren't missing the chance to capitalize on Kirov's death.'

'It was all over the TV,' Jack said. 'The networks covered it live.'

'What about Stonebridge?'

'He was there. We caught up on old times. Then he threatened me, and not just out of nostalgia.'

'What does he know?' Cal asked.

'He thinks I have the Glass memo.'

'But he doesn't know for sure,' Cal said. 'He could just be fishing.'

'Deduction backs him up on this one. Isaac didn't know that many people.'

'Did he mention us?' Jack said.

'No.' He hadn't mentioned Faye either, so I could hope he didn't know about any of them. 'He offered me a deal: the letter in exchange for a get-out-of-jail-free card.'

I hadn't realized at the time how bizarre it was to see Stonebridge trying to play good cop. It was like spending three hours in a bar before you noticed that a dog was playing the piano.

'I don't think we're blown. If Stonebridge knew everything he wanted to, I wouldn't be here.'

'What are you going to do about him?' Cal asked.

'I'm going to stick to the plan. Speaking of which, where are we with the names in the memo?'

'We've chased a few of them down,' Cal said.

'Have they all disappeared?'

'No. We looked into the religious men first. You were right about Rabbi Tenenbaum: he was a constant critic of the Elders, and he died of a heart attack.'

'Did you find anything connecting those two facts?'

'Nothing. Tenenbaum had never even been arrested. The Medical Examiner's report said everything it should. Some of his family have their suspicions, but nothing to back them up. If Glass's men killed him, they've covered their tracks.'

'And Father Fiore?'

'He's gone,' Jack said. 'It's out of character, to say the least. His congregation has filed a missing persons report, and the police are moving on it. As far as we can tell, nobody at the federal level is interfering.'

'How about the numbers?' I asked. 'Did your people find out what they mean?'

Cal shook his head. 'We kicked them upstairs, but nothing came back. They've never seen them before.'

'Tell me something I don't know.'

'We got somewhere with two more of the names,' Jack said. 'Sarah Johnson and Martin Drysdale.'

'Johnson,' I said. 'Wasn't she that lawyer for the American Civil Liberties Union, back when it still existed?'

'Our people did some digging. Johnson was involved in several Church and state cases before the Adamson regime. Word is, she embarrassed more than one powerful Revivalist in the court-room.'

'Any names?'

'Everyone we talked to was too skittish to get specific,' Jack said.

'And what does she say?'

'We don't know,' Jack said. 'She suddenly decided to move to Europe two weeks ago. None of her friends knows where, or if they do they aren't telling. One of them let drop that he wasn't surprised she'd left after what they did to her.'

'He didn't go into details?'

'He clammed up right after, realized he'd said too much.'

'Okay,' I said. 'I think it's a safe bet that Johnson is on that list because someone wanted payback. What about Drysdale?'

'Maybe the same motive,' Cal said, picking up where Jack left off.

Sometimes I felt like I was talking to a double act.

'He's a painter-decorator who owns his own business and works all over the city. No iffy friends or associates that we know of. We talked to a few people in the business, and word had got around that Drysdale was in some big dispute with one of his clients. No names again, but everyone agreed Drysdale was getting ready to sue.'

'We need to figure out what connects these people,' I said.

'Otherwise we're never going to get a handle on the Fishermen.'

'A priest, a painter, a lawyer and a rabbi,' Jack said. 'Put 'em all together and what have we got?'

'If they walk into a bar, the beginning of a joke. Otherwise, I have no idea.'

'What about Emerson?' Cal asked.

I gave them my account of his life. 'He doesn't make sense yet,' I said. 'Emerson's up to something, but he doesn't act that way.'

'Maybe he's just a good actor.'

'I'm not talking about him being nervous or erratic. Anyone who's involved in his kind of duplicity behaves with more caution, even when he's doing everyday things. It's an unconscious response to keeping secrets. I haven't seen anything like that in the last three days. His life is too damn comfortable.'

'Maybe you're overthinking this,' Cal said. 'He could just be selling Justice files, and they haven't grabbed him yet because of his father.'

'Glass is a political animal. He wouldn't mind covering for the son if it meant the father took up residence in his pocket. If that were true, why tell Stonebridge about him at all?'

'Maybe they're negotiating,' Jack said. 'Or Glass really is going to lock him up, but wants a smoking gun. I thought this scenario was your idea.'

'It is, but something about it doesn't sit right,' I said. 'I'm going to stay on Emerson until he makes another drop. I need to find out what he's selling and who's buying it.'

'Maybe it's time to make contact,' Cal said.

'I've only been on the guy for three days. I don't want to tip my mitt just yet.'

'The Fishermen could grab Emerson at any time,' Jack said. 'We need to move before they do.'

'We barely know anything about him,' I said. 'Emerson might even be on our side.'

'All the more reason to approach him now,' Cal said. 'We need to see where he stands. If he's with us, he should be warned. Hell, I'd consider warning him even if he isn't, just for the sake of basic decency. Either way, we need to know why Emerson has a special place in Glass's heart.'

'I'll think about it. Did you get anywhere with Cassandra?' I had decided not to tell Cal and Jack that Cassandra and I were in contact, at least until I knew more about my mysterious friend.

'To put it simply: bad mojo,' Cal said.

'Is that a direct quote from your boss Jefferson?'

'More or less. He told us she was dangerous.'

Two people I'd never met were both telling me the other was trouble. Wonderful.

'Her? He used that word?'

'Yes. He was very interested to know that Glass was looking for her.'

At least I knew that my friend was a woman. Now I just had to figure out who she really was and what she wanted. 'Jefferson didn't say why she might top Glass's hit list?'

'Not exactly,' Cal said. 'As soon as I mentioned that name, he went all coy, like I've never seen before. Part of his warning was that she was the reason the CIA got broken up and sold for scrap.'

'How?'

'He wouldn't say. Jefferson talked about her in a familiar way, like he knew her. He was very interested in her whereabouts.'

Cal and Jack looked at me and waited.

'Search me,' I said. 'Did Jefferson say anything else?'

'He said if I ever heard the term "Rudashevsky Group", I was to tell him immediately. He said this right after I asked about Cassandra. You ever heard of that?'

'Do you have a secure internet connection here?'

'Sure.'

I showed them the video of the Houston Commission hearings, without telling them how I found it.

'I thought I'd heard that name before,' Cal said. 'Senator Lee seemed pretty damn informed, didn't he?'

'A lot more than your average senator,' I agreed. 'Maybe Cassandra was his Deep Throat in the CIA. That would explain why your boss said she had something to do with the agency's demise.'

The CIA hadn't outlived the war. The administration had dismembered the agency with bureaucratic knives: covert ops went to the Pentagon and analysts to the Defense Intelligence Agency. The leftovers were scattered around the rest of the intelligence community, or went to the private sector.

'But the CIA was toeing President Adamson's line,' Jack said. 'The fucking director is carrying their water right there.' He pointed to Director Foyle, face frozen in surprise at the first of Senator Lee's questions.

'It doesn't matter,' Cal said. 'If Cassandra was CIA and fed that information to Lee, then the institution as a whole was suspect. Foyle couldn't be trusted to keep his subordinates in line. If President Adamson had fired him, there would be no guarantee that Foyle's replacement would have better luck. The only way to be sure was to eviscerate the entire agency.'

'What did Jefferson want you to do if you ran into Cassandra?' I asked.

'Tell him immediately, and stay out of her way.'

If Jefferson was DIA as Cassandra claimed, and he knew her, he might be a refugee from the CIA's demise. Jefferson wouldn't be too well disposed to the catalyst for the agency's destruction, especially when she was planning to expose the country's secrets.

I had about a dozen other questions I wanted to ask Cal, most relating to the Founder Initiative. That was the DIA programme Cassandra said Jefferson was running, with Cal and Jack being members of one of his cells. I couldn't think of a way to bring it up without admitting I was in contact with Cassandra. If I told Cal he would tell Jefferson. I didn't want him to know until I figured out whether it was him or Cassandra I should trust.

'I'll stay on Emerson, you keep digging into Cassandra. If we're going to have a chance, we have to make one of Glass's enemies our friend.'

SEVENTEEN

A loud buzzing sound woke me shortly before eleven. I was at my desk. I looked around. There were no signs of a struggle. I had probably fallen asleep, not suffered another seizure. Now that my computer was gone, there was no way to be certain.

The buzzing was the receiver telling me that Emerson's car was on the move. He was following his usual route to work, but he hadn't worked late before, or gone back to the office. I jumped in my rental car, hoping this was the break I'd been waiting for.

I was waiting near the DOJ offices when Emerson arrived. The whole block was federal offices, and all of them were dark. I didn't bother stashing the car this time: foot traffic wasn't a problem, and I could always park it if a meter maid got the jump on me. Emerson parked in his space, but didn't leave the car. If I was lucky, he was waiting for his fat-fingered benefactor.

Five minutes later another car pulled into the lot. It wasn't the same car that he'd met at the tattoo parlour, nor was the same man driving it. It was Emerson's Titan bodyguard. If he'd been following Emerson for security reasons, he wouldn't have been so far behind. The guard waited until Emerson climbed in, and then drove north.

We drove up Centre Street for a few minutes, and then turned into Alphabet City. The tattoo parlour was on the other side of the Village. They stopped on Seventh Street, just before it ran into First Avenue. I couldn't stop without giving the Titan man a chance to see they were being followed. I saw them enter an old red-brick townhouse before I had to turn.

I parked around the corner and came back to the building. A small sign identified it as a boutique hotel of the kind that had become popular in the last few years; mansions that had been broken up into flats were broken up again. What was left were very small rooms at a reasonable price.

Some people used these joints as a more respectable version of Isaac's boarding house, but that wasn't why I was so familiar with them. Surveillance had made playing around more difficult now than at any point in the last forty years. Straight hotels were a risk: you never knew if the clerk was on somebody's payroll, or who was hanging around the lobby. These places filled the gap, making it easier for couples who were unmarried or wed to someone else to meet and canoodle in peace.

The system worked like this: a hotel, even a tiny one, couldn't sell rooms by the hour without getting attention. Some of the rooms were rented by the month as a cheap crash pad; the rest were farmed out to touts who sub-let them on an hourly basis. The hotel had no record of this going on, so the risks were pretty low.

Nobody took a room in a place like this because they couldn't face the commute home. I didn't think he was here to meet Fat Fingers either. Handlers and contacts had routines for a reason. Emerson was probably just playing doctor with the wrong patient. After seeing his wife, I almost managed a flicker of indignation. Whatever he was up to I'd have something to hold over his head, whether Emerson was an angel or the other kind.

A tout lingered outside the hotel. Emerson had gone right past him, so he had a room of his own or knew someone who did. The tout saw my interest and sidled up.

'Fifty for the hour, two hundred for the night,' he rasped through yellowed teeth. He was dressed in trousers and a sports coat that didn't exactly match, and both were strangers to his tie. The man reminded me of a high school guidance counsellor who had fallen on hard times. Once I pressed a fifty into his hand, the man became free to consider other aspects of the world around him. It was then that he noticed I had no companion.

'Hey,' he said, dropping the key into my hand, 'what are you going to do in there by yourself?'

'Spend an hour with someone I love,' I said, and pushed past him.

The lobby had once been someone's drawing room. A small clerk was sandwiched between a desk in front and a boarded-up fireplace behind him. He didn't look up when I came in. In this racket blindness and deafness were the ultimate kind of personal service.

A spiral staircase was the building's spine. It went up two floors, splitting into rooms at crazy angles only a Victorian could have come up with. The room the tout had rented to me was on the first floor. I didn't see Emerson there, so I kept going up. He made it easy for me to figure out which room was his by leaving the bodyguard outside. I stopped in front of the door next to him – about three steps away – and pretended to look for my key.

The first mistake the bodyguard made was not noticing that I still wore my fedora. Gentlemen don't wear hats indoors. His second mistake was ignoring the dark sunglasses perched on my nose this close to midnight. These errors all flowed from the man's original sin of playing with his phone instead of doing his job.

I turned and closed the distance (it was only two steps, not three), grabbed the arm that held his phone and jerked it forward. The bodyguard resisted my force like any surprised person, and that only made him stumble forward, his head leading. I brought my other fist down on the back of his neck, and the Titan man collapsed into my arms like a fainting lover.

I rested him against the wall and listened. No sounds of movement or alarm came from behind Emerson's door. The Titan man was packing a revolver and a Taser, so he could play Jekyll or Hyde depending on the day. I relieved him of the latter: a non-lethal option might come in handy in a minute. Emerson hadn't trusted his minder with a key to the room, so I was going to have to knock the hard way. I didn't mind that especially; I'd grown too fond of the sound of a collapsing door when I worked with Seventeen. There was something about the splintering sound that came after the boom of a wooden door being dislodged that I found satisfying.

The door crushed inwards under my heel. Emerson was inside, sitting on a faded, crushed-velvet couch. Standing a few feet away was a woman in her late twenties wearing the legal minimum of clothing. She opened her mouth to scream.

I covered Emerson with my gun, and stuck the Taser in the woman's face. 'Hold that thought.'

I stepped inside and closed the broken door. Emerson had rented what passed for the penthouse in this joint. We were in the suite's sitting room. The couch Emerson sat on was across from the door. There was another chair beside it. A small table that had once occupied the centre of the room, where the woman was now standing, had been moved against a wall. There were two other rooms in the suite: a bathroom on my left, and a closed door on the right that I assumed led to the bedroom.

No one spoke. The clerk downstairs hadn't heard my forced entry, or he thought it was another thing he was paid to ignore. Neither Emerson nor the woman looked like they were in any hurry to make conversation. Since I was the one with the weapons, I got to speak first.

'I guess your marriage isn't so happy after all.'

The woman prepared to weep. As I saw the water gathering in her eyes, I noticed that her face was already streaked with diluted eyeliner. I'd seen more than one mistress turn on the taps when she was discovered, but never before I entered the room. What had been going on in here before I arrived, that this woman was both half naked and in tears?

'If it's money you want . . .' Emerson began, reaching for his wallet.

'Put your hands behind your back.'

Emerson did as he was told.

'Unplug that television and tie him up,' I said to the woman.

There was a small flatscreen mounted on a bracket in the corner of the room. She wound the cord around Emerson's hands and then tied it off. I inspected her work, and it was solid.

'Is there anyone else here?'

The woman shook her head.

I opened the bedroom door and motioned her inside. The woman picked up the ring of discarded clothes that surrounded her and did as instructed. Emerson looked like he was about say something, so I undid his hand-painted silk tie and gagged him with it.

The bedroom had a king-sized bed, another wall-mounted TV, and a carpet that should have been replaced years ago. The woman sat on the bed and I closed the door.

'Are you going to rape me too?'

The question threw me. It explained the old tears on her face, but there had been no signs of a struggle in the other room. 'I'm here for Emerson,' I said. 'If I put the Taser away, will you promise not to scream?'

She nodded.

'What's your name?' I asked.

'Jennifer,' she said, pulling on her wrinkled clothes. She was short and lithe, with dark roots showing in her shoulder-length blonde hair. Jennifer was in the neighbourhood of twenty-five, and her heart-shaped face would have been pretty if it wasn't in so much pain.

'Okay, Jennifer,' I said. 'Why don't you tell me how you got here? Start from the beginning.'

'He' – she couldn't say his name – 'came to my house while my husband was at work. He said my husband was suspected of anti-American activities, and that they were going to arrest him.'

'Who's they?'

'His bosses.'

'Emerson doesn't work for the criminal side of Justice.' Jennifer didn't know what I was talking about. I forgot civilians didn't see these fine distinctions, perhaps because they didn't exist any more. Either way it was irrelevant; as far as I knew anti-American activities wasn't officially on the statute books. 'Did he show you a warrant?'

'No, something else. He called it a "Task Order".'

There was that term again. 'Did it say what your husband is accused of?'

'I didn't understand it,' Jennifer said. 'It was all codes and numbers.'

'Why did you believe him?'

'Because he was from the government,' Jennifer said. 'And he had pictures of us. Dozens of them. He had transcripts of phone calls, bank records, recordings.' She stopped and hugged her feet to her knees, tried to take up as little space as possible. 'He had our entire life.'

'What did Emerson want?'

'What do you think? He said he could make it go away, if . . .'

'If you met him here.'

I wanted to feel sick, horrified. That was the normal reaction to what Emerson had done. It wasn't that I was indifferent to Jennifer's suffering, or that I expected it. The part of me that could express disgust or outrage was simply exhausted. 'How long has he been doing this to you?'

'About a month.'

'Does he ever talk about who he works for?' I asked. 'Does he ever brag or anything like that?'

'What, you mean like during pillow talk?' She looked away, the disgust I couldn't feel appearing in her face. 'The only thing he ever talked about was himself.'

Jennifer retreated inside herself, and I let her go. There was no point in interrogating the poor woman when I had the bastard tied up in the next room.

'Are you with the government?' Jennifer asked. 'Are you here to arrest him?'

'I'm here to make sure he never hurts anyone again,' I said. 'Leave it at that. Jennifer, I need you to go home and forget you ever saw me. Try to forget about him too, if you can.'

She didn't believe me or wasn't satisfied with the answer. It didn't matter.

Jennifer followed me back into the living room. Emerson was where I'd left him. The eyes behind the expensive gag were fuming, but he looked too in love with himself to try anything. I yanked the tie out of his mouth.

'Do you know who I am?' he said, through a gasp.

'I know exactly who you are, David Emerson. That's why you're coming with me.'

Jennifer reached into her bra, and suddenly a razor blade was at Emerson's throat. 'Why did you have to come tonight?' she said. 'Why couldn't you have come before, when I didn't have the courage?'

'Listen to me very carefully, Jennifer.' I wouldn't get to the

Taser in time, and the convulsions it caused might put the razor in Emerson's throat. 'I know Emerson has it coming.'

'You don't know a fucking thing,' she said. 'You have no idea what it's like, to be raped for a whole month, to try and be with your husband . . .'

'I didn't rape you,' Emerson said. His eyes were scared, but his voice had the smooth timbre of a professional liar. 'We made a deal.'

'Shut up or I'll let her do what she wants,' I said.

Emerson closed his mouth.

'Let me tell you what I do know, Jennifer. Emerson is part of a system. No matter what he's told you, he's just another moving part that can be replaced. If you kill him, they'll give the job to someone just as bad, and your husband's name will still be on file.'

Jennifer swallowed hard. She was a bit calmer, but the razor wasn't going anywhere.

'I'm sorry,' I said. 'I can't give you justice. I can't even give you the hollow satisfaction of killing him. All I can say is that there are others. The only way this stops is if I can get to the people he works for, before they get to him.'

Neither of them believed me. I showed her the Glass memo. Jennifer didn't understand what she was reading.

'Who is General Glass?'

The colour began to leak from Emerson's face.

'They're coming for him, Jennifer. Look at him.'

Jennifer looked down at Emerson's pale face, the sweat collecting just below her on his brow.

'Have you ever seen him this afraid?'

'What will they do to him?'

'God knows,' I said, 'but I guarantee it will be worse than anything we can come up with.'

The razor came away from Emerson's neck, but he didn't look that relieved.

'I'll make you a deal,' she said. 'You forget about me, and I'll forget about you.' Jennifer picked her purse up off the floor and opened the door. She stopped when she saw the body on the other side.

'He's alive,' I said. 'Would you mind bringing him inside?'

The bodyguard had at least fifty pounds on Jennifer, but she managed it. She was out the door before I could say thank you. She didn't look at Emerson, or me.

Emerson stared at his bodyguard with fascination. I think his situation had finally made a dent in the thick armour of privilege Emerson had been swaddled in since the day he was born. I doubted that he liked the bodyguard – he was the help, after all – but he might be the first person Emerson knew to whom anything bad had happened at all.

'Are you going to kill me?'

'I would have let your victim do the honours if I was,' I said.

Maybe Jennifer had believed what I'd said about the worse punishment, or she was one of those rare people who knew that inflicting pain almost never made you feel better. Whatever the reason, she'd shown an amazing amount of restraint.

'Who are you? Who do you work for?' Emerson said.

'I know you're unfamiliar with that side of an interrogation, but I'm the one who asks the questions.'

'That memo is a fake,' Emerson said, but his heart wasn't in his words. It was somewhere on the floor trying to burrow into the carpets. He hadn't even seen the memo yet, and I guess he didn't need to. The whirlpool in his gut was the only authentication he needed.

'What's the number next to my name?'

Emerson was the kind of man who skated through life on his charm. On the rare occasions that had failed, he'd had family connections to fall back on. Emerson had never had to bargain for anything in his life, and his inexperience was showing.

'Why do you want to know?' I said. 'Want to find out what you're guilty of?' There was confusion on his face for a second, and I knew I'd stumbled.

'The codes have nothing to do with the crime,' he said. The old feeling of invulnerability was coming back. 'You don't know what you're talking about.'

'One hundred and ninety-nine.' It was the number next to Father Fiore's name.

Emerson blinked. He tried to breathe and swallow at the same time, and what came out was a cough. 'Is that my number?'

When I'd first seen the numbers, I'd assumed it was a code for the person's sin. They weren't normal police codes – a 187 was a homicide, but none of the others fitted – so I had assumed they were references to whatever secret law the person was accused of breaking. Judging by Emerson's reaction, I had it backwards: those three digits didn't represent the past, but the future Glass had planned for him.

'It could be. There are two ways you can find out: help me, or go home and wait.'

'No, no,' Emerson said, to himself, not to me. 'This can't be happening. They'd never make me a client.'

A client. That's the term Cassandra had used. 'Is that what you call the people you murder?'

'Fisher Partners doesn't murder people,' Emerson said. 'Not often, anyway.'

Fisher Partners. That was another point in Cassandra's favour. Emerson had used the name without any prompting, so I decided to play along. If I asked him about the company I risked looking ignorant again, and I had to convince Emerson I was in complete control.

'If you give me the complete list of clients' – the word tasted dirty – 'you'll get a head start.'

Emerson laughed. It was nervous, crazy laughter, not

mockery. He was barely aware of me, too lost in his own self-pity. Emerson seemed inclined to stay there, and I didn't have time to nurse this fortunate son.

'I don't have the whole list,' Emerson said. 'It's compartmentalized. Otherwise I'd already know my fate, wouldn't I? We only deal with New York. And even if I had it I'd never give it to you.' He shut up and wouldn't meet my eyes.

I didn't let him give me the silent treatment for long. 'Okay, it's your funeral.' I rose and went to the door.

'Where are you going?' Emerson said. 'I'm tied up.'

'So you are,' I said. 'If you don't want my help, that's fine. I'm sure the Fishermen know all about this place. They'll be here before anyone else misses you. I guess I could save everyone a little time and just leave you like that in Times Square.'

'When the police find me, you'll go down on a kidnapping charge.'

'If the police find you first, tell them all about me,' I said. 'Knock yourself out. You won't make it to the station, let alone a trial.'

'We'll see. You don't know who my father is.'

'The Fishermen care for your preacher father about as much as I do. They have their orders.'

Emerson didn't say anything. I put my hand on the doorknob.

'Okay,' he said. 'If I get you the New York list, I'm going to need more than a head start.'

'You'll get it,' I said. 'How long will it take the Fishermen to figure out the list has been stolen? Twelve hours?'

'Less. The computer people will notice it when they come on shift at seven.'

'Then as of seven o'clock, you will be their lowest priority,' I said. 'Once he finds out the list is missing, Stonebridge will tear the city apart looking for it. He knows what the price is for failing Glass.'

'And I know what the price is for betraying him,' Emerson said.

'The point is, I'll be a nice big diversion. With your money and connections, you could be out of the country before dawn.'

Emerson stared at the floor. 'If I give you the list, you'll tell me my number?'

I didn't understand Emerson's obsession with his bureaucratic classification. Knowing that I was wanted by Glass's pet organization would be enough to put me on the run, no matter what they were planning. Maybe the number would give Emerson a clue to who had betrayed him, or whether the Fishermen intended to target his family. Whatever the reason, Emerson was offering me leverage, so I took it.

'It's a deal.'

'Untie me.'

I loosened the cord. I didn't need restraints or a gun to keep control of Emerson now. He'd accepted the logic of my offer, saw it as the single tiny window of escape I wanted him to.

'Where is the list?'

'I can access it from my office.'

'Let's go.'

Emerson pulled on his coat as if in a dream. I pushed his forgotten hat on to his head, and helped him out the door.

We took the bodyguard's car and headed back to his office. He drove and I rode shotgun. As I'd expected, there were no screams of help or attempts at heroics. Emerson knew that he was marked, and no one could help him now.

'What did you do to piss your bosses off?' I said.

'Figure it out for yourself.'

'I'd rather you tell me than try to imagine something worse than what you were doing to that woman.'

'Don't listen to that slut,' Emerson said. 'We made a deal, that's all. A transaction. And she liked it anyway.'

'If you'd held a gun to her husband's head and demanded sex, no one would call it anything but rape,' I said. 'Your way isn't any different just because paperwork is involved.'

Emerson glanced at my face and reconsidered what he was going to say.

'So what was it?' I said. 'Embezzlement? Espionage? Is that what was going on with your friend in the parking lot?'

Emerson shook his head. He was bemused. 'You don't know who you're dealing with, do you?'

'I know the major players,' I said, 'probably better than you do. I don't know the organization. Why don't you tell me about it?'

'I never said I'd play twenty questions.'

'We've got five minutes of driving to kill,' I said, 'and I know you're dying to tell me how important you used to be.'

I saw Emerson's back tense where those last words had hit.

'My father didn't raise a family, he bred a personal army,' Emerson said. 'My job was to go to law school, and then burrow deep into the secular hierarchy. He wanted me at Justice in case some east coast fag ever came for his Bible.'

'You thought you were worth more.'

'I am. Fisher Partners recognized my potential.' Emerson laughed bitterly to himself. 'You know what's almost funny about my situation? I got here by doing my job. When Fisher Partners first hired me, I expected a more glamorous position. Instead I got stuck in logistical support for Acquisitions.'

'Acquisitions?' I said. 'Is that grabbing people?'

'What company ever uses an accurate name for its operations?' Emerson threw back. 'That's what you saw me doing in the parking lot. Sometimes the Acquisition teams need more information about their clients. I use the Justice files to provide it. The position wasn't what I'd expected. I didn't really fit in. Acquisitions is run by military people, and I never served. Plus my boss is a complete asshole.'

'Is Stonebridge your boss?'

'Do you know him?'

'Unfortunately.'

'Yeah, my feelings exactly,' Emerson said.

'Is everyone in Acquisitions Task Force Seventeen veterans?'

'I don't know what you mean.'

'Did they talk about Tehran?' I said.

'The older ones did. The rest swapped stories about the Holy Land. It was Greek to me either way. I wanted to be in Marketing. That's where the real action was.'

'Marketing?'

'Acquisitions is the client service side. They're obedient and boring, just like the military. Marketing is all about creativity and initiative.'

'I bet it's also where the money is.'

'Like I said, it's a business. Each unit competes with all the others to generate the best leads.'

'You compete to rat people out?'

'We don't even know them. Everyone in Marketing has top-secret clearances. They use intelligence from the NSA, FBI, you name it. We've been keeping track of troublemakers and un-desirables for years, but never had the money or the will to do anything about them. Marketing is like a big filter on top of all that information.'

'And they decide who is taken?'

'Leads are sent to the board, who have final approval. The more leads that pan out, the bigger the unit's performance-related bonuses. It's a meritocracy.'

I resisted the urge to vomit out the window. A meritocracy based on competing to find the most people to disappear. 'How were you going to get into Marketing?' I said. 'I doubt Fisher puts out a call for résumés.'

'A few months ago, someone in Homeland Security

approached me. I'd never seen him before, but he carried a letter of introduction from the Secretary and a DHS ID. He offered me what he said was an exciting opportunity.'

'Whose pound of flesh did they ask for in return?'

'Piotr Kirov's.'

'You're a liar,' I said. He had to be. Emerson had seen Kirov's name on the news and woven it into his delusions of grandeur.

'Why would I lie?' he said. 'Kirov and I got along. Piotr was ambitious, like me. I fed him information from my father's connections and he shepherded my career in return. That's why they approached me. They wanted me to feed him some information that terrorists were holed up in that building that blew up.'

'Did you know what was going to happen?'

'Of course not. I only realized when I saw the news.'

For the briefest of moments I saw what might have been remorse on his face. It could just as easily have been indigestion. 'Why didn't you run then?'

'I have a family. I couldn't just pick up and leave.' That was what Emerson had been telling himself the last few days, but there was more to it. Anyone with a realistic opinion of himself would have seen the writing on the wall.

'What did Kirov do? Why did they kill him?'

'I didn't ask and they didn't tell me. Acquisitions never know why someone is a client. It's the same with Marketing; they don't know how their leads are punished, or if they're scooped up at all. We only see aggregate numbers. The only reason I know about both is that I was supposed to be moving from one to the other. Everything is compartmentalized.'

Even more than the letter, this arrangement had the stamp of General Glass. If a Fisherman, who knows the punishment, also knew the crime, he might think one didn't fit the other. He might be tempted to show mercy. He might even begin to question the entire programme. I doubted that the Fisher Partners board, packed with worthies as it was, knew the full extent of what was going on. Like Cassandra had said, they'd sleep better if they didn't. Everything was compartmentalized, so no one was accountable.

We got to the DOJ office. Emerson parked beside his own car. 'You can't come inside.'

'How stupid do you think I am?' I said.

'There's twenty-four-hour security. You'll have to show ID and submit to a fingerprint scan to get a guest pass. Do you want to do that?'

It was a good question. I had been operating on the assumption that the Elders' truce with the Bureau still held, but the hairs on the back of my neck were starting to raise doubts. The Elders wouldn't want it known why I was a person of interest, but Emerson had just explained how that wouldn't matter. If my name was on the New York list, there wouldn't be a hint of what had happened last year beside it. Like Emerson, there would just be a number, a doom in three digits.

'Give me the keys to the other car,' I said.

'What?'

'Your car keys.' I held out my hand. 'I'll listen to the radio while you're gone.'

Emerson handed them over. He seemed reluctant more from a general sulk than because I'd thrown a monkey wrench in his escape plans. Under other circumstances I would never have given a man like Emerson this much leeway, but this was new territory for all concerned. If Emerson called the cops, his situation wouldn't improve one bit. It didn't matter that I believed the Fishermen were coming for him. He did.

I locked the bodyguard's car and recovered the bug from Emerson's. It was last year's Lexus with all the bells and whistles. I got in the passenger seat, but didn't turn on the radio. It would have used the battery, and that would activate any other tracking devices attached to the car. I sat and waited with my hands in my pockets. I didn't want my fingerprints to sully the leather interior.

It took Emerson twenty minutes, just long enough for me to start wondering if I'd misread him. He exited the office alone and walked double-time to the car. He got in on the driver's side and handed me a manila envelope. Inside was a list of names and codes printed on Fisher Partners letterhead. The list went on for pages and pages.

'My God,' I said. 'How many people is this?'

'Around a thousand, I think,' Emerson said. 'It may take you a while to find who you're looking for; they're sorted by priority, not last name.'

'Why?'

'The list itself doesn't matter. All that's important is who's next.'

A thousand people, just in New York. I tried to think how many there could be nationally, but there was no way to extrapolate. This list could be the longest in the country, ground zero for what was happening. It could also be just the beginning.

On the top of the first page was a single word: Leviathan. 'What does that word mean?'

'That's the name of the programme,' Emerson said.

Leviathan. Something Glass had said during our first interview came back to me: 'The United States must become the Leviathan.' He'd finally gotten his wish. The difference was that he wasn't breaking the will of some foreign enemy, but his own people.

'You've got what you want,' Emerson said. 'I've even brought you a little bonus.' He showed me another folder. 'These are the codes. Before you see them I want my number.'

I put the memo face down on the dashboard. Emerson

snatched it and put the folder in its place. A gang of conflicting emotions had a turf war over his face. There was shock at this fresh bludgeoning by reality, fear of what was coming, and an odd kind of relief.

According to the second file, Emerson's code – 825 – meant public liquidation. 'I don't see what you have to be relieved about. They want to kill you.'

'There are worse things. If they're planning to kill me in public, they want my death to be known. That means they'll leave my family alone.'

Emerson hadn't shown so much concern for his family an hour ago. It was a cognitive dissonance I'd seen in cheating husbands a thousand times: worrying about his wife and children being exposed to public shame while he rented the motel room.

'I was afraid they'd scheduled me for full erasure.' The code for that fate was the subtle 666. 'They don't just render you to some secret prison. They take your entire family, and then do their best to erase all record of your existence. Anyone who remembers you will learn not to say so. They annihilate you.'

Emerson took his keys and was about to start the car when I put my hand on his arm. 'One last question,' I said, angry at myself that it hadn't been my first.

'Jesus Christ, haven't you got enough? I have to get my family out of the country.'

'There was a Titan man guarding Stonebridge, just like your sadsack. His name is Isaac Taylor,' I said, forcing myself to use the present tense. 'Have you ever heard that name?'

'No, I've never heard the name. I don't know anyone at Titan. In fact, I don't know anyone at all. Now are we fucking done?'

I removed my hand and got out of the car. There was nothing more to say. Calling him bad names for what he'd done was pointless, and I certainly didn't wish him luck.

My rental car was still parked in the East Village. I had two folders under my arms, and I was afraid of both of them. When I'd flipped through the names I hadn't seen anyone I recognized, but that might change once I got home and took a proper look. My name could be in there, or Benny's, or Faye's, maybe even Iris, though I might not recognize it if it was there. My office was still a mess after the break-in, and I was so desperate to put off going through the list I considered doing something about it. I was still weighing the possibility when the blast knocked me to the ground.

Instinct had me up and taking cover behind the nearest vehicle before I knew what was happening. Bits and pieces of Emerson's car were all over the parking lot. What was left, a skeleton of steel, was on fire. Another bomb in New York City.

The blast had shredded the bodyguard's car, blown out every window and set off every car alarm in the surrounding area. There wasn't much other damage. This wasn't a terrorist car bomb; it was a hit. Public liquidation. The Fishermen had done exactly what they said they would, and Emerson wouldn't be the last.

I headed in the direction of my car. I couldn't be seen here, and I had to get on the road before the cavalry shut them down. When I turned the block, Emerson's car was still on fire, the smoke taking what was left of him – his ashes and his crimes – high into the air.

LEVIATHAN

May those who curse days curse that day,
those who are ready to rouse Leviathan.

– Job iii, 8, New International Version

EIGHTEEN

Nine years ago

The Lab was what passed for entertainment on campus. It was a chemistry teaching lab that had been converted into a bar. Boxes of Erlenmeyer flasks, beakers and retorts had somehow survived the invasion, and were now used to serve alcohol smuggled along the same routes the Pasdaran used to transport arms. I wouldn't be surprised if the Revolutionary Guard was taking a cut. I hadn't come here much when I was on regular duty, and didn't come here at all after my new assignment. Task Force Seventeen kept itself separate. Task Force Seventeen kept itself pure.

Benny sat at one of the lab stations with Judge and two other Airborne soldiers from another platoon. Judge saw me first, and whispered to the two men I didn't recognize. I didn't need to read lips to know what he was saying. It was being whispered all around me as I approached them. It had started with the British. Some clever Royal Marine had called one of us 'Steve Seventeen'. It had become 'Psycho Seventeen', 'Scary Seventeen', and then just 'SS'. The initials were intentional. The room had seen the mark of Seventeen on the helmet under my arm, and knew something evil was in their midst.

As I reached the table, everyone but Benny got up. They

brushed past me without a glance or a word, even Judge. Benny stared at his test tube of whisky.

'This seat taken?'

Benny shrugged, and I had no choice but to take it as a yes.

'How are the others?'

'Mitchell bought it last week. Mortar attack,' Benny said. 'Everyone else is okay.'

I didn't know what to say. I hadn't seen Benny since I joined Seventeen, and there hadn't exactly been a party to mark my departure from the unit. I'd expected a thorough cursing out, but not this wall of silence.

'This is kind of a one-sided conversation, Benny.'

'I don't know what you expect me to say. I'm glad you aren't dead, Felix, but beyond that I'm struggling. What are you doing here?'

'I wanted to say hello.'

'Well, mission fucking accomplished.'

We didn't say anything for a while. I could feel the eyes of the whole room burning a hole in my back. Benny was risking ostracism just being seen with me.

'I shot a mother a few days ago,' I said. 'I shot her twice, actually. I didn't kill her the first time.'

'Your colonel is the one who doles out the medals, not me.'

'It probably wasn't the first mother I, or you, had killed.'

Benny didn't like what I'd said, but he didn't argue with it either. We both remembered the women who had joined their men to fight us with assault rifles and bare hands, headscarves intact to protect their modesty.

'What's your point?'

'We did some horrible things during the invasion, but we did them to survive. This woman was armed. We were looking for her husband and took her son instead. He died in a mortar attack just after we returned to base.'

I hesitated. I felt Glass's gaze more than all the other eyes in the room combined, and he was far away. The next thing I said would cross the line from private unease to disloyalty. 'I'm actually relieved about that. I was afraid of what we were going to do him.'

Benny kept his eyes on his drink. I wasn't sure if he was even listening to me. He finished it off, swore in a reluctant way, and looked at me. 'You knew what Seventeen did when you joined.'

'Those were rumours, and they weren't the only ones.'

'So are you here to tell me Seventeen isn't as bad as I thought?'

'No.'

'Then what?'

'What they're doing, what I'm doing, it's wrong, probably criminal. It's killed people who didn't deserve it, and it will probably kill a lot more. I can't do it any more.'

'Then don't do it.'

'I can't exactly quit, Benny.'

Benny had this look. He would scrutinize someone through half-closed eyes, stare right through them. He called it his bullshit detector, and he'd never used it on me before.

'It's worse than the rest of Military Intelligence? I've seen them play pretty rough before.'

I told him about 6524 and Stonebridge. I could have been court-martialled for talking out of school, but I didn't care.

'Fuck me,' Benny said, 'they really think this guy is their intellectual property?'

I nodded. 'Stonebridge would have tortured the prisoner until he said what he wanted. If he'd died in the process, that would have been a bonus. There'd be no worries about a later recantation.'

'You need to tell someone,' Benny said. 'CID maybe.'

Criminal Investigations Division, the army's cops. 'How can

CID investigate?' I said. 'What they're doing is practically un-official policy.'

'It was practically unofficial policy at Abu Ghraib, and they investigated that,' Benny said. 'There are a lot of good people in this army, Felix. If you bring some evidence to them, something will happen.'

'The only something that happened after Abu Ghraib was the prosecution of a few grunts.'

'You wanna sit here and justify yourself, do it without me,' Benny said, rising. '"Just following orders" doesn't sound any better now than it used to. You aren't stupid, Felix; you know the way back to the human race.'

Benny left, and I didn't bother trying to stop him. Once his mind was made up, that was it. Without Benny's protective company, the hostility in the room felt twice as strong. A group of Stillwater mercenaries sat at a lab station near the blacked-out windows. One of them – a big, bullet-headed son of a bitch with at least two inches and twenty pounds on me – made no attempt to hide his interest. I had the feeling he wasn't looking for a date.

Bullet Head stood up and walked over. 'I got a message for you from a friend.' His voice sounded like it was coming through a ton of gravel.

'You must have the wrong guy,' I said. 'I don't have any friends.'

'You get anything out of the prisoner, you tell Janus first,' Bullet Head said. He had a heavy Russian accent. I guessed he was ex-Spetznaz, Russia's Special Forces. 'They'll make it worth your while.'

'By Janus, you mean Stonebridge,' I said.

He didn't respond.

'If I refuse?'

Bullet Head leaned in. His breath was hot and smelled of bootlegged gin. 'That wouldn't be smart.'

The hostility of the room had already **put my** nervous system on notice. Now that this gorilla was getting intimate, my amygdala was lighting up like a Christmas tree. I had a bad feeling about how this was going to end.

'Tell him to stick his intellectual property where the sun never shines,' I said. It could be his ass or his heart; either one had more than enough space.

Bullet Head smiled. I knew what was coming.

I rolled off the stool as the first blow came down, a big meat hammer that was his left hand. The blow glanced off my back as I moved, giving little more than a sting. I threw three quick punches to disorient him, and got my body into the last. Bullet Head laughed in my face. He grabbed me, and the next thing I knew, I was airborne in the direction of a nearby table.

I hit the black plastic top, and felt the last round of drinks break and settle into my vest for the ride. The table's former occupants had moved against the wall along with the rest of the bystanders. Together they formed a ring with just enough room for us to kill each other.

I grabbed one of the vacant stools and held him off just like they did with lions at the circus. The crowd loved it: some laughed, others called me a coward, a few could walk and chew gum at the same time. Bullet Head played along, roaring for the crowd.

Bullet Head's accomplice was still sitting at their table. He was watching the circus, but showed no interest in joining in. He was there as a friendly witness in case my Russian foe became too enthusiastic. This encounter was supposed to look like a bar brawl; people might ask questions if it became obvious that it was a message. He wouldn't join in unless I gave Bullet Head a run for his money.

I kept the stool and my head pointed in Bullet Head's direction, but left a corner of my eye watching his partner behind me.

As I inched closer, the partner's hands formed into fists on the tabletop. He was waiting for his chance, that innocuous second when he could play the part of a drunken bystander joining in. I wasn't about to give him the chance. I stepped back, pivoted, and swung the stool into his face.

The blow knocked the Stillwater man off his seat and into dreamland. The crowd's verdict was mixed: most took it as further evidence of my perfidy, while a few had eyes to see the logic. Bullet Head's next roar wasn't for the crowd. I guess he and the other jackass were friends. Bullet Head stepped forward and kicked with one of his tree-trunk legs. I wasn't fast enough to get out of the way, but I got the stool between my chest and the sole of his boot.

I've been hit by softer cars. The kick sent me flying again, this time into the tender arms of the crowd. A miasma of sweat and beer-drenched breath swallowed me. I couldn't tell faces apart; the crowd was a single mass of disgust, laughter and misplaced anger. Anonymous mouths yelled and screamed, but those nearest my ears just whispered, 'SS.'

Arms held me, then raised me to my feet. Just as I was about to find my balance, strong hands pushed me back into the make-shift ring. Bullet Head was waiting. He picked up an Erlenmeyer flask half full of vodka from a nearby table and smashed it against the edge. It gave me time to realize just how wrong I'd been about this man. He wasn't ex-Special Forces, just a big motherfucker used to coasting on his size. I had to show him why humans were known for their brains.

Bullet Head threw jabs at my face with the broken glass. I danced out of the way. The flask had added to his advantage in reach. He stabbed again. I dodged, but the glass tore a gash down my forearm. I couldn't close the distance to hit him, and I wasn't going to live long enough to regret many more mistakes.

I got lucky. Bullet Head swung hard and high with the broken flask. I dropped and drove my heel into his left foot as hard as I could. You can build and harden a body until doomsday, but none of it helps the little bones in the feet.

Bullet Head cried out. I straightened up and drove my fist into the soft tissue of his armpit. Another cry, and this time he dropped the flask. I swept his leg while he was off balance, but the big galoot grabbed on. We stumbled around for a moment and then fell against a table.

I elbowed him in the head, and this time the medicine worked. The top half of him lay on top of the table, his tree legs a tangled mess downstairs. A shard of the flask was still on the table. I picked it up and held it against his neck. Bullet Head was conscious enough to see it, to know what it meant. He stared at the triangle of glass – already bloody from where it cut into my bare hands – and saw nothing else.

'SS, SS,' the crowd chanted. My victory hadn't brought them around. There was still hatred in their voices, mixed in with a little respect and backhanded admiration. I was the black knight, the Sheriff of Nottingham, the villain everyone loved to cheer.

I looked at that piece of glass in my hand and saw a doorway. I'd probably go to prison, but not for long. It would be called manslaughter, and there was no better phrase for the act on earth. I could stop hunting, killing, and delivering others to cells from which they would never return. The cost of the ticket would be one more life.

I thought of the joy this murder would bring to Stonebridge, and what it would do to my only friend. Benny was the only person who'd remember me in a year, and if I did this he would regret he'd ever met me. I might as well not exist.

I dropped the glass. Behind me, MPs yelled from the door. I had just enough time to put up my hands before they Tasered me.

★

They held American prisoners in shipping containers not far from the airport. I'd never understood why they didn't have a proper prison, but the accommodation wasn't that bad considering. I had my own cell and three square meals, more than I got when I was on regular duty.

They let us out for a few hours of exercise each day, though there was no yard to speak of. We were permitted to take a few steps into the desert and look at each other and the sky. Every day I counted my fellow inmates, and came up with a number around a hundred. Back in my cell I wondered at that number. It was small for the size of the force in the city, and as far as I knew this was the only prison nearby. Maybe they'd given up on a lot of prosecutions, because they needed the bodies or the crime had become a policy.

The detainee processing system was as fucked here as it was everywhere else, so I expected a long wait before someone informed me of my future. I didn't really mind. It was quiet in my cell, the lock as much a guarantee of peace as it was imprisonment. The world had decided to leave me alone for a while, and I was grateful.

Colonel Glass visited me on the sixth day. I stood at attention but he told me to sit on the steel-frame bed. He sat down next to me, and took his time speaking.

'How do you feel?'

'I didn't get busted up much,' I said. 'The only thing that hurts are the Taser punctures in my ass.'

'You were wearing a vest, son,' Glass said. 'The MPs had to improvise.' He offered me one of his stogies, but I declined.

'You gave that contractor a good beating, and put his friend in the hospital. They'll both live.'

'When do I go to jail?'

Glass made a non-committal noise in the back of his throat. I'd never heard him do that before; it was always one or the other with him.

'We may be able to avoid that.'

The prospect of remaining a free man didn't cheer me up as much as it should have. 'Stonebridge did this,' I said. 'That contractor threatened me on his behalf, said I had to give him anything 6524 said.'

'Do you think anyone who was in that room will testify to that?'

I thought of that wall of faces baying for my blood and shook my head. 'No one else would have heard.'

'Then it doesn't really matter. The fact that you fell for it is what's important. Stonebridge was smart. You should have known no one in there would back you up.'

'Sir, what will happen to prisoner 6524?'

'Aren't you more concerned about your own future?'

'I'm relatively safe here,' I said. 'I can't say the same thing about him.'

'Prisoner 6524 was handed over to Janus the day after you were arrested.' He put a hand on my shoulder to keep me from rising. 'I had no choice, son. We can't afford to wait, and your future in this army is still in doubt.'

I wanted to say that Stonebridge would torture him until he heard what he wanted. I couldn't stand by and watch us destroy another man, but I knew that appealing to empathy was the wrong way to go in this task force. 'Stonebridge's incompetence will ruin any intelligence value the prisoner has, sir.'

'I think you're being too hard on your colleague,' Glass said. 'Stonebridge is over-enthusiastic in his pursuit of the truth, but his heart is in the right place. He's loyal, and he understands the sacrifices we make to do our jobs. You haven't been with me very long, Strange. I think when you accepted my offer you had a very different idea of what your work would be, and that is my fault. I had hoped you would figure out the rest on your own.'

Glass knew I was about to speak before I did, and held up his hand.

'Let's go outside,' he said, and opened the container as if we were stepping out on to the veranda after dinner.

Glass lit his cigar and took a few puffs to get it going. 'Do you remember when I said you had an investigative mind, Strange?'

It was during our first interview. 'Yes, sir.'

'You can't leave things alone; you have to take them apart and see how they work. That's why you're one of the few people who truly understands what we do here. My boys are only concerned with killing bad guys. That's why I chose them. You try to figure out who the bad guys are, and that's why you have doubts.'

I denied it without thinking, a reflex reaction, but Glass put up his hand again.

'It's a good thing, Sergeant. That doubt is why you're so useful to me. You are a rare combination: you have the capacity to do what is necessary, and the decency to realize it is horrible. That's the problem with Stonebridge: he's so happy to be on the winning team it damages his perspective.

'Americans are good people. They love their families, pay their taxes and drive on the right side of the road. They go to sleep believing they live in a more or less decent world. We know that isn't true, and part of our job is keeping that truth from the country we love.

'We've both been shot at, Strange, and we know it's not as bad as it sounds. When our leaders talk about the sacrifice we make, that's not what they mean. We do these horrible things, take these sins upon ourselves, so America can believe it leads a blameless life. The task force bears the greatest share of this weight. We wield this power because no one else will.'

Glass fell silent and looked across the Tehran skyline, a thousand broken fingers of concrete and steel. From this distance I could see smoke lingering in the air from a recent airstrike, but no people. 'Look at it,' he said, his cigar hand sweeping across the remains of a place millions once called home. 'What decent person could do that?'

I didn't have an answer.

'Just bear with me a little longer, Strange,' Colonel Glass said. 'All this may be over soon.'

I knew he hadn't chosen my imprisonment as the reason for this lecture. 'Has the prisoner said something, sir?'

Glass smiled. I realized he was excited. It was another emotion I'd never seen in him before. 'We know where they are.'

It took me a minute to figure out what he was referring to. 'You mean nuclear weapons?'

'Prisoner 6524 gave up damn near the whole programme. After Houston, the Supreme Leader ordered their weapons programme to be split up and hidden. Some of it was smuggled into Afghanistan, the rest buried deep in the desert. He couldn't tell us where, but he knows of one more device, and it's in the city.'

'In Tehran?' I could hardly contain my amazement. 'If they were looking to hide nuclear material, that's not a very safe place.'

'In this case, they weren't. The Supreme Leader wanted an ace in the hole. The prisoner thinks they'd planned to use it if the city fell, and just aren't desperate enough yet to nuke their own people.'

It didn't make any sense. If the mullahs had wanted to go out in a blaze of glory, they would have planted the weapon somewhere else. A single large device could blow radiation over the Straits of Hormuz or make oil fields inaccessible for years. If they were really crazy enough to entertain this idea, they would have tried to smuggle it near Israel and hold the country hostage. Putting your last, suicidal option in the middle of your own people just didn't make sense.

'What did they do to the prisoner, sir?'

'Nothing we haven't done before,' Glass said. 'I supervised Stonebridge's interrogation of the detainee myself. He used nothing physically coercive; sleep deprivation, disorientation and the Conveyor.'

The Conveyor was a method of continuous interrogation. A team of interrogators led by Stonebridge would have questioned the prisoner non-stop in shifts. Being asked questions you didn't want to answer sounded like nothing more than an uncomfortable job interview. Imagine that job interview going on for days, without interruption, while the cuffs on your arms rub them raw and ruin your best suit.

'Sir, do we have any corroborating evidence for this?'

'We will,' Glass said. 'I've put together a mission. Once we hit the bunker and recover the device, we'll have all the corroboration we need. I'd prefer it if we had time to gather more evidence, but the tempo of this war doesn't allow for that luxury. News this big can't be hidden from others, even if I wanted to. Prisoner 6524's intelligence has gone all the way up the chain of command. That's where the authorization comes from.'

The colonel could only mean President Adamson. If the Commander-in-Chief had given the order, then the momentum behind this mission was unstoppable.

'Sir, I request that I be added to this mission.' It was a presumptuous thing to ask of an officer, especially a full colonel, but by the smile on his face I knew he'd anticipated it. It was probably the reason for his visit.

'I thought you might be interested, Strange.'

He slapped me on the back. From another officer it would have been insulting, but Glass could display a warmth that felt both confusing and utterly genuine.

'Stonebridge will see it as an attempt to get a piece of the glory, but we know why you want to go. You're crazy enough to risk your life just to prove him wrong. It's one of the things I like about you. You leave in four hours.'

'Sir, I'm not sure I'll be allowed to go anywhere.'

'You mean this?' Glass said, as if he were noticing that we were in a prison for the first time. 'I'll get your day of reckoning postponed. By the time it happens, you'll be a hero.'

NINETEEN

I walked away from the sirens as fast as I could without attracting attention. Now was not the best time to be caught in a police dragnet. The streets had been quiet when Emerson and I were having our discussion, but that probably wouldn't matter. The police would hold anyone nearby just in case, like they had done to me after the Kirov attack. I didn't fancy cooling my heels for another forty-eight hours in a police station.

My rental car was where I'd left it. As I got behind the wheel my phone rang. It was Faye, not Benny. At this time of night, it wouldn't be a social call.

'You have to help me,' Faye said, almost as soon as the connection was made. 'Someone's here.'

'Who's there?' I said. 'Is it the Corinthian?'

'No,' she said. 'I don't recognize them. I don't think they're his men.'

'Where are you?'

'My apartment. There's a blue van across the street with two men in it. They're watching me.'

Now that I'd discovered more than I wanted to about Faye's past, I knew to believe what she said. The Corinthian would have taught her to recognize a tail, and anyone who got in a car with him didn't scare easily.

'Are you sure they're only two?'

'That's all I can see,' Faye said. Experienced or not, I could hear the edge of panic in her voice. 'Please, just get over here.'

'Okay, Faye, this is what I want you to do,' I said. 'First, get that gun you told me about.'

'I already have it.'

'Good, then call the cops. I'm coming over right now. If anyone shows up at your door that isn't me or a cop with a valid badge number, put a bullet in them. Do you understand?' Silence. 'Faye?'

'Okay.'

'I'll be there before you know it.'

I headed for Queens. I didn't have time to check if Faye was on the list; I'd stuffed it in my trousers and hoped for the best. It didn't seem rational for the Elders to go after her, but none of what had happened so far made any kind of sense. They could be Fishermen whether Faye's name was on the list or not: Stonebridge might have sent some of his boys to tie off a loose end.

I hit Faye's block and took it slow. The blue van she'd spoken about was parked across the street from her building. I looked inside as I drove past and it was empty. Faye's number was busy. I told myself that was fine. She might be on the line with a 911 dispatcher.

I found a parking space around the corner and walked back. The light in Faye's living room was on, but the blinds were down. I was the only one on the street. I hoped that meant the men in the van didn't have any back-up.

The latch on the front door popped as easily as it had the last time. The stairwell was empty. Faye's door was a little ajar, and people around here didn't leave their doors open by accident. I eased it open, leading with my weapon.

I got my second shock of the hour. Faye was standing in the centre of her living room. She had remarkable posture: it must have been the gun the gorilla had jammed into the small of her back. The Corinthian stood beside them like a chaperone. I was expected.

Faye tried to call out my name but the gorilla stifled it. I kept my eyes on the goon and my sights in line with the Corinthian's head. If I put a bullet where his heart should be I wasn't sure he'd feel it.

'Let's remain calm,' the Corinthian said. 'Young lady, my associate will remove his hand in approximately five seconds. I expect you to be silent.'

The goon's hand came away, and Faye kept her mouth shut.

'What the hell are you doing?' I said to the Corinthian.

'Beginning a transaction,' he replied. 'You have something I want. I have someone you would prefer not to die. I think we can come to an arrangement.'

'The only thing I have for you is in this gun,' I said. 'Where would you like them delivered?'

The Corinthian wasn't amused, and he wasn't angry. When it came to human emotions, he was never much of anything.

'You were fond of witticisms like that when you worked for me,' he said. 'I never understood the reason. Why do you say these things, Strange? What do you think you'll get for being such a funny man?

'You have something that belongs to Homeland Security,' the Corinthian said. 'A memo.'

There was no point in feigning ignorance. If the Corinthian was here, he'd done his homework. He couldn't know I had the list as well, or he would have demanded them both.

'Are you Stonebridge's errand boy now?'

'Don't try to bait me,' he said, 'you know it never works.'

'I haven't got this memo,' I said.

'Of course you do.'

'Stonebridge is delusional. He lost something and accused me of stealing it because we have a history.'

'You seem to have a history with a great many people.'

'I'm telling you, he was dropped on the head as a child,' I said. 'You work for him, you should know what he's like.'

'I don't work for him,' the Corinthian said. 'I'm an independent contractor.'

'Like a McDonald's franchise?'

'You can stop stalling,' the Corinthian said. 'Whoever you're waiting for isn't coming.'

'I'm not stalling,' I said. 'I'm trying to figure out how you got mixed up in this racket in the first place. It's not easy imagining you as a federal employee.'

The Corinthian sighed as if a child had asked him to read a story for the sixth time. 'I became aware of a business opportunity, and I pursued it. There is no mystery. That is simply how the system works.'

'You forget I've watched you operate. There's always another angle.'

'Perhaps, but imaginary angles have no bearing on where the guns in this room are pointed.'

'Even if I give you this memo, Stonebridge will never believe that I didn't make copies.'

'I'm sure he'll follow that up with you,' the Corinthian said. 'My contract is for the memo only.'

It was a lie of course. If Stonebridge really had put him up to this, then killing me would be the second priority after recovering the memo. Both men shared a fondness for grudges.

'Please, Felix,' Faye pleaded. There were tears in her eyes.

I didn't consider myself responsible for my client's safety. I wasn't a bodyguard, and lawyers were the greatest threat to most of my customers anyway. I frowned on violence against clients as a general rule – it was bad for business – and for people I liked a lot less than Faye. So far I hadn't lost a single one except Ezekiel White, and he didn't count.

'Just give him what he wants,' Faye said. 'I know I have no right to ask you, just because you served with Isaac in the Holy Land, but—'

Faye broke off. It was a simple mistake: Isaac and I had served together in Tehran, not the Holy Land. Had I not been looking right at her, I could have put it down to the new experience of being menaced with a firearm. There was as much fear on her face as there should have been, but I caught a flash of something else. It was a quick burst of anger, self-directed, an actress's disappointment in herself for misremembering a line.

'Shoot her,' I said. 'I don't have the memo. Tell Stonebridge he's insane. Tell me what Faye did for you,' I said to the Corinthian.

'I've already told you, Felix,' Faye yelled, but not fast enough to mask a flicker of confusion in the Corinthian's eyes.

'Don't be coy, I already know she was your employee. Who was the first?' I said keeping it vague so he couldn't fashion a plausible lie.

'I don't have time for your usual games, Strange.'

So Faye hadn't told him about our run-in. The Corinthian was a master of detail; if they'd concocted the story about Faye's bondage together, he'd know every word. Maybe she was afraid of what the Corinthian would do to her, or Faye had an agenda of her own. Her story was lurid enough to be a provocation, and the Corinthian would have told her about our violent history. After I got the list she probably would have set me on her boss, ready to go through our pockets when we were done killing each other. It might have worked if the Corinthian hadn't queered her timeline with this unscheduled piece of theatre.

The Corinthian was surprised. It was the best news I'd had all day. The gorilla looked to his master. His composure had returned, but the Corinthian didn't compromise himself any more with speech.

'Felix, what are you saying—' Faye said.

'How long have you worked for them?'

'I told you—'

'Not before, now.'

'You're making a mistake, Strange,' the Corinthian said.

'Am I? I know she worked for you.' I realized the Corinthian had given me the outlines of his scam without being aware of it. 'Isaac worked for Stonebridge. If Faye got close to him, then you'd have a man on the inside.'

'He promised he'd get Isaac back if I gave him the memo,' Faye said. 'Isn't that what we both want?'

'Save it,' I said. 'I can't believe a word you say.'

'You know I will kill her,' the Corinthian said.

Faye pleaded with me with her eyes. She'd stopped acting; the fear was real and burning her up inside. Everyone in the room agreed that the Corinthian wouldn't hesitate to kill her. Whatever her role had been, she was definitely a hostage now.

'Maybe you'd like me to do it for you,' I said. I moved my gun in line with Faye. 'There's about six feet between us. At that range, with this calibre, I might get two for one.'

'Don't be stupid, Strange,' the Corinthian said. 'I know Faye isn't the only woman you care about.'

Something grabbed a fistful of my guts and began to twist. Before I had a chance to ask the Corinthian what the hell he'd meant, the gorilla panicked.

He should have moved her left. The gun was in the gorilla's right hand. He should have pulled her left to cover his body with hers and clear a path for his gun. It should have been left.

The first round hit Faye in the chest as the gorilla pushed her right and dived left. I saw a flash from his muzzle, a quick starburst, but I didn't feel anything. I fired two more shots, and they found the man they were looking for.

The Corinthian was gone. I heard a crash in the bedroom. The window that faced on to the alley behind the building was open. I caught a glimpse of the Corinthian on the fire escape before I had to duck a burst of automatic fire from the street below. I stuck my gun out the broken window and fired back. I heard squealing tyres and peeked out the shredded window frame. The Corinthian and his back-up were gone.

I went back to the living room. The whole apartment was quiet, except for the sound of blood seeping into Faye's lungs as she tried to breathe. The police would be on their way, an ambulance too. I tore a piece from Faye's blouse and tried to slow the bleeding. She was drowning in her own blood. Faye was already dead, and her body would realize it before help arrived.

'Faye,' I said, 'I need to know where Isaac is.'

'Pretend. That's what he wanted me to do. What I always did. Find the memo.'

'Where is Isaac?'

'I don't know,' she said, through stolen breaths. 'You were right. I was supposed to get close to Isaac. He disappeared before it could be set up.'

'What about the pictures?'

Faye didn't look surprised that I knew about them, but she was past a lot of things now. 'Fakes.'

I'd looked at the pictures briefly, in bad light, so it was possible they were composites. I kicked myself for not lifting one when I had the chance, but it had been too easy to believe my lying eyes.

'He told me to play the worried girlfriend, see who turned up. He didn't expect you.'

Her breathing had become a series of short rasps.

'Where is he?' she said.

'The Corinthian is gone.'

'No, the man who shot me.' She had the unfocused eyes of a blind man. They looked clear and healthy only because we saw a mirror there, instead of a window. 'I met him before, but I can't remember what he looks like,' Faye said. 'Do you know who he is?'

My gun was still warm. It had discharged three rounds. Two were in the hired help. The other was somewhere inside my arms. I hadn't meant to hit her, even when I realized she was working full-time for the Corinthian. I hadn't meant to, but that didn't change what was going to happen.

'Don't be afraid,' I said. 'He's gone. He's not coming back.'

'Stay with me,' she said. 'I don't want to die alone.'

I put a pillow under her head. It was all I could do. I held her hand and listened to her breath slow and fall away. Even when one part of my brain knew she was dead, the other refused to let go. Only the sound of approaching sirens made me flee from what I had done.

TWENTY

I was back on the road, driving away from sirens for a second time that night. Sooner or later ballistics would match the bullet in Faye with the rounds I'd fired at the Starlight last year. It should have bothered me more than it did. There were so many terrible things in motion right now, the few days it would take to make the match seemed like the distant future.

The only other woman I cared about was Iris, and she'd told me she was staying at the Excelsior Hotel. It was also in Queens, so I didn't have that far to go. The news was full of the Emerson bombing. The authorities hadn't leaked any details yet, which showed an unusual probity on their part. Commentators spanning the range from ill-informed to disingenuous all but announced that twelve-foot super-Arabs had set the device while selling white virgins into slavery. I turned the radio off. I wasn't in the mood for light entertainment.

When I got my first glance at the Excelsior, I thought maybe Iris had given me a false address. It was a motel, no matter what the name said. Ten rooms stood side by side with parking in front, the manager's office forming the perpendicular end of the building's L-shape. It wasn't far from Grand Central Parkway, and probably depended on the highway and Shea Stadium for its business. From the look of it, the Excelsior was grateful for whatever it could get.

I parked in a space in front of the office and went inside. Before the door had closed behind me I'd had to re-evaluate my first impression of the place. Outside, the paint was peeling on the aluminium siding and the motel windows had an unhealthy sheen. The office inside was clean and correct in every particular. The linoleum under my feet was swept and in good condition. The courtesy chairs facing the window had no shiny patches on the arms or tears in the upholstery. The front desk was dusted and polished to a professional standard, and even the wallpaper looked new. I couldn't reconcile the pride and means on display inside with the indifferent shabbiness outside.

The woman behind the front desk only made me more suspicious. She was old but not frail, a small woman who gave the impression she had once been taller. She didn't have that professional weariness that afflicted people in the service industry the way miners came down with black lung. Instead of a false smile for sales purposes, I felt my measurements being taken.

'Excuse me, I'm—'

'I know why you're here, Mr Strange.'

Her sharp brown eyes jumped a little when I reached for my gun. It was such an automatic reaction it took me a second to realize what I was doing.

'Sorry,' I said, but left my hand on the grip. 'Have we met before?'

'No, Mr Strange,' the woman said. 'But everyone here knows who you are.'

When I added the woman's diction to the mismatched decor, it became clear what kind of joint I was standing in. The Excelsior was a safe house for the Crusade of Love.

'I'm Mrs Brown,' the woman said.

'I figured,' I replied, pointing to the brass nameplate resting on the desk. I wished that the rest of Mrs Brown's dialogue had subtitles. She was not an easy woman to read.

'Are you looking for Iris, Mr Strange?' Mrs Brown said. 'I'm glad you showed the manners to call here instead of her room.'

'I don't know which room is hers, and it's kind of an emergency.'

I wasn't expecting Mrs Brown to panic, but I was surprised how little effect the word 'emergency' had on her.

'Is she involved?'

'I don't know,' I said. 'Threats have been made by a man who can make them reality.'

'I haven't seen Iris in three days. That isn't unusual,' she said, as she saw the blood in my face find a new home. 'She's a very independent girl.'

They had her. Whether it was the Corinthian or Fisher Partners didn't matter; Iris had helped me figure that out. I didn't have any evidence for my conclusion, and that might allow me to deny it for as long as I stayed within the walnut-panelled confines of this office.

Mrs Brown was biting the bottom right corner of her lip. I sensed this was a sign of intense worry on her part, probably brought on by whatever train wreck my face resembled.

'I need to see her room.'

Mrs Brown led me to room five, unlocked the door, and left without a word. Whatever I discovered in there, she wasn't ready for it yet.

When I looked inside, I realized how much I'd been hoping that Iris had made the place her own. I was tired of hotel rooms, inside and through a lens at a distance. I was tired of searching their lumpy beds and battered nightstands for signs of bad judgement and weakness. I was tired of chasing people I knew wouldn't be there.

The closet was full of clothes owned by a woman too classy to stay here. Shoes were arranged below the dresses, accessories in a curio box on a desk across from the bed. I looked through the small teak drawers – inlaid with an Asian pattern I didn't recognize – but all I turned up was treasure.

The bathroom was clean in every sense of the word. I ended where I had begun: standing in the centre of a room that had no answers. I looked at the skirting board and considered getting my hands dirty. Mrs Brown wouldn't like it, and Iris wouldn't have ripped up the room for that reason.

On the nightstand was a picture of Iris and Brother Isaiah. It was from the distant past: when she was still a junkie, and he was still alive. The background was a church hall: people mingling in front of a long table where old ladies made tea on an industrial scale. The scars of Iris's unsaved life hadn't begun to fade yet. She looked tired, afraid and grateful to be alive. Brother Isaiah looked the same as when I'd first seen him, lying on that bed in Manhattan and waiting for his death to be solved.

When I put the picture back on the nightstand, I noticed that the lamp beside it was unplugged. It was heavy and vaguely rococo: the kind of lamp housewives assumed the aristocracy would have owned if they'd had access to moulded plastic. I checked the cord and base and everything seemed to be in order. The neck was a single cylinder screwed into the other two parts. I took off the shade and unscrewed the top.

A single sheet of paper was inside, as white as the lamp's neck.

Felix,
If you are reading this, then something has gone wrong. I found out where they took my friend Salda. They held him in a warehouse near La Guardia. The sign on the

building is for a company called Executive Transport Services. I'm going to sit on the place for a while and see what turns up. Maybe I'll live long enough to show it to you.

You were right to tell me to leave. I had no idea what they were capable of. If you want to repay me for helping you, then don't come after me. I know you'll want an excuse to feel guilty; nobody understands that better than a good Christian. Let me go. Wherever I am now, I want to know that you are somewhere else, a safe place where you are happy, healthy and pissing someone off.

Iris

I couldn't process what I'd read. I was caught in the moment after a flashbang detonates: the overloaded retina transmitting that single, frozen image of the world just before the explosion. It was like the moment I realized my mother was dead.

Iris was gone.

I looked up and saw Mrs Brown standing over me. She was doing it in a protective way, putting her body between me and whatever shadows might come through the crack under the door.

I gave her the letter. Its contents caused great pain, but no surprise.

'You already knew they'd taken her, didn't you?'

'I suspected, but I knew as soon as you arrived,' Mrs Brown said.

'I'm going to that warehouse.'

'She wouldn't want you to.'

'I know,' I said. 'But what's happening is bigger than her.' The words were bitter; I had to force them out with my tongue. 'Mrs Brown, you know what I think of your organization, but take the advice of an old enemy: get everyone you can out of the country now.' The old lady was tough. Even after what she'd just read, Mrs Brown didn't seem shaken. 'If you have any doubts, talk to the veterans in your organization. Tell them Task Force Seventeen has come home.'

I wasn't sure she was convinced, but I'd said everything I could. I picked up the picture on the bedside table. 'May I keep this?'

She nodded.

'I'll find her, Mrs Brown.'

'I pray that you will,' she replied. 'As for myself, I have no doubt I will see that dear girl again.'

I knew she meant their reunion would be in the next life. After her statement, Mrs Brown allowed herself to weep. I took the old woman in my arms and let her cry for both of us. I was too angry for tears.

I didn't want to imagine what they'd done to her, but I didn't have to. It had been done by six men – that was the usual number – masked and all in black, Satanists who only knew one ritual. Four had held her down while the other two cut the clothes from her body. The shreds had been bagged. A sedative was administered by anal suppository. They photographed her before she was swaddled in diapers and clothed in an orange jumpsuit, gift-wrapped for a waiting van. If the team knew its job, the whole operation took around five minutes. That was the average time for the old pros at Seventeen.

'I'll give you a moment,' Mrs Brown said, suddenly ashamed of her pain, and left the room.

I sat on the bed and pinched the chenille between my fingers. The material was already intimately familiar, a déjà vu in my fingertips. I had a vision of myself, sitting on a bed in an endless succession of rooms just like this one, waiting for some sign of her from a God I did not believe in.

The warehouse was right where Iris said it would be. The main building was a three-storey aluminium box, windowless and taciturn with rust. Smaller outbuildings clustered around it. 'Executive Transport Services' was written on the side, in blue and gold, the words floodlit in the darkness of an empty part of town.

I sat on the building for an hour, but no one came or went. The security set-up was odd. The perimeter was your standard chain-link fence topped with razor wire. What aroused my interest was the lack of foot or vehicle patrols, and the complete absence of cameras.

I'd stopped at an all-night chain store and picked up a few things I thought would come in handy. In the brown bag on the passenger seat was a set of bolt cutters for the fence I'd assumed would be there. There were some other things in the bag as well. I hoped they were just along for the ride.

The new cutters made a me-sized hole in the fence without much effort. There was about a hundred yards of illuminated concrete between my position and the main building. I played hopscotch with its smaller brothers. That got me within thirty paces of a side door. I charged across the rest.

I unscrewed the bulb above the door for some privacy, and started on the lock. It was difficult work. The lock was rusted, and would have been stubborn even if I'd had a key. My great temptation during those awkward, fiddly moments was just to kick the fucking thing down, but old training kept my head on straight.

The door opened into a series of storage rooms separated by metal sliding doors. There were no wood splinters, broken pallets or other litter that would suggest an active place of business. I entered each one expecting trouble, but even vermin had become particular about inhabiting a place like this.

The last room gave way to a much bigger loading area that made up most of the building. Naked bulbs hanging from the ceiling illuminated the only cargo awaiting pick-up. There were seven rows of naked box-spring beds, twelve beds to a row, each one perfectly spaced from its neighbours. It looked like the remains of a shelter set up in the aftermath of a disaster.

Like the smaller rooms, the floor had been swept completely clean. I grid-searched the room with a pocket light. There were no old bags or receipts, dead cigarettes or paper cups with smudges around the edges, none of the pocket lint of modern life that snoops like me depended on. It took a lot of discipline to leave nothing behind. Even professionals made mistakes.

I found that mistake under the fourth bed in the fifth row. A chain had been hooked to the bed frame. At the other end was a standard-issue handcuff. I walked my light over it. On the inside of the hinge were a few brown spots. I would have thought it was rust if I'd had less experience with dried blood. Logic told me it couldn't be Iris's, that she was probably taken somewhere else, but my imagination said otherwise.

Seven rows, twelve beds to a row. Eighty-four people were handcuffed to these beds, blindfolded, headphones on to muffle each other's cries. Eighty-four units of human cargo waiting to be shipped to an undisclosed location.

There were two sets of old tracks from a big vehicle in the cargo dock, eighteen-wheelers most likely. You could fit eighty-four people in two trucks if you packed them tight enough. That didn't tell me how many shipments they made. Did this warehouse empty once a week, or twice a day? Just how much volume could Fisher Partners handle?

I searched the loading area again. On the third bed in the second row I found something I'd missed the first time.

Scratched into the bed's grey paint were two letters: 'MA'. There were smudges of dried blood around the initials; one had a few whorls that might have been part of a fingerprint. The occupant of this bed had scratched his or her initials into the paint with a fingernail and had paid the price. Pain and blood to remind someone, anyone, that they had existed.

I'd never know what those initials stood for. The person who had scratched them into the iron could be a man or a woman, young or old, everyone and no one. Two letters were all that was left of a human being, and that was more than would remain of the others who had passed through here.

The warehouse was completely silent. I had expected the Fishermen to return at any moment, or at the very least for some rent-a-cops to notice my work on the door. I wondered why, after taking so much care with everything else, they'd left the beds at all. It could only mean that they were coming back. Whatever had happened here was not even close to finished.

TWENTY-ONE

I retreated to my office and closed the blinds against the world. I had no real leads, and even less evidence to convince someone else of what had happened. I sat in my chair and tried to think of my next move. Anything was better than sitting here waiting for things to get worse.

I may not have had any clues, but I did know a man who might give me one. Stonebridge was out there right now, doing something offensive like spending his blood money, sleeping well, or breathing. He wouldn't tell me much, and if I put the screws on the coward he'd sing whatever song he thought I wanted to hear. The one thing I could count on was that Stonebridge wasn't nearly as careful as the men who'd swept that warehouse. I might find something useful lying around the house, after I killed him.

Taped under the sink was an old snub-nosed thirty-eight. I'd taken it off an irate husband who'd been dumb enough to take his mistress to the same hotel for two months in a row, but smart enough not to take a shot at me. God knows where he'd found it; odds were on the gutter. I suspected there were already a few bodies on this piece of tempered steel. It wouldn't mind one more.

I got together everything I thought I'd need. After I visited Stonebridge, I'd be in the wind. I had the microdot blow-ups and the Fisher Partners list. The burglars had missed a small stash of medication hidden in a bag in the toilet tank. Adding in what I had in the storage locker near Grand Central, I had enough to last me for three months, give or take.

In finding space in my pockets for the pills, I took out Cassandra's phone. She was the only one who seemed to know anything about the Fishermen; the only one not trying to kill me, anyway. Once I killed Stonebridge my path would be fixed. I'd have to leave the city in hours, and Benny would have to face a lot of questions about why his old friend had just murdered a federal official. Cassandra might be able to give me an alternative. I was too old to believe in fairy godmothers, but too desperate to care.

I called the only number in the phone's memory.

'I've been expecting your call,' Cassandra said. It was the same mechanical voice: sexless, ageless and difficult to trust.

'They took her,' I said.

There was a silence. I thought Cassandra might have hung up.

'Tell me her name,' Cassandra said.

'Iris.' It had become such a difficult word to say.

'Is she a blood relation? Someone you love?'

I told Cassandra the whole story: the meeting in New York, her connection to the death of Brother Isaiah, how a woman whose real name I didn't know could mean so much to a poor sap like me. It was a crazy thing to do, maybe even dangerous, but I had to tell someone.

'You said one day I'd need your help,' I said. 'Today is that day.'

'I can't do that, Felix,' she said.

'I'm begging you.' I would have been on my knees if the eyes on the other end of the line could see me.

'I didn't say won't, I said can't. I want to help you, Felix, you have no idea how much I do, but she's gone.'

'They can't disappear her into the air or send her to the moon. Iris is still alive, Cassandra, and she has to be somewhere.'

'I know what I'm asking of you, but please do not pursue this woman. You will not find her, and you'll probably get yourself killed.

'We don't have much time,' Cassandra said, when I didn't speak. 'Fisher Partners will kill Director Sands tonight. His plane will crash on its way to New York. Without him, you will be as naked as the day you were born. Find a quiet corner to put your heart in, and listen to what I know your head is telling you. Iris is in the system now, and the rabbit hole only goes one way.'

I killed the line. I would have thrown the phone across the room if it hadn't slipped from my lifeless hand. Iris was gone. Those three words kept bouncing around my brain like a low-calibre bullet. The walls of my home and place of business, one of the few places I felt safe, began to march in.

Something Cassandra had said was bouncing around in my head too. The line about my life being in danger wasn't surprising: there's no better way to gain someone's confidence than pretending that you're looking out for their safety. It was what Cassandra had said about FBI Director Sands that I couldn't stop thinking about. For a lie it was very specific, and very soon.

I hadn't looked at the list yet. The night had been busy, but I couldn't delay reading it any longer. I started at the top and skimmed for names I recognized. I usually had the news on when I worked, but I was ahead of it this time.

I got a shock at eighty-six. David Presmore, the assistant director in charge of the FBI's New York office. He was Benny's boss. I picked up the phone to call him and put it down again just as fast. If Presmore was on the list, Benny might be as well.

Benny was the hundred and ninth name. I looked at it, typed in neat black ink like any other document, and felt the blood in my head rush for the safety of my feet. I didn't pick up the phone this time. My line to the FBI was supposed to be secure, but I couldn't trust that now. Before tonight I never would have imagined that the Elders would attack the upper ranks of the Bureau. They were going after Presmore, and Director Sands was only one more rung on the chain of command.

All bets were now off. I'd have to go over to Benny's place, even if that plan had risks of its own. He'd never believe me unless I told him in person anyway.

I shoved Cassandra's phone in my pocket and ran out the door.

For once traffic was going my way. I was off Williamsburg Bridge and on to the expressway before I allowed myself to think about the obvious implication of Benny's name being on the list. If he was there, then so was I. We'd both heard White's confession, so taking one without the other was pointless. Benny and I came as a set.

Wherever I was on the list, it was below one hundred and nine. I knew I should have been worried, scared maybe, but all I felt was a little relief. Ever since that night, I'd expected them to come after me sooner or later. I was almost glad the wait was over. With my name so far down the list, I'd obviously made less of an impression than I thought. I'd have to make them regret their decision to leave me in the wild.

Benny had moved to a new house three months before his daughter had been born. The third-floor walk-up they used to live in had become impractical once prams were involved. Their new place was a post-war red-brick house; the kind of starter home he would have been able to buy fresh out of the army if he'd come home from a different war. Being a Bureau agent in

New York had always been a hardship. The cost-of-living adjustment to an agent's salary had never kept up with inflation. A few years ago this house would have been out of Benny's price range, but now a government job was one of the few regular pay cheques around.

I opened the glass outer door and worked the knocker hard. The sound seemed to reverberate off the entire quiet street. Benny wasn't going to be happy to see me. Saving his life might not be enough to improve his mood.

A light went on inside, which cued the muffled sound of wailing. Benny opened the door wearing a frayed housecoat and his wife's pink slippers. A shotgun pointed in the vicinity of my head completed the outfit. It was a toss-up whether his face or the weapon had a more threatening expression. When he saw who it was he lowered the shotgun, but not by much.

'I'm not an intruder, Benny.'

'It's four in the morning, you've woken my child, and I haven't had a decent night's sleep in six months,' Benny said. 'Let's hear your excuse first. Then I'll decide.'

'The truce is over.'

'Is this one of your crazy hunches?' Benny said.

'They're coming after all of us, Benny, even the director. I've got more proof than you'll ever want to see.'

Benny's face grew darker still. I was relieved the expression was directed at someone else. He leaned the shotgun beside the door and waved me inside.

'I'll make some coffee,' he said, leading me to the kitchen. 'Start from the beginning, you sleep-murdering fucknuts.'

'We don't have time, Benny. The director is in danger. The Elders are going to hit his plane.'

Benny was so stunned he didn't immediately ask me what the hell I was talking about.

'He's flying down tonight, isn't he?'

'How did you know that? No one outside the Bureau is supposed to know.'

'I'll explain everything, Benny, I promise. Just stop him from getting on the Bureau's jet. If I'm wrong you can have me committed later.'

'If you're wrong, the director will sign the papers himself. Gimme a minute,' he said, and disappeared upstairs.

I waited for the coffee to brew and looked around Benny's brand-new kitchen. A glass sliding door led to the back yard, an old barbecue just visible in the darkness. On the brushed aluminium fridge were pictures of Sharon, their little girl, plus bills, a list of emergency numbers, and a reminder for Benny to call his mother. It felt like a home, a place they would think fondly of after they were forced to flee. I wished they'd had more time here to make memories they could be nostalgic for.

Miriam wandered in, rubbing sleep from her eyes. She was a petite woman with wide hazel eyes and long dark hair left to roam free in the night. She wore a pink robe, faded with repeated washing, and was barefoot after Benny's larceny. Miriam was easy on the eyes at any time of day, but I kept that fact to myself.

'You picked a funny time to visit, Felix,' she said.

'I'm sorry, Miriam, it couldn't wait.'

'It never can. I suppose if I'd wanted peace and quiet, I shouldn't have married a fed.'

Miriam and I had one of those strange friendships formed through an intermediary. I could tell you about her fondness for blueberry pie, her preference for shades of red, but I don't think I'd had a conversation with her for more than five minutes that didn't involve Benny. She'd taken an interest in me the way a kind heart keeps an eye on strays, but I'm sure it was the same for her. We mostly knew each other through the reports of her husband.

I was about to ask her about the baby, when I realized Miriam was staring at me.

'Did somebody break your heart, Felix?'

'Excuse me?'

'You got that look on your face; I can recognize it a mile off. What was her name?'

I felt something inside me trying to get out. Back at the office I'd locked my grief in a brand-new cage, and I wasn't about to let it run free now.

'Iris.'

'So what happened?' She was as direct as her spouse.

'She left,' I said. 'Disappeared.'

'No Dear John letter or anything?'

'It wasn't really her decision.'

'Still, what kind of woman . . .'

Miriam trailed off when she caught me staring, though this time it was over her shoulder. Benny stood behind her in the doorway, paler than I'd ever seen him. He looked like he'd seen a ghost, or heard that someone close had recently become one.

'Miriam, give us a minute.'

'Benny, what's going on?'

'Just one minute. I'll come up later.'

She looked at us like conspirators plotting against her peace of mind and left. I slid a chair out from the kitchen table so Benny could collapse into it.

'What's happened?'

'Director Sands was already on his way. The plane crashed outside Baltimore. No survivors.'

I had never been so unhappy at being correct. 'I'm sorry, Benny.'

'The secure line is going crazy. The Bureau's in chaos. They don't know whether it was an accident or terrorism.'

'We know what it was.'

I showed him the list. I pointed out ADIC Presmore's name, and told him what the number next to it meant. Benny was in a dream. I wasn't sure if he could even hear me.

'Sands wasn't a kind man,' Benny said, to someone I couldn't see. 'In a different time, he might not have been considered a good one. But he was the only one willing to stand up to those Jesus freaks. He was the last man in this country with a fucking spine.'

'Benny,' I said, grabbing his shoulder, 'you have to get your family ready. Go up to Canada. That number beside your name, it means erasure. They're going to wipe out any trace of your existence, reverse your birth. They did it to Isaac, and they'll do it to us.'

'The Director's name isn't here,' Benny said.

'This list is only for New York. A Fisher Partners team in DC would have sabotaged the plane. Do the math Benny: your boss is on list, and so are we.'

'I have to warn Dave,' Benny said, meaning Assistant Director in Charge Presmore, his boss. 'I called him right after I heard the news. He didn't pick up.'

There was a good chance they'd already gotten to him. Benny knew that, but he was going anyway.

'I'm coming along.'

Benny nodded and stood up. 'How am I going to explain this to Miriam?' He sighed, and walked up the staircase like it ended in a scaffold.

I poured a cup of black coffee and stirred it for want of any other way to keep my hands occupied. I hadn't really thought about my next move after coming here. I still entertained the idea of hunting down Stonebridge, but I didn't want Benny involved. After we discovered Presmore's fate, Benny was going to Canada if I had to drag him there myself.

The crying upstairs resumed as the voices grew louder.

'Presmore was my rabbi at the Bureau, Miriam. You've been to his house, met his children. He's guided and protected me. The least I can fucking do is try to warn him.'

'And then what? You don't sound like you're coming to Canada.'

'Of course I fucking will.'

'When?'

Benny took his time answering. 'Felix and I have to get to the bottom of this.'

'Have you lost your fucking mind?' Miriam said. It was the first time I'd ever heard her swear.

'It's my job, Miriam, and I owe it to the director.'

'And what about your family? What do you owe us?'

'You knew what I did when you married me.'

'And I accepted it. It was my decision. Sharon doesn't get to make that choice. Now I have to ask if today is the day my little girl loses her father.'

'Nobody's gonna die tonight,' Benny said.

It was obvious to me, one flight down, that he wasn't positive about that.

'Did Felix put you up to this?'

'What the hell are you talking about?'

'I adore Felix, you know I do. But he's crazy. You've said it yourself. He hasn't been right since the war.'

'Felix didn't put me up to anything.'

'You're an agent with the FBI, for God's sake. They would have left you alone if it wasn't for him.'

A door slammed. Sharon had stopped crying, or the sound was now locked away. I stared out the window. The light in the kitchen was too bright. Instead of the house next door, the glass showed the unwelcome sight of my own reflection.

Miriam came into the kitchen. Her eyes were red with furious tears. I'll never forget the way she looked at me for as long as I live. It was a kind of hatred, born from the most sympathetic of fears.

'Miriam, I—'

The slap hit hard. I'd been on the receiving end of a smack before, but when women hit that way it was usually symbolic. Miriam's hand was meant to cause pain, and it did in many different ways. Before the sound had echoed off the floor, she grabbed my face and pressed it close to hers.

'You bring my husband back to me in one piece,' she whispered in my ear, 'or I'll hunt you down.'

She let go. Miriam refused to look at me again, and went upstairs to her child.

Benny came down a minute later fully dressed, his face set like a mask for war.

We stood there for a little while. I don't know why. Benny took one last look around his kitchen, as if he already hadn't seen it for years.

'Let's go.'

TWENTY-TWO

Presmore's place was out in Connecticut. I called Cal's contact number while we were on the road. It took more rings than before to get an answer. There was no hello, as usual, and the silence sounded hostile this time.

'I have a rush order,' I said.

'What's your address?' the woman asked, trying to shake the sleep from her voice.

I read off Presmore's address. 'It's a large order, ma'am. We'll need all the cigars you have.'

'Understood. Delivery will be about an hour.'

I hung up.

'Who was that?' Benny said.

'Friends of Isaac's. I have a feeling we'll need all the help we can get.'

Before Benny could ask, I filled him in on the whole rotten story. I think the part that surprised him most was Isaac working with Cal and Jack. Neither of us had thought he had something like that in him.

'So you think this Jefferson who's handling Cal is Defense Intelligence?'

'Cassandra said the Founder Initiative is a DIA operation. They have people like Jefferson all over the country recruiting veterans to be the Pentagon's eyes and ears. They're building their very own red, white and blue orchestra right under the Elders' noses.'

'Wait,' Benny said, 'isn't Cassandra that other motherfucker we haven't met and shouldn't trust?'

'She was right about the director.'

He didn't say anything for a while. I had the feeling whatever he was turning over in his head wasn't good.

'Everything I've done since the war, all those ways I tried to make something out of that hill of shit they gave us, it's all going to disappear tonight,' he finally said. 'Ten years of my life, and the Elders are just going to wipe it away.'

Benny opened his mouth again, but no words came out. This man who had once been in contention for the title of worst mouth in the army had no oaths that could express his anger. Instead he hammered on the steering wheel so hard I thought he was going to crash the car.

'You still have Miriam and Sharon. The Elders can't take them away from you.'

He reminded me with a look that we both knew that wasn't true, but it calmed him down a little. We drove the rest of the way in silence, too hurt to nurse each other's wounds.

We parked a few blocks away from Presmore's house. Dawn was threatening to break when we got there, but it had only shown itself at the bottom of the horizon. The street was as quiet as you'd expect. Not even dogs had noted our arrival.

'Time to cowboy up,' Benny said.

He got out of the car and I followed him to its rear.

'You've got your little black bag, I've got the trunk of doom,' he said and popped the back.

Inside were two armoured vests, three flashbangs, a set of burglar tools, a spare tyre, the wadded remains of half a dozen drive-through meals, and a box of shotgun shells.

314

'Ah, fuck,' Benny said. 'I forgot the shotgun at home.'

'That's it?' I said. 'This is your fucking arsenal?'

'I don't see you bringing anything to the table. Take one of these,' he said, shoving a vest at me, 'just in case you're still interested in staying alive.'

I strapped on the vest, and pulled my suit jacket over it on the off-chance I had to look respectable. I claimed one of the flashbangs as well.

'Ready?' Benny said.

I shrugged, and that was as good as yes.

Assistant Director in Charge Presmore's house was a white-washed colonial affair, pillars holding up the porch and three chimneys reaching for the sky. It was bigger and fancier than I'd expected. 'Pretty swanky for a fed,' I said.

'He married money.'

The properties around here had a lot of lawn between them, and Presmore's was no exception: there was enough grassland to graze cattle on. The good people who lived here had paid good money for that land, to protect their privacy and their views. It made me feel exposed.

'Come on,' Benny said, starting up the cobbled path to the door. 'Let me do the talking.'

When we got to the front door, we found it half open. All the lights in the front room were on, as if they were expecting guests.

'Shit,' Benny said under his breath. We drew our weapons and went in.

The inside was trashed. To our left was a kind of sitting room, two sofas arranged to make the most of the floor-to-ceiling windows that flanked the front door. A lamp had been thrown off a nearby end table. Books from the shelves on the back wall were on the floor. The furniture was slashed and turned over. It was too methodical for a burglary, and they'd left the stereo and the TV.

The track lighting showed us an irregular blood trail. It started a few steps in from the front door, and led towards the back of the house through the central corridor.

'Do you know where that trail is going?' I asked.

'The kitchen, I think.'

Down the central corridor were stairs leading up. There were open doorways to the right and left.

Benny knelt near the bookshelf. He stood with a photograph framed in gold and broken glass. It was the Presmore family: two parents, two girls, and a little boy. The background was a church, maybe Presbyterian, the photo the product of a fundraiser or some other congregational event. They smiled at the camera in their Sunday best, everyone happy and well-behaved.

'What was the number next to his name?'

'One hundred and ninety-nine. It's the code for secret rendition: they kidnap him and then deny he's in custody. They should have left the family alone,' I said. 'Maybe they're staying with relatives.'

Benny didn't say anything. His eyes were still on the picture.

'We might as well see if they left anything behind,' I said, knowing the chances weren't good. 'I'll take the blood trail, if—'

'I'll do it,' Benny said. 'If they're there, I want them to be found by a friend. You take the upstairs.'

The lights went out. Benny and I didn't need to consult with each other to know that diving behind the torn sofas in the front room was the best thing to do. The room had become an outline bathed in a greyish-orange light, the mix of moon and street light filtered through cream drapes. The front door was about twenty feet away, but those twenty feet were exposed to all three door-ways.

The Presmores had laid down real hardwood for their floors and stairs, and I silently thanked the pile of heiress money that had made it possible. Creaks came from the direction of the staircase. Benny signalled towards the left doorway and I nodded. I popped the pin on my flashbang and rolled it towards the stairs.

The sound was deafening, the hands over my ears little protection. I was up first. Behind us it sounded like an asthmatic had entered the room, a spasm of coughs further shredding the long-suffering furniture.

I got to the doorway first. I felt rather than saw a shape to my right, the lizard part of my brain warning of something near before I could process what my eyes were showing me. I caught the Fisherman's arm with mine as he tried to bring his gun into line. Once I had a hold of his arm, I could feel where the rest of his body was. I sensed the distribution of his weight, and the location of his other arm. As the old song went, all his bones were connected.

I found a soft point just below his wrist and dug in my thumb. The pain released his hold on the gun, which made an incredible racket in the silent house when it hit the floor. I twisted his wrist towards a point just past his shoulder. He got off a hook that rattled my skull, but without his balance he couldn't make it count. He was leaning towards me in an uncomfortable way to stop his wrist from breaking, and it put his head right where I wanted it. I struck the Fisherman in the neck with the soft part between my thumb and forefinger. He fell down coughing, and I put my heel to his temple. The whole thing lasted maybe three seconds.

I ripped the night vision goggles off his face and retrieved the sub-machine gun. Benny took a few shots through the doorway to cover me. When I put on the goggles, memories staggered me for a moment. Half my time in Tehran had been spent in this flat, greenish underworld. I'd hoped never to go back.

The room we retreated into must have been Presmore's study. A heavy oak desk, one of those Victorian revival jobs, faced a solarium that had been added to the side of the building. I could see awards and souvenirs on the walls, markers of a lifetime in public service, but there wasn't enough light to read them even if I'd had the time.

I poked my head around the corner, and saw two men taking cover behind the remains of the furniture. One would cover the other's advance towards the doorway. Before I had a chance to appreciate their training and discipline any further, the Fisherman at the rear opened up. It was lucky I crouched as I took cover; the rounds went right through the plaster and wood I was hiding behind. I fired blind into the room and retreated back to Presmore's desk. Benny added a little music of his own.

I remembered the throwaway piece I'd brought with me and slid it to Benny. He fired it and his own weapon at irregular intervals to try to convince the Fishermen there was another person in the study. Their ignorance of our true numbers was the only reason we were still alive. Behind us was a corridor that probably connected with the main one on its way to the kitchen. We couldn't defend one doorway, let alone both. Once they figured out there were only two of us, they'd hit us from both sides and that would be it. Considering the training I'd seen on display, our life expectancy was less than a minute.

I signalled a plan to Benny. He'd throw a flashbang into the front room. While they had that to play with, we'd drag the desk into the solarium. He gave me the finger. I shrugged back, which meant I was willing to entertain a better idea if he had one. Benny pulled a flashbang from his vest while mouthing a stream of profanity so wide it would have burned ears in a square mile had it been audible.

Benny threw the flashbang. We grabbed the desk with our eyes closed and dragged it to the entrance to the solarium. We vaulted over the desk and lay flat.

'Well, we've taken cover in a fucking glass house,' Benny said. 'I hope you know what you're doing.'

So did I. To my right was the street. The fence that separated the Presmore property from the next house was too high to vault over. The solarium was surrounded only by grass, which must have it made it a nice place to be in the mornings. What it meant for us was a dash across open ground to the street. If we threw our last flashbang, and there were only two Fishermen, it might distract them long enough for us to make it. Otherwise, we'd be ventilated before our shoes touched concrete.

My phone vibrated and I answered it. Benny gave me the dirtiest of looks and put a few rounds downrange.

'We're out front,' Cal said.

I could see a van parked across the street and a silhouette on the driver's side.

'Where are you?'

'Inside that solarium to the left of the house,' I said. 'Did you bring your big toys?'

'Enough to start a war.'

'Light the house up.'

'But you're inside,' Cal said.

'Just light it up,' I said, and closed the phone.

Benny was about to ask a question when the pre-dawn silence was broken by a sound that had never been heard in this part of the world. From behind their van, Cal opened up on the front of the house with a Squad Automatic Weapon. The light machine gun shattered the front windows, tore up the whitewashed façade, and hopefully made life hell for anyone in the front room.

There was answering fire from the windows on the first floor. Cal took cover. I saw another silhouette that I assumed to be Jack, holding the outline of an RPG. There was a glow and a whoosh as the grenade flew into the upper window, and then the contents of the first floor were blown out on to the lawn. Cal resumed his work with the SAW.

'Go,' I yelled to Benny, and popped up to cover his retreat. A Fisherman was waiting for me in the rear corridor. It felt like two swift punches to the chest. One of the bullets pushed against my cracked ribs. It was that pain, and not the impact of the bullets, that sent me through the solarium wall ass-backwards.

I half sat half fell on to the lawn and tried to get back the breath the bullets had stolen from me.

'Are you okay?' Benny's voice said above me.

'Vest,' I wheezed.

Benny grabbed me by the vest collar and dragged me back towards the street.

'I can walk, damn it,' I said, when my breath had returned.

Benny ignored me and kept firing at the solarium. I had no choice but to join in.

I struggled to my feet when we got to the road, hoping my suit wasn't as ruined as I thought it was. Sporadic fire was still coming from the windows. I could see a few silhouettes in the neighbouring houses, shadows behind a curtain topped with peeking, frightened faces. The police wouldn't be long.

'Get in the back,' Jack yelled, returning fire with an M4. We didn't need to be told twice. Benny and I dived in, safe under a blanket of automatic weapons fire.

Cal got in the driver's side. Jack took shotgun, still firing his rifle. We left the scene as fast as the old vehicle could accelerate. A final volley of fire punched holes in the side of the van.

'Benny, meet Cal and Jack,' I said, when we were a few blocks away from the Presmore house. 'They're friends of Isaac.'

'My ass is still where it should be because of you guys,' Benny said.

He and I were thinking the same thing: there was no good reason for us to be alive. The Fishermen in that house weren't the lifers and zeroes that Stonebridge had deputized and surrounded himself with. They were professionals, probably ex-Seventeen. I'd seen them work before, and didn't fancy our chances if we met them again.

'The cops will be on their way,' Cal said. 'They could be setting up roadblocks right now.'

'Let's find somewhere quiet,' I said.

Jack directed us to a small parking lot surrounded by forest. It was a place for day-trippers and nature lovers to leave their technology behind for a few hours. At this time of morning, it was completely empty. We got out to stretch our legs and figure out a plan.

'Why did they hit the director now?' Jack said.

'They had to eventually,' Benny replied. 'All missing persons cases go through us. Sooner or later an agent would have connected the dots. Even if he kept his mouth shut, word would get out eventually. They couldn't take the risk of leaving us independent.'

'Some of the agents might still be loyal to his memory, and willing to resist,' I said.

'If they resist, they won't win. The Elders have been seeding the Bureau with their own assholes for years, creating new positions if they had to. Add in the careerists and the followers, and the odds aren't good.'

Benny struck the side of the van and said something obscene in Hebrew.

'We have to fight them now,' Jack said.

'There was one team in that house,' I said. 'We surprised them, Jack, and we barely got out alive. There are hundreds of Fishermen, and a few thousand more thugs at their beck and call.'

'I think it's time you gentlemen met our mutual friend,' Cal said.

'That's a good idea but we need to split up first. I've got someone to see, and Benny has a family to meet.'

'This isn't a good time to be making social calls,' Cal said. 'Do you need to warn someone?'

'I have to meet Cassandra.'

Cal's white brows knitted together. 'You told me you didn't know where she is.'

'I don't. Now that we have the list, I'll arrange a meeting.'

'It's too much of a risk,' Cal said. 'Without the Bureau, you'll have no protection. You'll get picked up by the cops or worse.'

'I'll worry about that.'

'Jefferson has told me to secure you both and the list,' Cal said.

Jack was as surprised by Cal's tone as we were. I wondered if he knew who he was really working for.

'That doesn't sound like a request, Cal. Last time I checked I don't work for Jefferson.'

'Jesus Christ, Felix, what's your problem?' Jack said. 'We've saved your ass twice. What more do you need to trust us?'

'I've trusted both of you with my life. How much do you know about Jefferson, Jack?'

Jack hesitated.

'He works for the Defense Intelligence Agency.'

Jack turned to Cal. His disbelief was genuine. 'We're part of a DIA operation?'

'I couldn't tell you, Jack. I'm sorry.'

'You take a copy of the list to Jefferson, and I go my own way. Everybody wins.'

Cal reacted to my offer by pulling his sidearm. Benny was going to draw his iron when I stopped him with a look.

'What the hell are you doing?' Jack said.

'Everyone here took an oath,' Cal said. 'We swore to defend the constitution, and if people had kept their word we wouldn't be in this mess in the first place. My country asked for my help, that's all I know. I don't turn my back on my family. You shouldn't either.'

'You know my history, Cal, you know who abandoned who.'

'Why is Cassandra so important to you?'

'She's promised me an explanation.'

'I can't let you take the list to her,' Cal said. 'My orders are to prevent the list from falling into the wrong hands.'

'Wrong hands? We should be trying to get this list into as many hands as possible. Hell, we should be screaming about it from the fucking rooftops, whether it does any good or not. Did Jefferson tell you why he wanted the list kept secret? Of course he didn't,' I said, when Cal didn't respond. 'It's need-to-know, because if you knew you wouldn't be pointing a gun at me.'

'Jefferson wants to deal with the Elders,' Benny said. He could see where I was going. 'The Bureau tried that, and you've seen where it got us. We're all just pawns in a bureaucratic turf war.'

'Even if that's true,' Jack said, 'Jefferson will stop the Fishermen.'

'The list would be useless to them if they did,' I said. 'The Pentagon wants the Elders under its thumb, and as long as the Fishermen stay away from its people, it couldn't care less what happens to the rest of us.'

'You're lying,' Cal said.

'This is about leverage, Cal, not justice.'

Cal could see what I was saying, but it wasn't persuading him to lower his gun. Jack stepped between us.

'What are you doing, boy?' Cal said. 'We have our orders.'

The pain in his face came as much from pointing a gun at his young friend as the thought of disobeying Jefferson.

'I don't know if Strange is right, but you are. We're family. I can't remember the faces of men I served with who died; in a few years, I'm afraid I'll lose Isaac too. Aren't enough of us dead? We have the list. That's enough.'

Cal lowered his gun. I gave Benny the list and he supervised Jack photographing each of its many pages. Cal and I stood around and avoided each other's eyes.

'You won't survive for long on your own,' he said.

Instead of answering, I wandered closer to the tree line. From here, the forest seemed to go on for ever. I was tempted to walk inside and keep going, to walk away from everything like I'd always planned to. Back then I hadn't wanted to, and now I knew better. Sooner or later I'd walk into a highway or a power line, something made by human hands, and I'd be the property of civilization once again.

I dug the satellite phone out of my coat pocket and called the number.

'I have the list,' I said. 'Tell me what to do.'

CASSANDRA

For the time will come when men will not put up with sound
doctrine. Instead, to suit their own desires, they will gather
around them a great number of teachers to say what their
itching ears want to hear.

They will turn their ears away from the truth and turn aside
to myths.

– 2 Timothy iv, 3–4, New International Version

TWENTY-THREE

Nine Years Ago

'It's good to have you on board, Strange,' Lieutenant Blake said. 'If this mission had happened a few weeks ago, I might have thought you were here to keep an eye on me.'

Blake and I hadn't seen each other since the day that mortar attack killed Sykes and the young detainee. He would have heard about the fight in the Lab and my stint in holding. More gossip circulated around here than at a church bake sale. It was a by-product of us being constantly on edge and bored at the same time.

'Keep an eye on you for who?'

'The colonel, of course.' He laughed when he saw the confusion on my face. 'I guess you aren't aware of your reputation.'

'They closed down my fan club last week, if that's what you mean.'

'Some people didn't care for the interest Glass took in you. They thought you were a world-class kiss-ass.'

'Something changed their minds?'

'The dust-up in the Lab. That place ain't exactly friendly to our kind, but you went in flying the flag. I guess you knew no one in there would help you if things kicked off.'

'I knew,' I said, 'but I didn't really care.'

Blake came a bit closer and dropped his voice. 'Have you seen the intelligence on this?'

'I've seen the prisoner and read the interrogation transcripts,' I said.

'You didn't talk to him yourself?'

'Janus vetoed it, on security grounds.'

Blake was as impressed by that reasoning as I was. 'Any corroboration?'

I shook my head. 'We have the word of one man,' I said, 'and Janus has given him a lot of attention.'

Blake knew what that meant. 'Thanks, Strange,' he said.

I shouldn't have told him any of that – Glass didn't like his hunters' minds cluttered with too much information – but Blake deserved to know more about the mission he was leading.

'I never thought you were as big an asshole as people said.'

'My pleasure, Lieutenant.'

Blake went back to his men. I tried to figure out the latest addition to our safari: three engineers and a PackHound. It was basically a walking table, a metal pack animal that would carry any buried treasure we found. There wasn't a wheeled vehicle in the army that could get through the mess of the bazaar, and no one wanted to carry a nuclear device home on their backs.

The engineers interested me more than they usually would. Two were Corps men and the other obviously wasn't, no matter what the uniform said. In fact, he was too loose in general to be a military man. I figured he was the OGA – Other Government Agency – contribution to our group. OGA was what we called anyone from the intelligence community, since we weren't cleared to know who they actually were. I'd say the man coming with us was Defense Intelligence Agency if I had to guess, but I couldn't be sure. He was never more than five feet from the PackHound, attached by an invisible leash. He was here to take ownership of whatever we found, or to declare victory once we dug up something.

The bazaar district was a defender's dream: a labyrinth of lanes and alleyways defined by lots of small buildings. It was practically impervious to air power, a fact the air force had set out to prove when we invaded. They'd pounded the area for almost a week before they sent the grunts in. All that had accomplished was the creation of broken, irregular terrain that was even easier to hold.

American forces had pulled out of the bazaar and the mosque as soon as we'd declared victory. The area was acknowledged by commanders as the Pasdaran's, no matter what Pentagon spokespeople said. We would be the first Americans in a long time to have the dubious honour of venturing so far into bandit country.

We set off at night. The rangers in our company had been taught to move silently, reconnoitring territory without leaving any trace of themselves. Having myself and the engineers along would have queered their game, but the PackHound made it pointless. It gave off a shuddering growl, and practically stamped the ground with every step it took. We would have been less conspicuous if we'd brought along a Tin Pan Alley band and a platoon of majorettes.

The city was the same as it always was: dead and yet alive. Other creatures were in the ruined maze with us, but they were felt rather than seen. The rangers formed a ring around us, waiting for attacks. We were too attractive to be left unmolested.

I watched the man in front of me and turned the facts of the operation over in my head. What Glass had said to me still didn't make any sense. After all this time searching for WMD – forget nuclear material, we would have settled for a tube of concentrated mustard – the task force had come up empty. Before I'd joined Seventeen had been all over the country, and they had only a few broken centrifuges and some paperwork from a civilian nuclear programme. Everyone knew there were nukes somewhere, it was repeated so often we'd ceased even thinking about the question. All we had to do was find the evidence that had to be out there.

Some Pasdaran officers had confirmed the existence of the programme after someone from Janus had smacked them around, but none had been able to provide concrete evidence. Prisoner 6524 had dropped everything we needed in our laps, gift-wrapped by his screams. Nothing in this city was that damn easy, which was one of the reasons I had to see it for myself.

I was on the ground. There was a singing in my ears, a tone so loud it made everything else sound like it was underwater. I could feel hands on my arms, but the sensation was distant, as if it were happening to another set of limbs I'd left at home. The slap on the face, however, felt right where it should be.

'Strange,' Lieutenant Blake said, his head hovering above me.

I blinked, and finally realized I was wounded. My hands examined my body, especially the crotch.

'Don't worry, all your junk's where it should be,' Blake said. 'What's the damage?' he said to another pair of hands that belonged to a person I couldn't see.

'Shrapnel's ripped up his leg pretty good.'

'I need to see,' I said.

'Maybe you should wait until we get some morphine in you.'

I ignored Blake's suggestion and struggled into a sitting position.

My right leg was fucked. Flying metal had torn it up all the way to the thigh like a buckshot wound. The pain didn't come home until I saw the ranger medic inspecting the exposed anklebone.

The medic held me down while Blake stifled my screams. 'Morphine,' he said again to the medic. After a while the pain retreated. It didn't go away completely; just withdrew to a safer distance.

'It's not as bad as it looks, sergeant. The shrapnel didn't hit anything major. Reyes has got you stabilized. Your ankle is fractured, but I don't think you'll lose the leg.'

Blake helped me sit up. The medic, Reyes, was binding my leg. The other rangers had formed a defensive perimeter around the engineers and us.

'What was it?' I said.

'IED,' Blake said. 'An old artillery shell wired with a pressure trigger, I'd guess.'

Two bodies lay on the edge of the perimeter. The first was the soldier who must have stepped on the IED. Both his legs had been blown off, and the rest of him was burned into anonymity. The man in front of him lay face down, back and neck covered in shrapnel. I should have been lying there with him. Perhaps the soldier's body had absorbed most of the blast, and the shrapnel I got had flown between his legs to me. More likely it was just dumb luck.

Blake stood up and got on the radio. 'Moses, this is Crusader. We just hit an IED. Yes, two of my men and Sergeant Strange. Strange is stable but not mobile. He needs immediate casevac. The others are already gone.'

There was an incredible weariness on Blake's face, a heaviness in the eyes that seemed to pull down the rest of his face. There was some grief, but it was mixed with exhaustion at the thought of writing two more letters home. There had been no gunfight, no wild-eyed jihadis wielding AKs and screaming the name of their God. The person who had set that IED was probably a kid who had died before we ran into his handiwork. Blake could tell the families of those men that they had done their duty, but there would be no face upon which all the grief and anger could be hung.

A look of consternation grew on Blake's face as Glass spoke in his ear. When he responded, Blake kept the look on his face and his clipped, professional tone separate. 'Sir, that's against regulations. If casevac isn't available, we'll wait or send two men home with Strange. It's not far.'

Glass was chewing him out. When it came to my life and the mission, there was no confusion where the colonel's priorities lay. Blake looked at a building fifty feet away from us. The skeleton of its four storeys was intact, though everything inside the walls had been burned. A spiral staircase now exposed to the elements connected the floors.

'Understood, sir,' Blake said. He wouldn't look at me.

'It's all right, sir,' I said. 'You have your orders.'

'That isn't good enough. We don't abandon our own people.'

'Think of it as leaving someone to cover your rear.'

Blake shook his head. 'Not even a pound of shrapnel can slow down that mouth of yours.'

He gestured to the medic. They got me on a stretcher and carried me towards the building Blake had been looking at.

'Is that where you're stashing me?' I said.

'It's the best I can do. Up there you won't attract any attention.'

Getting a stretcher up a spiral staircase was no easy feat. Blake and the medic struggled up every floor, the staircase just wide enough to accommodate us. They put me down on the roof, in the shadow of a wall that might have housed the building's water tank. The medic gave my bandages a final once-over and went down. Blake lingered.

'At least you got your wish,' Blake said. 'You won't have to see the bazaar again.'

'I never wanted it to come true this way, sir.'

'I know. Do me a favour and keep your mouth shut. The Pasdaran won't look up here.'

'Watch yourself in there, sir,' I said. 'I'm not just talking about the enemy. Just because the colonel thinks there's a pot of gold at the end of that rainbow doesn't mean there's anything to find.'

Blake nodded. 'I've chased geese before, Sergeant; I know how it's done.' Blake took my radio and fiddled with it. 'You're on my frequency now. I'm sure it's against all kinds of rules, but if you can't be there for the game, you deserve at least to hear it.'

I thanked him, but Blake didn't go.

'I'm all right, Lieutenant. You'd better get a move on before Glass calls again.'

'I don't like this.'

'Nobody does.'

He offered me his hand and I took it.

'We'll be back soon. Who knows, we might just win this war in the meantime.'

'If you do, don't forget to pick me up before the parade.'

Blake raised his hand in farewell. On his way down the stairs I heard him call in.

'This is Crusader. We are Charlie Mike.'

After a while, I realized the medic had given me more morphine than usual. Time had taken on an elastic quality, and I felt more at ease in no-man's-land than anyone but Death had a right to be. I felt pretty good in general. My other wounds hadn't been nearly this much fun.

I'd come on this mission for a reason, but I was no longer sure what it was. It might have been to prove something to Glass, or prove Stonebridge wrong. Whatever it was, I was sure it had something to do with all the horrible shit I'd done. It must have been important for me to volunteer for a mission with a better-than-average chance of sudden, violent death.

Four storeys wasn't that high, but we'd done a good job of bringing everything low. I could see the Butcher School from here; just its outlines, not the sentries on its roof, my former comrades.

I could also see the Central Library, which dominated that part of the skyline by default. I imagined Glass looking out from its broken top, though I knew he was down in its entrails. He was looking out over the city, watching Blake, the task force, and me, judging us all.

'Crusader, this is Moses,' Glass said over the radio. 'What is your status?'

'We are approximately a hundred Mikes from Point Delta. We are—'

Gunfire drowned out the rest of Blake's response. I had my rifle level before I realized the sound was on the radio.

I heard Glass calling out between the gaps in the firefight. There were two explosions, but no response from Blake.

'Crusader,' Glass said. 'Crusader, respond damn it.'

'We've been ambushed, sir,' Blake said. 'Pasdaran, at least thirty. I believe we are surrounded.'

'Casualties?'

'There are only four of us left, sir. Myself, Reyes—'

'What about the engineers?'

'They're all dead, sir.' There was more gunfire. Blake was yelling at what was left of his platoon, trying to form some kind of defensive circle in the rubble.

'Crusader, where is the PackHound?'

Blake didn't respond.

'Crusader, where is the package?'

'The PackHound is in enemy territory, sir,' Blake said. His voice was as calm as the last time we'd spoken. 'I don't have the manpower to retrieve it.'

'Understood, Crusader. Withdraw immediately. I repeat, withdraw immediately.'

There was an explosion, and then static.

'Crusader,' Glass said. 'Crusader, respond.'

They were all dead. I didn't need to see the bodies to be sure. Fifteen men, and they hadn't lived long enough to find out if the mission to which they gave their lives was a fraud. Glass would try again, use the whole task force if he had to. More men would die before Stonebridge was revealed as a fraud, and there was nothing I could do about it. Even if both my legs were working, I couldn't prove a negative.

I turned the radio back to the old frequency. I was about to let command know I was still alive when a bright flash in the distance blinded me. Through my fingers I saw a ball of light near the ruins of Khomeini Mosque. I thought of those illuminations of holy visitations. There was a bright and fiery aura, but no saint floated in its centre.

The light called up a divine wind, one that buffeted me with stone, dust and the ashes of human remains. It howled louder than the explosion that had put me on my back, a screaming that seemed to start inside my head. I yelled into the radio, but I couldn't hear the sound of my own voice. No one was coming.

I curled up as best I could, and hid my face from whatever new evil had crawled into this city to be born.

TWENTY-FOUR

'Wake up,' I said to Benny, dozing in the passenger seat and mumbling in Hebrew.

'Are we there?' he said, taking his hat off his face and sitting up.

'Almost.'

We'd driven from New York down the Baltimore–DC corridor in a stolen car, pushing our luck a little further every time we passed a highway patrol. The only thing I'd known about our destination was a set of grid coordinates Cassandra had given me. They were in the concrete hinterland between Washington and Dulles International Airport, but the spot they pointed to was just a blank space on the map. The area was covered in office parks and industrial sites, each one full to the gills with government contractors and lobbying shops.

The map ended at a private road that connected a network of residential streets to the outside world. It reminded me of a gated community, but instead of a gate the entrance was blocked by a thin strip of yellow tape, an unspecific 'Danger' stamped on its face.

'That's encouraging,' Benny said, squinting at the tape. 'Why did Cassandra send us to a toxic suburb?'

'This area is ground zero for contractors doing classified work.'

Benny's eyes slid my way. The grin that appeared on his face had nothing to do with our present surroundings. I'd been forced to replace my ruined suit with a grey abomination bought off the rack at an outlet store in New Jersey. Benny had been laughing at it the whole way.

'Aren't you done yet?'

'No. You still look like an idiot.'

I showed him my long sleeves and they set off a fresh round of laughter. I'd bought the jacket a size bigger than the trousers to accommodate my gun, and was no longer sure they matched.

'It's not as if I had time to get it altered,' I said. I took my whole schedule of medication – red, green and blue pills – and swallowed them with the dregs of cold roadside coffee.

'You've done enough already, Benny,' I said. 'Only one of us has a family, and he should be on his way to join them.'

'We had this argument when I said I was coming.'

'I still don't get it.'

'I told you about my grandfather, my old man's old man, who fled Warsaw when he was young,' Benny said. 'He'd come for Passover and tell me stories about the old country. The fields he worked in when he was a boy, the little houses of his village. I didn't know why he was sweet on the place: no electricity, no toilets, no TV. The place sounded like a dump. I was just a kid, I didn't get it. He loved this country – told me never to take it for granted – but his home was always that village in Poland. The Nazis and then the Soviets took that away from him.

'He never went back. He was losing a fight with cancer when the Soviets threw in the towel. He got to see that at least. Sharon's going to be a refugee for a little while; there's nothing I can do about that. But I'll be fucked if I let the Elders force my daughter to grow up a stranger to her own country.'

Benny got out of the car, which was his way of saying the matter was closed.

We got what we needed from the trunk: vests, a new shotgun and that sub-machine gun I'd taken off the Fisherman at Presmore's house. No young mothers or curious children opened their curtains to see two men getting ready for war.

We walked down the road's centre line. No car or man met us on the way.

'Can you hear anything?' Benny said.

There were no silent places in New York: population density and thin walls saw to that. Even in the quiet parts of town, there would always be a car on the street, a pair of heels on concrete, or the sound of distant music. I listened for children playing, a lawnmower, the purr of an air conditioner, the machine-gun sound of a sprinkler on a lawn. The white noise I'd filtered out since childhood was noticeable in its absence. Even the power lines, which always gave off a low hum, were silent.

'You think it was some kind of attack?' Benny said. 'Chemical or biological maybe?' He left out nuclear, though he knew without a Geiger counter we could be drinking rads by the quart and not know it.

'We would have heard about it,' I said.

Down the street, it was McMansions all the way – seven different species of overgrown dwelling pushing hard against the property line. The front lawns showed signs of only recent neglect: seeded and cared for, but allowed to grow more than was proper. Their health ruled out the nuclear possibility anyway.

'GPS says about two hundred metres more,' I said.

The satellite phone rang. 'You've arrived. Don't bother,' the voice said, when I started to look around. 'Do you have the list?'

'Do you have a face?'

'Take the next left. I'll meet you in the fourth house on the right.'

We turned left. The sign called it Maple Street. It looked the same as the last street. Without the signs it wouldn't be hard to get lost in this suburban labyrinth. I wondered how many times residents had walked into the wrong house by mistake.

The fourth house on the right was the same as the others, except that its front door was open.

Cassandra was waiting in the living room. The woman standing in front of us was short and in her early sixties. Her grey hair was tied in two plaits that reached halfway down her back. A pair of reading glasses hung around her neck on a chain. She wore a loose blue dress, faded with repeated washing, belted at the waist by the two pistols she carried in holsters on either hip. At first glance she looked like an earth mother with a unique perspective on gun rights.

For a moment we didn't say anything. I think we were all surprised that we'd lived long enough to meet one another.

'You the Wizard of Oz?' Benny said.

She smiled. 'My name is Julia Platt,' she said. 'I used to be chief of the Directorate of Intelligence at CIA, when such a thing still existed. Call me Cassandra; I haven't answered to the other name in a long time.'

'What the hell happened around here?' Benny said. 'I wanna know in advance if my balls are going to fall off.'

'They were taken,' Cassandra said, indicating two worn chairs.

Neither of us accepted the invitation.

'The Fishermen did this?'

Cassandra nodded.

'Why would they take an entire fucking street?' Benny said.

A street, a whole community that didn't appear on maps. 'It was an intelligence outfit,' I said. 'Company, or maybe NSA.'

339

'A place of rest for men and women who'd served their country for too long. Just because an employee retires doesn't mean their enemies do. They weren't in deep cover, just retirees going about the little business all retired people do. We hid them in plain sight as a precaution no one thought they'd need.

'Their patriotism made it easy. Even after so many years of Elder rule, the deference to authority was automatic, unthinking. They spent their lives working for their country, and that led them to assume that anyone with a badge was one of their own. The Fishermen showed up in the middle of the night with all the bells and whistles: hazmat suits, unmarked vans, guns and badges. All they had to say was terrorism, and the residents of Maple Street got in the vans on their own, like good little lambs.'

'Why now?' Benny said. 'The CIA has been out of action for more than a decade. Who cares about some old ex-agents? No offence.'

'You're asking the wrong question,' Cassandra said. 'It's not "Why now?" but "Why did they wait so long?"'

Cassandra took her own offer and sat in one of the chairs. 'My friend owned this house. His name was Zachary Middleton. He was CIA, a brilliant analyst and a good man. He dealt with retirement better than I did. Zach took that rigorous, brilliant mind of his and used it to build a wonderful garden. I wish I could show it to you, but I don't have the green thumb he did, and there's always someone watching,' she said, pointing up to the clear blue sky and the eyes that hid behind it.

'Every regime tells itself lies. It has to convince itself that it's legitimate, that it has an unquestioned right to rule. In the old days kings said they were chosen by God. Then we grew up and realized that power could only come from the people. There has been some backsliding of late.'

'So the Elders believe they were chosen by God,' Benny said. 'What else is new?'

'Some do, but the rest are more – venal is a better word than practical. They told themselves an even bigger lie: they were representatives of the people. Breathtaking, isn't it? That such a monstrous idea could not only survive, but flourish for ten years. There was some opposition, but they could be written off as cranks and perverts, a few bad apples in the Godly barrel. Everyone else went along to get along. The Elders were free to live in their self-delusions, because we were too afraid to say otherwise.'

'Until it became obvious that they weren't everyone's best friend,' I said. I knew Cassandra and I were thinking of the same thing: the Battle of Christopher Park.

'You were there, weren't you?' she said to me.

I nodded. I'd seen the running gun battles, the buildings gutted by fire and explosives, the blood on red brick. I'd seen the same things so many times, the memory didn't affect me until I reminded myself it had happened in Greenwich Village.

'I guess it isn't easy to tell yourself that bedtime story after an armed rebellion in the biggest city in America.'

'The Old Testament voices grew stronger,' Cassandra said. 'They reminded the Council that people were wayward children who needed a good spanking. The Elders saw their own blood on the pavements of Christopher Park, their own bodies against the wall. They made the same evil bargain with Glass that we'd made with them: keep us safe, and we'll do anything you say.'

Cassandra held out her hand. 'You've seen my face,' she said, 'now show me the list.'

I hesitated, and she noticed. I didn't give Cassandra the list so much as hold out my hand and let her take it. I gave her a moment to skim through the names. Cassandra sighed, and let the pages rest in her lap.

'I expected more names,' she said.

'That's the New York list. The whole operation is compartmentalized. Glass is probably the only person with access to all the names.'

'I suppose it will have to do.'

'You're welcome,' Benny said.

'Why these people?' I asked. 'Director Sands, people like us I understand, but I don't recognize most of these names.'

'The fear has driven them crazy,' Benny said. They're fighting shadows.'

'They're not mad,' Cassandra said. 'Leviathan is not a pogrom or a lynching. Some of the people on this list have expertise, knowledge or influence. Others are unwilling to tolerate cruelty to another. The rest might simply be decent or courageous enough to be a problem. I doubt most of these people know each other, or have even thought seriously about opposing the Elders. These names are the seeds of any future opposition movement. Glass is applying the same doctrine at home as they use abroad: if there is a one per cent chance a person will oppose the Elders in the future, they are dealt with.

'They have more than enough material to work with. The war kept a lot of criticism out of the official press, but that didn't stop everyone else from giving their opinion. Speaking their mind was their right, after all; it's in the constitution. People called the Elders crooks and fools, and they did it in bars, over the phone, and on video over the Internet; an amazing cacophony of voices, more afraid of being ignored than heard by the authorities. Our culture was a modern miracle that everyone on the western side of the world had taken for granted since before I was born.

'God, this used to be such a wonderful country.'

I thought the sentence was going to end in tears, but the look on her face was worse than that. It was disillusionment so massive and brutal that it seemed to distort the light around her with a gravity of its own.

'Considering how many decent people are in the country, wouldn't rounding them all up be a smaller operation?' I said.

'If the scope of Leviathan was limited only to the great and the good, it would be a few thousand names at most. Do you remember that document I sent you?'

'That intercept of the Fisher Partners board congratulating itself?'

'Four Elders sit on the board. Every Elder is a stockholder; together they have the controlling share. When a task order is sent to Fisher Partners, who do you think pays the Fishermen's salaries, the cost of transport and logistics? Who do you think pays to have the clients held in an undisclosed location and tortured?'

'The government,' Benny said. 'From the black budget, I'd expect.'

'And Fisher Partners, like any other company, pays dividends to its stockholders, and rewards those who bring it new business. What a coincidence that the Elders are both.'

'The more people the Elders order disappeared, the more money they make,' I said.

'To make that money they needed more names, and here we leave politics and enter the realm of psychology. Who is more deserving of punishment than those who had personally wronged the Elders? The popular kids who had picked on them in school, the smartasses who had mocked them in government and television, the better men who had stolen women they believed to be theirs. The culture wars left a lot of scores un-settled, at least in their long and petty memories. You could see Leviathan as the frustrations and insecurities of twenty-four old, bitter men unleashed on the world.

'But even when you add every person who ever looked cross-eyed at an Elder, it's still not enough. All those reasons make a kind of sense, if you twist your mind enough. Citizens could still believe themselves safe if they did as they were told. That they think at all before they comply is still a problem. Here I have to borrow the thinking of my absent friend, our host. Zach was a connoisseur of government repression, studied it all over the world for the agency's benefit. He would say at this point that Leviathan becomes a statistical problem. It still needs the weight of numbers, a critical mass of death and terror that will frighten people beyond thought and into mute obedience.'

Cassandra's lecture connected two memories in my head. 'F. Lincoln Howe,' I said. He was an Elder and Secretary of State. 'At Kirov's funeral, he told the story of Abraham and Isaac, said it meant we had to have the fear of God in our hearts, that outward obedience wasn't good enough.'

'It is no coincidence that he also sits on the Fisher Partners board. He is the chief liaison between the Elders and the company.'

'He laid it all out, right in public,' I said. 'I just didn't understand it.'

'It wasn't meant for your ears,' Cassandra said. 'In the end, whether the names on that list are innocent or guilty doesn't matter. They could just as easily have used a phone book, or a dartboard.'

'Kill enough people, for whatever reason, and the rest fall in line,' Benny said.

'In fifty years, when everyone involved is dead, that is probably what they'll say,' Cassandra said. 'It's unlikely any single Elder is aware of the scale of what is happening. Even Glass probably can't see the full picture. Perhaps if you read every document, and then took all the Elders and dissected their black hearts one by one, you would know.

'If my friend were here, he would tell you one more thing: when a programme like this acquires a certain size, it takes on a momentum of its own. War can become the reason for war, and

344

that's what Leviathan is: the Elders' declaration of war on their own citizens. People will be executed because they've been shot, and disappear because they are gone.'

The silence of the street rushed into the vacuum Cassandra's voice had left. I listened in vain for something to break it, but its rule over this place was absolute.

'It almost sounds like you're making excuses for them,' Benny said.

I could see the Elders making similar pleas of ignorance at a trial I'd probably never live to see, if it ever happened at all.

'I want you to see what is happening as clearly as possible, because I know what your next question will be, and I want you to understand my answer.'

'So how do we stop it?' Benny said, when Cassandra didn't continue.

'We can't.'

'You said you could help us,' I said.

'I said we could help each other, which has nothing to do with stopping Leviathan.'

'Then what the fuck are we doing here?' Benny said. 'We've been shot at, other people we know are in prison or dead, and you're saying there's been no point to our fucking road trip?'

'The Elders are divided, brutal and incompetent. They also command the most powerful army in history.'

'And just how firm is that control?' I said.

'You're referring to your friends, part of the Founder Initiative,' Cassandra said. 'What do you think are the chances of the Joint Chiefs starting a military coup?'

'About as likely as a round of spontaneous public demonstrations that forces the Elders from power,' I said.

When Cal and Jack had first shown me the fruits of Leviathan in Grand Central, my strongest objection to the whole idea was that it would have to be public to have its intended effect. I was right, and as usual it was in the worst way. It was impossible to keep Leviathan secret for ever: it would leak out to the public in bits and pieces – enquiries about missing friends, the sighting of Fishermen, maybe a body or two seeing the light of day. There would be anger and outrage, but the fear would force people into their homes rather than on to the streets.

'So you were right,' Benny said to me. 'The Founders are about leverage, just like the Bureau. Wouldn't they still want to clip the Elders' wings? The Pentagon can't want the Fishermen running all over the country kidnapping people.'

'They haven't tried to stop it yet,' Cassandra said. 'Our only option is to go underground and wait. When enough people have been shot, it will stop.'

'Oh, good,' Benny said. 'I'm glad I risked my fucking life for such a brilliant plan.'

'The only thing we can do is isolate the Elders,' Cassandra said. 'That's why we need each other. I have some documents, but they're circumstantial by themselves. Strange has the list, but they won't believe a dishonourably discharged and visibly disturbed private eye from New York City.'

Benny's eyes bounced between the two of us. I shrugged to say Cassandra was right.

'I still have friends in the community,' she continued. 'Now that we have the list, they'll have no choice but to believe me.'

'You've been underground a long time,' Benny said.

'Europeans have long memories.'

'There's one more thing,' I said.

Cassandra smiled at me. Her eyes said I was an open book she could peruse as soon as she found a spare, rainy day.

'Tell me about the Rudashevsky Group.'

'The Elders fear the past as much as they do the future. Sometimes it is necessary for the dead to be dug up and shot again. It's best if you see it,' she said, noting the look on our faces. 'You won't believe me otherwise.'

She led us into the sitting room. Pictures on the walls went back thirty years, through a happy marriage, kids, and another generation smiling gap-toothed at the camera. I wondered how many of them were still at liberty, or at least alive. They might have left the children alone, but I had no facts to anchor that outburst of optimism.

Cassandra plugged a drive into the television that the room was designed around.

'What you are about to see are highlights from the last meeting of the Rudashevsky Group.'

A windowless room came on the screen. Four men in suits sat around a nondescript metal table. The room could have been anywhere in the world, or the far side of hell.

'You already know CIA Director Foyle,' she said. He was wearing the same suit in which he testified before the Houston Commission. 'This meeting happened two days after his testimony.'

'I'm guessing the topic of discussion is who leaked to Senator Lee and sandbagged Foyle,' Benny said.

'No, they'd already found out it was me,' Cassandra said. Her smile was infused with the pride of a lost cause. 'The meeting is about dealing with the fallout. On the left is Martin Doctorow, the last head of the State Department's Bureau of Intelligence and Research. Snarling at him is Gabriel Palmer, President Adamson's thug.'

Doctorow looked like a Harvard professor emeritus, his contempt for the proceedings almost hidden behind a patrician smile. Palmer was half Doctorow's age, around two hundred pounds of marshmallow stuffed into a suit that couldn't quite contain it. He glowed with zeal and rage in equal measure, a Davey before the term entered the vernacular.

'Who took this video?'

'The man who keeps his back to the camera, Roy Chambers. He ran NSA at the time. The Pentagon should have been there as well, but after Senator Lee's testimony they forgot to attend.'

'Why the hell did he tape it?' Benny said. 'That has to be illegal.'

'Everything happening inside that room is illegal. Roy was smart enough to want some insurance in case Adamson turned on him later, so he taped the group's meetings. I've kept the tapes for the same reason. I'll fast-forward to the good parts.'

The men argued, paced and rolled their eyes at ten times the normal speed. Palmer's body language was even more aggressive sped up, pacing, jabbing his finger at the air. Doctorow and Foyle barely seemed to move.

'Nothing Senator Lee said was a lie,' Doctorow said, when the tape slowed down.

'Nothing I said was a lie either,' Foyle said. The anger on his face was palpable even at the video's low resolution, but there was none of the indignation of a man who felt his conscience was clear.

'You just left out certain details,' Doctorow said, 'like the fact that we can connect Rudashevsky to Syria, Saudi Arabia and Egypt. The fact that Rudashevsky could have sold the uranium we found at Houston to any or all three. The fact that we still don't know how the device reached Houston or who brought it there. The fact that—'

'Enough,' Palmer said. 'You know why I'm here. The President has no doubt that Iran is responsible for Houston. He doesn't want there to be any in the public's mind either.'

'There is always doubt,' Foyle said.

'Our leader disagrees.'

'Not all of us are lucky enough to have a personal line to God,' Doctorow said.

'Watch your mouth.'

'What are you going to do, whelp?' Doctorow said. 'Wash my mouth out with soap?'

For a second I thought Palmer was going to hit him.

'I don't see how any of this matters,' Foyle said.

There was a moment of silence.

'The public have been calling for blood since the attack,' he continued. 'If we told them Canada was involved, they'd be demanding we slaughter every man, woman and child north of the 49th parallel. Just because the President's fig leaf has slipped a little doesn't change things. The die has been cast.'

'This is a question of loyalty,' Palmer said.

'She has been dealt with,' Foyle said. 'The President has his pound of flesh. What more does he want?'

It took me a moment to realize what was being said, or, more importantly what wasn't, because the sins on display were all of omission. There had been no smoking gun, no bloody handprint or DNA that made Iran a slam dunk, just a collection of connections that could lead in different ways depending on what angle you approached them from. That was the real story: the President's faith versus Doctorow's catalogue of unknowns. It wasn't the Rudashevsky Group that had sealed Iran's fate, but a single man, alone on his knees, believing that God had made him a vessel for His truth. That knowledge flowed into the lower depths of my heart, and blossomed into something I could not name.

I ran, past Benny and his open mouth, Cassandra's sad eyes, through the back door, just in time to vomit in the garden that had once been Zachary Middleton's pride and joy.

Benny found me retching into the wild remains of a bougain-villea.

'What's wrong?' he said. 'Do you need your medication?'

I shook my head, still unable to speak. There was no pill for this condition.

'Then tell me what the fuck is wrong before I break your ribs doing CPR.'

'Didn't you hear what they said?' I straightened up, but it was still a struggle not to choke on my own breath.

'They didn't give us the whole story on Houston. Governments never do.'

'They lied.'

'They didn't lie,' Benny said. His voice was less emphatic than his words. 'You heard what Foyle said. It's still possible Rudashevsky sold Iran the uranium used on Houston.'

'After everything that happened in Tehran, is a maybe good enough for you?'

Benny shook his head. He lit a cigarette to give himself some time to think.

'We signed up before any of that happened, swore an oath to go wherever they sent us.'

'But you didn't volunteer for Task Force Seventeen,' I said. 'You didn't deliver people up for torture and death to find something that wasn't even there. It was like you said then, nobody put a gun to my head. Glass called, and I answered.'

The sun seemed impossibly bright. The weather hadn't changed, I just found it more painful.

'I thought I could somehow make up for Seventeen. Not all at once, but in instalments, a good deed here and there, as much as I could afford. All those things I did and helped to do, they were all in the service of a lie. All those people brutalized and dead, for nothing.' I wiped my mouth with the back of my hand. 'What the hell am I going to do now, Benny?'

Benny took a long drag before he answered.

'I was so angry at you for joining those Nazis, you have no fucking idea,' he said. 'You were dead to me. You know it was

Isaac who convinced me to visit you in the hospital? I'd seen people torn up more than once, but that first day, when I saw what was happening to you . . .'

Benny dropped his cigarette and ground it out.

'Felix, don't you think these last ten years have been payment enough?'

I didn't know what to say. There was no one who could decide that. Those I had wronged were dead and gone, their families following not far behind.

'Come on,' he said, handing me my hat, 'we'll get you a towel and a breathmint, and then we'll get the fuck out of here. We've been in this ghost town too long.'

An alarm went off in the basement. Cassandra stuck her head through the back door.

'They're here,' she said, as if calling us to dinner. The monsters had come to Maple Street.

TWENTY-FIVE

Cassandra had transformed the basement into a command post. A bank of monitors watched the approaches to the house and Maple Street, while a row of plasma screens spat out satellite data and the results of an analysis I couldn't follow. There was about half a million dollars of computing power in a server rack enclosed by a metal cage. The rest of the machines I couldn't even identify.

'You knew they were coming?' Benny said.

'As I said, someone is always watching.'

'Why the fuck didn't you tell us? We could have had this little pow-wow on the goddamn road.'

'If they caught us out in the open, we wouldn't have had a chance,' Cassandra said. 'Here, our death isn't guaranteed.'

Through one of the monitors we heard Stonebridge's voice blaring out of a speaker on top of the van. 'Strange, we can work this out. I just want the list, give it to me, and you and your friends are free to go.'

'Does he think we're stupid?' Benny asked.

'I guess so.' Only the black van was visible on the monitors. 'Stonebridge couldn't bring real Fishermen: they'd hear about the list and report him to Glass. He has to use his own people, those he thinks he can trust to keep their mouths shut. It looks like all his friends in the world can fit into that van.'

'He'll have a sniper in position somewhere,' Benny said. 'Maybe more than one. You got any weapons in this joint?'

Cassandra led us to a small room off the main basement. It had been the laundry room once, judging by the washer-dryer combo gathering dust in the corner. A gun rack was on the opposite wall. Two shotguns, a high-powered rifle with a scope and a sub-machine gun identical to mine waited for trained hands. There were seven handguns of various makes on a smaller rack, and two boxes – one with grenades, the other packed with pale bricks of C4 – on the floor.

'Holy shit,' Benny said, speaking for us both.

'You can buy just about anything in Virginia,' she said, 'except a drink on Sunday.'

Benny took the other sub-machine gun while I stuffed my pockets with ammo.

'So what's the plan?' he asked.

'I'm going to talk to him.'

'So, we're as stupid as he thinks we are?'

'I need Stonebridge alive, Benny. I've got a question or two to ask him. I'll go out alone. How good are you with that rifle?' I asked Cassandra.

'Better than you deserve.'

'Then find a good spot and cover me. Benny, keep your sights on the van. If things go wrong – and they probably will – fuck up their vehicle. That might give the two of you a chance to run.'

'The getaway car is around back, packed and ready,' Cassandra said. She threw Benny the keys. 'Good luck,' she said to me, and disappeared out the back door with the rifle. Benny followed her.

I made sure my gear was in order. It felt a lot like a mission in Iran. That meant it would go badly, but this time I didn't really care; as long as Benny and Cassandra got away, whatever else happened was fine with me. I checked my hat in the hallway mirror. It looked good.

Benny was waiting for me outside, a new cigarette burning in his hand. I'd been wondering how I avoided the sentimental goodbye.

'What?' he said. 'You wanna die alone?'

The sky was clear, the sun bright, and a bird or two had finally found their way here. We took the road towards my old colleague, right down the centre line.

Stonebridge and his gang formed a rough perimeter around their vehicle. They were the same men I'd seen at Kirov's funeral: they had bigger guns today, but there'd been no similar upgrade in the brain department. I'd had enough experience with their type to know they spent their lives looking out for number one. I doubt they'd been housebroken long enough for that to change.

The house on my left looked like all the others, except for a low stone wall that ringed the property, painted white before nature had taken its course. It was the only one I'd seen in the whole development, which must have made it the hot topic of the last homeowners' association meeting. The houses on the other corners were as quiet as the rest. If Stonebridge's back-up was hidden in there, they were doing their job.

Stonebridge didn't say anything right off, so I kept silent too. Maybe he was looking for signs of other accomplices, but more likely he was enjoying his victory before it had happened.

'The prodigal son and his sidekick,' Stonebridge finally said.

'That's rich, coming from Glass's butt-boy,' Benny replied.

'General Glass,' Stonebridge said. 'We know why we're here, Strange, so I'll get to the point. If you return my property, I'll let you and your friend go.'

My friend could only mean Benny. Maybe he didn't know Cassandra was here.

'I find that hard to believe,' I said.

'You're lucky, Strange,' he said. 'Like I told you, the old man would prefer it if you stayed alive.' His eyes drifted away from mine for a moment. 'I've never seen the general get sentimental before. I don't like it, but I do as I'm told. Besides, nobody cares about you that much. It will be a month at least before your task order comes up. By then you and Benny can be safe in the Holy Land. It's where you belong anyway.'

'And if I make trouble later?'

Stonebridge smiled. I braced myself for bad news.

'I have some insurance. What's her name again?' He paused out of pure sadism. 'Iris, she said. You'll have to forgive me, I deal with so many names.'

I couldn't hold it all in. Stonebridge saw the signs: the blink, the tightening of the mouth, the single breath exhaled with too much speed. He saw it all, and in the depths of his eyes he danced with joy.

'I want to see her,' I said.

'You're in no position to negotiate, Strange. She's alive,' he said. 'I guess I could have done something from a movie like put her on the phone, but you'll just have to believe me. Iris will stay that way, as long as you behave. Now give me the list, and we never have to see each other again.'

Stonebridge was lying. Iris was already in the system, maybe already dead. Either way, Stonebridge didn't know.

Benny looked from Stonebridge to me, and back again. He knew there was an even chance I'd throttle the shitbird right then and there.

'Before we do this, there's something I need to know.'

Stonebridge could barely contain his boredom. 'What is it?'

'Tell me what you did with Isaac.'

The confusion on his face was genuine. 'I don't handle every name on that list personally, you know.'

'He isn't on the list. Isaac Taylor. He was your Titan body-guard, until you had him killed.'

Stonebridge remembered. I couldn't enjoy his discomfort as much as he had my own.

'He also put his hands on my property. I had him dealt with.' Stonebridge's voice had a tone people usually reserved for inter-rogations about their breakfast. 'I didn't learn what he was really up to until later, when it was too late to have him questioned. Beyond that I can't remember.'

I didn't think he was lying. Stonebridge had done so much harm from a distance, his victims had blurred together. He saw names on paper, documents to be filed, targets to be met. The people he destroyed were just widgets to be moved through a system of Glass's design.

'No more stalling,' Stonebridge said. 'Give me the list.'

'Perhaps you should hear my offer first.' The voice was the Corinthian's. It came from further up the street, but the voice was being broadcast from more than one place, almost impos-sible to pin down.

Stonebridge was as surprised as I was. His men became restless, hands on their weapons, eyes looking for the new player none of us could see. Stonebridge quieted them with a look. Maybe he still believed the Corinthian was on his side.

'Jesus Christ,' Benny said. 'What is this, a fucking reunion?'

'That list is a valuable commodity,' the Corinthian said. 'I know a more generous buyer than the man standing in front of you.'

'Why don't you come down here and we'll talk?' I said.

'I haven't forgotten our last negotiation, Strange,' the Corinthian said. 'This operation has been delegated to my employees. I am supervising from a remote location.'

'What the hell are you doing here?' Stonebridge said, not quite sure where to direct his voice.

'Looking after my interests.'

'You work for me. You're my man.'

It wasn't the first time I'd laughed in Stonebridge's face, but it might be the last. 'Did you hear that?' I said to the air.

'Now you see what I have to put up with, Mr Strange,' the Corinthian said.

Circumstances were replacing my first, unlikely plan with one that might be a little better: getting the Corinthian and Stonebridge to have a cockfight while the rest of us ran like hell.

'Who's your buyer?' I said.

'A consortium of economic interests who have been forced into exile by the current regime.'

'I guess they want to make some trouble,' I said.

'And some of those names on your list are friends of theirs. I heard what Stonebridge offered, and I can do better: transportation to a country of your choice, and a hundred thousand dollars for your trouble. You might even save some innocent lives if the leak persuades the Elders to stop Leviathan. That's worth something to you, as I recall.'

'You won't get away with betraying me,' Stonebridge yelled at the sky, as if he were blaming the gods for being outmanoeuvred. 'The Elders will see to that.'

'You never understood the realities of business, Stonebridge,' the Corinthian said. 'What you call betrayal is simply diversification.'

Stonebridge fixed his gaze on me. 'Give me that list, or no one leaves here alive.'

'I hope you brought friends,' I said in the direction of the Corinthian's voice.

'It would be best for you both not to find out just how many of them I have.'

'Confusing, isn't it?' I said to Stonebridge. 'You're not used to picking fights with people who can hit back.'

'Don't you get it?' he replied with a sneer. 'He's the one who sold your Iris to me.'

Something broke two doors down. One of Stonebridge's thugs jumped and his gun went off in the sound's general direction.

After that, all hell broke loose.

Two of Stonebridge's thugs fell; by Cassandra's hand or the Corinthian's, I couldn't tell. I used the distraction to give Stonebridge a quick double tap in the face with my right hand, just to see if anybody was home. By the way he reeled back, I guessed the space between his ears was vacant. I grabbed Stonebridge by the lapels and threw him over the wall, following close behind.

I peeked back over to check on Benny. He was pinned behind a car across the street but unhurt. One of Stonebridge's goons had crawled under the van, while the other two had taken shelter in the house to my left. They fired at a house two doors up across the street, and the house answered with muzzle flashes from the windows. There was too much lead in the air for us to move.

'You okay?' I yelled to Benny.

'Terrific,' he yelled back.

I could see silhouettes between houses and hiding behind cars. New gunfire came from the top of a house to Benny's right, firing above Stonebridge's goons at the other house. They must have been Stonebridge's reserve in case I'd resisted going to slaughter. I wouldn't have been surprised if thugs had started coming up from the sewers and raining from the sky.

'Who do I shoot at?' Benny said.

'Flip a coin.'

Stonebridge had come to his senses. He bolted for the house behind us.

'Get the bastard,' Benny said. 'I can take care of myself.'

I crossed the front lawn at a low run. Stonebridge opened the front door and ran inside. I followed, but as soon as I opened the door I had to stand aside for some bullets that were on their way out. I caught a glimpse of a front hall, a corridor of floral wallpaper, and Stonebridge disappearing around a corner.

The front room was a retiree's studio. An easel in the centre of the room and a single chair against the back wall were the only furniture. The beginnings of a watercolour sat on the easel, brushes and spots of desiccated paint ready in case the artist should ever return to complete his work. The paintings on the walls were all vaguely European landscapes, each one signed 'Crumb' at the bottom. I didn't have much time to get a sense of the painter's work, as Stonebridge kept interrupting from the next room.

'You should have taken the deal, Strange,' Stonebridge said, and fired down the hall.

There never was a deal. Stonebridge would have been an idiot to leave me alive, and I would have been that idiot's dim-witted kid brother if I'd believed him. He'd put on that show at the crossroads in the hope I'd do his job for him. Stonebridge was still looking for the easiest way, just like he had in Tehran.

I leaned out of the doorway and fired back, but my heart wasn't in it. I'd told Benny that I needed Stonebridge alive. That wasn't the whole truth. I wanted him alive, and the fact that I was willing to risk my own for that purpose only showed how little I valued it.

I'd copped one of Cassandra's grenades, and it was about to come in handy. The hall was wide, about three paces. I'd probably have just enough time to cover that distance. I threw the grenade into the kitchen and chased after it as fast as I could.

When the grenade had landed a few feet away from him, Stonebridge had lost a second in blind panic. He'd spent another running for the back door. By the time Stonebridge had figured out I hadn't pulled the pin, he'd turned back just in time to meet the butt of my gun. He took it better than I expected.

I surveyed the kitchen while Stonebridge found his feet. It was small for a McMansion. The left wall was a sink and dishwasher topped with a counter covered by tins and dust. An oven and a refrigerator bigger than both of us were against the opposite wall. A flat-pack dining-room table took up most of the floor space. Stonebridge's pistol was in the corner near the back door. If he went for the gun I'd have my boot on his neck before he could use it.

I put my sub-machine gun on the counter. It was time to settle this the old-fashioned way.

'I've learned a thing or two since the last time we fought,' Stonebridge said.

'I'll prepare myself to be impressed.'

I couldn't recognize anything in his stance. He still looked like the clumsy fucking oaf I remembered, all bluster and no finesse. I decided to give him a swing or two and see just how many storeys below contempt I should put him.

His guard was close and high. Someone had taught him a little Muay Thai, or maybe he'd watched a lot of mixed martial arts. The first punch was so telegraphed I could hear the Morse code in my ear. I let it go past, and walked right into a low kick. The burning sensation in my right thigh wasn't nearly as annoying as Stonebridge's laugh. Maybe he'd picked up a thing or two after all.

'Are you a pacifist now?' Stonebridge said.

'Come closer and find out.'

Another high right, again so clear he might as well have written me a letter and thrown it in the mail. His punch was the first to leave the station, but mine arrived ahead of schedule. It was a quick jab, an insult more than a blow. He stepped back, and we circled each other as much as the space allowed. He kicked low again. I intercepted his leg with my own. He stumbled back against the rear door that led to the garden, his left ankle now as tender as a newborn baby's.

I showed him my right palm, pointed at the sky, and waved him forward.

'Third time lucky.'

A metal cylinder appeared in Stonebridge's fist. God knows where he'd been hiding it. He flicked his wrist, and the cylinder grew into a baton.

'I should have known a fair fight was against your religion,' I said.

I took the first blow on my forearm, which was better than the part of my face he'd been aiming at. It stung like a whip. I backed off and Stonebridge came on, a hell of a lot better with the baton than his own hands. He got inside my guard, and the baton found one of my injured ribs. It seemed like every person who meant me harm could see them glowing in the dark. Stonebridge laughed as I doubled over.

'Not so cocky now, Strange.'

I affected an injured lurch to the right, to put the table between us.

'I'm not going to chase you,' he said.

I kicked the table hard. With a squeal of outrage from the floor, the table skidded back and pinned Stonebridge against the oven. He had to use both his hands to push the table back, and I took that opportunity to grab a tin from the counter behind me. It was made of thin, brushed aluminium, 'Flour' written on the front in old-time lettering. I brought it down on Stonebridge's head.

The tin crumpled, spraying flour over us both but not doing much damage to Stonebridge. The owner of this kitchen must have had a real fondness for cheap shit. The blow gave me enough time to trap the arm with the baton. I grabbed his index and pinkie fingers, and snapped them both.

Stonebridge howled while I took the baton. The table was still between us. Stonebridge tried to run around it to his gun. That play had been a bad idea before, and it was a bad idea now. I gave him a kick in the ass that sent him head first through the glass of the back door and into the garden.

It was in good condition, like the garden that had once belonged to Cassandra's friend. Perhaps a couple had lived here, one painting, the other tending the plants. The lawn was thick and tall like the others in the community. Herbs grew against the house. A corner had been prepared for flowers, but most of them had died without their keeper around.

I let him stand up before I hit him again. Now it was his turn to protect his head from the baton. I worked the extremities: left thigh, right arm, left arm when he grabbed for the baton. I faked, he flinched, and I hit him in the left arm again. The baton was meant to stun, not injure. The hollow aluminium wasn't strong enough to break bone, unless you swung it really hard.

Stonebridge's weakened ankle gave in. I felt the break through the baton, through my arm directly into the pleasure centres of the brain. Stonebridge collapsed to the ground and I kept hitting him: right leg, left leg, top of the head, upper back, lower back, back to the legs, up to the arms. He was screaming, pleading, but someone else heard it, not me.

I only stopped when he stopped screaming. I knelt and found a pulse. Stonebridge's eyes had rolled far back in his head. I grabbed him by the lapels of a suit that was too good for him and dragged him across the garden. In a corner was a bird bath, a heavy stone bowl held up by three cherubs. The authorities would have called the three naked figures child pornography if wings hadn't been attached to their baby flesh. I gave

Stonebridge a quickie baptism to focus his attention. He was in dire need of having his many sins washed away.

'How much?' I said. 'How much did you pay for Iris?'

'Ten thousand. I don't know where she is now,' he said.

I threw him to the ground.

Stonebridge curled himself into a ball on the wild, green lawn, hands up to protect his face.

'What do you want?' he said through broken, swollen lips.

The hatred, greed and envy had leaked out of him along with the blood on his face and shirt. What was left could barely fill the suit he'd arrived in.

'Do you want me to say I'm sorry?'

I wondered now if he wanted me to kill him. It would be yet another easy way out. Stonebridge had the same future as every rabbit and gazelle on the planet: a lifetime of watching your back, imagining claws at the end of every rustle and squeak. The difference was that the dumb animals couldn't see the future, couldn't be caught between dreading that inevitable moment and hoping it would finally happen.

'When he catches up with you, the general will not turn the other cheek,' I said.

'It doesn't matter what the general does to me; I'm dead anyway. You don't know, do you?' Stonebridge said when he saw my confusion, a little of the old bravado coming back. 'It's fatal, Strange. That secret Pentagon study I told you about? Almost all of us are dead: cancer, organ failure, strokes; our bodies fall apart.'

Stonebridge spat out some blood.

'Nobody lives to forty. It's a lottery.'

Benny crashed through the garden fence, turning around to send a few shots back in the direction he'd come before he gave us his full attention. The sight of the two of us stopped him for a second. I was still covered in flour, my face the colour of a pale, angry ghost. The water in the birdbath had mixed with the flour and blood to make a brownish goo that stuck to Stonebridge's face and shirt.

'The Corinthian's and this shitbird's shitbirds are still killing each other. It's time to say goodbye to this gated community.'

If the Corinthian had shown I would have stuck around, whatever the consequences, but I knew he didn't make the same mistake twice. It was time to leave before one group finished off the other and came looking for us.

'Let's go.'

'What do you want to do with him?' Benny said.

I looked at Stonebridge, still on the ground, bloody and broken. Glass had built Task Force Seventeen to destroy a society. I hadn't known it then, but that's really what all his talk about Leviathan had meant. When he created the Fishermen, Glass learned from his mistakes. The company was in every state, an organization that was massive and autonomous at the same time. Fisher Partners was a machine that chewed up humans on an industrial scale. All I'd done was find one small, replaceable part, and snap it off.

'Leave him,' I said. 'Let the general take out his own trash.'

We turned our backs on the battle still raging next door.

'They'll come for you, Strange,' Stonebridge said to my back. 'No matter where you go, the Fishermen will find you.' There was admiration in his voice, as if he was talking about himself rather than a corporation. Even now, Stonebridge was desperate to side with the strong against the weak, even when the poor bastard in question was himself.

TWENTY-SIX

I'd left Benny and Cassandra on a road outside DC. It wasn't safe for me to follow where they were going. We stood on the hard shoulder and waited for their ride, an SUV full of Mossad agents en route from the Israeli embassy. Benny chain-smoked, trying to make up for all the cigarettes he'd abstained from since Sharon was born.

Benny looked at his watch. 'Miriam and the baby should be over the border by now. In another hour or two they'll be on a plane to the Holy Land.'

'Your family can go anywhere, and they decide Israel is the best place for a little peace and quiet?'

'Do you remember when the Bureau loaned me out to the Israeli police?'

'Sure,' I said. 'The Bureau kept you out there for two years, and if you were working with the police, then I'm Judy Garland.'

For a second Benny looked like he might argue the point. 'I have friends over there, is the point I'm trying to make. It's not too late for you to come along.'

'I'm not exactly part of the diaspora, Benny.'

'Your mother became an Orthodox Jew in good standing,' he said. 'The rest can be finessed.'

'I thought the Israelis were more particular of late.'

'It's a point of contention. They say reformed Jews aren't really Jews, while the Jesus freaks are intent on shipping over anyone who's seen *Fiddler on the Roof.*'

I was surprised the Elders didn't play along; they could say the only real Jews were four guys in Jerusalem, and declare the gathering over.

'Whether you've got friends there or not, I don't see why Shin Bet won't put you in chains as soon as you hit the tarmac. They need the Elders.'

'And the Elders need them. It's an ugly marriage, with a lot of secrets on both sides. We'll both be fine. Mossad still owes Cassandra a favour; they'll make sure she reaches her friends in Europe. You sure you won't do the smart thing for once? Just try it, you might like it.'

I could see my future in Israel: sitting in bars and cafés, parks and my single empty room, looking for something I'd already found. I shook my head.

'*Cherchez la dame*, huh? Do you really think you can find her?'

'I want to find out.'

Benny kicked at the dirt and lit a new cigarette from his dying one. I could tell he wanted to say something more, but he didn't know what it was.

'Could you get a message to Judge for me?' I said. 'He deserves to know what happened to Isaac.'

'I can swing that.'

'Thanks. Hold on to this for me.'

'It's Isaac's, isn't it?' Benny said, taking the diary.

These old pages, dragged from one war zone to the next, were a record of the banal atrocities the three of us had witnessed, abroad and now at home. If it ever made its way into a museum as part of the chronicle of the Elder regime, the exhibit would talk about a person with the courage to face what was happening and do something about it. Isaac wasn't a great man, but his actions put him head and shoulders above most of the assholes sucking oxygen on this planet. It was a good story, even if the ending wasn't a happy one.

'Take care of it for me,' I said. 'It's all that's left of him.'

Benny nodded and stuck it in his pocket. He tore an empty packet of Lucky Strikes in half and handed one part to me.

'I'll give the other half to my Mossad contact, should you need a friendly Jew. He moves around a lot, but you'll find he'll be there when you need him. His name is Gideon, and he already knows who you are.'

'How will I find this Gideon?'

'You won't need to.' Benny inhaled half his cigarette, but didn't seem to enjoy it.

'When I'm gone, there won't be anyone left to keep your ass out of your trouble.'

'I know.' When Benny was gone, there wouldn't be anyone left at all.

A black SUV arrrived, exactly as I'd predicted. It was full of men in dark suits and darker sunglasses. They didn't say hello. I wondered if they, the Corinthian's men and the Secret Service all shopped at the same store. Benny went over to speak to the driver. Cassandra came over to me.

'Do you think telling other governments about Leviathan will do anything?' I said.

'It's the best we can do,' she said. 'At the very least, we'll make the Elders pay for what they're doing.'

'Did any of the Rudashevsky Group pay for what they did?'

'Only when they tried to sleep.'

'I bet Adamson never lost a wink. I don't understand why other countries just took them at their word.'

'They didn't, but it's hard to call your most important ally a liar to his face. Our friends have been holding us at arm's length since then, and every day the arms get longer. After Leviathan, they might let the Elders go entirely.'

Benny motioned Cassandra over to the SUV. She lingered.

'I wish I knew what you were up to,' she said. 'You're too smart to think you can get this woman back.'

'Her name's Iris,' I said, 'and I know which way the rabbit hole goes.'

Cassandra smiled. The driver of the SUV tested out his horn. Cassandra pressed my hand, and then let the Mossad agents help her into the back.

'I'm not done with you yet,' Benny yelled at me, which was his way of saying so long, goodbye, we'll see each other soon.

I waved, and the SUV went back the way it came.

I returned to New York by train. I paid cash, kept my hat on, and watched the news for an outdated picture of my face. No wanted posters materialized. Either Stonebridge was still in the wind, or Fisher Partners intended to deal with me privately. I hoped the Corinthian was too busy covering his own ass to send someone after me, but he'd always been a good multi-tasker when it came to evil. I kept my eye on the carriage doors the whole way home.

I'd come back to the city for two reasons: to get my emergency stash, and burgle Stonebridge's townhouse. The second job was almost as easy as the first. Stonebridge had left only one of his goons to guard the hearth, and that dumbass had been easily dealt with. A five-minute toss of his office was all it took to find what I needed. I should have just given a nickel to a toddler and taken the afternoon off.

I didn't find anything about Iris or where Stonebridge's clients had ended up; it was a little early for Christmas. Glass's compartmentalization was doing its job. What I did find was a paper trail for almost all the Fishermen under Stonebridge's control.

The Fishermen operated all over the city, but their expenses were a trail of itemized breadcrumbs. I found the team that had probably taken Iris from the mileage they drove and the places they ate, in the window of days when she was taken. The turn-over in Fisher Partners was heavy: of the six men in the original team, personnel records showed that two were now in the Holy Land, and the other four had been scattered all over the country. Glass would have moved his men around to make sure they stayed inconspicuous, and to stop them from developing any local attachments that might compromise their performance. The forms only identified the individual Fishermen with ID numbers, but it would be enough.

When the Fishermen found Stonebridge, he'd tell them every-thing, including the Corinthian's betrayal. He may have seen his attempt to sell Fisher Partners' secrets as diversification, but Glass would react only one way. The Corinthian was smart enough to know all this, and I knew the bastard well enough to know there was only one place in the country he'd feel safe. It used to be known as the Strip, the Elders had renamed it the Las Vegas Special Enterprise Zone, but everyone just called it Babylon. It would be my first stop.

The panic kit the Bureau had given me had everything I needed to be someone else: a passport, driver's licence, social security and two credit cards. They were genuine documents, better than any forgery I could get on the black market. The papers were in the name of Peter Braithwaite. I tried the name on for size. It didn't quite fit.

Even with real papers, the airport was an unnecessary risk. The trains were guarded by amateurs, and then only sporadically. I had enough medication to last me for three months, much more than I'd need. The FBI was riven by internal politics and time-servers. Local police were kept busy with terrorism scares and enforcing the Elders' rule. Real journalism was non-existent. In the America I grew up in, I wouldn't have had a chance, but now I might just live long enough to do what I planned.

I had a list of my own now, four numbers and an AKA: the Corinthian. He'd found Iris and sold her to Stonebridge; just another transaction for a businessman only interested in crooked things. I could find him and the others, if I wanted to.

The Fishermen kidnapping and killing people right now would probably never be held responsible. Maybe they'd try a few of the peasants in twenty years, but the architects would never see the inside of a courtroom. They'd walked away before, and should someone dredge up their crimes from the sea of black ink where they were hidden, a dozen heads would be on TV within the hour telling us it was all for the good of the country.

If I couldn't find Iris, I'd find the men who took her. I knew if I killed these men the Elders would hire someone else. Like Stonebridge, they were easily replaced in a country full of desperate men. It would settle nothing. It certainly wouldn't make up for what I had done. It was only a direction, but that was what I needed.

First I said goodbye to the city I loved. I'd walked as much of it as I could, told the parks and delis, junk shops and taxicabs that I wasn't coming back. I'd lived other places, but only New York had ever been my home. I tried to hold those memories in my head, fix them in amber, but the torrent of propaganda and myth was already overwhelming them. When I thought of the Chrysler Building and Mott Street and the subway, the way they appeared in tourist videos was already beginning to replace the way I had seen them, the streets in my head captured by the lens of a camera, not my eye. The only thing I could do for my city was tell her the truth, whether she wanted to hear it or not.

The shrine between tracks twenty-six and twenty-seven was almost the same as when Cal and Jack had first showed it to me. There might have been a few new additions to the wall, but it was hard to tell. There were so many faces, and Stonebridge hadn't been responsible for them all. I matched the pictures and names to Stonebridge's files, and began to write.

MAGGIE PYM. White female, 42, 5' 8", brown hair, hazel eyes, caesarean scar on midsection. Shot twice in the head during a routine traffic stop by agent 1446, who was impersonating a police officer. Body left in car, valuables removed to suggest carjacking gone wrong.

PAUL GANZ. White male, 36, 6' 1", black hair, green eyes. Strangled on 32nd Street. Remains transferred to Waste Management.

SHANE LEWES. Black male, 51, 6' 2", shaved head, brown eyes. Client acquired on 115th Street. Client transferred to Transport.

ZACK MITCHELL. White male, 63, 5' 8", grey hair, grey eyes. Client suffered heart attack during preparation for Transport. Remains transferred to Waste Management.

STEVEN WATERS. White male, 39, 5' 10", brown hair, green eyes. As per task order's special instructions, client was beaten to death in his residence. Collateral damage to home applied to suggest home invasion. Articles 133449, 133450 and 133451 left in home to suggest client was afflicted with homosexuality.

LISA KEMP. White female, 26, 5' 2", blonde hair, blue eyes. Client acquired at JFK International Airport. Client transferred to Transport.

ANTONIO DIAZ. Hispanic male, 43, 5' 6", black hair, grey eyes. Client acquired at Lima 43.090356,-73.499495.

LISA JONES. Black female, 48, 5' 8", black hair, brown eyes. Contrary to intelligence, client's family was at her home at time of acquisition. Client resisted. In process of acquisition, client's daughter became collateral damage. Client transferred to Transport. Supplemental report attached.

MARK JINTAO. Asian male, 51, 5' 9", black hair, brown eyes. Client and all known blood relatives acquired. Transferred to Transport.

STEPHEN JACKSON. White male, 16, 6' 2", blond hair, blue eyes. Client acquired on Interstate 86. Transferred to Transport. Transcripts of enhanced interrogation to follow.

And on, and on, and on.

I had faces of my own to add to the wall. I tacked up the picture of Isaac that Faye had given me, the only one that was real. Below it I wrote: 'Murdered by the Department of Homeland Security'.

The last picture to add was Iris's. I'd made a copy of the one Mrs Brown let me take and cropped out the old bastard Brother Isaiah. There was nothing to say, so I just wrote: 'Iris. Whereabouts unknown'.

It was only after I was done that I noticed I had an audience. Gathered around me in a semicircle were commuters changing trains, men on business trips, a few confused tourists, staff on break, and some cops who should have **been** arresting me. No one said a word. One or two sobbed.

I turned to them, and I waited. No one came forward. Part of me had hoped the Fishermen would come here. I'd wanted them to step from the embrace of the crowd, to show for a moment the true face they didn't want these good people to see.

Ever since I'd parted ways with Benny and Cassandra, I'd been waiting for the Fishermen to come. In alleys and deserted streets, around dark corners and on empty platforms, I expected to see figures I would recognize, shadows that would know my name but not what I had done. Every day, I waited for my old friends.

I looked up at the sky – the facsimile painted on the ceiling, not the real one. It was the way humans saw the universe, not the way it was. Stars were displaced, galaxies out of whack, gods and monsters drawn backwards. It looked the same, but it was wrong, all wrong.

I pushed through the crowd. No one tried to stop me. I had a train to catch, all the way to the open, lonely west.

BACKGROUND READING

Boyer, Paul, *When Time Shall Be No More: Prophecy Belief in Modern American Culture*, Belknap Harvard, 1992

Conquest, Robert, *The Great Terror: A Reassessment*, Pimlico, 2008

Gourevitch, Philip, and Morris, Errol, *Standard Operating Procedure*, Picador, 2008

Mayer, Jane, *The Dark Side*, Doubleday, 2008

Ricks, Thomas E., *Fiasco*, Penguin, 2006

Scahill, Jeremy, *Blackwater*, Serpent's Tail, 2007

Shorrock, Tim, *Spies for Hire*, Simon & Schuster, 2008

Wright, Evan, *Generation Kill*, Corgi, 2005

ACKNOWLEDGEMENTS

I am indebted to my agent Rob Dinsdale for his critical eye and my editor Kate Parkin for her faith in buying two books before they were written. Both keep me on the straight and narrow, editing-wise.

All of the books in the reading list provided insight and raw material in one way or another for this novel. Robert Conquest's *The Great Terror* was indispensable in constructing Fisher Partners' own reign of terror. The failures of strategic thinking that Thomas Ricks catalogues in *Fiasco* helped me design the endless war in Tehran, and *The Dark Side* and *Standard Operating Procedure* were vital for Task Force Seventeen's detainee program. Lastly, Tim Shorrock's *Spies for Hire* helped me design both Janus and Fisher Partners, and to understand the intelligence community they operate in and feed off.

The website biblegateway.com was the source of scripture cited in the novel. The fighting in this book is inspired by the teachings of Sifu Andrew Sofos and Sifu Mark Green.

As for Alice, what can I say? Words are simply not good enough.

If you enjoyed *The Rapture*, the final novel of Elliott Hall's acclaimed Strange Trilogy is available now.

THE CHILDREN'S CRUSADE

Elliott Hall

Only one man stands in their way . . .

PI Felix Strange is working his last case. The woman he loves has been taken by Fisher Partners – America's for-profit secret police – and, though he suspects he won't find her, he's going to do the next best thing: kill everyone involved.

As he works his way down the list, Strange is offered a secret deal, which could lead him straight to Iris. Across the American South, the militant Sons of David are on the rise. Their leader, the prophet Joshua, promises a new world to replace the sinful old. To free Iris, all Strange has to do is assassinate this new messiah. The problem? He's twelve years old.

Now read on . . .

www.elliott-hall.co.uk

ONE

A Highway

The first round hit the engine block. A hood covered my face, but they hadn't bothered with headphones this time. I heard and felt the old petrol monster die, its V8 thrum replaced by tyres screaming as we drifted into the median of whatever road we were on.

When we came to a stop I could hear only two voices. The man in the front passenger seat was reporting to someone over a phone while the other to my right returned fire with a SAW light machine gun. The driver was probably dead, killed by the same weapon that had brought down the vehicle.

The SUV's interior and the hood over my face made it impossible to separate the gunfire. It seemed to come from all around us, the opposing fire pebbles thrown by an angry child when they hit the SUV's bodywork. There were still hostiles out there, but maybe they weren't hostile to me.

'Assailants unknown,' the man in front said into his phone. 'Request immediate reinforcements.'

An explosion jammed its hand into my chest and then imposed silence. Ringing ears, confusion. The drugs hadn't quite worn off yet. I thought about running, but the chains hadn't gone anywhere. I was still alive, so I waited. If a bullet was coming, now would be the time.

The door across from me opened. I felt a hand, and then I was looking at a man wearing a ski mask, surgical gloves, chinos and an aquamarine golf shirt. His rifle was on his shoulder, at rest safe in the knowledge that everyone in the truck's interior was restrained or dead. Behind him was the desert – not the clean sand of a movie, but an arid expanse of little flora, a seabed minus the water – and beyond that what appeared to my disoriented eye both a rising and a setting sun.

The man put a light in my eyes and seemed satisfied with the way the pupils dilated. His own were a faded brown, determined to tell me nothing. The man didn't climb into the SUV; instead he unlocked my chains and shoved aside the corpse so I could get out. My late captor had been ventilated through the door he was firing from, some bullets meant for him coming to rest in the seat beside my head.

I climbed out, legs unsteady from the shot they'd given me and long periods of enforced idleness. There were four other men in the same uniform as my rescuer, an office that had decided to shoot up traffic as a team-building exercise. Three cars waited for them on the opposite side of the road. The other men stood a little apart and waited for their leader to finish with me.

'Are you Felix Strange?' the leader said.

I stared at him, and it wasn't because the man had spoken in Hebrew. I couldn't remember the last time someone had used my real name.

'Is that your name?' he said, switching to English.

I nodded.

He pressed a key into my hand and pointed at a motel in the distance. The man turned away and rejoined his subordinates before I had a chance to ask for a ride. I could see them putting their surgical gloves into a single plastic bag, to be destroyed along with the masks when I was out of sight. After the guns went the same way, they'd be another collection of nameless faces.

I began to walk. The motel was about a mile down the highway. I dragged my lead feet along the pebbled shoulder and noticed the lack of cars in both directions. The sun was brighter than I remembered, the light almost alien. The wind made up for it. It was a tepid breeze that could only be felt if you paid attention, but it was real, honest-to-God wind, not air filtered through the guts of a machine. I wondered where I was, which country, how long I'd been there – here.

After a while, I could see a sign identifying the buildings I was aiming for as the 'Restful Slumber Motel'. The embossed plastic keychain said someone had reserved number nine.

I walked.

A parking lot encircled the motel like a moat. Past it was a veranda that connected the buildings; tile, stucco and sharp-edged plants from a thirsty climate. If someone in the office saw me, they didn't come out to say hello.

I opened the door expecting a thrown-fist or guns-drawn welcome, but the room was empty. There was a double bed, nightstand, and a wardrobe built into the wall. On the nightstand was a phone and an old flip calendar. I laid it face-down, not yet able to believe that I had been gone so long.

A shoulder holster was draped over the coat rack beside the wardrobe. Resting inside was a forty-five pistol with the serial number burned off. I felt the weight and checked the action. It wasn't mine, but it would do.

In the wardrobe were two pressed white shirts, half a dozen ties of varying taste, and one dark suit. In a pocket of the jacket were car keys and a roll of hundreds of respectable size. In the other was my medication, pills red, green and blue. The only thing my benefactor had forgotten was a decent hat.

The last item in the room lay on the bed in plain sight. It

was the picture of Iris, the only one I'd ever had. It was from just after she'd dragged herself from the streets, long before I knew her, when the scars of a short misspent life were still fresh.

I sat on the bed. The cover was chenille. I pinched it between my fingers and thought of her. When I closed my eyes, I didn't see the girl in the photograph, but the woman I'd first seen in New York turning heads and disrupting traffic. Iris had worn a tan trenchcoat and her dark hair long. At the time she'd worn sunglasses, but I'd rubbed those out and replaced them with her beautiful grey eyes.

I was a private investigator at the time, and Iris a spy for a bunch of deranged moral hypocrites. I'd tailed her around Chinatown and then chased her halfway across Central Park before I even knew her name. It was complicated, then almost as much as now.

The photograph was rough around the edges, one corner smudged by my hand. I'd rubbed it between my thumb and forefinger for what now seemed like my entire life, hoping it would grant wishes I knew wouldn't come true. I turned the picture over, then thought better of it and placed it in my inside pocket. Someone wanted me angry.

Fisher Partners – the for-profit secret police whose guest I'd been until recently – would be responding to their dead employees' calls for help. They wouldn't search this place for a while. The reasonable assumption was that I'd been whisked away, not forced to walk a fucking mile of highway. I could linger for a while in room number nine.

Iris had written me a note before she was kidnapped by Fisher Partners' man in New York, Peter Stonebridge. I hadn't managed to return the favour, occupied as I was trying to kill everyone involved, especially the man known as the Corinthian. They still had her, somewhere, but now was a good time to write some things down before my second chance ended with handcuffs or a loaded gun.

I wanted to try to explain to her what had happened, how I'd gone from being a shamus in New York to what I'd become. The hotel's complimentary pad didn't look like it had enough paper for that, but I picked up the branded Biro next to it and started anyway.

Iris:

You told me not to look for you, that you wanted me to be somewhere where I could be happy, healthy and pissing someone off. I passed up the chance to leave the country, so I guess I only managed the last one. I couldn't let you go.

The Corinthian led them to you. He sold the information to Fisher Partners, just like he sold anything else he could get his hands on. The price was high because of my history with Stonebridge. They used you to get to me, and it worked.

I didn't expect to live this long. It's been pretty confusing, sweetheart. I knew I couldn't find you, but I knew where the Corinthian was. I thought if I killed him, and the Fishermen contracted to kidnap you, it would make a difference.

The prob

The phone rang. I drew my new forty-five in its direction before I realized I was being an idiot. The phone kept ringing. I put it to my ear.

'This is Jefferson,' said a voice I'd never heard before. 'We have work to do.'

Read more . . .

Elliott Hall

THE FIRST STONE

The first book in the Strange Trilogy

Private eye Felix Strange doesn't work homicide cases. He saw enough dead bodies fighting in Iran, a war that left him with a crippling disease that has no name and no cure. So when Strange is summoned to a Manhattan hotel room to investigate the dead body of America's most-loved preacher, he'd rather not get involved.

In a race against time Strange must face religious police, organized crime and a dame with very particular ideas, while uncovering a conspiracy that reaches the very heart of his newly fundamentalist nation.

'Chills the blood . . . ingenious and witty' *Daily Telegraph*

'A knockout debut' *Guardian*

Read more . . .

James Frey

BRIGHT SHINY MORNING

A dazzling story by the controversial writer of *A Million Little Pieces*

Bright Shiny Morning takes a wild ride through the ultimate metropolis, where glittering excess rubs shoulders with seedy depravity. Frey lingers on a handful of Los Angeles' lost souls, bringing vividly to life their egos and ideals, hopes and despairs, anxieties and absurdities. The backdrop is the relentless drumbeat of millions of other lives. In his trademark searing voice, James Frey describes a city, a culture, an age.

'An absolute triumph of a novel' Irvine Welsh, *Guardian*

'Engrossing' *The Times*

'Totally addictive' *Time Out*

Order your copy now by calling Bookpoint on 01235 827716 or visit your local bookshop quoting ISBN 978-1-84854-047-7 www.johnmurray.co.uk

Read more ...

Kevin Brockmeier

THE BRIEF HISTORY OF THE DEAD

The critically acclaimed, spellbinding novel about life, death and everything that follows

Imagine a place between heaven and earth. A city where everyone ends up after they die. This city looks like any other, with trees and houses and newspapers, where people work, drink coffee and fall in love. And here they remain, kept alive by the memories of those left behind on earth.

Kevin Brockmeier's magical novel tells the story of this city's inhabitants, as they try to make sense of the world where they now find themselves. And it is also the story of Laura, a girl trapped in the Antarctic fighting for her life. How these two stories connect is brilliantly revealed. *The Brief History of the Dead* is a novel that lives long in the minds of all who fall under its spell.

'Highly impressive' *Financial Times*

'Brockmeier is a lyrical yet subtle writer . . . A powerful read' *Time Out*

'His confident voice, observational brilliance and playful humour dazzle to the end' *The Times*

Order your copy now by calling Bookpoint on 01235 827716 or visit your local bookshop quoting ISBN 978-0-7195-6830-5 www.johnmurray.co.uk